north of
tomorrow

A NOVEL

north of
tomorrow

Cindy McCormick Martinusen

TYNDALE HOUSE PUBLISHERS, INC. | WHEATON, ILLINOIS

Visit Tyndale's exciting Web site at www.tyndale.com

Designed by Julie Chen

Edited by Lorie Popp and Ramona Cramer Tucker

Published in association with the literary agency of Janet Kobobel Grant, Books & Such, 4788 Carissa Ave., Santa Rosa, CA 95405.

Scripture quotations are taken from the *Holy Bible,* King James Version.

Scripture quotations are taken from the *Holy Bible,* New Living Translation, copyright © 1996. Used by permission of Tyndale House Publishers, Inc., Wheaton, Illinois 60189. All rights reserved.

Library of Congress Cataloging-in-Publication Data

Martinusen, Cindy McCormick, date.
  North of tomorrow / Cindy McCormick Martinusen.
    p. cm.
Includes bibliographical references.
  ISBN 0-8423-5237-6
  1. Concentration camp commandants—Fiction. 2. Holocaust, Jewish (1939–1945)—Fiction. 3. Fathers and daughters—Fiction. 4. Grandfathers—Fiction. I. Title.
PS3563.A737 N67 2002
813′.6—dc21   2001006999

Printed in the United States of America

08 07 06 05 04 03 02
7   6   5   4   3   2   1

To Cody, Madelyn, and Weston
For your todays and tomorrows

Then your children will ask,

"What does all this mean?"

EXODUS 12:26, NLT

AUSTRIAN WOODS NEAR CZECH BORDER
April 12, 1945

"Our strength cannot carry another step.
  And so we die tonight."
Brigit Kirke raced through the woods, out of breath, expecting a bullet to blast into her back at any moment. Her brother, Edgar, was faster, always just ahead. He became her goal to keep moving when she felt she could go no farther. Ducking tree limbs and brush, they ran, the moist leaves and pine needles quieting their hurried steps. Finally they reached their closest hiding place and crawled beneath the low branches.
  "In the darkness, forgotten from the world.
  We die tonight."
They had run faster than she'd thought possible to this spot where silence was required. But her heart wouldn't calm, and her breath wouldn't even. As she gasped loudly for air, Brigit's lungs burned.
  "Keep quiet, or we will be found," Edgar whispered sharply.
  She covered her mouth and rested her back against the tree trunk, resolving not to move or make a sound.
  Fear kept her still.
  "We wanted to walk the fields of spring. We dreamed and hoped in vain.
  We die tonight."
Brigit didn't want to hear this song that played in her thoughts. Written and sung by a woman who would later die

in Brigit's arms, now the lyrics returned not as a comfort but as the night's curse.

Edgar touched her arm, and she turned only slightly, as if even that movement might reveal their location. He was trying to reassure her as he did when he patted the top of her head or winked her way. Always the older brother, even now. She wished to see his eyes, his expression, but the night was too dark.

A breeze stirred the leaves.

"We were almost free," Brigit whispered in sudden grief.

"Almost, but—" The breeze died away before he could answer.

Brigit held back the tears and wished someone would make this all right. She was tired of merely surviving. She wanted to live but was weary of fighting for just one more day. It shouldn't be this way now, not with the war nearly over and all the obstacles she'd already endured. No one should die just steps from freedom. Somehow reality always intruded on what she believed should be right. After surviving hell's fury, now they might die on the eve of life.

"Who will remember if we all die tonight?"

For a time she and Edgar had become comfortable, believing no one had tracked them across the Czechoslovakian border and into the Austrian woods. They had played cards, told stories, and dreamed dreams while hiding in the safe house where food was delivered by the old woman they'd learned to trust. Over the past week they'd seen planes flying overhead with Allied symbols on their sides. Edgar said soon they'd taste the Coca-Cola he'd promised, see the great statue of a woman holding her torch of hope, and find new life in America. Brigit had almost believed him and had given moments to wondering—perhaps they could find their parents or some of their old friends from Prague. There'd be no more hiding. Never hiding again. And no more fear.

But plans had given way to truth. Truth had come this evening in the sound of a vehicle moving slowly up the mountain road. There had been little time to flee and few options for escape. The road and woods on one side would now be watched. Brigit had seen only four soldiers moving toward the cabin before she and Edgar disappeared into the woods—but four was enough. Behind them was a sheer precipice. A V-shaped cliff that Edgar had said was seventy-five meters tall when they'd stood at its ledge many weeks ago. It had frightened her to stand there—frightened her to imagine dying that way. She'd crept to the ledge and sent a scattering of rocks down . . . down . . . down to the bottom far below.

Now the soldiers and cliffs were a tight noose around them. Brigit and Edgar knew they were trapped—as did the soldiers and most certainly the man who had hunted them for almost a year. Edgar had found several temporary hiding places, but the coming daylight would expose them . . . if the men cared to wait that long.

Another gust of wind and Brigit moved, gathering her legs close to her chest. She rubbed them through her dirty wool pants and the feeling returned.

"Miracles happen," Edgar said softly, breaking their vow to speak only in the wind. "We might make it."

Brigit shook her head. "No America or statue or Coca-Cola. Do not say there will be," she replied in turn. Not that she blamed him for trying. Seeking to protect her in every way, he often made promises he couldn't keep.

Edgar didn't respond for a long moment. Then, finally, under his breath he said, "We must separate."

"We promised to stay together," Brigit begged.

"You move south, but watch for the cliff—thirty meters off," he insisted. "We will meet at the next hiding place."

"No."

"I will go forward and hide until they pass me. If we hold

out, perhaps till morning, we might be safe. If one survives, we help the other. The Allies are close. Berlin will surrender; it might have already. They know their time is short. That could save us. Brigit, just make it one more day."

She stared at his profile, a darker darkness in the night. Was this the last memory she'd have of her brother?

The leaves crunched loudly as he stood and pulled her up beside him.

"There is hope if we split. One can hide better than two."

Hope. It wanted to grow inside her, but she knew it was too tempting. Although his logic worked in theory, she feared what he intended. He might try to protect her by giving himself away. The delay could save her, but she wouldn't allow it. They would kill him.

"I am not a child." Brigit's mind sought some escape. "We can bargain with them. He needs us to get the location. We will help him get the Empress Brooch. We will tell him to escape before the Allies arrive. He wants the brooch, not us."

It was a fairy tale even to her own ears. Brigit knew the man who hunted them had already pursued and killed many before them—all for the quest of the Empress Sissi Brooch and its priceless emeralds.

"Why would he let us live?" Edgar suddenly put up his hand. She heard and saw through the trees as he did. "Lights. We cannot let them take us—it will be worse to die their way."

She hesitated, unwilling to plunge into the unknown beyond him.

"Let your fear drive you—but think smart." Edgar grabbed her tightly by both arms and kissed her forehead. "Now go!"

Her legs faltered momentarily. Then the blood rushed to her veins, and she plunged into the dark, unsure of the direction.

Once she left Edgar behind, fear came quickly. She began to run, her arms wildly swiping branches away from her face. Her footfalls sounded loud, loud enough for the whole world to hear. Which way was south? She'd forgotten to ask. A maze wrapped around her as minutes passed like hours.

"*We die for nothing.*

And, yet, we die tonight."

She heard shouting and stopped, trying to hear above her own breathing.

"Run, Brigit! Go to *drei!*" Edgar was telling her to go to their third hiding place.

Then a gunshot cut the night. Brigit dropped to the ground. Leaves pressed against her face. She felt no pain. She wasn't shot.

Edgar.

Brigit wanted to go back, but panic drove her as she got up and moved forward, the branches tearing at her flesh. Their third hiding place wasn't far now.

But ahead the darkness opened. She stopped just in time. A scuffle of rocks slid down the cliff into the engulfing mouth below. Crawling on hands and knees, scratched from brush and bleeding from rocks, Brigit searched the ledge for the pathway or some miracle.

She rose quickly when she heard someone behind her. She wished for Edgar but knew it wasn't him. The footsteps slowed through the dense brush; then a man's image appeared against the night sky. Brigit felt naked and exposed on the cliff's edge as she stood before him.

"Tell me where to find it," the voice said. The voice she remembered well.

"Where is my brother?" Her fear for Edgar made her sound strong.

"Fraülein Brigit Kirke. You are a smart girl. You know of your brother. You know where your family is. What does it feel like to be the only one alive?"

She backed to the ledge.

"It has taken a long time to speak with you again. What a journey until this moment."

"You will kill me," Brigit stated.

"You are what—nineteen years old now? Many things you have endured. So long have I searched for you. Finally the end comes, and we meet face-to-face. You know why I seek you. You know what I must have."

She was shaking. His voice was calm and assuring, as if he hadn't just killed her brother . . . as if he wouldn't soon kill her. "Why would you do this to us? It is only a piece of jewelry."

"The Empress Brooch is much more than you will ever know." He spoke with a hint of anger.

"I have seen it—how can it be worth this?"

"You have seen it—I knew it. Tell me. Tell me where it is."

"You tell me why. Why do you want it so badly that you would do this to us?"

He didn't answer. Brigit recalled her father saying before the first deportations, "If they could see us as people, perhaps they would not persecute us."

"I am just a young girl. My brother was only twenty-one."

"You will take me there." She had heard this tone in his voice before. "I will keep you safe. I give my word."

But as he reached for her, she knew his words were utter lies. Truth was here. Hope had died with Edgar.

She had one moment to choose.

"*Tonight we die.*

We die."

Brigit turned and jumped.

part *one*

And so ended that horrible long war that refuses
to be forgotten. Life went on. It went on despite both
the dead and the living, because this was a war that no one
quite survived. Something very important and precious had
been killed by it, or perhaps, it had just died of horror,
or starvation, or simply of disgust—who knows?

—HEDA MARGOLIUS KOVALY, *Under a Cruel Star: A Life in Prague 1941–1968*

CHAPTER ONE

PRAGUE, CZECH REPUBLIC
Present Day

The blackness pressed around her, suffocating her breath and keeping the night in her eyes. Amanda Rivans struggled to rise, to break from the tangle of invisible arms that wrapped around her.

The old nightmare had come again; Amanda could see the children's faces, solemn and still. She felt great relief in awakening, even as she tried to remember where she was.

She tugged the thick comforter over her legs and attempted to shake the nightmare with logic. *I'm awake now. It was only a dream.* Yet in what hotel in which city was she this time? Her feet touched the cold wood floor and she shivered. When her hand sought a light and knocked over books, the sound jarred her memory.

Stefan's books.

Amanda was in Prague, in the apartment of Stefan's cousin, Petrov. Stefan Keller slept in the room below, after giving her the loft where he usually slept when in the city.

She pulled the lamp chain, bringing a circle of light to the bedside table. She felt the relief of sight.

No one stirred in the house. Rising from the bed, a simple box spring and mattress in the center of the narrow loft, Amanda walked to the railing. As she peered over it into the kitchen, strands of her blonde hair fell across her face. She heard the swish of air moving through the apartment's radiators; outside, the remnants of a storm pressed hard against the windows and eaves. An antique wall clock ticked softly, reminding her of childhood and home.

Was it the storm or this place that had brought the old dream's return? Drawn to the lone window on the gabled end, Amanda made her way toward it, bending her head to escape the sloping rafters.

Outside, the city of Prague was the illusive place where much of her past was centered . . . and possibly her future. She pressed her hands against the cold, frosted glass of the window, and the wind and sleet pushed back. A streetlight appeared fuzzy, wrapped in a blanket of swirling snow.

In her line of work Amanda was familiar with generic hotels and strangers in the rooms beyond closed doors. But this place exuded calm, a sense of safety. It wasn't just this high-tower apartment with its steep vaulted ceilings and plaster walls or the oddly comforting scent of a centuries-old building. It was that the people beneath this roof could find a real place in her heart. And that realization also struck chords of caution within her.

When she'd agreed to come visit, Stefan had told her that the apartment was Petrov's, but Stefan's mother and grandmother had been living with him for seventeen years. Before Amanda asked, Petrov had answered her question of his bachelor status, stating that with two women in the house, who needed another? Amanda had laughed at his comical expression.

Amanda met Stefan last summer in Paris at a weekend conference that had focused on children of tragedies, including survivors of the Holocaust, the wars of former Yugoslavia, and other European countries in crisis. Several colleagues from the History Network had attended, along with other journalists she'd met over the years. As a researcher for History Network, Amanda was covering the event for a short piece to air on the weekly *History News Today*. Such seminars and conferences not only were covered for program use, but they provided the chance to network with others in a field where making contacts proved invaluable. She'd already found friends in historians and documentary filmmakers who later helped with the History Network productions.

Amanda recalled her first impression of Stefan Keller. He had a casual stance but an intense way of watching the world around him as if he were processing it all as a filmmaker would critique a scene of life. He was a new and handsome face, drawing interest from several of the single female journalists. Stefan had arrived with a male reporter from CNN but spoke little in group conversations. Someone discovered he was there as a guest and that he worked with some religious group. Amanda saw him walking on a parallel pathway in the university garden. She tried to look ahead to see if their paths would eventually cross, but friends called from behind and she turned away. He attended the author readings without comment and some of the extra late-night discussions, then slipped away when everyone else made plans for hitting the clubs. Amanda sized him up as arrogant and aloof.

One evening of the conference Amanda went to the small café beside the university building. After ordering, she realized there was a hole in her wallet and the coins had fallen to the bottom of her purse. While digging, she dropped her purse on the floor.

"I'll cover you," a voice said, and she caught a very slight accent. She saw his arm first, reaching to hand some coins to the vendor. When he knelt beside her to help pick up the contents of her purse, Amanda realized who it was. She bumped his head as they stood.

"I'm not usually this much of a klutz," she said with an embarrassed laugh.

"We all have our days." He handed her a tube of lipstick, rubbing his forehead and smiling—the first she'd seen from him. He had a great smile.

The attraction she felt was immediate and strong. And in that instant, she wondered if he recognized it too.

They sipped their coffee at a tiny table outside, missing a workshop in the process. Amanda asked him if he wanted to go with her and some of the others to a club that night.

He shook his head. "I promised someone I'd get pictures of Paris for her."

"I understand." Amanda assumed he meant his girlfriend since he didn't wear a wedding ring.

"Emily is seven years old."

"Is she your daughter?"

"No. Her parents are good friends of mine in New York. She wants to go to Paris to see where Madeline lives. That's a character—"

"From Ludwig Bemelmans' books. Yes, I read them as a child myself."

"Well, I'm Emily's hero because I was coming to Paris. Tonight I must get a photo from the top of the Eiffel Tower."

"Sounds fun."

"I heard there can be long lines. But I've never been up there, and I couldn't disappoint her. She promised to bake me cookies and mail them to me every week for a month."

"Seems like a worthwhile trade. I've never been up to the top either." She hadn't meant it as a hint, though later he would tease that she had.

"Would you like to come?"

Amanda was tired of the club scene, and she had never viewed the city from above, and at night no less. "I was told to never go anywhere with strangers."

"I was told that too," he said.

The Eiffel Tower was crowded with people at the ticket counter and on the lower deck. It gave them plenty of time to talk. The night turned cool with a quick wind on the upper level. They'd been dressed for a warm day—Amanda in a sleeveless shirt with slacks and Stefan in a thin cotton dress shirt. They were cold at the top, but they rubbed their arms and stood close for warmth. The view was spectacular, and they spent an hour pointing out parts of the city.

After that night in Paris, Amanda wondered if Stefan would really e-mail as he had promised. He was spending a week in Africa doing relief work; then he'd be back at his friend's apartment in Amsterdam. It took one week exactly, and instead of e-mailing, he phoned. Each day after that, her days were brightened by his screen name appearing in her in-box. She laughed with him across wires and phone lines. They shared thoughts, favorite books, and music, and even debated from time to time about favorite TV shows, though only touching on politics and his devout religion versus her tolerance for any religion. Through it all they formed more than a friendship. It became harder and harder to be apart. And yet their worlds were so different, she wondered how they would ever come together.

Now she'd spent her first day in Prague, in Stefan's world, but it had gone too fast. Though she'd been unable to reach the sites for her research, it allowed time to enjoy Stefan's family. Yet now Amanda had only one day left in Prague. The day would bring good-byes too soon as she left for her home in San Francisco. Two days may not be enough for her research, and they certainly weren't enough time with Stefan.

A hard burst of wind rattled the window, and a chill crept through the back corner of the loft. Dawn would come in hours. She needed rest before the day ahead—a day to concentrate on finding a piece of jewelry long lost. The Empress Brooch that could open the door to developing a program at her workplace and even answer questions about her own past.

Amanda returned to bed and shivered at the remembered nightmare. It had been years since she'd had it—time enough to believe it was gone forever. Perhaps it was this place getting too close . . . or maybe the work she tried to trivialize. *It's just a piece of jewelry,* she told herself. What could the search for an antique brooch do to her?

Yet she could never fully forget the warnings. Twice Amanda had been warned about seeking the Empress Brooch. "There is a curse on that brooch," her aunt had told her bluntly. And her Uncle Martin had also advised against searching their family's past: "Some things are better left alone."

"It's my job," she had told Uncle Martin, though it wasn't fully the truth. This was also personal—something that brought back childhood stories and a promise she'd once made to herself about her father.

Tomorrow she'd seek what she'd been warned against. Maybe somewhere inside she'd allowed the warnings to become a fear. And that fear had crept in where she couldn't fight back—in her dreams.

Through the glass and pelting sleet, Amanda peered at the orange glow of the streetlight. The answers could be close.

Pulling the covers up under her chin, Amanda settled back with a sigh. For the moment she felt safe in Stefan's place, surrounded by the insulated silence found only on a snowy night. It brought a comforting warmth, but she sensed the cold just beyond.

The dawn should bring her answers. Perhaps she would find the link to the Empress Brooch. And then, perhaps she'd find her own family's story.

Whatever she found—or didn't find—Amanda hoped the search would make the nightmare leave her, for good.

⋅⊶⊷⋅

A few hours later church bells clanged through ancient streets, awakening the city. The scent of sausage and the movements of someone in the kitchen below made Amanda stretch and look for her house slippers.

Amanda stood on tiptoe and examined herself in the mirror hanging on the wall, while attempting to do something with her hair. The blonde, shoulder-length cut was flat as expected and soft shadows beneath her pale green eyes spoke of her lack of sleep. She needed a shower, but with one bathroom for five people, Amanda wondered how to get one or if there'd be any hot water left. She grimaced. There were some advantages to impersonal hotels. Peeking over the loft railing, she saw Stefan's mother, Pavla, stirring a large pan of potatoes beside the sizzling sausage. Breakfast looked greasy and fattening, what Amanda rarely ate, but her stomach growled in yearning for what her father would call "real food."

"Good morning," Pavla said cheerfully as Amanda walked down steep, creaking stairs to the kitchen. "Coffee, yes?"

"Thank you," Amanda said sheepishly, aware of her sweats, oversized sweatshirt, lack of makeup, and bed head.

In contrast, Pavla's hair was tucked into a neat bun, and her gray slacks and white blouse were mostly covered by an apron. She poured a cup of coffee, which appeared as thick as espresso, and set the cup on a small tray with a silver creamer and a dish of sugar cubes.

"Stefan, he go to market," Pavla informed her. "He buy fresh bread for morning meal. You sit here?" She patted the top of the chair and smiled, revealing slightly yellowed teeth and dimples in her cheeks.

"All right." Amanda noticed the closed bathroom door and the crooked crack of light at the bottom.

"You sleep good?"

"Pretty good," Amanda said, again thinking of the nightmare.

"I work in little time," Pavla said, glancing at the antique wall clock. It let out a low bong as if to confirm her words. Stefan's mother worked at a school across town, Amanda recalled, though she'd meant to ask more details the day before. *How had one day gone so quickly?* Amanda thought once again. She wanted to know much more about this family than she now had time for.

"You teach children the Bohemian arts, right?"

"Yes." Pavla pointed to a collage of photographs stuck beneath various mismatched magnets on the old refrigerator.

Amanda rose from the table and examined the smiling faces in brightly colored traditional clothing.

"Our country grows fast in technology and change," Pavla continued. "Our children and young people not have to live under Communism as we do. They want everything like America. But we not forget old ways. I teach music, dance, art, and crafts from wood."

"I, too, believe in the importance of history," Amanda said.

Their eyes met in silent understanding.

"Yes, yes. I know. You work for television history show, no? Today important day in your work, yes?"

"It could be," Amanda admitted. "If I find the information I'm looking for."

Just then footsteps creaked up the long stairway beyond the front door.

Amanda smiled. It had to be Stefan. Because the elevator

was in constant need of repair, she knew he had trekked up five long flights of winding stairs.

"Stefan buy bread fast today," Pavla said with a wink as she returned to the stove.

The lock clicked across the room, and the top of Stefan's ash-blond hair appeared first as he entered. *"Dobre jitro—,"* he began, then spotted Amanda. "Good morning." His eyes, so pale blue, held hers, and she wondered again if he felt the intensity between them.

Pavla interrupted their locked gaze as she retrieved the bag of bread from Stefan's arm. He took off his coat, heavy with melting snow, and sat on an old wooden bench by the door. Running his hand through his wet hair, he shook his head and kicked off his black boots.

So this is who Stefan is, Amanda thought. This was Stefan on all those days he wrote about going to Prague for the weekend. This was where he'd come and bring the morning bread. He'd take off his coat, kick off his shoes just like that, and say good morning. And today she was here to see it.

He was looking at her again, but this time she felt self-conscious. He'd never seen her in the morning without makeup or her hair done just right; he'd never seen her not wearing the career clothes she wore at conferences, let alone sweats.

"It's cold again but will clear by afternoon," Stefan said. "And you'll be working underground all day."

He reached beneath the bench to the long basket overflowing with shoes and worn-out slippers to find his own pair of misshapen slippers that had earlier reminded Amanda of something Mr. Winifred, her elderly landlord in San Francisco, would wear. She'd teased Stefan about it until she realized that the loaners from Stefan's grandmother that she'd been wearing were even worse looking—and a size too small.

Amanda thought about yesterday when Stefan, Petrov, and

she went through Petrov's slides and newspapers covering the 1989 Velvet Revolution. Amanda, fascinated with the stories of Czechoslovakia's independence, wanted to hear everything about their experiences during such a tumultuous time. But Stefan was unusually quiet, and his silence reminded her of how little she really knew about him. Although they had written each other for months after their initial meeting in Paris, there were huge pieces of Stefan she still didn't know.

Stefan said he needed to run an errand. After he left, Petrov explained that for older people like himself who'd lived their entire lives under Communism, there had been a complete change of mind-set during the transformation. But Stefan had been young when Communism fell, and his best friend had died during that time. Amanda wondered what thoughts had filled Stefan's mind then and why he'd left Prague as soon as his country found freedom. Was it because of his friend's death, something he'd rarely spoken about?

Stefan soon returned in his usual light mood, carrying the new fleece-lined slippers that she now wore. Her questions were quickly forgotten when Pavla brought out Stefan's baby photos.

Now it was the day of her departure and neither knew when they'd see each other again. "If my work goes well today, perhaps I'll have time to see some sunshine," Amanda said.

"Work fast," Stefan said with a smile.

"Let us eat." Pavla turned from the stove with a large iron skillet in hand. Amanda set plates from the dish drainer around the table as Pavla followed, scooping healthy helpings onto the plates. Before Stefan sat at the table, he greeted his grandmother, coming from the bathroom, her hair neatly tucked into a bun much like Pavla's. She gave him a big hug, squeezed his face between her hands, and then chattered away in Czech.

"Petrov, can you come away from computer?" Pavla called.

Petrov wheeled on his computer chair from behind a wide bookcase that separated the kitchen from the living room. "You need not ask me twice. Babička, leave Stefan to be a man," Petrov said with a wink toward Amanda as Grandmother Ruza kissed Stefan's cheeks.

Ruza chided Petrov in Czech, even though Amanda knew she couldn't have understood what he'd said to her in English.

"*Dobre jitro,* Amanda," Petrov said, wheeling his chair to the corner of the table.

"*Dobre jitro,*" she replied in turn.

"Babička has yet to come to terms with the fact that I'm in my thirties now and that I'm not moving back to Prague," Stefan said, pulling a chair out for her.

"I'm sure a grandmother never does," Amanda said, though not from experience. She'd never known any of her grandparents. Yet she knew that one set had once lived not far from Prague.

"I will say the blessing over our meal," Petrov said, his gray hair falling across his forehead the way Stefan's hair often did. As he bowed his head, the rest of the family bowed with him. "First, I thank almighty God for the gift of Amanda Rivans in our home yesterday and this morning," he prayed in English.

Amanda shifted uncomfortably. She had yet to bow her head and close her eyes as the others had.

"We ask you, Father God," Petrov continued, "that protection be hers on the journey home this evening, that you guide her path in the days ahead and bless her with your love and peace. Please bless this food to nourish our bodies and keep our health. And . . . well, our food will be cold, Father, and so we thank you for your goodness. In the name of our Lord Jesus Christ, we say amen."

The others repeated his amen.

Amanda marveled at this mismatched family—at their solemn religion, their great love for one another, and their sudden voracious eating, as if Petrov's prayer that caused her pause was just an ordinary ritual they shared.

"Mother rarely makes such a breakfast except on holidays," Stefan said from beside her.

"We all benefit from your visit." Petrov spoke what she assumed to be the same words to Ruza, who smiled and nodded at Amanda as she ate.

Languages switched from English, which was often broken and hard to understand, to Czech and then to German. Stefan's grandmother spoke a little German, and Amanda was fluent in that language so it became the closest to common communication among them all.

Amanda tried to memorize the sound of family and drink in every detail of the place. The apartment's high vaulted ceilings showcased its dark wooden beams and white plaster. The upper stories of the building were colder than the lower ones, because the heat from the radiators rose but dissipated below. Yet Amanda loved the drafty old place and even more so when told the building dated to the late 1700s. Books and magazines sat in piles beside leather chairs and on shelves around the rooms. A bookcase under every window held volumes from Twain, Dickinson, Billy Graham, Margaret Mitchell, Grisham, Czech writers Kundera and Kafka, and others—and a few authors and languages she didn't recognize.

Amanda had spent some time getting used to Stefan in these surroundings, imagining this place as familiar to him. She had tried to picture it as he saw it—at least in the things that stood out to her. Like the simple pictures in thick wood frames, the glass figurines of peasants, a miniature Eiffel Tower, and a collection of floaty pens, with a different floating scene in each see-through pen, all obviously from Stefan's journeys. She wondered which family member he brought them home to— his mother, Pavla, who believed in the old ways; his grand- mother, Ruza, who'd shown off her postcard collection; or his intellectual cousin, Petrov, who studied theology for a hobby. What items had been here since his childhood? Stefan stayed here whenever he came to Prague, sleeping in the loft bed that had been his since he was a young boy and his father died. Each morning he'd awaken at dawn to the sound of bells ringing through the streets. It was Stefan's place whenever he came, left untouched when he was gone.

Amanda watched him across the table. The way he broke his roll in half and dipped it in jam before taking a bite. Throughout the meal and conversation he'd catch her eye and send her a half wink or a smile. Perhaps yesterday's blizzard had been the best thing for them. At least they'd had an entire day together—even if shared with his family. It was time they hadn't had since the day they'd met in Paris the summer before.

Amanda realized they were now discussing her reason for coming to Prague.

"Your work sounds interesting," Petrov said. "An entire channel devoted to history—and you work there. I find that fascinating."

"You live today also?" Pavla asked, but Amanda didn't understand what she meant. Pavla was smiling softly, and Amanda sensed there was great meaning in her words. "I know it easy to live in yesterday. You live today also, correct?"

Amanda nodded. She understood the depth of Pavla's words. It was easy to get wrapped up in the stories of the past and forget to look beyond career opportunities and ahead to what she wanted for her personal life.

Ruza spoke in Czech, leaning across the table to pat Amanda's hand.

"She says she hopes you find your family," Stefan said.

Amanda's gaze jumped to Ruza. "Thank you," she said, remembering their discussion of yesterday about her family. "I wish I had more time here. I hope to find information about my grandparents before their deaths. I'm not sure how long they lived in the village of Lidice before the Nazi invasion."

"Lidice?" Ruza said.

"You did not tell us they lived in Lidice," Petrov said. Suddenly the room was silent and all eyes turned toward Amanda.

"That is what I was told as a child," she said, taken aback by their obvious surprise and her slip of words. Amanda hadn't even told Stefan about her grandparents' fate in Lidice, and she certainly hadn't intended to tell his family the story until she had proof. Of course, any Czech citizen would know of the destruction and massacre of the village of Lidice by the Nazis. It was foolish of her not to have told earlier or foolish to have said it now without concrete proof.

"I had no idea, Amanda," Stefan said with sympathy.

"I never knew them. I'm not even sure what happened, except that neither my grandmother nor grandfather survived the war."

"We understand loss of family." Petrov glanced at Ruza and Pavla.

"All of you have lost much more than I have," Amanda replied. Stefan's father, grandfather, and uncle had all been killed during the various wars and uprisings in his country. The family had faced death and grief again and again.

"Yes, I understand. But you lost also. Their love and, how do you say, ah, heritage. It taken from you." Pavla nodded in sympathy. "I lost my father to the Nazis and my brother and husband to the Communists. But it is better times now."

"Are you ready for this day?" Stefan asked.

Amanda hesitated. She'd told him her newest project included the search for the lost Empress Brooch—a priceless piece of jewelry that had disappeared during the Nazi era. Her research could move the concept of a story on the lost brooch through development and into production at the History

Network. It would be a big step for her career. She'd also told Stefan that she planned to dedicate the project to her father, for his own work with Holocaust groups over the years. But she'd not shared her fears or the questions about her family she hoped would be settled today. The belief that Lidice was her grandparents' place of life and death could only be confirmed by finding a record of proof among the archives she'd soon search.

"I'm ready," she said with feigned confidence.

"Why don't you let me work with you?"

"Stefan cannot understand no." Pavla shook her head. "It his problem since he little boy. 'Stefan,' I would say, 'do not touch the stove.' He would. 'Do not play with Christmas eggs.' He break them. Again and again. Stefan, Amanda say yesterday that she get no work done with you at archive."

Amanda laughed at his mother's chastising, imagining a short little Stefan with decorated Czech Christmas eggs lying broken at his feet.

"We would have the entire day together. I'm not ready for you to leave tonight." Although Stefan spoke the words casually, she knew he was aware their time was falling away too fast.

"I will work quickly, find what I need, and then we will have the afternoon." She hoped it would be true. A huge part of her wanted him to help her, and she would let him if she was only searching for a brooch with no connection with her own background. But this was something she needed to seek on her own—for her future at the History Network, but even more for herself.

Pavla chuckled and reached for empty plates. "This wise girl, Stefan."

"And if I find a lead in the missing brooch, I may be spending much more time in Prague."

"We could get Stefan home more times too." Pavla reached for a thick knit sweater on the back of her chair.

"Time for Amanda to work." Stefan rose from his chair. "I have reserved the shower for you for the après-breakfast hour."

"*Dekuji*," Amanda said with a curtsy.

⟶═◉═⟵

Amanda took a quick shower in the old tile tub and used a hand nozzle to wash her hair. She packed her luggage in the loft and said good-bye to Petrov and Ruza—Pavla had already said her parting before going to teach the Czech school-children.

As Amanda prepared to leave, Ruza held Amanda tightly and spoke gentle Czech words. The old woman's face was heavily wrinkled from the hard years of life and her arms shook, but her eyes were the same crisp, pale blue as Stefan's. And, like his, they were unblinking in their gaze.

"Babička," Stefan finally said, putting a hand on his grand-mother's shoulder.

"What did she say?" Amanda asked as Ruza stepped away from her.

"Nothing. It is time to get you to the archives," Stefan put in quickly.

Ruza waited beside him.

"Tell me what she said, Stefan," Amanda insisted.

He sighed and glanced at the elderly woman. "She said something about caring for me and my heart. And that she wants you to seek God with all of yours."

Ruza smiled and then added a few words, patting her chest.

"'Seek God with all of your heart,' she says."

Amanda nodded. This wise woman had been through more than Amanda could imagine. Her heritage was one of sorrow and loss. Yet Ruza seemed joyful at the end of her life. "Tell her that I will try."

At the doorway Amanda turned back for a last wave at Petrov and Ruza. She detested good-byes. In one day and a morning she'd become attached to these people and this tower apartment. Now she was too quickly torn away. She could return, she reminded herself, though she'd packed her new slippers into her luggage instead of leaving them beneath the bench by the door. Perhaps next time she'd walk out the door with them mixed among Stefan's family's. Unless the archives revealed a different truth than she expected, Amanda hoped to return.

The only thing that bothered her was the slight infraction to the story of her heritage.

But soon she'd know the truth—and she'd have the answers she sought.

CHAPTER TWO

OAKDALE, FLORIDA

It was the hour of her discontent, Ms. Delsig believed. Why else would a woman of her age who had drawn thousands of sketches and created untold numbers of paintings now find herself struggling to move the pencil? Her arthritis wasn't bothering her hands. Her health was perfect as usual. The light and shadows worked with the Florida sun dipping behind her. Was it painter's block? Ms. Delsig didn't believe such a thing existed—there was always something to draw or paint.

Since after lunch, she'd worked on the five-by-ten-foot plot of garden granted to her by the Oakdale Home of Senior Living. She'd pulled those scraggly weeds and marveled at the new growth of bulbs and plants. She now sat on the bench with her eyes framing the section of garden she wanted to draw. Yet a half hour had passed, and she'd yet to choose a pencil from her art box.

Ms. Delsig sighed and shifted on the bench, distracted by someone being wheeled into the sunshine to her left. She smoothed the floral gardening apron over her lap and again took out the small sketchpad from her pocket where she'd placed it a few seconds before. This should be easy. She opened the wooden case and searched the upper tray of charcoal pencils—*6B extra soft would be the one,* she thought.

She flipped through the pages of sketches, seeking inspiration. Her years here at Oakdale were recorded in books such as these instead of photographs or journals of her life. She turned past diagrams of flowers, a profile of residents at the home, raindrop-laden plants, and rain streaming down the windows. Some were better than others. The arthritis made it tough to draw at times. Then she flipped past frayed top edges where pages had been ripped from the book—the disobedient drawings she didn't want to keep, the ones that seemed to draw themselves, arising from some horrible corner of her past. Finally she reached a blank page.

Her head cocked to one side, she rubbed her chin, gazed at the paper and then at the tiny plot of earth. She touched the pencil to the white page, but only for an instant. Her eyes turned again toward the garden.

Goodness sakes, she thought, glancing at the nurse's aide who was wiping drool from the chin of the woman in the wheelchair, *just the inspiration I'm looking for.*

She'd been waiting for a day like this—a day when the earth awakened from its rainy rest—and yet the image wouldn't come. She sighed again and sat back. The irises and paperwhites had been the first to rise from the rich soil; the tulips she'd ordered from Holland were close behind. Some kind of ivy crept carefully up the wooden fence, and a purple-flowered ground cover made a border in between.

This was the third year of her garden's rebirth, and Ms. Delsig felt pleased to see that an old woman like herself could learn new tricks. She'd decided to ignore the criticism and remarks of others as they compared her results to the gardening virtuoso who'd cultivated this area before her. "When Mr. Hill was alive, I declare there were flowers for every season." "How good of you to revive Mr. Hill's garden, though I'm sure he would have liked to give some advice. We've never had such beauty at the home since he left us."

Ms. Delsig would smile and continue planting and weeding and pruning. She was new to gardening, while Mr. Hill had been a retired nursery worker. He'd also been a favorite at the home, with its lack of elderly males to balance the female population. Mr. Hill had been handsome for a man of ninety-two and the prize to catch, or so she'd been told. He'd died two years before her arrival, and not one lucky lady had captured his heart before his well-mourned death. Few would remember Mr. Hill now with the fast turnover in nursing homes. Oakdale was no exception—Oakdale Home of the Aged and Decayed, as Ms. Delsig especially liked to call it. Yet even with Mr. Hill long gone, all current residents somehow continued to refer to her plot of dirt as his.

As she continued to sit in the sun, it warmed her face on one side and cast long shadows from the new green sprouts in the garden. When she looked behind her, she noticed the backyard dotted with groups and individual residents—or inmates, as her friend Alfred Milton called them—as they warmed cold bones outside. The grounds had been pelted with rain for many days so the lawn was soggy, causing metal walkers to get stuck and shoes to get slushy—her own walker and Keds tennis shoes included.

She gazed back to her garden that occupied the left side of the yard, considering what to sketch. She tried to draw a line across the page, but nothing came to her.

"They will be lovely."

Into the falling sunlight stepped Ms. Delsig's roommate and the one female resident at Oakdale she truly considered a friend. In a minute Janice Reynolds sat on the bench beside her, rocking softly back and forth as she always did when sitting.

"Right now I love the garden best," Ms. Delsig said, patting Janice's hand. Her roommate's skin was smooth—unlike Ms. Delsig's own worn epidermis that was covered in veins and dotted with age spots. Janice was young in her book. Fifty-three was a lass compared to Ms. Delsig's own seventy-six years. Someone like Janice shouldn't be in a place like this, and Ms. Delsig often said so. But Janice's tendency toward unexpected seizures and constant rocking motions had been her ticket to Oakdale.

"Why do you love it best now?" Janice said, rocking slightly faster.

"I'm not sure. Perhaps it is anticipation of what will come or maybe that wonder I find in flowers. I planted those bulbs on the right three years ago. They will be purple irises in a few months—it took me two seasons to remember their names. But I planted them, they grew, they faded, and I cut the stalks. They popped from the ground last spring, and we went through the stages another time. Now I see them growing again—all from those bulbs I planted. I have watched every day from the window of the recreation room or hobbled out here on a sunny day. Sometimes I just want to dig down a little to see if they are really coming. Then, suddenly, here they are."

"But the flowers, that's when the garden is truly beautiful." Janice rocked with her arms tight against her chest.

"Ah, but the flowers mean that soon I will be cutting them down to dirt again. Right now, I have each day to see them grow and the bud to appear surrounded in green. It is the time of greeting now, not the time of good-bye."

Janice was silent for a long time. Her rocking would slow, then increase at intervals. That meant she was thinking, Ms. Delsig knew.

"I need to tell you something, Ms. Delsig."

"And what would it be, dear?"

Janice stared at the green buds, not looking at her. Her forehead was scrunched in thought, and stringy auburn hair fell across her cheeks.

"What is it?" Ms. Delsig asked again as the pencil rolled from her hand onto the grass.

Janice retrieved the pencil and held it tightly with two hands. "You remember my sister's husband died six months ago. Well, Monique is alone now. Monique says she gets scared at night and that she misses me. Remember how you always say I don't belong here?"

Oh, here it comes, Ms. Delsig thought. "I remember."

"Well, I should have told you earlier about the possibility. It's just that I was afraid it might not happen and afraid to tell you. But Monique asked me to come live with her in Georgia."

Ms. Delsig gently took the pencil from Janice's grip and put it away in the wooden case. She closed the lid and snapped the latches. "I thought you didn't like Monique." She recalled their many conversations across the room they shared. Unlike many of the other roommates at Oakdale who fought for their halves of the room, Ms. Delsig and Janice had become as close as sisters, or so she had thought.

"She wrote me a long letter asking for my forgiveness. She said her husband wouldn't let me live there and forced her to put me away. She wants to get help for me—is already searching for doctors in her area." Janice bit her lip. Her rocking stopped for one moment. "We were close when we were young," she continued. "She took care of me. I called her Mama sometimes."

"Yes, I know." Ms. Delsig smoothed Janice's hair.

"Are you happy for me?" Janice glanced furtively at her.

"I am very happy for you. Really."

It was the truth, and Ms. Delsig hoped Janice believed her, even if the words sounded forced. She was just so surprised, shocked actually. It never crossed her mind that she'd lose this woman. Everyone knew what it meant to be a permanent resident here. It meant that Ms. Delsig wouldn't need a forwarding address ever again. When she finally left this place it would be in the white hearse she'd requested in writing to take her from Oakdale Home of the Aged and Decayed to the Oakdale Home of the Dead and Soon-to-be-Buried.

Ms. Delsig had arrived here reluctantly and had tried her best to be the grouchy, old crow she wanted to be. But the staff was lovely and the food passable, except on taco-salad Thursday (at least they said it was taco salad). And she did have Edith and Tess, whom she'd known from her previous life on the outside—even though both women had died within the first year of Ms. Delsig's arrival. The passing of those two friends had left Ms. Delsig with only two friends— Janice Reynolds and Alfred Milton. And her biggest ray of happiness at Oakdale was rooming with Janice. Janice's young age ensured that Ms. Delsig would not lose at least one of those remaining friendships until her own white-hearse departure.

"I'm a little afraid, Ms. Delsig. Isn't that silly? I am afraid to leave this place. Did you know I have been here for nine years now? I was so young when I came. I still am young compared to so many here. But I'm afraid to be out there."

Ms. Delsig hugged her, joining the rapid rocking to and fro. "You will be all right. We will both be all right." She wanted to be strong for Janice, but a great tiredness swept over her. The sun felt hot and her sprouts of green seemed to mock her. *It won't be long and you will have to cut us down too. It is always good-bye for you.*

"I'll come back and visit. My sister already said she'd bring me. I told her I had to or I couldn't leave."

"Of course you will visit, of course." She pulled back and held Janice's arms.

"I'll send you some of my favorite banana bread."

"That would be wonderful." Ms. Delsig tried hard to smile.

"We could e-mail if you would learn how to turn on the computer." There was such hope in Janice's eyes.

"I may have to do that since I know your record for writing real letters."

"And I'll never tell your secret. Never. Not even to my sister."

Ms. Delsig stared at Janice. "My secret. What do you mean?" She felt a strange sense of wonder. "I do not have any secrets."

"That's right," Janice said. She moved her fingers over her lips and then tossed away the invisible key.

A chill swept across her. Why would Janice say such a thing? Ms. Delsig didn't have any secrets. Not any that Janice knew about.

"I am so forgetful. Sometimes I forget what I have told you," Ms. Delsig said with a smile.

Janice smiled too. "Well, it meant a lot that I could be there for you for once. How many times have you helped me? If only you were my sister and able to care for me," she said wistfully.

"You have helped me too," Ms. Delsig said, wondering how to ask Janice what exactly she'd shared—and when. She sought her memories for a time and only came up with the night many months earlier when she'd awakened in terror but couldn't remember the dream. Janice had been patting her shoulder, saying words of comfort. Had she revealed something then without knowing it?

"Well, I have an appointment to make final arrangements with Mr. Bartlett. Meet you at art class, okay?" Janice said as she left her on the bench.

Ms. Delsig watched her shuffled departure toward the open French doors. Surely it didn't matter if Janice knew of her past; it was long ago. Yet she could feel this hour turn from discontent to sudden fear. Why couldn't she remember? Some things in yesterday could still be harmful, and she had planned to carry them safely away in a shiny white hearse.

Whom could she trust if not herself?

CHAPTER THREE

The basement documentation center was two stories beneath the snow-covered streets of Prague. The hands of the clock had moved round and round since Amanda's arrival. Her eyes had stayed downward toward the piles of folders of papers of data of words. The load of information was immense.

The seventh hour ticked past. Stefan had called twice to check on her. Each time she had admitted failure and asked for more time. Now the day was gone, and she'd spent it all in this basement, lighted by the buzz and flicker of a fluorescent tube and surrounded by stacks of files and open boxes. Seven hours, and she'd accomplished little. Disappointment had been keen in Stefan's voice as well as in hers. But she had been determined to keep looking. She couldn't leave Prague tonight with nothing. If she could find just one name or one lead to follow—anything.

Her toes inside her left boot felt frozen. Amanda recalled the loose string in her wool sock that had begun the unraveling process earlier that morning. Her neck muscles ached and the metal chair pressed against her bones. It felt like days had passed with her being trapped in these gray rooms of the former Secret Service building. During the Communist era, it had been a place for the Czech secret police to hold meetings and interrogations; now it was an archive storage that held the paperwork of lives, covert missions, and lost stories waiting to be voiced.

If she were in the United States, a simple run of various computer searches would move her through thousands of documents. But this was a former Communist country. Time was required, with many old files only recently released from secret government vaults and many still beyond the use of a search engine. Amanda also met another challenge when she'd arrived that morning—the Internet server was down, making any computer file impossible to retrieve.

Amanda stood and paced. Pacing often worked to stir ideas.

Her thoughts returned to the beginning. From her initial research she found two leads that possibly placed the Empress Sissi Brooch in the Czech Republic. The story of the brooch began in Austria. One large emerald with two smaller ones on each side, this brooch had been owned by the Austrian empress, Elizabeth—called Sissi by her adoring subjects. One day in the 1800s, when the empress was riding her horse, she'd fallen off. A Jewish man, Herbert Lange, had helped her and then, at her request, kept the fact that she was riding a horse a secret. So Empress Sissi had given the brooch to Lange as a symbol of her gratitude. The brooch had then passed to Herbert's son, Simon, but Simon died in a concentration camp. The brooch was never recovered. Simon's daughter, Celia Lange, the rightful heiress to the brooch, had last seen it in her father's care before she escaped Austria during World War II. Unfortunately, Amanda couldn't interview Celia Lange because she had died recently. She had talked by phone to

Celia's granddaughter, Darby Evans Collins, but Mrs. Collins had little new information to offer, except for a few places they knew the brooch couldn't be located, due to their own searches.

But Amanda had two possibilities of her own to pursue.

The strongest lead was information she'd uncovered after gaining permission from the Lange family to pursue the brooch as a possible feature for the History Network.

The last man known to have the brooch, Simon Lange, had hidden at a home in the Alps that was owned by Simon's friend Jan Kirke, who lived in Prague. Jan Kirke made one last visit to Austria during the time of Simon's hiding to see his old friend. Soon after Jan's return to Prague, Simon Lange was captured by the Nazis and died later at Mauthausen Concentration Camp.

Amanda was following the slight lead that on the last visit between old family friends, Simon had passed the brooch into the care of his friend, Jan Kirke, for safekeeping until the war was over. Someone in the Nazi Party must have believed this also and followed the Kirkes to Prague, which was occupied by the Germans at that time. Yet Amanda needed a record that this was true, along with some record of the Kirke family after WWII.

There was also the weaker yet very personal lead that had brought her here—a bedtime story told to Amanda when she was a little girl. The tale linked her own lost family with a unique and beautiful brooch that had belonged to an Austrian empress. Since her grandparents had lived and died near Prague, finding them could uncover some link with her family and the brooch. Whether there was a link or the story was a fairy tale, she couldn't guess. But she hoped she could find something about her grandparents—it would be a gift to her father and one he'd long deserved. Amanda had often pictured her father's reaction as the full story of his parents was revealed. It would bring his world full circle in a way. And her own.

Returning to the papers in front of her, Amanda made an unconscious reach for the mug on the table. For the second time that afternoon her lips tasted the bitterness of old coffee. She set the mug down quickly, and black liquid splashed on the papers. The wet stain reminded her of an inkblot test. For a moment Amanda tried to discern a pattern. Then she grimaced. She'd been in this basement too long. What she'd give for fresh, strong coffee that would heat away the chill that crept through her.

Wiping away the coffee, she gazed once again at the list of names of people who died in the Lidice massacre. Hours earlier she'd searched these names, then set them aside before going through stacks of connected information. On one of these lines, she should find her grandparents, Kurt and Hilde Heinrich. When she'd first gone through the paper that morning, she hadn't found them. But they had to be there. She had to try again.

Her eyes stung from hours of bad light and many words in several languages. She touched each name on the pages, looking for names even somewhat similar. Why weren't her grandparents here?

Amanda heard a heavy door slam somewhere above, then the light footsteps of the assistant provided to her by the documentation center. Jirik Novak appeared in the doorway, a cup in hand. He jumped in surprise to see her still there.

"*S dovolenim,*" Jirik stuttered in Czech. She smiled at his embarrassment. Jirik had stuck with her for five hours, searching files and bringing boxes for her perusal. He supposedly knew English, or so Amanda's assistant, Tiffany Hammon, had assured her when making the arrangements with the archival office. Yet Jirik knew little more English than Amanda's Czech, which only helped her find a bathroom, order coffee, and say thank you.

"You long work." Jirik took a sip of something steaming from the Styrofoam cup. Evidently he caught her longing glance and looked down, suddenly streaming off what she supposed was an apology for not bringing her anything. She tried to assure Jirik even as her stomach protested her scanty lunch of a pack of airplane pretzels and bottled water.

Taking several quick steps to the table, Jirik held out the cup in offering. Of course, it *was* hot coffee, what she'd been longing for. If she hadn't just seen him take a drink, she might have accepted his offer.

"*Ne, ne,*" she said, trying to look busy.

Jirik nodded, then picked up her list of needed information. Without her list written in both English and Czech, Jirik would have been completely unable to help her.

"More copies?" Jirik asked as he sat on the edge of the cold metal table. He stretched his thin arms above his head. Jirik, though only in his mid-twenties, appeared to have worked in the basement much too long. His pasty white skin and slight frame conjured up the image of a laboratory mouse that was rarely fed or given attention.

"This is good. You've made enough copies, thank you," she responded, but he looked confused. "*Ne more, dekuji.*" She leaned back in her chair and stretched to relieve the aches in her shoulders and neck. Jirik had already copied a pile of documents for her to go through once she returned home. Picking up a stack of now closed folders, she dropped them back into a box beside her. The fluorescent light above continued to tick and flicker intermittently. Everything in the room was gray—the walls, metal shelves, tables, and chairs—a memory of the long Communist era in Prague.

"O-kay." Jirik muttered, popping out a cigarette from his

coat pocket and lighting up. He gazed over the papers and exhaled a whiff of smoke. "Boyfriend come back."

Amanda grinned at Jirik's cool manner as he believed he communicated perfect English. Next time she'd ask her assistant to double-check what it meant to speak English by having Tiffany actually speak to the person in advance.

"My friend will be here soon," she said, checking her watch. The time had flown. Her program manager at the History Network would not be pleased. Sylvia Pride already had the working title "In Search of the Empress Brooch." Researchers were working on the back story of Austria's beloved Empress Elizabeth and pulling any related images.

"More stay in Praha?" he asked.

"*Ne*, I fly back to San Francisco tonight."

Jirik nodded as if understanding and moved around a low cubicle wall to his desk. His chair scraped loudly against the cement floor and his dinosaur computer groaned to life.

"He'll be here soon," Amanda repeated to herself. With Stefan's arrival would come the warmth of his presence. She sighed. A tangled dragon of smoke from Jirik's cigarette hung near the ceiling and drifted slowly through the room.

She examined the list of names from the village of Lidice once more, allowing for some close variation. Her finger trailed down the last names. Turning the page, she scanned the columns. The paper was thin and yellowing after sixty years since it had first been typed and filed. Amanda had seen the Nazi SS typewriters with the swastika key that left the SS imprint on the headings of each page. Only the Nazis would produce a typewriter with their party symbol among the keys.

She dropped the list. They weren't there.

The many stories of her family's past were a mismatched setting she had hoped would come together into a perfect patchwork quilt. Now as she sought the answers, Amanda discovered more frays and pieces too unrelated to conjoin into any sort of pattern—patchwork or not. It was clear some piece of her heritage was missing.

All the papers surrounding her on the metal table and stuffed in these basement shelves represented lives, real lives. Amanda's work had revolved around investigating these lives, but it had become more than just her career—it was now her personal search. Only within the ink and lost lives of yesterday could she find the clues of what had happened to her family. And yet, even with all her searching, she couldn't find her own grandparents.

Faces came to her as she began to close folders, recalling the photographs and stories she'd spent the day with. Amanda knew from experience that these images would haunt her nights. Men hanging from light posts, children lying dead on the ground where people passed, and a mother crying in agony. In one photo a young man with a look of peace and determination awaited a bullet to the head. The next photo depicted him dead, his face in the dirt. Amanda lived with these images and moved past them as much as she could in her quest for links to her own past. She'd never known her grandmother and grandfather. Could any of the people in these photographs be part of her own bloodline?

They could be anyone.

"Ah! Computer!" Jirik said, rising from the cubicle wall with a wide smile stretching across his narrow face. Talking in Czech, he motioned Amanda over. She hurried around to his dungeonlike workstation. Old cups of coffee, bumper stickers, logos, and a picture of a music group whose members had pure white hair cluttered the space.

Jirik pointed at the computer screen. The server was working. He'd accessed the government files. The language was either Czech or Russian; she couldn't be sure. The program was old and outdated—a simple line of names and numbers against the black screen. Then she caught what he pointed to:

CZ45000K5
   *Kirke, Jan (Linz, Osterreich 30/11/98 Praha, CZ.
21/06/42)*
   *Kirke, Ilsa (Linz, Osterreich 07/02/05 Praha, CZ.
21/06/42)*
   Kirke, Edgar (Praha, CZ. 10/10/23)
   Kirke, Brigit (Praha, CZ. 27/07/26 Auschwitz)
   Kirke, Hani (Praha, CZ. 14/01/39 Auschwitz. 14/12/43)

The Kirke family. Or at least a possibility. *Osterreich* meant Austria, and *CZ* probably stood for Czechoslovakia. That gave even further evidence that this was the Kirke family she sought.

"What is this program?" Amanda asked, pointing at the top of the screen.

Jirik tried to tell her in Czech, but she didn't understand. His motions made her guess, as if this were a game of multi-lingual charades.

"Gov–gvr. How say?" he sputtered.

"Government?"

"Yes." He nodded. "Nazi govment."

"This is a Nazi file?"

"Russki keep."

"This is a Nazi file that the Russians kept after the war?"

He appeared a little unsure but nodded anyway.

"Can you print this? Print." She pointed to his dot matrix printer.

Jirik nodded with a smile that showed he was proud to have finally helped her.

"But why wasn't this information in those files?" She motioned to the many aisles they'd spent the day in.

He shrugged and pushed keys that made the printer jerk to life.

Soon Stefan would be here and he could ask questions for

her, she thought. Suddenly she had to consider the possibility that the Soviet government had long ago solved the mystery of the Empress Brooch. It could be sitting in a vault in Moscow at that very moment. Amanda gave Jirik an excited pat on the back, making him jump. They laughed together.

Finally she had something.

CHAPTER FOUR

Stefan was right on time.

Amanda heard him descend the stairs and stop at the first metal gate. Jirik jogged to unlock the gate that opened on squeaky hinges. Jirik held the gate and Stefan entered, ducking his head through the doorway. He carried two cups that sent whiffs of steam rising in the dim light. He smiled in his way that warmed her through.

"I'm here for my interrogation," he said. "Wasn't that the purpose of the room you've been sitting in the entire day?"

"I had the pleasure of seeing photographic evidence," she said, wishing away the remembrance of blood on the concrete below her feet and the instruments of torture laid out on a table much like the one before her.

"Perhaps if I could have helped—"

"You can help now," Amanda said, reaching for the coffee as if finding an oasis in the desert. "*Dekuji,* Stefan. You don't know how thankful I am for this. Come around here to what Jirik found on his computer."

"So something has been found after seven hours in the dungeon."

"Just come here," she said.

He brought two chairs from Amanda's worktable.

"Chairs—what a novel idea," she said, taking one from his hand.

"They make them in America too."

"Is that right? I'll have to look for one." Amanda noticed Jirik sitting in his chair, his head moving from one to another as they spoke. "This is why I couldn't have you work with me all day," she said.

"You would have found even less than the nothing you found." Stefan smiled wickedly.

She crossed her arms. "We found something. Well, Jirik did."

"All right," Stefan said, suddenly serious as he drew his chair close. He began asking Jirik questions. The two spoke for some time as Jirik scrolled up and down the data on the screen. Stefan pointed to names and words as Amanda watched from Jirik's other side and tried to discern something from the conversation.

"The program he is using, though it looks very outdated, is capable of searching for the listing of files that were kept secret under the Communist government until 1989. These names here are ones you were looking for, right?"

Jirik slid his chair back from between them, got up, and reached for his pack of cigarettes. Amanda and Stefan moved closer to the computer screen.

"Yes, I believe that is the Kirke family who lived for a time in Austria and may have had contact with the Empress Brooch," Amanda explained. "Possibly they kept it for safe-keeping when a friend of theirs was arrested. I phone-interviewed a woman, Darby Evans Collins, in Austria, whose grandmother was part of the Lange family—the heiress of the

Empress Brooch. But her grandmother had recently passed away, and she didn't know about the contact with the Kirke family."

"The listing of both Linz and Prague further confirms that this could be the same family." Stefan drummed his fingers on the desk.

"That's what I thought. But why wasn't this information in the archives?"

"Apparently, this is a type of serial number that indicated the file location." Stefan turned to where Jirik was sitting on top of a metal file cabinet enjoying his smoke. Stefan asked him another question and then relayed the answer to Amanda. "The serial number is either for a more secure file or for one that was taken back to Russia. Jirik said you'll have to contact the Documentation Center to proceed."

Amanda glanced at the wall clock. "The office is closed. And I'm leaving soon."

"If you can get permission from the Documentation Center after you are gone, I could stay the weekend, pick it up on Monday, and translate the file before sending it to you."

"Would that inconvenience you?" Amanda realized that she'd asked little about his work and plans in the day they'd been together.

"It will be all right. My grandmother and mother will be especially happy for me to stay a few extra days."

Amanda hesitated.

"Amanda, I will understand if you don't want me involved. This . . . well . . . there is a lot we haven't talked about—about us." She noted his sudden awkwardness. "But I know it's important that you get something for your work soon. I want to help if I can."

She nodded. He'd indicated more than he'd spoken. So he, too, felt a little unsure about what this was between them. They were different in a thousand ways, their lives on opposite continents, and their work vastly apart. Stefan's work for a missionary organization included travels that had carried him all over the world. He'd helped flooded villages in Africa, taught children in New Guinea, and was now assisting Eastern European countries. But Amanda didn't know about his real day-to-day work. She knew he was of an evangelical faith, but which one? Their two lives seemed an impossible mix, yet now she couldn't imagine him not in her life.

"I do need that information as soon as possible. If you are sure . . ."

"I'm sure." He took her hand and helped her up.

"Thank you, Stefan," she said softly, then became aware of Jirik's interest in them.

"Okay, what else?" Stefan glanced at the empty pretzel packets on the metal desk. "I suppose I should not have listened about lunch. You didn't eat, did you?"

She shrugged at his frown.

"Let's get some food before your flight."

As Amanda walked to her work area, she realized how hungry she was. A meal with Stefan before she had to leave sounded perfect. Jirik helped them return boxes and files to their metal shelves before Amanda gathered the documents, copies, and a few books into her satchel.

"Plenty of reading for the flight home," Stefan said, taking the bag from her hand. He paused and his clear, blue eyes examined her face as she examined his. "I didn't ask how the rest of your day went. With this information, will Nancy Drew solve the mystery?"

She laughed. "You couldn't be a Nancy Drew fan!"

"I am a fan of the sleuth standing in front of me," he said, chuckling. "And I must admit to some past Carolyn Keene admiration in my younger years. A cousin sent me used books from the States. It was like Christmas when a shipment arrived. For some years the books were mainly Beverly Cleary and the Little House on the Prairie series. Then came Nancy Drew. And she was your favorite?"

"Nancy was my childhood companion. I went around tapping walls in search of secret stairways for years."

"I received a few Hardy Boys books until my uncle wrote that I shouldn't have to read his daughter's books and included the great discovery of Louis L'Amour books."

"Not the Western writer? My dad still reads those books sometimes. You liked cowboys and gunfights?" Amanda stopped their pace to see if he was joking. Stefan, who read books about such topics as the effect of nuclear plants on village children, theological commentaries, and works of literature, was not the type she'd picture with a pile of Louis L'Amour books.

"Cowboys and the Old West. That's exactly why I loved him. I still watch Westerns with a kind of amazement—have you seen the movie *Shane* or *The Good, the Bad and the Ugly*?" Amanda shook her head, and Stefan smacked his forehead in amazement. "Those are some of the top movies ever."

"Are you serious? What about that list of foreign films you're always making me watch?"

"I just assumed you had already seen the great American movies."

"This is a side I never expected."

"I was a kid in Communist Prague—are you kidding? I loved that Wild West stuff. I made my own raccoon cap from my mom's old fur coat."

"I'm sure she loved that."

"She never knew," he said with a wink. "But you didn't answer my question."

"You get me talking books and Nancy Drew and I forget everything else." They walked back to the work areas, closing a metal gate to the files behind them.

"Do you foresee that file leading to this lost brooch?"

"I can dream such a thing."

"What if it did?"

"I would have one excellent program for the History Network. I would dedicate it to my father—a fitting honor for all the work he's done for Holocaust survivors. And if I find the brooch, a Jewish heirloom would be returned to its rightful place."

"Sounds noble enough."

Amanda noticed the list she'd left on the table. "This reminds me. Could you ask Jirik one more question? I asked him if this was the complete victim list from the Lidice massacre. He said it was, but we haven't communicated well today. You know what my Czech is like."

"What Czech?" Stefan teased. Amanda gave him the papers. He called to Jirik, who popped up from behind the cubicle. They discussed the list, and Jirik went through it with Stefan. "He says this is the official report and complete file."

"Then I am done for today."

"Did you find the names of your family there?" Stefan asked in concern.

"Could we talk about it later?" she said, not ready to face the disturbing questions of what it meant for them not to be there. Jirik had made a copy of the list, and she already had it inside her satchel. Perhaps she had a wrong spelling of her grandparents' names.

"Of course." Stefan spoke in such a way that Amanda realized he thought she'd found their names. He must think she was upset to see the proof before her eyes. She tried to think of how to tell him, but she wasn't ready to reveal that their names weren't there. If they hadn't died during the Lidice operation, did that mean they hadn't lived there either?

He shook out her coat and held it for her to put on. He turned her around and buttoned the front, untucking her hair from the collar. She watched him, feeling his closeness.

From his pocket Stefan pulled out a gray-and-burgundy scarf and wrapped it around her neck. "A little gift from Prague," he said, tying the scarf around her neck.

Amanda touched the twisted ends of the scarf and smiled. When Jirik cleared his throat, they turned in unison to face him.

"I think someone wants his cave back," Amanda said.

When Stefan gave Jirik the good news that they were leaving, the slight man actually seemed to have energy and even a tinge of excitement. He went to open the bottom gate while they packed the last of the papers and books into her satchel.

"You have plenty of work ahead," Stefan said.

"I'll go through them during those lonely nights at home."

"Yes, lonely nights at home." Stefan said it in a way that made her look at him. For a moment he gazed down at her satchel. "Time is short. Let's go."

It amazed her how his presence filled the spaces between them even when they were apart. Each day her thoughts would turn to Stefan. Yet sometimes she sensed that she could get hurt. Amanda had felt it from the beginning, since the first time they met. Yet how different he was—and even more intriguing—from the person she'd believed him to be in Paris.

Amanda thanked Jirik, who held open the gate and appeared indeed relieved to have his underground world returned to him.

"So what did you do while I was trapped below?" she asked Stefan as they walked up the stairs. They reached the ground floor, their footsteps echoing down empty corridors. When she'd arrived earlier, these halls had been full of people doing the business of an advancing government seeking its place in the free world of capitalism and democracy.

"I took my grandmother shopping for scarves. Yes, this is how I found yours. She always buys too many scarves this time of year—post-Christmas and pre-spring sales, you know.

I think I have received a scarf every year for my birthday, and it's in August. After shopping, we met my mother for lunch. They want me to move back to Praha. Lunch was their sales pitch for all the reasons why such a move would be right."

"Why don't you? You love it here, and it *is* your home—that comes through in your e-mails. You don't really have a home except for that room in your friend's apartment in Amsterdam and the dozen other mission headquarters on the Continent."

"You sound like my family. Let's save this discussion for another day."

Amanda wondered about his reluctance to talk about it. Did he not realize how much he loved Prague? It was so clear to her. Stefan's e-mails often told stories of his childhood in Prague, fishing attempts in the Vltava River, or hiking in the forested hillsides, along with the sights and smells of different seasons and favorite foods. Though he'd traveled the world, he always spoke most about Prague. What kept him from returning?

When they reached the exit, Stefan pushed the door open. The late-afternoon sunshine had already dropped behind the facades of buildings, but it still reflected from the snow. It was bright to her tired eyes that had spent a day in dim light. She was surprised to see blue sky peer through gray clouds. Prague had been lost to her beneath the late-winter blizzard. Now it awakened . . . just when she must leave.

"Next time you will see Praha. I will show you everything I promised."

"Next time?" she said, wondering when or if there would be another time here. She'd been all over Europe in the last few years, but this had been her first time to the city that had become a focal point for many tourist itineraries. Moreover, this was the place of her family's past. Amanda had yet to see the magic of this city, though she had made memories with Stefan and his family.

They walked in silence down cobblestone streets lined with old buildings that had enjoyed a resurgence of painting and redecorating. Pigeons cooed from sidewalks and porch eaves as Stefan and Amanda passed squares and carved monuments. Communist gray had spent over a decade disappearing beneath fresh whites and pale pastels. Flowerpots were filled with snow. Many shops had moved their displays outdoors. Fruits, marionette puppets, Matryoshka dolls, and racks of postcards drew the eye.

Amanda, always fascinated by Matryoshka dolls, paused to look at a colorful row of them. She'd bought a Polish version while in that country and had given it to a girlfriend's child. The little girl's eyes had widened as the large wooden doll opened to reveal a smaller one that opened to another until the very tiniest wooden doll was found.

"I think I should visit San Francisco," Stefan said.

"You do?" Amanda replaced the doll and they continued walking. She didn't know what to say.

"This isn't enough. We need more than this. Does that sound ungrateful?"

"No. I feel it too."

"Do you want me to come to San Francisco?" Stefan stopped and asked more with his expression than with his words. "I want to see your life."

"I want you to see it." She thought he might kiss her there on the ancient street of the Old Town. Instead he took her hand.

"Remember that crème brûlée we shared in Paris?" she asked.

"How could I forget?"

"My friend Benny says he found a place at home that makes the best crème brûlée in the world. He wants to wager that I'll like it better than the one in Paris. But nothing can compare with that night."

Stefan smiled as they recalled their post–Eiffel Tower hunger and how the custard dessert tasted like the best thing they'd ever eaten.

"Perhaps we'll have other nights that will compare," he said, then looked at his watch. "I want to show you something. We must hurry because our time is running out."

They walked quickly. Stefan carried her heavy satchel through narrow, winding alleys that ended in a busier street; then they took another turn to a quiet stone road. Old Town was a labyrinth of streets and alleys with the spires of cathedrals rising up against the sky. A crisp breeze that smelled of snow touched their faces. Few cars passed them, so they could enjoy the quaintness of this part of the city with its occasional sounds of horse-drawn carriages, footsteps, and gentle church bells.

"We didn't even touch the five," Amanda said, remembering their list of places he wanted to show her and why. He'd asked her to pick the top five. She'd chosen Wenceslas Square, the political center of Prague; the Old Jewish Cemetery in the Jewish Quarter; Franz Kafka's birthplace; Charles Bridge; and the Astronomical Clock in Old Town Square, where she could peek at the statue of Jan Hus with its inscription she'd seen in travel books: "Truth prevails."

Stefan stopped at the corner of a small square. "I know you must be hungry and we have to get to the airport soon, but let's take one moment in here. You didn't put this on your top-five list, but it's my favorite." He motioned behind them to a building with long, arched windows and white double-gabled peaks. It appeared to be the front of a humble church. No grand entrance or towers jutted upward like the many other structures that gave Prague the title of "city of a hundred spires."

"This is Betlemska kaple."

"*Kaple* is a chapel or church, right?"

"Yes, Bethlehem Chapel. You have heard of Jan Hus?"

"The Czech preacher whose teachings started the Hussite movement. Convicted as a heretic, he was burned at the stake, 1400s, I believe."

"You never cease to amaze me. The year 1415 to be exact." He walked toward the wide doors and reached for her. "Come with me. This is more than information. Jan Hus once preached here."

Stefan opened the heavy door. With their shoulders almost touching, they walked through the entrance into the sanctuary that was permeated with the musty scent of a well-aged building closed up during a storm.

"I used to come here a lot," Stefan continued. "They have concerts from time to time. I wish we had time to hear one together."

Amanda couldn't speak. She could almost hear the music streaming through this place. She recalled their time last autumn in Berlin at a boys' choir. The high-pitched voices sounded like angels singing from on high. If only they could have that here, in Stefan's place.

Bethlehem Chapel had little in the way of design or architectural wonder. The evening light was soft, diffused through the stained-glass windows. Long tapestries depicting different scenes from the Bible hung on the walls. Amanda understood that this was a refuge for Stefan. She could feel it herself. This was a private place where a person would beseech God, if that person believed in God. It was a peaceful place where someone like her could rest her head. She left Stefan's side to take a seat in a wood-and-fabric chair.

The silence of a church never failed to startle her. A weariness mixed with awe always swept over her, and she suddenly felt small in the scope of time and the universe. The strength she so depended on fell away, as if only here did she realize her many limitations.

Amanda had been in dozens of European churches. She could look over the artwork and shapes of windows and recognize the Gothic, Baroque, and rococo styles. She'd step into churches and synagogues and many other places of worship in an attempt to understand why these places endured the centuries—what was it in men that required the search throughout all generations? What did they feel that made them return to these places?

Stefan walked to the end of the pews at the foot of the altar. She wondered why he'd brought her here. His work was part of his faith and his life revolved around it. Amanda's faith was in herself and in her work. She believed in preserving history for tomorrow's generations. She'd thought a dozen times, *If only one generation could learn from the mistakes of the past.* But each generation believed itself modern and better than the one that had gone before it. As a result, people made the same mistakes and walked in newness only by the vastness of their destruction. Perhaps she and Stefan weren't so different with their desire to open the eyes of today and tomorrow—he to faith, she to history.

Closing her eyes, she savored the feeling of sanctuary. Her mind roamed over her worries—the lead in the Kirke family and then the Lidice list that was missing her grandparents' names. Her eyes opened as she recalled something Stefan's grandmother had said that morning: *"I hope you find your family."*

She knew that Stefan's family was drawn to her heritage because it mirrored their own. Until this search she'd never realized how much of her life had been built upon the heritage of grandparents who had been victims of the Lidice massacre. Her father's lifework had been based on honoring the memory of parents he couldn't remember. Her love of the past and job at the History Network were the products of the stories and lives of survivors her father sought to help. This undefined yet deepening relationship with Stefan had begun at a conference for children of Nazi and Communist victims. Her life was built on yesterday. And now that foundation seemed shaky indeed.

"Are you ready?" Stefan was waiting for her.

"No," she whispered. He took her hand, and they walked down the aisle and into the descending evening. They would go and eat, get her things, and say good-bye. If only it were as simple as that.

Perhaps it was nothing. Some part of the story was wrong and would be easily fixed. Then everything in her and her father's life could continue on as it had in the past. But with her grandparents' names missing from the list she felt the glitch, the foreboding. Maybe she didn't want the truth. Maybe the story she'd always known was the one she wanted to keep. Yet it was already too late.

The unraveling had begun.

CHAPTER FIVE

The curtain between them was open as usual, and the night-light glowed from the wall between their hospital beds. Every night Janice flipped on her light as the sun fell and they would talk for a short time. Then Janice would fall asleep and Ms. Delsig would lower her metal railing to get up and turn off the night-light. In the still darkness, she would listen to the quiet breathing of her friend and find rest. It was a ritual. Ms. Delsig wondered if she could sleep without it.

In the first months after Ms. Delsig's arrival at Oakdale, the curtain had separated them throughout the day, but especially at night. Ms. Delsig's adjustment to life on the "inside" had been hard, and even harder was her decision to have a roommate instead of paying for a single room. Ms. Delsig could easily afford the single, but a golfing partner had told her, just prior to her admittance into the home, that it was important to have a roommate. "You live longer with someone there—even if you argue all the time. All alone, you just fall into death's clutches." Ms. Delsig was still receiving Christmas cards from this woman, so the theory had been proven at least once. Yet Ms. Delsig feared having someone in the room while she slept. She was afraid of what she might reveal in the midnight hours.

When Ms. Delsig had looked over the facilities at Oakdale, she had met Janice, who had the window side of the room available. The window side was usually viewed as treasured ground—something you didn't mess with or people got hostile. But Janice didn't like to sleep by windows, she said. It gave her the creeps. So Ms. Delsig had smiled at the mousy woman and decided to give it a three-month trial.

It wasn't perfect at first. Janice was terrified of falling asleep in the dark and her night-light was too bright. She said she didn't mind awakening to darkness; it was just that she couldn't enter sleep that way. Soon enough they were talking in the evenings as they prepared for bed and continuing their conversations as they snuggled into the covers with the curtain open between them. Janice always fell asleep first, and her presence became a comfort to Ms. Delsig. What a surprise it had been when the three-month trial ended and the routine that would last for years had been established.

"Are you awake?" Janice queried now.

"Of course, dear." Ms. Delsig turned over to face Janice. The night-light brought odd shadows to her friend's features.

Janice clutched the blue blanket up to her chin. The rocking motion that usually stopped beneath the cover of blankets had resumed. "Ms. Delsig, can I tell you something?"

"Of course."

"You may think less of me."

"Never."

"Well. It's just that I'm so appreciative of my sister. And it's exciting to think of leaving. But, well . . . there was a time right before I came here that I did something foolish."

"What foolish thing could you do?" Ms. Delsig pushed the button on the armrest to sit up a little more.

"Oh, it is embarrassing. You see, I was in the bathtub at my sister's house, and a spider fell from the ceiling and landed in the water."

"Uh-oh. I know what you think of spiders."

"Exactly. Well, this time I really freaked. It was floating right toward me with those long sticky legs flipping around in the water. I'm not sure what happened, but I started screaming and running and all I could see were those legs. I ran outside—"

"Without a robe?"

"Yes, without a robe, or so I'm told. I can't remember much of the rest except for a neighbor running over and all sorts of noise. It brought on a seizure, and when I finally woke up, I was in the hospital. I couldn't blame my sister for putting me here, or her husband—though I never liked him. After all, it was only a spider. But now . . ."

"You are afraid something like that might happen again?"

"Yes."

"Make your sister have a bug man come," Ms. Delsig said, trying to bring a smile to Janice's pinched expression. "Okay, it's not just spiders, is it? Tell me specifically what you are afraid of."

"Out there."

"Going into the world?"

"Yes. Spiders, noise, that huge busy place."

Ms. Delsig could imagine Janice's mind full of fast cars, playground chaos, quickly turning traffic lights, honking horns, impatient cashiers, and policemen awaiting a citizen's mistakes—not to mention bugs and spiders lurking to attack. Once when they were watching a television drama about working in an ER, Janice had muttered, "How do they survive a day?" Janice was overly sensitive inside Oakdale. She yelped when a tray was dropped, protested if her schedule was changed even slightly, cried and cried at any death whether she knew the person or not. How would she handle the outside world? Ms. Delsig wondered if she should protest this exodus tomorrow. The outside world would destroy the girl.

Janice stared at the ceiling, certainly envisioning the world too large for her. Her nervous rocking intensified, bringing jerking shadows against the opposite wall. It drew Ms. Delsig's eyes as the night-light's glow touched the framed pictures on the walls on Janice's side of the room. Then Ms. Delsig noticed that they were all "outside" pictures—a coastal sunset, a dockyard of sailboats, a gate opening to a luscious garden. Janice also saved every postcard she received from her sister and two nieces. Though Christmas and birthday cards were eventually tossed, she displayed the postcards from all over the world. Only one picture was of Oakdale, and Ms. Delsig had drawn it in pastels for one of Janice's birthdays.

She wants to leave. Deep inside, she wants this.

"Tell me what that spider could have done to you."

"Now you sound like Dr. Matthews," Janice said with a giggle.

"So Dr. Matthews has helped you work through the spider issues?"

"I think so."

"How frightening is your sister's house?" Ms. Delsig asked.

Janice turned back to face her. "It's not frightening at Monique's. The girls are grown and, of course, Lester is no longer there."

"You had a wonderful Christmas with her, the best one ever. So you can picture what it will be like."

"But what if she gets tired of me? Or what if something happens to her and I have to go get help? What if she insists on me going to the mall or grocery store? Monique can get irritated at my shyness."

Ms. Delsig smiled. "You tell Monique you don't want to go to the mall. Or perhaps you will feel brave and try it. And if she needs help, you will find the strength. If she gets tired of you, then you will be my roommate again. It is simple." She was saying it but knew how far from simple this was—especially for her, the one left behind.

"I don't know. It might be nice going to a real church or maybe someday seeing a movie at the movie house."

"That's the spirit. Now get some sleep. You have a busy day tomorrow."

"Thank you, Ms. Delsig. You truly are the best friend I've ever had."

"And you are the best friend I have ever had," Ms. Delsig whispered back, though she had the sudden image of her late husband. How she had once wished to share everything with him . . . he'd said the same thing in the beginning. It was strange how, looking back, she couldn't quite remember what kept them apart—the ghosts of the past, their own stubbornness, fear of vulnerability? How she missed what could have been.

Janice's breathing slowed, and Ms. Delsig lowered her metal railing to flip off the night-light. The darkness usually brought a strange comfort as if nothing bad could find her here. There were locks on all the doors at Oakdale, a fence surrounding it, and people out there on duty until dawn. Yet it wasn't helping her sleep tonight. She considered asking for a sleeping pill to overcome the way her heart raced at the thought of Janice not being across the room tomorrow night.

She turned in her bed again and again, unable to find rest. It was another sleepless night, when loneliness and despair nearly blinded her completely. Her hands shook as the room molded and shaped itself into the memories—yet they seemed so real she could hear the moans of dying voices and smell the stench of death around her. She gathered her blankets high to her neck and long, slow tears began to fall—unwanted and unbidden.

And into the night Ms. Delsig whispered a silent plea: *God, oh God, I am afraid of being alone again. I am so very, very afraid.*

--==○==--

Richter Hauer bought a newspaper at the gas station and walked back toward the row of run-down motel rooms. He tugged the black stocking cap further over his ears as he stopped to watch the sun rise over the craggy mountain peaks. The Canadian Rockies reminded him of the Austrian Alps, and the view made him miss home just as it had every morning for the past two weeks since his arrival in the small town outside Banff, Alberta, Canada.

Unlocking the door, he walked inside the motel room that contained a lumpy, king-size bed, a dresser with TV, and a miniature bathroom. He kicked the heater below the window and heard it rumble to life.

He checked his watch. There were a few hours left before the arrival of the people who had promised to help him. Richter wondered again if he'd made a mistake. He'd aligned himself with the wrong groups of people several times before, and it had always cost him something. Once it nearly cost him his life.

But Richter had counted his money every few days, and every few days he found it dwindling. With over six thousand dollars in Canadian money, he had enough for the present but not enough for the long term. He was tired of worrying about money, tired of living a frugal man's life. There were no jobs available for a man on the run. He was a fugitive now, a wanted man—someone who couldn't gain legal employment. At first, he rather liked that image of himself—the outlaw in hiding—but the amusement quickly wore thin. He'd left everyone he'd known and had never experienced such loneliness in his life. He'd shared drinks with a few people in different bars as he traveled from Toronto toward the west. A few women had shared his bed but for one night only. His German accent always brought questions, and questions brought lies—and lies could eventually trip you up.

He packed his duffel bag as he considered his plan of action. Every detail must be thought through to precision. Richter knew he'd made serious errors before—ones that should have cost him his life. It wouldn't be like that this time.

Richter divided his money into separate small bags. He'd get a new identity soon. No more dumpy hotels, hitchhiking, or small-town bars. Perhaps he'd go to Los Angeles or Miami, perhaps even back to Europe if he dared.

He picked up an old photograph of the Empress Brooch and slid it into the portfolio. The people he was to meet wanted information about the Empress Brooch, and he could give it to them—for a price. Then Richter would be free to do whatever he wanted.

⋆═◉═⋆

The sun was shining. Of course it would shine on the day Ms. Delsig wished for rain. Rain was more fitting for this day— more truthful, more acceptable.

Through her recently washed and squeegeed window she could see dewdrops on the plants in her garden. She was sure more green bulbs had sprouted in the night. Her rosebushes had leaves, and buds popped from new stalks as if she hadn't cut them back only a few months earlier. It never ceased to amaze her how those roses could burst anew after such a painful pruning.

When she'd lived at Sweetbriar Estate, her former residence, Ms. Delsig had paid a gardener to give her the desired horticultural results. Now new life rose miraculously from the work of her own hands. She always felt that one day she'd find her rosebushes gone, stripped and ripped from the ground by a tropical storm or burnt to nothing beneath a summer sun. They'd leave without the chance for good-bye. Yet so far they continued to grow.

Today would bring a good-bye.

Janice continued to say she'd return for visits, but Ms. Delsig knew the truth. Janice might come a few times. Then weeks would pass and Ms. Delsig would receive a call or a guilt-induced letter. Finally Janice would pull free except for an occasional memory and waning thought to make contact. It was better to allow Janice the belief, easier for the younger woman to leave that way. But Ms. Delsig couldn't allow such fantasy for herself. It was better to face reality right away. More painful at first, but in the long run, she had a greater chance of survival.

Ms. Delsig's gaze caught the thin line of blue Atlantic waves. She wondered about those waters and the beaches pressed against them. People would carry their umbrellas, towels, and sunscreen to those white Florida sands. They'd toss Frisbees, fly kites, surf the waves. What would it be like to leave Oakdale today? to drive along the beach roads and perhaps stop and put toes in the salty sea?

She had asked herself for years if an old folks home had been the right choice. She pictured the sprawling grounds of her house and the airy, wide rooms. A young family resided at the estate now. Had the toddler written on the wallpaper she'd ordered from Italy, or had the older boy broken one of the stained-glass windows she'd installed? It always bothered her to think about the home she'd abandoned for a shared room at Oakdale. A time of weakness had brought her here.

Ms. Delsig and her friends had all talked about it—that magical age of rest-home admittance—around pots of tea or while driving across the green. It could be seventy or eighty or ninety—no one was quite sure of an exact age. When one from their group would say good-bye and leave her home and life-time of possessions for the few suitcases that now composed her life, the topic would always resurface. Ms. Delsig had watched several friends have a birthday and then a month or so later disappear into the void called Nursing Care. There was something about old-aged birthdays that brought families together for discussing, "What are we going to do about Grandma?"

But that was for other people, she had thought. There was no family to convince her of her importance in the outside world. She'd been spared the evening dinner and surprise family attack: "But, Grandma, it's for your own safety. And how nice to have someone serve you healthy meals around the clock. We'll come visit you as often as we can. You'll have friends your own age. We think you'll like it better there than in this old drafty house you've been in for so long."

Ms. Delsig had heard her friends' stories. She remembered how Phyllis had cried for days, finally relenting beneath her son's pressure. But then there was Margie, who had actually looked forward to leaving lonely nights at home for the activity of a nursing facility near her grandchildren. Her annual Christmas newsletter was proof that it could work. But while Ms. Delsig claimed, "Each birthday is one step toward that eternal green without the need for golf carts," inwardly she knew that decisions must be made about a "permanent residence."

Without family and someone calling her Grandma, Ms. Delsig had few choices. She could end up locked in her bathroom for two days like Gladys, or perhaps she'd have a stroke and be unable to reach a phone. She could fall down and break a hip—the beginning of the end for many a feisty old woman.

Perhaps worse than family members deciding your admittance into an old folks home was having to decide it on your own. On her seventy-third birthday, after a burglar started hitting the homes in her neighborhhood, Ms. Delsig made the choice to relinquish her freedom and check in where you don't check out—at least, not many did.

The change was radical. The loss of freedom turned many people into angry individuals or caused early death. Some gave up and lived a listless life for years while awaiting the end. Ms. Delsig had tried to prepare for it mentally. She sought out the garden for something of her own and something to keep her busy. She took her vitamins as usual, though her old 2.8-mile walk four times a week had dwindled to ten minutes on the treadmill three times a week. Well, at least she was still consistently exercising. Janice couldn't be a more perfect roommate, and the dapper Alfred Milton always made her smile. She'd made the right decision. But . . . there were many *but*s that she tried to ignore. A slice of sea between the sky and the top of a fence was just the beginning.

Ms. Delsig turned from the window and sat in a white wicker chair facing Janice's side of the room. Today it would be bare of the things that made it Janice's. Already several filled boxes waited at the doorway, and Janice had gone to breakfast to say her good-byes. Unlike herself, Janice had made many close friends in the home. Ms. Delsig knew many considered themselves friends of hers, but she hadn't allowed her heart to make an investment. There were few securities to rely on. Strange how Janice didn't fear friendships—only spiders and the world outside.

The quick steps of a staff member echoed down the corridor and stopped at her door. "Ms. Delsig, we've been looking for you." *The petite girl must only be twenty at the oldest,* Ms. Delsig thought. "It's art time."

Ms. Delsig glanced at the clock in surprise. How had it become ten-thirty already? "I didn't realize, and today is Friday?"

"Come along, dearie. Is your memory giving you trouble?"

Ms. Delsig detested how some of the employees treated her like a small child or an adorable pet. This was a newer nurse's aide, another someone she'd not taken time to know.

"My memory is fine. I've decided to skip today."

"Oh, but the group will be so disappointed. Belisa says you are her best student."

"That's because I teach her the techniques." Ms. Delsig's voice amplified her annoyance. "If my memory still works correctly, isn't art a voluntary activity?"

"I'll have to mark it in your chart that you were irritable and chose to avoid the group."

"You do that. And I will write a complaint that you were condescending and pushy."

The young woman's mouth dropped, as if a child she was baby-sitting had just disobeyed.

"Excuse me, Vickie Ann." Janice entered the room and walked to Ms. Delsig's side. She was rocking gently, but she gazed intently at Vickie Ann. "You must remember to be sensitive to us at Oakdale. This is our home, and we were once people just like you. You might be surprised to find that we're still people."

"I know that." Vickie Ann looked insulted. She turned sharply, like a private in the army. They listened to her hard steps echo away.

"Leaving is giving you some confidence, I see."

"It is," Janice said with a wide smile. "You should have heard what I told Kisser Bob."

"Oh, do tell me."

Janice sat on the edge of Ms. Delsig's bed and leaned forward with a sparkle in her eye. "Well, it happened this morning on the way to breakfast. I rounded the corner and as usual, there he waited. He smiled that mischievous smile, looked from side to side, and was just about to pucker up when I said, 'Mr. Bob, we are all aware that you like to kiss the ladies, but if you ever want a kiss back, you have to be a gentleman.'"

"Marvelous girl," Ms. Delsig replied. Usually Janice was too timid to complain if her food was cold or a service hadn't been given. This was courageous for her.

"He puckered but I ran for it." Janice walked to the door. "Come to art with me," she begged. "It will be our last one together. Because of you, it's been the highlight of my weeks here."

"Why is that?"

"I love to see you work. And I love that I can draw some things now—not very good, but you can tell what they are. And I love how it's often you who teaches the class and Belisa doesn't realize it."

Ms. Delsig smiled, but her body felt achy from a night of little rest. "I don't want to go."

"For me?" Janice tilted her head and smiled sweetly. She could look so young and dear even with age lines around her eyes.

"You use all the dirty tricks." Ms. Delsig tried to sound annoyed.

Janice followed Ms. Delsig's slow pace down the hallway to the recreation room. As they approached the doorway, they heard the voice of Oakdale's recreation-and-exercise therapist, Belisa, doing her basic explanation on shadow and shading. Surely she had her red apple on a tray to demonstrate.

"There they are," Belisa said as they entered the large, decorated room that Janice had described well as looking like a kindergarten classroom. Residents' artwork was plastered across two walls, one side wall had exercise stretching instructions and cutout articles about nutrition and health, and the other side wall had a long row of beautiful white-grid windows with French doors that opened onto a patio. It was the newest addition at Oakdale, a gift from a deceased resident. Ms. Delsig had to admit it was an inviting room. Usually she enjoyed it, gazing over the newest art attempts and watching the light through the windows. Yet today it seemed too bright and loud.

"You nearly missed art, Ms. Delsig, and Janice, I hear this is your last day." From their tables and easels around the room, residents sighed and displayed sorrow at Janice's leaving. Ms. Delsig wondered if they'd really miss her or only felt envy that someone was returning to the land of the living. From where she stood at the windowed end of the room, Belisa waved them inside. A bright red apple sat on a podium in front of her.

Janice followed Ms. Delsig to the back corner of the class where their two easels awaited.

"As I was saying," Belisa continued, "next week we hope to be back outside for the spring and summer. That should brighten up our artwork."

Yes, we can paint the garden and fence a hundred times more, just like last year and the year before.

Ms. Delsig didn't like the sarcasm that pulsed through her. Yet it sometimes arose during the scheduled art time that would surely awaken the creative spirit in all of them—on your mark, get set, create! Belisa truly meant well, she was sure. But Ms. Delsig had studied under true artists and found her patience in kindergarten instruction failing fast.

"Ms. Delsig, are you working in pencils or pastels today? And your last pastel was very beautiful—it reminded me of one of the French impressionists."

"Probably because I copied it from a French impressionist, a man I met once when I was very young. His name was Claude Monet—ever heard of him?"

She heard the chuckles through the room. They thought she'd made a joke.

Belisa turned toward her quickly. "You didn't meet Claude Monet. He's been dead since—"

"December 5, 1926. And I will probably go with pencils today."

"We're going through the color wheel again for those attempting oils this summer and for those newcomers. You can just do what you'd like, Ms. Delsig."

"Very kind of you," Ms. Delsig retorted.

She opened the wooden case connected to her easel and found a sketching pencil. Today she didn't struggle as she had the day before. The pencil moved easily across the paper. She was unsure what she wanted to sketch but knew it was some-thing for Janice to take to her new home in Georgia. Flowers . . . Janice liked flowers. But Ms. Delsig soon crumpled the paper and began again. It wasn't working, she thought with another crumple and toss. This couldn't be happening again.

Something was there, wanting to be drawn, but Ms. Delsig avoided it. She tried the steeple of a church. A cabin by a stream. An abstract of her flower garden. A pile of paper grew around her feet.

"We've covered shadow, line, and mood this month." Belisa's voice was irritatingly loud for those without hearing problems. Perhaps distraction was the problem. "Today let's try a work of our own. First, bring to mind one of the artists we've studied. Chris Van Allsburg and his dreamy scenes of a sailboat cruising the night sky. Or Marc Chagall's fiddler, which draws upon his memories of the Russian village he grew up in." Belisa wandered among the potential artists. She paused at Ms. Delsig and whispered, "Of course, you don't need this pitch. Anything you'd like to add today?"

Ms. Delsig shook her head. Her eyes seemed unable to move from the white canvas that now waited on the easel, so lonely and full of anticipation. The colors were already there in her mind. She never painted with drab colors. The images were there. Images she'd taken from her thoughts and revealed on paper or canvas only to destroy them once out from their spell. Belisa continued her monologue of artists' works—Matisse, Hopper, Gauguin. Ms. Delsig just stared and wondered if she could stop herself from creating what so desperately wanted to appear.

"Search deep inside for what wants to come out," Belisa instructed, "a memory, a feeling, a moment. And let's see what we find within. Of course, this may take several weeks to complete, so just get the image started today."

Ms. Delsig set the pencil on the easel tray and reached into the lower tray for her paints and palette. She mixed colors and began to work. The room faded away and she found herself falling, falling into the scene as her hand painted it all around her.

Time passed. She knew it as she set her last brush on the palette. Over an hour by the hands of the clock. The class had dispersed. No one had dared come to gaze at her work. They'd earlier learned to await her finale, sometimes waiting a few classes before she would allow a display. Even Janice had left her to work uninterrupted. Ms. Delsig sat in the silence of herself, hearing the distant noises of Belisa straightening up and Oakdale life outside the room.

The images can't be stopped sometimes, she thought with her eyes on the shades of gray, purple, and black—with the deep red hung in the center nearly dripping from the canvas. This one reminded Ms. Delsig of a Munch painting of a face with hands clasped over ears and a horrific silent scream escaping the gaping mouth. Ms. Delsig knew such a scream, heard it audibly in her ears at times, and felt it deeply within herself.

"How did you do—?" Belisa had come up behind her—"oh my."

No one had yet seen this side of her art. When such images came and she felt forced to draw, Ms. Delsig had always destroyed them in the end. This was why she'd been unable to sketch her garden. This thing, this image from inside her, had insisted on not being ignored any longer.

"Perhaps it is time for you to speak of it," Belisa said softly.

"Speak of what?" Ms. Delsig asked without moving her eyes from the painting.

"The past. Perhaps you should speak of your past." There was compassion in Belisa's eyes when Ms. Delsig turned to look at her. It angered her.

"Why would I speak of my past?"

Belisa bent down beside Ms. Delsig's chair. "Many of the staff know about the number tattooed on your arm. We've had Holocaust survivors here before. Many, like you, keep what happened inside, but it's much more harmful that way. You can be free of it—by telling the story, through art or writing. Don't you think it's time?"

Ms. Delsig was shaking now. She was shaking with anger so deep and strong it overtook her. The staff knew about her? They knew nothing. And yet this woman talked as if she knew all about it and could fix it easily. Ms. Delsig clamped her mouth shut, afraid to speak, afraid of what words would come out. No words could ever say enough.

"You do not know . . . ," she finally said. "Janice is leaving. That is what this painting is about."

"Ms. Delsig—" Belisa knelt and put a cold hand on her arm—"people who endure catastrophic events are able to suppress the past for long periods of time. But they are never able to heal without facing the demons and conquering them."

At those words Ms. Delsig's strength returned and she rose from the chair, reaching for her walker. "You have a degree in recreation, not psychology. Now go back to your arts and crafts. I need to tell my best friend good-bye."

CHAPTER SIX

Stefan was behind her now. A continent, an ocean, and thirty thousand feet separated their lives. The Boeing 777 flew toward North America; then it would make its southwestern turn from Canada into U.S. airspace and down toward San Francisco, California.

This was the first trip in a long time when Amanda didn't feel her usual relief at returning home. As much as she loved to travel and experience new places and cultures, the time away always brought a heightened sense of home. Her mind would switch from the faraway place she'd been to wondering what her father and best friend Benny Dunn had been doing while she was gone; whether her dog, Hemingway, would think she'd abandoned him; and always what was happening at work. Her production leader, Sylvia Pride, would give new advice on how to succeed in a man's world; Troy Donley, Webmaster for the History Network on the Net, would have some bizarre new trivia for her; her assistant, Tiffany, would relay her latest dating woes and adventures; there would be some new office romance or scandal, some new program to develop, or a birthday luncheon, company night to a concert or benefit—it took a week to catch up on everything.

Yet on this return, Amanda didn't feel interested in what had happened while she was off on another continent. This time she felt as if she'd left something important and undiscovered behind.

The tearing away from Stefan had been painful. Their time together had been too short, a tease as it brought stronger feelings that were unresolved between them. Amanda had been drawn closer to Stefan by sleeping in his loft, eating at his family's table, walking the streets of his city, and sitting in his church. Yet the attachment did nothing to assure her. There were no promises except that he would come to her city next. She'd promised nothing either, except that she wanted him there.

Her thoughts moved in rapid succession. Since her grandparents were not on the Lidice list, could she have the wrong names, wrong spelling, or had they died somewhere else? Should she tell her father anything until she had the facts? What would she find—if anything—in the Kirke file? She needed more time than the twelve hours of flight to figure this out. Though she flew above the world from one continent to the next, Amanda wished to stay suspended in the sky long enough to sort out the mess that grew high around her.

In the next few weeks she'd get to meet Darby Evans Collins, the living heiress to the Empress Brooch. The woman and her husband, Brant, divided their time between the United States and Austria. Amanda had done a short phone interview with her weeks earlier but had many more questions. Everywhere in Amanda's work there were possibilities, and she was tired from the weight of them all.

The in-flight movies played over the tiny TVs attached to the back of the seats. After the first plane meal, Amanda had dozed for a while and then listened to some music while updating her electronic organizer. For once no one sat beside her. Amanda pushed the buttons on the armrest to flip through the TV channels. The map on the screen showed they'd made over half the journey.

Halfway. Not here nor there. Like a glitch in time.

She flipped the light on and stretched slightly in her seat. Business class was a definite improvement over coach, where she often traveled, but Amanda found little rest on airplanes. She longed for her bed, with its down comforter and pillows she'd bought in France, and the safe, cozy walls of her very own cottage.

Amanda was avoiding the work she had with her. After the day of staring at papers and this being nighttime in Prague, she'd excused herself from it. Her satchel was shoved beneath the seat in front of her. The data she'd obtained in the archives was inside, unorganized and holding three inches' worth of possible information about the Empress Brooch or perhaps even something about her relatives. Usually she loved to hunt for data. She loved to seek dates, events, or places that would then click with other information she already knew or would soon find.

Once while doing a short piece on a Holocaust survivor and his experiences in the Bergen-Belsen Concentration Camp, Amanda had had an idea to further appeal to the viewers' identification with the man. She had included film footage of the camp after liberation, with the captured SS guards hauling bodies over their shoulders to a mass grave. Then she'd connected the survivor's story with Anne Frank, who had died at the same camp. The survivor she interviewed had been a year older than Anne, which touched on that human element. The clips inside the Frank secret annex and a reading from Anne's diary, telling of Anne's death, were mirrored against the survivor's childhood photographs with family members who perished during the war. They ended the story back with the survivor standing at the Bergen-Belsen gate fifty years later. The program, targeted for teen viewers, had won Amanda her first documentary award.

The Empress Brooch story would follow a similar pattern, this time putting human faces with the mystery of a lost brooch. The villainous Nazi officer who sought the brooch would be investigated next, adding to the intrigue. And if Amanda made a great and miraculous find, the program would conclude with the discovery of the brooch's location.

This was the pitch she'd given her program manager. Yet Amanda had kept the personal element of the Empress Brooch to herself. Her father had told her this version of the story when she was a child, saying that his aunt had told him. Amanda's great-grandfather had served for years as the emperor's carriage driver. As her great-grandfather's wedding approached, the emperor promised him the treasured Empress Brooch as a reward for his faithful service. The young man was thrilled and planned to give the brooch to his wife on their wedding day. But a beguiling visitor had other plans. Unknown to the carriage driver, the visitor deceived the Austrian empress into giving her precious pin to him instead of Amanda's great-grandfather.

It was a story she requested again and again—her father's steady voice carrying her to that magical land mixed with royalty, evil, and adventure. This was the only story without a pat "happily ever after" ending. Her father would end it, "And no one knows what happened to the Empress Sissi Brooch."

This was much better than a happy ending. It stirred her imagination and brought a string of questions: "Where do you think it could be, Daddy? Maybe we can find it? Can we go to Europe someday and find the palace?"

Growing up had put a little girl's quest into lower priority, but the questions and the longing for answers had never left her. Her initial indecision on what to major in was replaced by her decision to major in history after she began her internship at the Documentation Center of Popular Culture. This eventually led to her work at the History Network for the last nine years—where the world opened up to her. Amanda had been to Europe countless times. Once while in Vienna, she'd toured one of the palaces where the empress had resided. In 1998, for the Austrian celebration of beloved Empress Sissi's birthday, Amanda had spent a week in Austria, eating Sissi chocolates.

But it wasn't until she happened across a recent article about a missing brooch that had belonged to Empress Sissi and was lost during the Nazi occupation of Austria that Amanda returned to the story of her youth.

She knew the story she'd heard as a child was probably one many children had heard. If through her research she discovered that she was somehow connected to the Empress Sissi Brooch, how much more interesting—not that it would change the development of the network program. Amanda knew objectivity was essential. She had to distance herself through the research to get the facts, make the connections. The focus was the Empress Brooch, but what fun to also seek after a bedtime tale from her childhood.

Amanda reclined her seat back the few inches it allowed and flipped off the television. She put her travel pillow behind her neck and closed her eyes.

She'd heard many more stories as a child—some about her lost family and even more about their friends. She'd always believed them, never questioning the truth of the storyteller. Yet one memory of her youth still disturbed her. Although she'd dismissed it as an old woman's senility, she hadn't forgotten it. The words had come at a time when Aunt Helga had not been herself so Amanda had never told her father about it. Now in retrospect, Amanda found her great-aunt's words even more distressing.

The story of her grandparents' fate was always the same. The peaceful village where Kurt and Hilde Heinrich lived had been interrupted one night by Nazi soldiers. A rumor that the assassins of a high-ranking Nazi had found refuge in Lidice had brought the fury of Adolf Hitler himself upon the community. Amanda's grandfather, along with the rest of the village men, had been executed against a stone wall of the Horak Farm. His remains were buried in a mass grave, twisted among the limbs of his neighbors. Amanda's grandmother and the other women villagers had been sent to Ravensbrück Concentration Camp after a chaotic and horrific separation from their children. Most of the children were murdered—except for those with Aryan features. Those "lucky ones" were sent to orphanages or to Germany for adoption; some were even adopted by high-ranking Nazi officials. Any child in any occupied territory throughout Europe could be taken from his or her family and given to a German family—never to be seen again and some never to know of their true heritage.

Amanda's father and brother had not been among the children that week; they had been staying in a different village for a short holiday when the Nazis marched in. Ravensbrück was too hard for Amanda's grandmother; she became ill with typhus and died. At least that was the story Amanda heard from her great-aunt Helga, who had also told her father that story when he was young.

Yet it was in Aunt Helga's later years, and only once, that the story changed slightly. Just one detail—the date of Amanda's grandmother's death. Amanda recalled it now as one of those frightening moments of youth that would always associate itself with her aunt, fighting to block out the good memories. Aunt Helga had lost her dentures the morning they'd come to visit. While Amanda's father searched beneath the bed and in empty cups around the house and in the bathroom, Aunt Helga motioned Amanda to her side.

"Come closer," she said with a smile of sunken lips and

gums. Her words came through smacking jaws, and her breath smelled of something like medicine and old age. "Did I tell you about your grandmother? She was my sister, you know. A good little sister, but unhappy when I move to America. She died, you know. Died too young."

"Yes, I know," Amanda said.

"No, you do not know. You do not know. May 21, 1945. That was the day my sister died. But do not tell anyone, okay? May 21, 1945, my little sister died." Her voice held a melancholy tone. "She was too young to die. Promised me she would come get her boys in America. I still wonder about her death."

She chewed her lower lip and shook her head sadly. Amanda touched her aunt's shoulder in comfort.

Then Aunt Helga had grabbed Amanda's hand and squeezed with surprising strength. Her eyes flared in great fear. "Do not tell. Not anyone. No one can ever know."

It was the only time the story varied. Later that day Amanda asked her father to tell what happened to his parents. She hadn't asked in years. He told the story that was told to him by his aunt and uncle—the usual Lidice story. She asked the date of the massacre. June 1942.

"My mother died at the camp in 1943, I believe."

At fifteen years of age, Amanda had many other thoughts than to wonder about dates so long ago, even though their family history was very much a part of their lives.

Her father read book after book of WWII history and enjoyed the company of Holocaust survivors and their families. He and his brother, Martin, had inherited from Uncle Hans the apartment building and small corner grocery along Powell Street in San Francisco, where they'd lived since childhood and where Amanda had been raised. The brothers had become known for helping families and new immigrants of any race to find housing, even offering small loans. It had almost cost them their business and became a source of argu-

ment between the brothers. Amanda's father always was too
generous, while Martin wanted to create a larger company
with more responsible business practices.

For Amanda, life was always brimming with new people and
things to do. She had started dating and decided to run for
student government. There was never a need to tell anyone
about Aunt Helga's "secret." Perhaps in her age and senility,
Aunt Helga had been confused. Several times Amanda had
tried to push it away, not wanting to remember her loving
aunt in the one moment that never failed to bring a shiver
down her arms.

Amanda moved the seat up, flipped on the overhead light,
and searched her satchel for the booklet describing the village
of Lidice, located in what was no longer Czechoslovakia but
the Czech Republic. She went through the story and confirmed again the date June 10, 1942, as the death of a village.
Amanda had seen many of the photographs taken before Hitler
decreed that the village must be "wiped from the face of the
earth." She'd read the history of this rural settlement that had
begun in the thirteenth century. There was a monument for
those killed during World War I, a school, a church. Pictures
depicted a theater group, a fire brigade, an ice hockey team, a
celebration for Corpus Christi Day, and children lined up for
their school photos. Later came the photos of the bodies. They
were all men, and Amanda had spent time in the past searching what she could see in those faces. She'd wondered if one of
those men was her grandfather. Had that been his coat and
hat? that lost shoe?

But now things had changed. Kurt and Hilde Heinrich could
not be found on the list of victims. If Amanda added that to
Aunt Helga's information, maybe the entire story was different.
It could mean that Hilde Heinrich might have been alive when
the war ended. Perhaps her grandmother had survived the
concentration camp. Perhaps she was still alive. Often records

were confused after a war. Yet Hilde had never come to America to reclaim her boys.

"Can I get you something to drink?" the flight attendant asked at her row.

"No, thank you," Amanda said, then closed her eyes as the woman moved on. Amanda should spend the remaining hours on the Empress Brooch. But the questions were beginning to fall in around her. Questions that broke the comfortable walls of security and challenged the one safe area in her life—her father. While people had come and gone, especially her mother, Henry Rivans had been the constant in her life. He'd raised Amanda alone, survived cancer, and always remained a stable man, dedicated to his beliefs, his work, and his daughter. What would it do to him if the story of his life were untrue?

Since an early age, Amanda had worked to build her security by considering routes of escape. Her childhood *what ifs* were not much different from the ones she'd established as an adult. Then she had worried, *What if something happens to Dad? What if I get Mr. Brown for my fourth-grade teacher? What if Shawna won't be my best friend anymore?* Now Amanda thought, *What if something happens to Dad? What if I'm caught in company downsizing? What if Benny gets married and I don't like his wife?*

The questions always initiated a plan of action. When her best friend, Shawna, had become best friends with Melinda Taylor in sixth grade, Amanda was safely prepared. She'd not revealed her darkest secrets and had kept a large circle of friends. She barely missed Shawna. When her father battled the worst of his cancer, Amanda was at his side, determined not to miss a day in case it was his last. Even sitting in her seat now, she knew exactly which exit to take out of the airplane in case of a crash. She often checked fire-escape routes at the hotels she stayed at. She knew what to do if an earthquake hit while she was crossing the Golden Gate or the lower level of the Bay Bridge. She faithfully put a tenth of her income into investments or savings.

But there seemed to be no escape route when it came to wondering how to deal with a different past than what you had always believed. Did it matter? Would it really change anything to find a different heritage than the one she'd always believed?

Amanda knew it would. Her relationship with Stefan had begun with the common thread that their families were both Holocaust survivors, and her father's life had revolved directly around his family's past.

The plane rumbled toward home. Amanda wouldn't be half here and half there for long. And once she touched ground, the vast unknown stretched ahead.

※═◎═◎═※

Stefan Keller walked the quiet streets alone. His mother and grandmother were thrilled to have him for the weekend. His grandmother had squeezed his cheeks, proclaiming again that he should return to Praha. Petrov had laughed at the display of motherly affection both women pressed upon Stefan. They'd talked around the table for hours as they always did when he came to visit. They had asked general questions about Amanda's search at the archives. Petrov was most interested, believing he might have some contacts who could help with the Kirke information and Amanda's family. Stefan tried to carry the evening as if it were any other, but he knew they perceived his struggle. His mother invited him to meet her for lunch tomorrow. Stefan knew that would be her concerned discussion time about Amanda.

After his mother and grandmother had gone to bed, Stefan had put on his coat and gone outside to walk for a while. He'd spent many hours walking and praying whenever he wrestled with something that felt beyond his control. While he knew what was bothering him, Stefan was unsure of a solution. He hadn't intended for his feelings for Amanda to run so deep. Yet, looking back, he'd known it was a possibility that first day they'd met at the conference. He'd sat behind her at a workshop, where she couldn't see him. As she read some of the speakers' histories on their outlines, Stefan watched her pull her hair into a clip without breaking concentration, as if it were a natural motion. He noticed the smooth lines of her neck, the soft fair hairs that fell from the clip, and the small hoop earrings hanging from tiny earlobes. Later he'd seen her in line at the outdoor vendor. Stefan wasn't thirsty but he'd stepped in line behind her anyway. He was curious but didn't expect to even talk to her. Though she dressed the professional part, with clothing and hair in perfect style, there was something warm and intriguing about Amanda Rivans. Then she had dropped her purse right in front of him, and he'd been there to help.

Over coffee, he'd noticed her infectious laughter. And her passion for the stories they'd heard over the weekend mirrored his own. Her eyes drew his stare and the way her mouth moved while talking and smiling created in him a powerful longing he'd never felt before. That's when he'd known he should be careful; she could be dangerous in ways he couldn't quite see. But he'd found himself telling her about the photos he'd promised to take and wanting her with him on a night's excursion to the top of the Eiffel Tower. After all, it was only one night in Paris.

But thoughts of her persisted during his mission work in Africa. His work felt different as he recited what he'd tell Amanda about the African sunset and the joy he found in the children. He couldn't wait to hear her voice again. As the weeks passed, Amanda and Stefan grew closer.

Months later, they'd met in Berlin again. Berlin had hosted

another seminar for Amanda and meetings with a mission leader for him. They'd met every spare moment and even had one evening to themselves.

Yet he'd never quite expressed the whole truth of who he was. She knew he worked for a Christian missionary group. But his faith wasn't just a label or a part of his life. It was who he was. It was how he perceived the world and how he lived each moment. Perhaps he had delayed telling her because he feared it might be too much for her to understand. Or maybe he worried she wouldn't care and would want to continue as they were. Stefan knew his faith and her lack of faith would eventually pose problems. He had determined to date and eventually marry only a woman who believed as he did. How could he spend his life with someone who didn't understand or share the strongest part of who he was? It would tear them apart—Stefan knew this to be true and had seen it within his own family.

Stefan crossed a small square. Other late-night wanderers meandered the square or sat close to heaters at an outdoor café. Stefan bought a coffee and kept walking. His every trip to Prague brought him visiting family and friends and the places he loved. He would note the amazing changes of the city, from the new cars that had begun to replace the old beaters to the restoration of buildings with new paint and face-lifts. Billboards with American actors and models and Hollywood movie posters covered bus stops and buildings. He saw words like *Internet Café* and the *Gap*.

As a teen, Stefan hadn't known that his city lived in the Dark Ages until Communism lifted. Then he'd found the shocking truth in the United States. He was in awe of the world he saw, and yet now he regretted the many changes in his hometown. Along with democracy came the rush of pornography, organized crime, and prostitution that had not flourished under the Communist regime.

Stefan realized how close he'd walked toward the river and the chapel that had changed his life. He had wanted to share it with Amanda—at the beginning in trying to explain to her who he really was as a Christian. It couldn't wait. He had to talk to her—*before* he went to San Francisco.

He stared into the waters of the Vltava River for some time. The night had grown cold, so his face and fingers were numb when he finally climbed the stairs to Petrov's apartment. Everyone was asleep. Stefan crept up the loft steps and sat on the edge of the mattress. Amanda had made the bed this morning; there was a yellow sticky note on the pillow. He flipped on the bedside light to read it.

> *Stefan, I wish we had more time to see your city, but I will cherish the hours we spent together. Thank you. Amanda*

The note first brought a smile to his lips. Then a powerful loneliness followed—she was far from him already. In the corner of the room he noticed crumpled yellow papers inside the tiny trash can. He rose to retrieve them and smoothed out Amanda's first attempts at a note to him.

> *Stefan, I can't thank you enough. What you mean to me . . .*

> *Thank you, Stefan. I wish we had every day . . .*

> *You don't know what these days have meant . . .*

He smoothed the three notes and put them with the one she'd finally decided upon. Lying against the pillow, he rested the notes upon his chest.

God, I don't know what to do. I want what you want for me. I never expected to feel this for someone who doesn't know you as I know you. Amanda and I are different. We don't believe in the same things. But I can't get her out of my head. I hardly trust myself right now. If she were here, I don't know how strong I could be. Help me walk the path you've planned and to know that path when I see it.

Long ago, he'd vowed to do whatever God had designed for his life. Yet sudden fear arose when he thought of losing Amanda. He longed to hear God speak to him.

But he found only silence in the deep of this night.

CHAPTER SEVEN

Amanda pulled her luggage along the bumpy path beneath the glow of the streetlight, through the side gate of the old Victorian house, into the small backyard, and on toward the mother-in-law quarters that was her little home. Built after the great quake of 1906, the main house had once been of San Franciscan society. Although a bit worn and faded under the care of its lone elderly heir, Mr. Winifred, the place was pretty and clean with fresh pots of flowers and a gardened back patio separating her tiny house from the main one. Her cottage was a hideaway in the midst of the city.

Amanda dropped her luggage on the porch and turned at the sound of Mr. Winifred's back door creaking open. As expected, her golden retriever bounced from the steps and raced toward her.

"Welcome home, Amanda!" Mr. Winifred called from the doorway with a wave.

"Thanks, Mr. Winifred," she called, kneeling beside her dog. Hemingway's tail wagged at an extraordinary speed as he leaned into her hug. "How are you, boy? Did you miss me? Did you take good care of Mr. Winifred?"

She heard the creak of Mr. Winifred's door closing as she opened hers. Hemingway ran inside and plopped down in his favorite spot beside the desk in her bedroom. The clock reminded Amanda that she had ten minutes before meeting her father for dinner at their favorite restaurant. She'd be late.

Plopping the suitcase on her bed, she opened a window to cleanse the stuffy old house, hurried to the bathroom for a quick spritz to her hair and makeup. She changed from her stagnant airplane clothing.

Then she hit the button on her answering machine. "You have sixteen new messages," the electronic voice announced. She scribbled down the list: an old coworker, a salesperson . . .

"Are you home yet?" It was Benny, her best friend, and he sounded annoyed. He was never known for patience. "You haven't called. So call."

"Thought you might come in tomorrow, Amanda." It was Sylvia Pride, her program manager, next. "Hope to hear about any advancements on the brooch idea, and I need to give a heads-up for next week. If you don't show, we'll chat early Monday."

Messages five and six were Benny again: "I know you must be there. I'm almost positive you said you'd be home yesterday. Your cell phone is off and now your office is closed. I have much to tell and much to hear. Call."

"Amanda, a little surprise . . . yes, this is your mother."

At this message Amanda stopped with only her head and one arm through a cream-colored turtleneck. "I'm in New York. But the bigger surprise is that I'll be in San Francisco on the sixteenth for several weeks. I hope we can spend an evening together, perhaps even more time than that, depending on our schedule. Consider attending my reading in a few weeks. Please call and let me know your schedule. It would be wonderful to get together. Perhaps your father could come with us."

The machine skipped to the next message. Amanda sat at her desk and scribbled on a sticky note: *Mother*. She seemed unable to write more. Her mother was coming to San Francisco? Remembering the date, Amanda realized her mother was already here, which meant no time to get mentally prepared for such an event. She wanted Amanda to attend a poetry reading, which was even worse. But that her mother wanted to see her father—no way.

Amanda tried to recall the last time Patricia Marley had taken any interest in her father's life. Probably not since the day she'd left him when Amanda was three years old. Why the sudden interest? Perhaps she'd gone through all the husbands she'd wanted and now thought she could return to the beginning. Perhaps she'd heard that the man she'd married so long ago was no longer the struggling co-owner of a grocery and apartment building.

Her father's message broke her musing: "Hi, honey. I know you're coming in today so give me a call if our plans change or if you get in early and want to tell me you made it safe and sound. I had a call from your mom—yes, talk about ghosts of decades past." That brought a smile to Amanda's lips. "She's coming to the house tomorrow night and I really want you to come too—please say you will. Talk to you soon, tonight at Italia. It puts your ol' dad's heart at ease to have his girl home."

Benny was the final message. "It's Friday now. I gave you another few days so you *must* be home now. I'm coming over later tonight, so grind the hazelnut espresso. Ciao, or however you say good-bye wherever you've been."

Amanda glanced at the clock and realized she was already five minutes late meeting her father. He would be early as usual. She saved the messages, grabbed her handbag, patted Hemingway where he already slept, and walked out the door.

⋆⟩⟨⋆

The streets were full on this Friday evening downtown.
Amanda parked in a garage and walked two blocks. The night
was cool and she caught the salt air from the bay. Approaching
the green canopy with the word *Italia* in script writing,
Amanda paused at the line of windows. There he was—her
father—at their usual window table. The waiter was standing
next to him; her father would be ordering her the portabello
ravioli. He wore his ever-faithful gray sport coat and a white
shirt. His hands were folded on the table. During those long
days and nights when she didn't know if he'd survive the cancer
that ate through his bones, Amanda had promised herself to not
take him for granted again, to take long moments to really see
him. It was a promise she'd kept for two years.

Amanda opened the restaurant door to the full scent of Ital-
ian cuisine. At a small stage in the back corner a female vocal-
ist and a male guitarist performed a folk tune. Amanda walked
beneath tiny amber lights toward their table. It was a restaurant she enjoyed more than her father did, though he most
often insisted they meet here. Her father faced away from the
entrance. She admired the line of his back and the bald spot
half covered beneath peppered gray hair, which he'd combed
into proper order except for one rebellious cowlick that
popped up in back. In his mid-sixties, Henry Rivans sometimes seemed much older, not in spirit, but in the way he
enjoyed the company of elderly people more than those his
own age, how he'd play chess in the park, or feed the pigeons
for fun. He found beauty in the simple entertainment of
anything around him. He looked calm and thoughtful, awaiting her arrival.

"I'm late," she said, touching his shoulder as she moved
around him.

"I always enjoy the wait." Henry rose to greet her. He kissed her cheek, and she felt the prickle of stubble he seemed unable to shave completely smooth. The feel of his face reminded her of childhood stories and good-night kisses. It also confirmed that he was no longer sick, no longer under the power of the chemo and radiation he'd endured.

Henry pulled out her chair and scooted her in, then took her coat to a nearby coatrack. His chair scraped softly when he returned to the table. Beneath the amber lights, he looked younger, and Amanda's own weariness rose in the comfort of her favorite restaurant and her father's presence.

"Now I am content." He patted her hand. "My daughter is home from yet another journey."

"My flight was delayed when I changed in Munich. I barely made it."

"You are tired; we could have done this tomorrow."

"I wouldn't miss portabello ravioli for anything," she said, taking a sip of the wine her father had ordered for her. Henry had already eaten one or two rolls, evidenced by the crumbs on his plate.

"And what is this?" She picked up an envelope on her appetizer plate and noticed his smile.

"Open it later, but it might have something to do with two season tickets for a particular baseball team."

"This year was my turn to buy."

"I only said that so you wouldn't argue when I bought last year. Anyway, your travels keep you from over half the games—so it's my treat and no arguments."

"Yes, Daddy," she said with a laugh. "This year, the Giants are going to the Series—I can feel it."

They talked about the coming season with games at the new Pac Bell Stadium where they'd cheer wildly as Barry Bonds hit homers over the wall and into San Francisco Bay. They missed cold and windy Candlestick Park only for nostalgia's sake, but the new stadium built over the bay and in the downtown area was secretly their favorite.

"And I have something for you." She reached for the small bag inside her purse and handed it to her father.

"A floaty pen?" he said, obviously surprised. "I used to love these."

"I thought I'd start bringing them home from my travels," she said, watching him dip the pen back and forth, moving the tiny boat up and down the Vltava River. "A friend gave me the idea."

"A friend?"

"Anyway, I didn't want to ruin my meal before it arrived," Amanda said, avoiding the topic of Stefan, "but tomorrow night is Mother?"

"Ah yes, you heard my message then. Dinner tomorrow, but please be there." He gave a look of comic desperation. "What a surprise that she called."

"A shock. Why did she call you?" Amanda wished he'd told the woman he was too busy.

"Can anyone explain the unexplainable? I look back at our years together and simply marvel that she stayed as long as she did. Your mother is one of those people not made for this world."

"I would agree with that," Amanda said.

Henry gave his best fatherly frown. "She wants us to attend one of her readings in a few weeks. We talked quite a long while actually."

As he reflected aloud upon their conversation, Amanda took in his slight smile. It brought a rush of annoyance. Somehow she could not allow her mother to suddenly glide into her father's life after nearly thirty years. Amanda's mother always ended relationships with a graceful departure that left havoc in its wake.

"Your mother didn't know about the cancer." He sounded somewhat hurt.

"I never told her," she said firmly. "I didn't think she needed to know."

"Ah, you are right. We have been divorced a very long time."

"Dad, she didn't have the right to know. I didn't want her sending some poem about how she felt so far away and the guilt she must carry as payment for her abandonment. She would have made your illness her cross. I couldn't stand that. And besides, I knew you'd come through just fine."

He nodded as if understanding fully, but there was a hint of something unspoken.

"You still think I should have told her?"

"Oh no. That is your choice, and I agree it was difficult enough without your mother's presence intruding."

"You aren't saying something." Amanda searched his expression. The past few years had taught her to read him well, especially during his illness. She'd ask how he felt and his assurances were either believable by the clarity of his gaze or found to be false by the slight expression in his mouth, the rise or fall of his eyebrows, a look of avoidance in his eyes. "Dad, we don't keep secrets, remember?" Even as she said it she thought of what she'd learned, or unlearned, in Prague. But it was right for her to wait before telling him.

"I had a doctor's appointment while you were gone."

The room froze in her eyes for an instant. "They found something."

"It's probably nothing," he said soothingly. "Even the doctor thinks so. But, of course, they want to make sure."

The music halted, as if the guitarist and the singer felt her shock. Amanda hadn't known about the appointment. She knew he had one in June—it was on her calendar. For every appointment, she braced herself for news. This one caught her unprepared.

"Why didn't you tell me you were going in?"

"It happened when you were gone. I kept having some aching in my side, so I called for an appointment. Now, honey, get that look off your face. There's nothing to worry about yet."

Nothing to worry about—yet. Amanda didn't want this again. She couldn't. Her father sat there across from her, with his kind, dark eyes and his thin frame so healthy and strong. She couldn't see him in another hospital gown. She couldn't attempt cheerfulness when he was obviously walking death's roadway. For so long, she had lived day by day with the fear of losing him. In just the last six months, after nearly two years of good reports, Amanda had felt she'd finally quit holding her breath.

At odd moments even now, Amanda would catch a whiff of that hospital smell. She didn't know what it was—the cleaner they used in the hallways, the mixture of disease and medicines, rubber-soled shoes, and disinfected everything. But when she caught that scent in a grocery aisle or somewhere else, it brought her back—back to long nights in the waiting room, coffee from a machine, waiting and waiting for test results or a doctor to do his rounds. They'd had two years of freedom from that place and those smells. It wasn't enough time.

"I'm sure it's nothing," Amanda said with an attempt at optimism. She felt instant shame for her unwillingness to walk the cancer path again. She'd suffered nothing compared to her father. Sleeping in chairs, awakening to her clothing stuck to her back, a sore neck and back muscles, hospital food—she knew what soup went with which day of the week by the time he was released. Yet he was the one who had been probed with knives, who had things cut from his body. He had the collapsed veins in his arms and the consuming sickness from the chemotherapy. How could he sit there as if in peace?

Her father moved on to another subject. They didn't know anything right now; it could be nothing. Henry Rivans would find no need to worry or fret. She noticed a thread had come loose on the sleeve of his sport coat. It bothered her. She kept watching it and thinking of those days and nights in the hospital, and the days and nights in his small apartment where the scent of the hospital followed them. His hands moved as he talked now, those hands that she remembered holding books and leafing through papers, stacking cans on shelves, patting her shoulder when she was troubled. The loose thread fluttered as he continued to speak. Didn't he notice it? Did he know that pulling it could fray the material? Of course he did. Henry Rivans would patiently wait till he was home and there take out his cuticle scissors, carefully snipping it away. She wanted to pull it out right now.

"You don't have to if you're too busy," he said.

"What?" she asked, unable to recall what he'd been speaking about. The singer at the back of the restaurant began to sing again, a lonely song that reminded Amanda of the Scottish moors.

"Dinner tomorrow, with your mother and me."

"Sure, Dad."

"All right, now tell me everything about your trip. First to Budapest and then to Prague. What did you think of your two days in our homeland?"

How easily he passed from the possibility of devastating news to what she didn't want to speak about. She needed some family facts from her father or uncle without them asking too many questions in return.

"Well, a storm kept me from seeing most of it. Prague looks worth another trip."

"In more ways than one, I suppose?"

Amanda smiled, knowing he meant Stefan. She wasn't ready to go there yet either.

"I wish I could remember Prague. Aunt Helga said she loved the city."

"When did Aunt Helga come to the United States?"

"In the 1930s, after she married Hans."

"Do you remember anything about living there before being sent to Aunt Helga in America?"

"Not really." He looked thoughtful.

"You and Uncle Martin came to America in the early forties?"

"We came in 1943. I was four years old and Martin was around three."

"How did you get here?" Amanda realized there were many details she didn't know.

"Aunt Helga said that a family who knew our parents smuggled us first to Argentina, and then we made it to the States. Guess it took something like nine months for us to arrive. I seem to remember being told to stay away from a railing and looking down at water and waves. I was sick a lot as a child so perhaps that's what happened to my memories."

"What about memories of your mother and father?"

"I remember my mother most. She liked working with her flowers, and I had this small shovel and would help her. She was pretty, it seems like, though I can't quite remember her face. I was four when we were separated. I think I remember my father. I recall polished boots and a uniform—Aunt Helga said he was in the Czech Army."

That was new information to her. She could look in Czech Army records for her grandfather's name.

"I can't imagine being four years old and having to leave both parents behind," she said, vaguely recalling her mother's departure when she was three.

"Unfortunately, such things happened a lot during that time. It's lucky that we were sent away."

"A blessing," she replied. The waiter walked toward them, his arms laden with plates.

"What?" her father asked.

"Oh, Stefan says things are a blessing instead of luck."

The waiter stood before them. "Portabello ravioli for the lady and lasagna for the gentleman. Can I get you anything else?"

They both thanked him before his departure.

"Tell me about the Budapest conference. It was about Eastern Europe in current times or something, correct?"

Amanda nodded as she took a bite of pasta, then began telling about the days of speakers and workshops that projected what would soon change in the emerging countries. She'd been sent mainly as a rep for the History Network to talk to university professors and politicians from the countries represented. The History Network and its parent company, World Television, had a growing interest in the opportunities opening in such countries.

"It was mainly for networking. The Czech Republic has been doing a lot of films, and Hollywood has discovered it's a cheap place to make movies. Other countries may try to follow the lead. The History Network may establish an Eastern European headquarters in one of the capital cities. There's a lot of talk. I was there to build bridges."

Her father gave Amanda's hand a squeeze. "Your life amazes me. I couldn't keep up with such a schedule—flying all over the world, creating these programs, networking—there's too much for me to list."

"Thanks, Dad. I am enjoying it, but . . . I don't know. Sometimes I just wonder if I'm missing a few things in my life."

Henry nodded while taking in her thoughtful musing. She knew he only offered advice when she asked.

"Have you talked to Uncle Martin since I've been gone?"

"No," he said simply without looking up from his plate.

Amanda shook her head but decided not to push him since he didn't push her. She'd already given him a long talk about the importance of family and the need to stay connected. She wanted both father and uncle during the holidays. But her comments didn't help. The rift between her father and his brother was a mystery neither had yet logically explained to her. After seeming close her entire childhood, they had pulled apart the last three years. It irritated her. Their foolishness was costing them more than they knew.

Amanda watched her father talk and eat his lasagna. She realized anew that he could be sick again. He wouldn't have contacted his doctor unless he, too, was concerned. They ate their meal with too many worries close at hand. She thought of the ending lines of a Longfellow poem she'd memorized in sixth grade.

> *And the night was filled with laughter and the thoughts that possess the day,*
> *Shall fold their tents like the Arabs and as silently, steal away.*

If only every night could close in such a way. Amanda wished it could come true.

CHAPTER EIGHT

Amanda had made the loop past weariness back to wakefulness. Her clock read 10:30 P.M. It was morning in Prague.

She took papers from her satchel and piled them on the large maple desk in her bedroom. It was a beautiful desk, a gift from her father when she had graduated from college weeks before she started her summer-intern position at the History Network West Coast. She tried to keep her desks organized and succeeded with the one at the office, but this home work area was in constant use and always looked it. Sticky notes lined the back shelves with reminders of groceries to pick up, people to call, research Web sites to remember. There were stacks of books she used often, printouts, a coffee cup, the computer, the printer, and her favorite antique lamp with tapestry shade that she'd bought at a flea market in Paris.

Quickly straightening up and organizing what she'd brought home from Prague, Amanda waited for Benny's late-night knock on the door. She expected him anytime, especially after the new message she'd found when she arrived home from the restaurant: "Don't forget I'll be there tonight, a little late."

Amanda had put up with Benjamin Dunn's sometimes demanding intrusions since childhood. The grandson of her father's closest friends, the Levs, who had lived in their apartment complex, Benny had grown up in New York and came to visit on certain Jewish holidays and for a few weeks each summer. The same age as Amanda, they were often put together. Every visit would begin with their staring at one another with an equal mixture of suspicion and curiosity. As young children, one would woo the other with a toy, and then they'd run through the house like old playmates. Preadolescence brought only stares and awkward conversations.

Benny had given Amanda her first kiss—a not-so-pleasant experience—the summer before high school. Benny had come with a guitar and his cassettes of hard-rock music like Led Zeppelin and AC/DC, and the new-wave music of Tears For Fears and Depeche Mode—he wasn't sure what he liked best. Amanda slept a floor below the Levs' guest room and would drift asleep to the sound of his thumping music. He fascinated her with his rebellious ways and how he seemed to know everything about what was "in" and what wasn't. As they talked one night on the steps outside the apartment building, he claimed he'd kissed a bunch of girls, and she admitted it hadn't happened for her yet. He reached across the guitar and pulled her close. Somehow they missed first contact. When their lips did meet, someone whistled at them from the street. Neither liked the kiss anyway—Amanda said it was like kissing a brother; Benny said it was like kissing a mom. That had done wonders for Amanda's pursuit of boys at school. It took several boyfriends before she felt assured that she didn't kiss like someone's mother.

Amanda checked the clock and wondered when Benny would arrive. The scent of hazelnut coffee filled the small house. She flipped on the bedroom television and turned to the History Network, then picked up a fax her assistant had sent. It was a list of phone messages during her time away. She perused the information, stopping at the name Darby Evans Collins. Since Darby and her mother were the last living heirs of the Empress Sissi Brooch, Darby had already agreed to an on-camera interview about her own failed search for the family heirlooms and the story behind the loss of the Empress Brooch during WWII. The faxed message read that Darby planned to return to California in a couple of weeks and would be ready for the interview. Amanda had considered telling Darby about her own childhood brooch stories and her thoughts of how they could be connected. But she'd decided to wait until their in-person interview.

Sleepiness crept over her, but there was no way to reach Benny. He had a cellular phone that he never kept on because he didn't want to turn into one of the "common followers of technology with their ringing pants and briefcases." Sometimes he drove her crazy.

She heard the side gate open and his footsteps along the flagstone to her entrance behind Mr. Winifred's house. Amanda always checked the peephole to see one of Benny's crazy faces—she often said that if he could market his expressions, he'd be rich. Through the peephole she saw the misshapen image of her front porch and Benny, hanging himself with the tie around his neck. A tie on Benny Dunn? She unlocked the door.

"The last time you wore a tie was to Grandma Lev's funeral," she said, closing the door behind him. She leaned against it and admired the sight of Benjamin Dunn in an actual suit—coal black pants, shoes, and jacket with a cobalt dress shirt beneath. If he cut his dark brown hair and took out his earring, his parents might actually approve of his appearance.

"Let's not discuss it right now. And what kind of greeting is that after over a week without me?"

She hugged him and kissed his cheek. "Is that better?"

"Yeah, but you still kiss like my mother." He laughed and picked her up, pinning her arms down and swinging her around. "I'm just kidding. I'm so glad to have my Amanda home again! You aren't going to punch me now, so I can let you go?"

"You will let me go and I will punch you."

"Truce? Uncle? Forgiveness? Sorry? Peace?" He dropped her and raced around her brown corduroy couch as she tried to catch him. Hemingway ran from the bedroom and joined the chase with tail wagging and a few barks. Finally they collapsed on the couch, laughing, and Hemingway jumped on Benny's legs, awaiting a few hearty pats. Amanda punched his arm.

"Ouch." He flopped down with his head on the arm of the couch in his usual spot and began pushing her off the other end with his feet. "Honey, I've had a hard day. Would you please take care of me?"

Amanda moved to the high-back chair and let Benny have his spot. She never sat on the couch at Benny's end; he'd spilled drinks on the arm so many times she'd given up on the stains. With few visitors coming over anyway, Benny claimed it as his own messy side.

"Did you eat?" he asked, which meant he hadn't.

"With Dad at Italia's. I might have some leftovers in the fridge if someone is nice to me."

"So you just got home tonight?"

"Yes. I noticed by your messages that you pay a lot of attention to when I tell you I'll be home."

He brushed his hair back from his face. "Want some coffee?"

"Of course."

"Great, get me some while you're up."

"Oh yes, Master Ben." She put her feet on the coffee table and leaned back.

"You know, Hemingway and I are really tired of you traveling. What are we supposed to do when you're gone?"

"Hemingway has an excuse—you need to get a life."

"I'm trying," he said.

"What is it now?"

"What do you mean?"

"How are you trying to get a life—more graduate work, a new religion du jour, a special someone? Something important made you dress like that."

"I've decided to give up." His hands covered his face. It took a second to register what he meant.

"No!" She couldn't hide her surprise. "Not that."

He nodded. "It's my destiny, Obi-Wan Kenobi, and I cannot fight it any longer. The force was against me."

"Benny, this is a very important moment."

"I'm trying not to think about it."

Amanda started to laugh at his grimace, his tie hanging loose and crooked, his body uncomfortable in the unfamiliar clothes. It made her laugh harder. "I'm sorry," she said, unable to stop. "You just look so, so miserable."

The corner of his mouth twitched, as if he had to fight to keep his scowl. Then he chuckled. "I told myself I'd rather jump off the Golden Gate before joining Dad. Perhaps I really should hang myself with my tie." He grabbed the end and yanked it up, feigning a choking expression.

"When did this happen?"

"End of last week. Dad came to hear me play at the club—you know, his Friday night escape from Mom. We talked for a few hours and he actually made sense. Perhaps I was momentarily weakened because I was days away from pawning my amplifier and selling my artwork at the flea market."

"I'd buy it all first, except the amplifier."

"If you'd quit leaving town so often, perhaps we could have talked. You could have talked me out of it."

Amanda didn't respond.

"Right?" he demanded.

"I don't know. You've tried everything in the world except teaching, so why not give it your best shot and see what you think?" Amanda recalled Benny's art endeavors, his several bands and then solo work, his jobs as restaurant manager, actor, horticulturist, not to mention the various religions he'd sought, much to the horror of his Jewish parents.

"Those were my thoughts over the weekend. Then the week began. I'm working Monday through Saturday—yes, Saturday school for those juvenile delinquents. Talk about insanity."

"You might like it."

"Why do I share my life? You should know me better than that."

"I think you'll make a great teacher. Are you doing some music and drama too?"

"Yeah."

"You relate so well to kids since you haven't really grown up, even if you are thirty-four."

"You are close at my heels, dear one. And what makes you so mature? You let a strange, wandering man into your house at all hours of the night."

"Some truth there."

Benny lowered his dark eyebrows until they were one. "Anyway, I'm giving it a shot. There are a few students I kind of like—some with no potential according to the outside world."

"Kindred spirits, no doubt."

"Enough of your ridicule. Now you owe me a cup of coffee. I've had a long day, remember?"

"And I'm still on someone else's time zone, remember?" She

stretched as she rose and then walked to the kitchen. The sound of her feet on the tile floor brought a glance down at her new slippers she'd put on when she changed into her sweats. A wave of empty loneliness for Stefan swept over her.

"Tell me about the trip," Benny said.

"Do you really want to know?" she asked with humor in her tone.

"I asked, didn't I?"

Benny never appreciated her reminder of how he often talked about himself, expecting her to solve his problems, but then lacked interest in her life. Amanda's grand confession several years earlier had helped him see the light—but he was still working on it. She knew he thought he was greatly improved, while she'd drop the *greatly*.

Amanda brought two cups of coffee.

Benny sat up and put his feet on the coffee table. "What about the guy?"

"The guy?"

"Come on, give me the news. Did he propose after only eight months of e-mail and three real-life encounters? Will he try to sweep you off to some remote village, or can we convince him to come here? Will he hate me and I be forced to break up the wedding? Come on, the news."

"Let me start with the snowstorm." Amanda sat in the chair and went through the trials of her trip to Europe. They both laughed at how much was stacked against her. She was proud of Benny for listening so attentively without reverting to one of his own travel terror stories.

"And the guy—Stefanito or whatever his name is."

"Stefan," she said dryly.

"Yes, but it must be something like Stefanov or Stefanik in Czech."

"His mother named him Stefan."

"Kind of boring when you consider the prospects—Stefanovich?"

"Okay, Benjanik."

"I'll stop." Benny smiled. "Now tell me about seeing him again."

"Well, it was great. Troubling. Scary. I loved his family, and I think I could fall in love with him."

"Wow." Benny's feet dropped from the coffee table. "Wow."

"Yeah, I'm in a mess, aren't I?"

"It's a little nice to have *you* the mess for once. So you love him." Benny stared at her intently.

"I think I could love him."

"Why are you holding back? This could be the elusive one you've written letters to since you were nine and have painstakingly planned the bridal arrangements around."

"I can't even begin to share all the doubts I have." Amanda held her coffee on her lap, staring into the dark liquid with hopes that an image of the future might appear. "I don't know if it can work."

"Why?"

"I can't explain it."

"Okay, you like this guy, you could love him or are on the verge of love, which is a major thing for you."

"But my emotions aren't the best compass. Remember I thought I was in love with you a long time ago."

"I know. And I thought the same." Benny's dark eyes were pools of warmth to her. "But for once I was wise enough to know it would never work. It would destroy this."

"What *this*?"

"This friendship I need more than I need most anything."

Amanda smiled softly.

"But let us dissect Amanda Rivans' psyche once again."

"You know, I'm never wise enough to know."

"Know what?"

"I thought we should be together—back then. I understand it now. We would have eventually hated each other. But I didn't see it until after you broke my heart in tiny, tiny pieces."

"Knock it off. I didn't break your heart into tiny, tiny pieces. It broke mine more to do it."

"Let's not get back on that long-dead subject. I only used it as a reference as to how it's hard for me to know what's good for me or not." Hemingway sighed loudly from his spot on the floor between them. "See, even Hemingway agrees."

"Remember we were twenty years old then. You know a lot more now. Just start talking about why you're so worried."

"Let's see. Well, for one, just because he brings me coffee when I desperately need it, just because he's kind and sincere and strong in his beliefs, just because he . . ."

Benny leaned back with his arms behind his head.

"I'm crazy, aren't I?"

"Why are you determined to destroy the first really good thing to come along?"

Amanda wasn't prepared for this to turn so serious, so personal. She needed a few days away from her multitude of thoughts that simply renewed her fatigue and the desire to scurry straight to bed.

"I don't want to destroy it. But, Benny—" Amanda knew that beyond the doubts of distance, religion, and culture was the deeper fear that had planted itself within her in Prague and was sprouting by the time she arrived back home. "Something happened. It transcends his devout religion and how I am, well, Miss Relationship Failure. We were brought together by a common bond. And now I don't know if that bond is so common anymore."

"Now you've lost me. What common bond—I thought you met at some Holocaust thing and talked about your family stuff."

"We did. Stefan's grandfather and some of his extended family died in the Holocaust."

"And you have that similar situation. That village and all the men killed, the women off to camps where your grandmother died."

"That's what I've always been told." Heat rushed to Amanda's face. She wasn't ready to tell him or anyone, but here it was.

Benny hesitated with a confused expression. "So that isn't the truth?"

Amanda explained her search for her family on the Lidice victim list while searching for information on the Empress Brooch.

He set his coffee cup on the table. "They weren't there? What does that mean?"

"It means my grandparents probably didn't die the way we've always believed."

"This is bad. Does your father know?"

"No."

"You can't tell him." Benny's voice was firm.

"I was going to find the truth and then decide. Obviously his parents both died during the German occupation."

"Yes, but your dad—it's going to be hard, really hard on him, if this isn't true. That family history is as much a part of him as the lines in his hands. It's his identification with the survivors. Your dad once told Grandfather Lev that he often thought of his dead parents and believed it was his calling in life to do what they never had the chance to do—help survivors of the war. He wanted to make them proud."

They sat without speaking. The television in her bedroom flashed white light through the doorway.

"I guess it does affect you and Stefan too," Benny said after a while.

"It would probably change my relationship with him. His family now knows I'm searching for my family in Lidice."

"What a mess."

"Thanks."

"No, I'm serious."

"You aren't making me feel better."

"Come here." He reached for her and put his arm around her shoulder after she sat beside him. "I'm your friend. I tell you the truth and mix in a bit of sympathy, empathy, or exaggeration, but you've always been strong enough for the truth. I'm seeing it from this guy's side. Let's say I met a girl who was like me—yes, sounds scary. So our first common bond is that we both have a Jewish heritage and we liked insane music during our teen years, and we rebelled to avoid those roots. Then later I discover she's not even Jewish. Well, hate to be brutally honest, but it wouldn't work for me."

"I didn't lie."

"I know, and maybe this Stefan is a better man than me, which wouldn't be tough. What other things have kept you together?"

Amanda pulled her blonde hair into a twist, then released it to fall back on her shoulders. "At least I know I'm really attracted to him."

"That's nothing. Most guys are attracted to at least a third of the women in their lives."

"Really?"

"Well, maybe, I don't know. But there must be more than attraction." Benny rubbed his chin in deep thought. "You need to find out who they really were, these grandparents. Then you can decide what or whether to tell your father and this Stefan."

"If it's completely different, I don't think I could lie to them."

"Of course not. But just find out before you say anything to anyone. Get into your research mode and get to the bottom of this."

Amanda nodded.

"Perhaps your grandparents were war heroes or something like that?"

She nodded again and knew that Benny was trying to cheer her up. But why would Aunt Helga tell a different story if something like that was the truth?

"Hey, I brought a movie from the school library."

"Benny, it's late and my sleep is already messed up."

"That's what coffee's for," he said, reciting one of their favorite lines.

"What movie is it?"

"*Willy Wonka and the Chocolate Factory*—now on DVD." He suddenly looked eleven years old again. Amanda couldn't help but smile.

"One of my old favorites."

"I know, and those high schoolers laughed when I said if they did good all week, we'd watch it Friday. Kids these days don't know great art."

"Put it on and our lives will be perfect for a few hours."

Benny refilled their coffee cups and put on the DVD.

Perhaps this was just the beginning of a long road she wasn't sure she was ready to walk. But ready or not, she was already on that road.

CHAPTER NINE

W hat do you think it means?" Dr. Matthews leaned back in his chair and pressed the fingertips of both his hands together. Ms. Delsig's newest work of art rested on the desk beneath his gaze.

They'd waited until after breakfast, when Ms. Delsig was sitting in the silence of her room, before sending the same nurse's aide who'd treated her like a child the day before.

"Good morning, dearie," Vickie Ann had said in her sugar-sweet tone. Ms. Delsig had scrutinized her tag to remember her name. "You have an important request from Mr. Bartlett to come down and visit for a while."

She'd been surprised and assumed it was to discuss the loss of Janice—whether she wanted a new roommate from within Oakdale or perhaps a single room. But this request felt like she was going to army headquarters. Vickie Ann had waited for her as she put on shoes instead of the slippers she wore in her room. Ms. Delsig chided herself for the bubbles of nervousness she felt. Fear always pulsed through her whenever she was sent to places of authority. Some things never went away.

Mr. Bartlett called her in that morning, her first morning without Janice, but not to discuss how she was feeling or what arrangements would be made in their room. He shook her hand, obviously not remembering her well, then broke the news.

"Dr. Matthews is at Oakdale today. He is our counselor and rotates among several of the senior facilities in the area. I would like you to talk to him."

Perhaps they believed she needed a counselor to get through the loss of Janice, she thought. Ms. Delsig didn't want to see this Dr. Matthews person, but she didn't do well standing up to men like Mr. Bartlett. And he hadn't really asked.

"He's waiting in room 15."

She had shuffled her way down. Vickie Ann opened the door, then left. Dr. Matthews sat at an imposing desk with the window behind him. She sat in the small chair in front of him.

And then Ms. Delsig saw the reason behind her summons. Her painting from the day before lay on the desk. Its dark colors seemed more disturbing inside the stark white room.

They began the usual chitchat. Dr. Matthews wanted her to be comfortable. He could become a confidant and friend. She could sit on the couch, or he could sit wherever made her feel at ease. He behaved as if she'd sought him out for help. There was no mention of Janice. After going through the small talk quickly, he had dived right in.

"What do you think it means?" he asked now for the second time.

She felt some confidence. "Art doesn't have to mean anything. It can express a feeling or a slice of imagination or tell a story or simply be."

"You are an excellent painter." He leaned forward with his

elbows on the desk, his fingers to his forehead, examining the canvas.

"Thank you." He didn't look up and she glanced around the room. There was a framed picture of trees and flowers on each wall—generic works. No photographs on the desk or shelf. Closed vinyl miniblinds. Jars of cotton and tongue depressors sat on a cabinet. The room must be used for various purposes, including the rotating shrink.

"What feeling, imagination, or expression caused you to compose this?" He seemed to be a patient man. She thought he'd probably seen every type of person and knew just how to draw each of them out.

"I can't really say. It just sort of happened."

"Does this happen very often?" He looked at her intently.

"From time to time."

"Where are those other paintings?"

"Usually they are sketches. I throw them away."

"Why?"

"Because I do not particularly like them."

"Why don't you like them?" Dr. Matthews asked.

Ms. Delsig knew he was taking her through his steps until she would be tripped up by his questions. She didn't respond.

He waited for a long time. Then he scratched his chin and pressed his fingers together, creating a triangle. "I think that perhaps this is a repressed memory from your childhood. Your Oakdale files have nothing about your childhood."

"You are incorrect, Doctor." She was suddenly ready to leave the probing eyes of this man.

"I assure you, the files have no information before 1960."

"No, I did not mean you were incorrect about the files. You are incorrect about this being a repressed memory."

"Then you know what this piece of art is about? Is it fantasy or memory?"

"Perhaps a little of both. But certainly not repressed. I think of this when I rise every morning and before my eyes close at night."

"Your time in a concentration camp, I presume. What camp was it?"

"I did not say I was in a concentration camp. Some nurse came to that conclusion."

"May I see the number tattooed on your arm?"

"You may not."

"So you don't deny that it is there?"

"I did not come here to be evaluated. So if you will excuse me, I would like to leave now."

"I have a friend who studies the works of people who have endured horrific circumstances. Would you mind if I took this with me?"

"Yes, I would," she said flatly. "Dr. Matthews, I appreciate that you think you can help me. But I am a seventy-six-year-old woman. Only God knows how many more years I have. I've lived my life and found happiness in it. That is all a person can hope for."

"I believe you are in denial."

"I believe I am too old to get my head fixed up."

"People live haunted lives when instead they can find peace."

"I have been told that death is the place to find peace. I am pretty close to that."

"Ms. Delsig, if you change your mind, I'll give you my business card. You wouldn't have to wait for my rotation. Call me. Anytime."

She was startled by his sincerity. His gaze appeared genuine. "I appreciate that. You may have the painting if you want something such as that. It's a little too dark for me."

He smiled—a surprisingly nice smile. "I'd like my friend to

see it; then I'll keep it for you. Your art should be in a gallery. Keep that in mind also."

Ms. Delsig left quickly, unable to push her walker fast enough.

⋆⁓═◉═⁓⋆

That afternoon Ms. Delsig was again attempting to sit in her room and simply stare for a while at Janice's empty side when Alfred Milton peered around the corner.

"Come with me," he ordered.

"No, Alfred," she said with a slight whine. Alfred was the only one at Oakdale who could truly understand what she'd lost in Janice. The three of them had spent many hours playing card games, telling stories, and watching old movies.

"It's time you learn the beast," he responded from the doorway. Alfred Milton always dressed for the day in pressed slacks, shined shoes, and a white undershirt she could see beneath his white dress shirt. They often talked about escaping Oakdale and running off to Mexico together. She wondered what "beast" he was talking about; then it hit her.

"Oh no," she said, standing.

He walked up with determined steps. "I won't let you sit here feeling sorry for yourself." He took her arm and slid the metal walker toward her. "Come along now."

"Alfred, please. I just want some time alone." But he was leading her to the doorway.

"It's time you learn." He prodded her down the hall.

"But I don't want to," she said. "They scare me. What if I ruin it or it explodes or something?"

"That won't happen."

"You don't understand. I cannot do this."

Alfred walked beside her. A few people looked their way. Kisser Bob sat at his corner. He'd quit making passes at Ms.

Delsig long ago, after she threatened to reach out and pinch him.

Before she knew it, Ms. Delsig stood in the doorway of the resource room. Her eyes went straight to the line of three computers that stared back with their blank, open screens. She was often drawn to the shelves of books encasing the room and the comfy chairs for reading. This place had been a quiet escape even with one old computer in the corner. But the generous donation of three brand-new computers to the resource room, once called the library, had changed everything. Ms. Delsig had to walk around the technology tables to her cozy spot in the corner. She'd watch people sit in front of those boxes and become lost to the world. It intrigued her at first, especially since she understood the way a book could draw her like a black hole away from this world and into the book world. Could computers provide such an adventure? Her curiosity was quickly curbed while spying frustrated users cursing or tapping angrily on the keys.

Agnes Scribbs, self-proclaimed librarian, put up signs for silence in the resource room. It began to annoy many of the regular readers, so when Agnes Scribbs started the Readers Against Computers group with its campaign to convince administration to move the computers out, Ms. Delsig put her name on the dotted line. It didn't work. The computers were becoming more popular, and some of the techno geeks—all in their seventies and eighties—decided perhaps the books should go. There were a few angry debates and plans for an Oakdale meeting. Alfred was Ms. Delsig's first friend to defect to the "other side." Janice's defection had come as a surprise. They both had tried to convince her, but to no avail.

"I am in the RAC group," she said weakly.

"Who cares what people think? You may even bridge the gap between readers and geeks, proving we can all exist in the world together." Alfred winked at her.

"I've never been much of a revolutionary," Ms. Delsig said, chuckling.

"Hello, Al," a voice called from the blue-and-green striped love seat across the room. Candy Banks waved and motioned him over.

Agnes gave a sharp *shhhh* from her desk in the checkout area.

"I'm busy right now, Candy," Alfred whispered.

"Huh?" she said loudly. Her bushy hair bobbed as she leaned forward.

"I'm busy with Ms. D."

"Really." Her penciled eyebrows raised high.

Ms. Delsig pushed her walker inside and gazed evenly at Candy. "Yes, Al is going to teach me the computer."

Eyes turned their way. Not only was another Readers Against Computers member about to defect, but now there'd be implications of them being the newest couple at Oakdale. The final goal in life for some women, including Candy Banks, was to snag themselves a man. Alfred was a prime target. Whenever a couple was established, the vicious words would fly. Ms. Delsig had kept herself out of it as much as possible. Strange how at their age, communal living brought back all the rules and conditions that she imagined an American high school to have. She had watched a television show about students in high school, and the parallels amazed her.

Residents often divided into groups. A newcomer would be asked, "What did you do for a living?" The answer often set their group. Interests, backgrounds, wealth—"Are you from family money or self-made, or are your kids doing well?"—all placed a label. Oakdale was supposed to be a new concept in assisted living, but residents who had been around revealed that it was much the same. The food might be better, the place cleaner, more nurses and aides available, but you couldn't leave when you wanted, you were expected to cooperate, and your initial label could determine the friends you'd have until death did you part.

"Well, isn't that nice of Al," Candy said with narrowed eyes. Then she whined, "Al, when are you going to teach me?"

"Perhaps I'll start a computer-learning class," Alfred said as he pulled out the chair for Ms. Delsig. "I'll test my teaching skills on this dear lady."

Alfred scooted close on another computer chair. Ms. Delsig stared at the buttons and strange symbols on the keyboard. Her sudden portrayal of confidence for the sake of Candy Banks now faltered as she recalled words like *hard-drive crash* and *computer virus.*

"Let's start at the beginning. This is the mouse."

"The mouse?"

"The mouse."

It took a few hours but by dinner, Ms. Delsig was beginning to feel comfortable with the plastic machine. Alfred showed her several times how to move the mouse, how to turn the computer off and on, and how the components of a computer worked together. She nodded, not really understanding half of it. But she learned what to click to get the results she wanted. And surprisingly, Ms. Delsig found that she *did* like the computer, especially when Alfred introduced the magical world of the Internet.

"This is the resort we'll run away to," he said, typing in *Cancún, Mexico.* Photos of white beaches, couples snorkeling, tables overflowing with tropical delicacies appeared. "Or we can visit my son's Web site and see my grandchildren." They read up on what was happening in the kids' lives, viewing soccer photos and a special note to Grandpa. Alfred e-mailed a letter back, and Ms. Delsig was amazed that the family could instantly read the note.

Finally, as the room cleared out, she asked him, "Why are you doing this? Why now?"

"You should know why," he said.

Ms. Delsig nodded. "Janice leaving."

"That is part of it. You do need to start e-mailing her. But there is more." He cocked his head. "I know about the meeting with Dr. Matthews. I wish I'd been a fly on the wall to see that one. You'll be expected to give a full story later."

"What do computers have to do with that?"

"Learning the computer can help you find some answers."

"About what?"

"About yourself."

"What—you think I'm crazy too?"

"If you are, then we all must be. No, this computer takes you into the world of information. Anything you want to know can most likely be found. Family you've lost. What your homeland is like today."

"Did Janice tell you anything?"

"No. I don't know very much about you, though I've been trying for three years to find out." He crossed his arms. "I know you aren't a native American—there is that slight accent, you know. And I heard the rumors about other things. But I want you to tell me when you're ready. And I want to help you find whatever you need. Any unanswered questions you might have, this will help."

"Alfred, I am an old, old woman. My unanswered questions are tucked away. I do not need to dig them out now. What would be the use?"

"We are still living, my dear. Life isn't over; it's just nearing the end. You need to dump that attitude and start realizing that if you have some life left—live it!"

She wanted to argue with him, tell him how tired she was, weary of living and sitting on the conveyor belt toward death. But perhaps there *was* some truth to his words.

"So tell me," Alfred said with an excited smile, "what is

something you've wondered about? Let's see if we can find an answer."

Ms. Delsig looked at the computer and back to Alfred. If she let herself consider them, she'd find many questions—some minor, some too fearsome to ask. But one came to mind. She'd wondered for years if anyone had found the hiding place. Now perhaps she could finally know.

"There was this brooch I once knew about. It was hidden during the war."

"Ms. Delsig," a woman in an Oakdale uniform said from the doorway, "I thought you might want to know—your new roommate has arrived."

"My roommate? I don't have a new roommate."

"You do now."

⋯⇒◎⇐⋯

Nothing was ever as simple as he planned. Richter should know that by now. He didn't want to be part of this group, and yet he knew if he wasn't careful they'd pull him right in.

The man and woman were Americans, brother and sister, he was told, though names were not exchanged. They had greeted him as if they were old friends in case anyone was watching, which they assured him there wouldn't be. Canada had been the perfect place for such a meeting they had said. The woman was attractive with her long curls and a small oval face. She watched him with a shy smile and blushed easily in that irresistible way he was drawn toward. He wished he'd shaved and cut his hair before their meeting, but she didn't seem to mind. The brother motioned her to sit across the booth from Richter as they sat in a dark corner of the bar. Richter reminded himself why he was meeting them. He'd get to the pleasure after the business.

"I've given you enough evidence to understand who I am," Richter began.

"We were stunned and pleased by your inquiry into our group—though I know it took some time for the word to reach us."

"You seem to have a careful chain of passing information," Richter said.

"We hope you will join us in the States and see exactly the operation we have in order."

Richter glanced at the woman and for a minute actually considered it. But there would be many pretty faces in the places he hoped to see. "I appreciate that, but I have some plans to figure out."

The woman glanced at her brother, who continued to stare at Richter.

"Is there a problem with that?" Richter asked.

"Is there a problem with your involvement with us? It becomes difficult to trust those who are not one of us."

"I can understand that. However, I am not planning on joining your group. I enjoy my independence. My plan was to give you some information you want, and for you to give me the new life I want. An easy trade."

"We can only work with people we trust." The man's words were clipped. "How do we know you won't give us false information? How do we trust a stranger? We like to work with those who believe as we believe."

Richter knew he was in a precarious situation. If they didn't believe he could be trusted, the deal would be off and he'd have to start all over. He was so tired of being on the run, wearing stocking caps, and spending hours in country bars. It wasn't his way of life. Yet he also didn't want to become tangled in a group who wouldn't let him out again. He knew these people had to be suspicious in their line of work, just as he did.

"I'd like to hear about what you believe," he said tentatively, wondering if showing interest in their cause would help them work together independently of each other. Richter didn't expect the man to launch into his neo-Nazi propaganda message, but he tried to sound interested in the ramblings.

"Most educated people know that life today was formed by organisms and different species developing and overcoming other species. We fight to keep things from extinction today. But some things *should* become extinct. As in other races of people."

It startled Richter to hear how this guy thought he had it all figured out.

"Don't get me wrong—I care about people," the brother insisted. "All people. I couldn't hurt anyone. But that's not the reality of life. For one to succeed, another must not. If you advance in your career, someone else doesn't. I enjoy a great New York steak, but some cow had to die for that. If one minority gets new rights, another doesn't. For any creature to survive, something else must not. This is our world—the cohabitation, the food chain, the survival of the fittest. I want white people to be in existence in a thousand years or ten thousand. So I fight for my race. Many other races do the same, only we are the ones who people hate. I won't intentionally harm another, but someone will probably not advance if we do. It's the nature of our world."

Richter could tell the guy thought his words would convert him. It sent a chill down his spine to realize how fully this couple believed in their cause. He needed to get what he wanted and get out.

"You have a noble cause," Richter said. He pulled a photograph of the Empress Brooch from his backpack and set it on the table. "It's something I may be very interested in someday. But right now I have one focus. I have information for sale, and I'm just looking for a buyer."

The man glanced at the woman, then down at the black-and-white photograph. Richter had the sudden feeling that he'd gotten in over his head. This time, perhaps he'd gone too far.

CHAPTER TEN

One day of warmth upon the city of Prague shrank the snow from corner pockets and caused roofs to drip, leaving wet streaks on the pavement. The wind would soon change and sweep across the hillsides, through the weave of branches, until everything would glow with bright greens and spring foliage. For the first time in years Stefan wanted to stay and watch the transformation. Over a decade had passed since he'd spent extended time in the country of his birth. The world had drawn him away, and he'd never thought to return except for a quick visit.

Stefan walked from the docile Old Town, Staré Město, into New Town, Nové Město, on his way to meet his mother for lunch. He pondered his family. They were all growing old fast. His grandmother would be ninety-five this year and though she remained fairly healthy, he noticed her increasing forget-fulness and how easily she became tired. The five flights of stairs made it extremely difficult for her to leave the apart-ment. His mother continued to work at the school and also tutored for an extra income, but she was beyond the age of most retirees with no possibility for rest on the horizon. Cousin Petrov was already in his fifties and made a small income playing his cello at weddings or on river cruises, and giving lessons, in addition to the unpaid work he did with local churches. Stefan's grandmother was especially proud to earn a little extra money by knitting Christmas ornaments. Earning extra money and being proud of it was a concept the Communist era would have construed as a bourgeois or capitalistic attitude. Life had changed dramatically for them.

They had a few conveniences they'd earned, like an old Fiat and a television. Stefan had given them his old computer when he bought a laptop. After spending many of their years under the rule of the Nazis and then the long decades of Communism, they were happy. None had seen America or the Western European countries except on television. They were content with life, thankful to God, rejoicing in the simplicity of everyday moments. Sometimes Stefan wondered if the many options granted to him were really blessings.

He walked down a shortcut he'd traveled often as a boy. His best friend had lived nearby, long before Stefan left the city and traveled the world. Thinking of the lunch with his mother, Stefan considered the daily bus commute she took to work long hours at her low-paying job.

His work at International Missions paid to support a single person well enough. But he could send his family only what money he made on side writing jobs. They didn't complain, but he worried about them because they didn't earn enough to stop working if his grandmother became ill. Petrov would never push, but it didn't have to be spoken that his cousin had long thought Stefan's place was in Prague. Even Amanda had said it, along with his mother and grandmother. What if he could move them all to the United States? he thought. Then he quickly dismissed the idea. His grandmother would never leave the graves of her loved ones.

"Stefan?" A woman stood in the darkened entrance of a building. "Stefan, is that you?"

He had been thinking in English, so the woman's Czech jarred him from his thoughts. He took a step toward the doorway, trying to recognize her face. A child with dark curls clutched her leg.

"It is Klara," the woman said, not moving from the shadows.

He walked up the stairs and studied her face. Her dark hair was curled and styled full around her face. She was beautiful even with the thick makeup.

"Klara, I heard you were still here," he said, giving her a hug. She hugged back with little emotion. "It has been a very long time."

"Since before you left Praha. At Ivanov's."

"That's right." Stefan remembered the party at the apartment of Ivanov, their old schoolmate. It had lasted until dawn as they celebrated the first months of their country's freedom. Klara Koubek had been drunk, and she had cried and begged Stefan not to leave the country.

But Stefan couldn't wait to get out of the country, and his opportunity had come. Tomas, a friend of his father's, had escaped the country before a round of political arrests and had become quite established in the States. He'd written that if Stefan needed a place and some help getting started in school, he would help. Tomas' and Stefan's fathers had vowed when they both had infant sons that if one made it out, they would help the other. Tomas' son had died as a child. Stefan's father had died as a political prisoner when Stefan was a young child.

"Is this your daughter?" Stefan peered down at this child, who hid behind her mother's leather pants.

"One of them. I have three daughters. This is the youngest."

"Amazing. You are a mother of three children." Stefan

shook his head at the thought. Klara still seemed like a seventeen-year-old girl, the little sister of his best friend, Viktor. He didn't see a wedding ring on her hand, so he didn't ask about that area of her life. "How is your mother?"

"She is very ill right now."

"I'm sorry to hear that." An uncomfortable strain settled between them. They had too many shared memories for small talk—memories he didn't want to recall and surely she didn't want to either. And surely both were thinking of Viktor.

"You still live in America?" Klara asked.

"No. I don't really live anywhere right now. I was in the States for about twelve years and then I started working all over."

"I would love to get out," she said with a sigh, running her fingers through the girl's curls.

"Home is a good thing, Klara."

"You can say that because you left." There was a depth to the sorrow in her voice. "But I must get to work now."

She walked down the steps and into the sunlight. He noticed her red leather pants, high-heeled boots, and black tank top. She looked like either a model or perhaps a prostitute—Stefan wasn't sure he wanted the answer. The little girl kept her large, curious eyes on him but hid when he winked at her.

"I'd like to see your mom. I'll be here until Monday."

"She would like that." Her expression softened. "She has missed you. We have all missed you."

"I have missed all of you too." He wanted to say something about Viktor. But even after all these years, there were still no words to begin.

"Where are you staying?" she asked.

"With my family—same place."

Klara nodded. "I see your mother sometimes. She is always nice to me. I go every Sunday to see my mother, if you want to come with me."

"Would you like me to meet you there?" he asked.

"I have a car," she said with a hint of pride. "I will pick you up."

"All right." Stefan watched her as she turned away. "Klara, what is your daughter's name?"

"Viktorie."

He waved at the child. "A good name. A very good name."

⋯≡◎≡⋯

Stefan's mother, Pavla, confirmed what he'd suspected. Klara worked as a dancer and high-paid prostitute. There were advertisements in the phone directory that promised every fantasy fulfilled, many with underage girls and boys, which was illegal in other countries. Stefan picked at his lunch as they discussed it and thought of Viktor's little sister doing such things. His best friend would have never allowed it.

Instead of the subject of Amanda, which Stefan expected his mother to approach, they talked about Klara and her ailing mother. Pavla had gone a few times herself to the hospital to visit the woman and had been told she would probably survive only a few more months.

Soon their short lunch was over. He could tell that his mother was even more concerned about him now than when he'd arrived.

"I'm all right," he said, giving her a hug. "I promise."

But within him was an unsettled feeling that wouldn't quiet. He knew what it was, but he wasn't ready to face it.

⋯≡◎≡⋯

Amanda knew her alarm clock had been buzzing and buzzing but was unable to pull herself from sleep. Finally she rolled over and knocked it off the bedside table. The buzz continued. Her hand searched through the air until she found the cord and yanked; then she rolled over and went back to sleep. The phone rang sometime later. She put her pillow over her head.

Finally Amanda ventured her head from beneath the pillow. She should have been working for hours. But it was Saturday, she told herself. Most people took the day off. She was breaking her rule to get on the current time zone, no matter how tired she felt. Yet that was what coffee was made for.

Her sleepy thoughts went to Stefan. His world seemed so far away. Yet, she wondered, what were his first morning thoughts? He'd once said that he prayed as he first awoke—but did he pray with his head on the pillow, or did he kneel on the floor with his hands clasped on the bed? Or perhaps he raised his hands and stood with the loft windows pushed open wide? What names did he utter toward heaven, and for what reason? Did he recite the same prayer like a mantra or reverently search himself for the proper words? Or did he use words that intoned a close friendship as she'd once heard in a youth pastor's prayers?

Amanda wished to know everything about Stefan, to understand everything about him, and thus felt an odd sorrow that she could never know it all.

She could, and would, ask him about his morning prayers. Her laptop was closed on her desk—the connection that brought them together across their worlds. The sticky note about Kurt and Hilde Heinrich on top reminded her of her goal for the day. Today she would find the answers.

There were three messages on her machine when she found her way to the small living room and kitchen.

"Sylvia Pride calling. I won't be in the office today, but let's meet early Monday. Ciao."

"Hey, it's Tiffany—ever faithful assistant. Troy, Erin, and a few others from the office are driving down to Santa Cruz to try a new restaurant and club. Call if you want some weekend fun! We leave at six."

Tiffany had become the coordinator for the office singles

and younger couples who liked going out on the weekends. Usually Amanda helped with suggestions or went along with the plans. There was always something of interest—a new gallery opening, a concert, or a festival. Even a karaoke night was fun as she laughed, watching her coworkers humiliate themselves.

"Amanda, this is your mother. I'm in town and would like to see you. Your father said you're home and that the two of you had dinner last night. I hear you're joining us tonight. But I would also like to talk to you about him, your father. I am staying at a friend's house. Here's the number . . ."

Already annoyed, Amanda saved the last message. Why did her mother want to discuss her father? There were lines her mother had not crossed in their brief meetings over the years. She would ask politely about him but then drop the subject. Her mother also never spoke of Amanda's childhood except for the period of time before Patricia left to "find herself." Now she was suddenly interjecting herself into the midst of Amanda's relationship with her father. Amanda had to be careful or she might say or do something she'd regret. Or even worse, she might begin to feel sympathetic toward her mother. To understand why the wandering soul named Patricia Marley must explore the world like the wind . . . always searching, always seeking. Amanda knew her mother could twist the truth to benefit herself. But the truth was clear—her mother couldn't commit, was unsatisfied, cared more about herself than anyone else. Amanda wouldn't let her mother's beguiling spirit turn the facts of her actions to sympathy.

Amanda worried that her father wouldn't see it as clearly. She decided to call him. "What time am I expected this evening?" she asked when he picked up.

"I'm not feeling well this morning, honey. Maybe I'll be better tomorrow." When he cleared his throat, she realized she'd awakened him. "I'll call and tell your mother."

"What's wrong?"

"Just a cold or sinus something. Nothing really. I'll just hang out and watch the Classics Channel and stay inside. The fog's here for the day."

"Are you sure it's only a cold?"

"Let me ask, hang on." She heard him blow his nose and imagined him in his recliner with a box of tissues in his lap. "Yep, it's a cold."

"I'll stop by later anyway. Get some rest. Don't just watch movies."

"Yes, ma'am. If you happen to come over, perhaps you'll bring something special?"

Amanda smiled. "I don't know what you're talking about."

"Oh, it must just be the sickness, but I thought you said something about pepper soup."

"I certainly did not, since I don't make pepper soup anymore. I keep the cap on the pepper shaker very tight when I make chicken noodle. Did you think I mentioned chicken noodle soup?"

"That sounds about right. And I foresee myself hungry after my nap." He blew his nose again for dramatic effect.

"I'll see what I can do."

Amanda hung up the phone, feeling that all was right with the world. Her father had a cold; he wanted pepper soup; he was watching classic movies. She still avoided calling her mother.

Heading for the kitchen in pajamas and slippers, Amanda passed her computer with the cords rolled up beside it. First the soup and Dad; then she would get to work.

The fridge held a variety of vegetables—all either shriveled or half turned to juice. She went to her landlord, Mr. Winifred, for his never-ending abundance of vegetables from his small greenhouse and weekly trips to the farmers market. Mr.

Winifred loaded her with veggies and gave his usual tip of the hat as she left.

Soon a pot of canned broth boiled on the stove as she cleaned and cut carrots and her father's favorite—brussels sprouts. The chicken would have to be canned chicken breast since her freezer and refrigerator were still bare. Her dad loved her chicken noodle. Well, at least he loved it now. Her first tries had always included too much pepper in the broth, hence the name "pepper soup."

With the soup simmering on her stove, Amanda was drawn to the computer. Stefan might be there. After hooking up the cords and phone line, she listened to the sound she loved— Internet connection—a sound similar to that of her espresso machine. It was music to her ears. Stefan's notes were usually shorter than hers, something Amanda had noticed in comparing female and male e-mails. Men were usually less talkative even on-line. There was a note from Petrov's address with Stefan's name in the subject heading among the long list of new mail she had received.

> Amanda, you're too far away already. I don't even know what to do anymore. Thank you for the note on my pillow. Soon I hope to put one on yours. I will try calling on your morning, and my night. I can't stand being so many time zones away. We share the sun for a short time.
>
> Soon.
>
> Stefan

She printed out the e-mail and read it over several times, then sent him a note back. For a while she went through her mail, deleting forwarded stories and jokes, sending responses if they could be short, saving mail that required more attention.

Later, soup locked in Tupperware, Amanda backed her car out of Mr. Winifred's garage and headed across town.

The day was indeed foggy. But such days were a comfort to

Amanda when she was staying indoors because of the air's muffled silence. However, driving in the city in fog was a harrowing experience in sitting close to the steering wheel and watching for drivers who ignored adverse weather conditions. It took seven minutes to reach the apartment building that once belonged to her father and uncle—where she'd lived much of her life. On the day her father's cancer was declared in remission, he had gone to the Realtor's office with only one condition of sale—that he could keep one of the units for himself rent free. The buyers agreed after negotiating the price and stipulations. Amanda was surprised when her father didn't request the two-bedroom unit she'd been raised in but instead opted for the less convenient one above. And yet she understood. The apartment he chose had been his closest friend's, the unit Henry had kept vacant for nine years after Mr. Lev's fatal heart attack.

The Levs had been the first tenants to move into 2B after Uncle Hans and Aunt Helga bought the brownstone complex in the late 1940s. Amanda's father, then a teenager, had spent hours with Mr. Lev, learning how to fix radios and electrical equipment, while Uncle Martin, the more outgoing of the brothers, spent his free time at the cinema or hanging out with friends. The Levs were immigrants from France, married with one young child. Mrs. Lev's first husband and two children had died in the camps. Mr. Lev had been a bachelor and lost his extended family, along with the family's three businesses and most of their wealth. Their one daughter later married and had one child—Benny Dunn. Mr. and Mrs. Lev lived the rest of their lives in 2B.

Memories sprang to Amanda's mind as she walked to the stairwell with the container of soup. She passed the hallway to the apartment she'd grown up in before going upstairs. It was still unfamiliar, having her father in the Levs' apartment. She'd open the door with the expectation of seeing Mr. Lev's old

leather chair by the window, where she'd once hidden within
the folds of the long, brown drapes. At nine years old, Amanda
had wanted badly to be included in the Lev family gathering.
That time the house had been full of guests who had come to
celebrate some honor given to Mr. Lev. As afternoon fell,
Amanda's father had declined their invitation to join the
family and guests for Shabbat, so the group would have pri-
vacy without the presence of outsiders. Amanda was more
than disappointed. She and her father were often invited to the
apartment for the Sabbath ritual. She wanted to watch them—
a group as diverse as the people on a San Francisco street
corner. Some men wore black clothing and hats; long ringlets
hung beside their ears. The children, including Benny, begged
that she stay. But her father would not relent.

"I'm going home," she had stated in anger. But instead she
had made a turn at the door and, with the help of Benny and
the other children, hid behind the drapes.

She heard her father bid his farewells and then the continued noise of a houseful of people. It was warm inside the
musty curtains and Amanda felt drowsy. Realizing how silent
the room had become, she peered from the folds, wondering if
everyone had disappeared in a poof of smoke. But they were
there, sitting around the two long tables that had been pushed
together and covered with a lace tablecloth.

Mr. Lev, with hands on the table and eyes steady on the
centerpiece of unlit candles, allowed several minutes to pass in
silence. He waited and waited, per the ritual, as the thoughts
of the day passed into remembrance. Mrs. Lev wiped away a
few tears as she'd done on the occasions Amanda had been at
the table. She wondered if every Friday Mrs. Lev once again
returned to that place called "the camps." Did she hear the
cries of her husband and lost children? What of Mr. Lev—was
this a weekly reminder of his journey in a derailed cattle car,
hiding in the woods, discovering that his parents and siblings

had been wiped from the earth? Or were those memories that happened long before her birth, back when her father and uncle were young, too far behind them now? Amanda wondered these things from her view in the curtains behind Mr. Lev's chair. She'd heard stories and overheard others that now filled her mind. As Mr. Lev began to speak words in Hebrew, as his fathers had before him, to a God so far away, Amanda thought about a heritage of sorrow and yet one that brought these people to the same table as one.

She could see the back of Benny's head and the cowlick at the nape of his neck. What did these weekly reminders do for him? Did he feel what she would feel—loved and part of a greater unit?

Mrs. Lev and Benny's mother began to light the candles. They gazed into the flame and motioned the smoke toward them in the most graceful movement she'd seen. It was as if they drew the flame toward them as silent protection from the world outside. Amanda had often copied the movement herself when she lit candles for special dinners with her father.

Then a gentle knock interrupted their Shabbat meal. She heard her father's voice. "I apologize for interrupting your Shabbat, Mr. Lev, but I have looked everywhere for Amanda. I am worried now."

Amanda hid farther inside the folds of the curtain.

"I believe I just found her," she heard Mr. Lev say. Footsteps came close, and a hand touched her head through the thick fabric.

Her father had been angry, something she'd rarely seen. He scolded and grounded her. Amanda had apologized, then stated, "But, Dad, I want to become a Jew."

Amanda smiled at the memory as she reached her father's door at 2B. The tradition and joining of people was what drew her toward organized religion. But the greater question of who God was always held her back. She unlocked the door with her key and entered, noticing the absence of Mr. Lev's chair by the window and the vertical blinds Mrs. Lev had put up when the drapes had faded.

"Dad?" she said in a tentative voice. "Pepper soup delivery."

There was no answer, and he wasn't in his usual beige recliner in front of the entertainment center. A classic movie was playing on the television. She recognized Gene Kelly as he started a dance number.

Amanda walked through the living room, noticing her father's familiar paintings of old San Francisco scenes—the construction of the Golden Gate Bridge, the 1906 earthquake, the fire at Cliff House, the city at night. She set the container beside the stove in the tight but space-efficient kitchen. Then she heard the voices.

"Dad," she said, louder this time.

"We're in here," a woman's voice replied.

It couldn't be. As Amanda's feet moved toward her father's bedroom, she was somewhat afraid of seeing who she knew was there.

"What are you doing here?" Amanda asked.

Her father was sitting up in bed, and Amanda's mother sat on the edge.

"Your father said he was ill, so I came to check on him." Patricia sounded hurt.

It had been two and a half years since Amanda had last seen her mother, and that had been for an hour at a bar in New York. The muted light from the bedroom window showed the age lines in her mother's face that the New York night lights had kept hidden. Or was it that she had aged that much since Amanda had last seen her? Even at fifty-six, Patricia Marley was exceptionally beautiful, with thick, raven black hair that held no sign of gray. Amanda knew some helpful surgeries were partially the cause of her lasting attractiveness.

"When were you going to return my calls?" Patricia rose

from the bed and smoothed the comforter where she'd sat until it was straightened again. She wore a tight sweater, jeans, and high heels.

"Later today," Amanda said. "It's good to see you again, Mother."

They hugged slightly and Patricia kissed both of her cheeks.

"Anyway, I was just leaving," Patricia said to Henry.

"But Amanda just got here. Don't you want to see her?" Henry asked. He looked from Patricia to Amanda, who felt the slight cut. It was Patricia's way. If you hurt Patricia Marley, expect it back. And Amanda's great sin was to not call in her mother's expected time frame.

"Of course I want to see her. Since your father is too ill for dinner, perhaps you'll have me. Unless you are too busy."

"Tonight will be fine. I'll have to give you directions to my place."

A cab was called. They waited with slight small talk among the three of them. Within ten minutes, her mother was gone.

"She does love you," Amanda's father said, swinging his legs to the floor and sneezing twice. "Before you arrived, she said how much she admired you."

"I've accepted what Mother gives me—I did that long ago. Now stay in bed. I'll get you some soup."

Before Amanda could heat him a bowlful, her father was in the kitchen.

"The cold medicine is kicking in. Your mother practically forced me out of the recliner. First time I see her in twelve or so years and I'm sniffling and coughing." He leaned over her shoulder and peered into the bowl. "Mmm, looks like the best pepper soup you've ever made. Aren't you having any?"

"Are you kidding? I know what I put in there. I wouldn't touch it."

He laughed.

She decided to have some also; she joined him in the living room with her hot soup.

"Well, I decided to call Uncle Martin next week," her father said.

"Really?" Amanda nearly dropped the soup from her spoon. "This is a shock. But a good shock."

"You've inspired me."

"In what way?"

"Remember how Edith Hopper has asked me for several years to be part of her living-history program in the Sonoma and Marin County schools, along with some community colleges?"

"Of course."

"She called again while you were gone. I decided to do it."

"Great, but what does that have to do with Uncle Martin?"

"Martin somehow took Aunt Helga's belongings captive when she died."

Amanda sighed. Her father had compassion and patience for just about everyone except his own brother. They'd always butted heads to some extent, but nothing like the last few years that had caused their battle of silence.

"Oh, Dad. You were sick when she passed away. He didn't take her things captive; he only stored them at his place."

"Yes, but he still never gave me the opportunity to see what she had in that old steamer trunk of hers. Martin said she'd saved many things from our school and childhood years. She also kept our family history, which I assume is in the trunk. I'd like to find some more facts before speaking as a living-history project."

She looked up quickly. Her father sipped the hot soup and dropped oyster crackers onto the top, unaware that he'd just spoken powerful words. Aunt Helga obviously knew that her sister and brother-in-law hadn't died at the Lidice massacre.

The truth could be with her in the grave, or it could be inside her steamer trunk.

Amanda stayed until her father fell asleep in his chair. She watched him sleeping in his cozy place. There were no IVs attached to his arms, and he was wearing his pajamas with a fuzzy afghan over his legs instead of a hospital gown and a thin blanket. He looked like her father again. Here in the building he'd lived in since coming to America as a young boy, Henry Rivans was home. Amanda suddenly realized that just as she'd helped him fight through his illness, she must now protect him from the change of what he'd always believed. There were always skeletons in the closets of family members, so why dig them up now? Nothing was worth destroying this. He had lived his entire life with the story of Lidice. What benefit would come with the truth?

"You've inspired me," he'd said.

Amanda knew she must contact her uncle before her father did.

CHAPTER ELEVEN

Ms. Delsig pushed hard against her walker and moved slowly down the hallway to her room. It was empty. Janice's side had been scoured clean; a Wet Floor sign rested in the center. The white vinyl curtain, which hadn't been removed from its hooks in years, was still wet from cleaning and now hung open, dividing the room.

Ms. Delsig had expected to have several days alone to process the change and grieve her loss. She'd decided to pay for a single room instead of adjusting to someone new. No one could replace Janice, and Ms. Delsig no longer felt the need for companionship as she had in her first months here. She again heard her friend's warning to always keep a roommate because loneliness brought death quicker. Did it really matter anymore? she wondered. If she had ten years or one year, in the end she was still dead.

Ms. Delsig turned from the room. Administration would be open, and she'd request the entire room before they moved the new person in. She lingered one last minute at the door, unable to quite take it all in—the emptiness of it.

Late afternoon was often the quietest time of day as naps and relaxation set the tone before supper. But today there was a commotion down the long tiled hallway. The voices were loud and the footsteps many. They moved from the main administration wing toward the resident rooms in a wide wave of people. It reminded her of a parade or group demonstration. At the helm an elderly woman the size of a large child was being pushed forward in her wheelchair. She was hunched forward, clutching the chair as she perused her surroundings. Her snow-white hair contrasted sharply with her dark complexion. Other residents came from their rooms to watch the new arrival and her entourage of family and several Oakdale employees. Ms. Delsig was surprised to see Mr. Bartlett among the group. The director of Oakdale was rarely seen in the hallways or near the rooms of the residents. This woman must be important.

Mr. Bartlett fluttered through the crowd to the wheelchair's side to navigate the way. As he pointed ahead, Ms. Delsig realized she was facing her new roommate. Janice had been replaced.

They stopped in front of her. The woman raised her head slowly, taking Ms. Delsig in with a searching eye.

"Ms. Delsig, this is your temporary roommate, Lilly Parkens." Mr. Bartlett motioned toward the room. "It is an honor to have Mrs. Parkens at Oakdale, as I'm sure you know."

"I do not know," Ms. Delsig said. Should she mention now her desire for a single room? "But it is nice to meet you."

"And nice to meet you, dear," Lilly Parkens said, her voice strong and quick compared to her tiny, hunched appearance.

"Mr. Bartlett, we agreed to a single room with a window," said a large woman who stood behind the wheelchair. She crossed her arms. "This was made perfectly clear upon arrangements, and thus this is most unsatisfactory."

"I apologize. I'm very sorry. I thought—" Mr. Bartlett stepped back and bumped into the doorjamb.

"Lorraine, calm yourself please. Mr. Bartlett and I discussed this. A room will be available in a month or so. With a window."

"Thank you, Mrs. Parkens." Relieved, Mr. Bartlett reverted back to his professional manager attitude. "Perhaps Ms. Delsig wouldn't mind trading places so you can at least have the window. She has been on that side for some time."

"Wait a minute." Ms. Delsig stood awkwardly half inside the doorway, a horde of eyes upon her. Glancing at the slight crack where the curtain hadn't been pulled across her little refuge, she was determined to go down fighting.

"I won't be taking your window place," Lilly Parkens said in a firm voice. "But soon I'd like a place of my own. Is that understood, Mr. Bartlett?"

"You are first on the list. One of our residents is planning to relocate to a home near her family very soon. Very, very soon. Now please make yourself comfortable. I'll send some staff to assist you, and I'll return after a short time." Mr. Bartlett put his hand on Ms. Delsig's walker. "Ms. Delsig, we need to resume our earlier conversation, if all of you will excuse us."

Mr. Bartlett went through the entire family—shaking hands, asking names, and patting heads of children—before leading Ms. Delsig down the hall. Once the Parkens family was behind them, he walked with sure steps, then waited for her to catch up. She would not be hurried, so she kept her own slow pace.

"Do you know who Lilly Parkens is?" he asked once they were around the corner.

"I don't know and I don't care. Is this the conversation you wanted to resume?"

"Lilly Parkens is a very notable member of Oakdale society. She's a well-known poet and has been involved in volunteer groups and civil rights organizations. This woman was invited to the White House on several occasions. We are very pleased to have her."

"Then what brings her to Oakdale? Her loving family wanted to rid themselves of her?"

"I'm disappointed in you, Ms. Delsig. This is not your usual behavior, and it will be excused only because of Janice's departure." Mr. Bartlett's tone chastised her; then he seemed to realize it. "I apologize for suggesting you give up your window side. That was insensitive of me."

"You wanted to speak to me?"

"Oh yes. Well, I did want you to know who you were rooming with. And I also wanted to ask about your time with Dr. Matthews." Mr. Bartlett pushed his glasses farther up his nose.

"Fine."

"Good. Then I'll let you get back to your new roommate. I'm sure you'll like her, perhaps even more than Janice."

Ms. Delsig stared at him as he turned away. Right then she decided to prove him wrong.

⋅✦⟾◎⟻✦⋅

Lilly Parkens' family stayed for hours, while Ms. Delsig avoided her room. They joined the residents for supper and after-supper music in the rec room. When weariness found her, Ms. Delsig finally pushed her way toward the room. She dreaded what it would look like, the changes she wasn't prepared to see. It was empty but she looked down, not wanting to see the new pictures that covered the white walls.

She was in bed with the curtain closed when the family and Lilly Parkens returned. They attempted quiet good-byes, but they lingered and kept shushing one another. A toddler boy found it a game to pop in and out of the closed curtain. He was pulled away, then popped back up and stared at Ms. Delsig with large black eyes. His tight curls were cropped so close to his scalp that Ms. Delsig felt a strange longing to pull him onto her lap and rub the top of his head until he giggled. Instead she tried to give a grouchy look that only brought a smile to both their lips. She hoped no one on the other side would know it. The rest of "the family," as she decided to call the entire group, promised to return every day and to spend Sunday afternoons with Grandma Lilly. Ms. Delsig wondered how long that promise would last. Guilt always brought such commitments—many broken by the end of the first week.

At last they left.

Ms. Delsig heard the creak of Lilly's wheelchair and a slow movement of feet. Lilly prepared for bed in their shared bathroom that both could reach through doors on each side of the curtain. She shuffled around slowly and finally there was the crunching sound of a mattress being sat upon. The metal bars weren't pulled up, but Ms. Delsig knew a nurse would be by in the night to move them into their nighttime position.

It was quiet now. Quiet throughout Oakdale. The lights were all turned off. Lilly Parkens didn't need a night-light. But she wasn't sleeping either. Ms. Delsig had sharp ears that would detect the deep breaths of slumber. She remembered her first nights here, sleepless nights—the smells so different from the home she'd loved and lived in for twenty-three years, the room and bed not her own, the closeness of another person after being a widow. Most of all, there had been the feeling that she'd made the worst mistake of her life. Was Lilly Parkens thinking these same things? Finally her roommate slept. Lilly Parkens, the great African-American women's crusader, grunted and coughed and snored all night while Ms. Delsig turned in her bed, wondering how Janice slept in the home of her sister.

She determined to get her roommate moved ASAP. Every snort and rumble brought heightened annoyance.

❧⟨◉⟩❧

It was later than usual when Ms. Delsig was awakened by movement and sounds in the hallway and bright light beaming through a crack in the beige drapes. She tugged the covers closely beneath her chin and tried to rid herself of the after-taste of nightmares she couldn't quite remember. It surprised her that she'd even slept. Then Ms. Delsig saw the window curtain being pulled aside. She sat up in aggravation. Lilly Parkens stared at her from her wheelchair.

"That curtain is not to be opened without asking me," Ms. Delsig said sharply. She pushed a button on the arm rail that moved the head of the bed upward.

"I must ask if you are a German woman."

"What are you talking about?" Suddenly she feared those unremembered dreams.

"I have tried to be a woman of forgiveness and grace. But Germans killed my little brother Felix. Germans murdered him after his troop surrendered. I am sorry, but though I do not hold you responsible, it is still a difficulty for me."

"That has nothing to do with me."

"I was in Europe at the end of the war. One of the few and first African-American nurses—"

"Don't assume that I want to hear your story. I don't. And I will not share mine."

"I cannot sleep in a room and listen to German all night."

"Listen to German all night? I hardly slept with the sounds you were making. I did not sleep until morning." Ms. Delsig dropped the metal rail; it clanged loudly as it fell. "And if you don't like it, then leave."

"Perhaps you could tell me about yourself—it might make it easier."

"I am going to get dressed and get to breakfast."

⊷⩵○⩵⊷

Lilly Parkens found Ms. Delsig later that afternoon as she worked on the computer. Ms. Delsig had tried to speak to Mr. Bartlett about the impossibility of sharing a room with Lilly, but he was gone for the day. So she'd avoided their room, sat far from Lilly at breakfast, and sought solace in the resource room. In one day she'd become addicted to the computer version of solitaire. Alfred said it gave her good mouse-maneuvering practice.

Lilly entered the room and introduced herself to Agnes Scribbs, who broke her own greatest commandmant of utmost quiet in the "library" by immediately raising her voice in exclamation: "You are the real Lilly Parkens!" Ms. Delsig moved the mouse, clicking on digital cards and carrying them into place as Agnes gushed and introduced Lilly to anyone who entered or passed the room.

Ms. Delsig had lost five times when she heard the motorized wheelchair pull up behind her.

"I want to talk to you," Lilly said.

"I am busy."

"It's very important."

"So is this." Ms. Delsig moved an ace to the top pile.

"Later?"

"Perhaps."

Ms. Delsig successfully avoided the little woman with the quick wheelchair through the early afternoon. But then, at last, she was caught in their room at nap time. Her anger toward the woman had grown throughout the day. It seemed everyone else immediately loved Lilly Parkens.

"I'm trying to apologize," Lilly said, opening the curtain. "It's something I rarely do and rarely do well."

"You are . . . a racist. How do you apologize for that?" Ms. Delsig jerked the curtain to separate them.

"Ms. Delsig." The curtain flew open. "I believe you are trying your best to anger me, and it's working. If you knew how I have fought against that word . . . in all my life I have never, *never* been accused of such a thing."

Ms. Delsig, surprised herself that she'd accused Lilly, couldn't give ground now. "Of course you wouldn't. But is it not the truth?"

"Of course not. I was trying to express my difficulty—and you should understand exactly because of your past."

"What past is this?"

"You are a Holocaust survivor."

"Why would you say that?" Ms. Delsig's voice was even and stern.

"A young woman who works here told me about you this morning."

"Rumors and gossip are more available around here than bedpans and medicine." With that, Ms. Delsig closed the curtain again and moved to the bathroom.

The family arrived later and kept Lilly occupied. Ms. Delsig remained on her side of the curtain, requesting that dinner be brought to her bed. No one disturbed her, and Lilly returned to the room that night without her family in tow.

Ms. Delsig fought to stay awake until Lilly's snores began. At first she was afraid to sleep and decided to ask Dr. Matthews for some sleeping pills. Then she worried about falling asleep. She'd thought she could trust herself with her own past. After all, the memories should remain in the deepest graves of her mind. Her childhood should be too distant to recall. True, bubbles of remembrance arose at inconsistent times, but she'd become well equipped at pushing them down and continuing on. Now others believed they knew. But they could never come close to comprehension.

The darkness of the past was beyond belief. And yet, it never quite left her.

CHAPTER TWELVE

Amanda tried Uncle Martin on her cell
phone in her car. His machine picked up so she left a message.
Driving past Golden Gate Park, she remembered that her
mother was coming for dinner. She'd stayed much longer than
intended at her father's. Turning toward her usual grocery
store, Amanda realized she'd never cooked for her mother. It
took a while in the grocery aisles to come up with a menu.

About an hour later Amanda carried an armload of groceries
across the small patio to her front door. It was unlocked. Her
mother was inside, sitting on her couch.

"I didn't expect you to be early," Amanda said as she
hurried in and dropped the brown bags on the counter.
Hemingway strolled out to see her, received his pat on the
head, and turned back toward his bed.

"Well, I should have called, but I was in the area. I met your
Mr. Winifred and sat in his lovely garden for a while. He let
me inside."

"Yes, Mr. Winifred is great." Amanda noticed a light blinking on her answering machine. "Just give me a few seconds to get settled; then I'll make some tea—or is it coffee?"

"Either one is fine. Take your time."

Amanda quickly put the food away and touched the message button.

Her uncle's voice played over the recorder. "I got your message and would love to meet—why not the old Sunday thing? It's been too long since I saw my traveling niece. I'll bring deli, you bring the thermos, and we'll meet at the museum bench. Let me know if that works for you. I'll be out again so leave it on my voice mail."

Stefan was the other call. "Amanda, it's me, Stefan. I'll try back later." She turned away, not wanting her mother to note her disappointment at missing his call.

"You have a cozy place here." Her mother was looking through one of Amanda's coffee-table books. She'd chosen *Lighthouses of the Western Coasts*.

"I like it." Amanda put water in a stainless steel teapot and set it on the stove. "I don't have any chamomile, but I have a few green-tea varieties."

"I drink green tea now," Patricia said from the chair Amanda usually sat in. She picked up a coffee cup stuffed with crinkled sticky notes. "I looked around this place where my daughter lives. This is where I call you from New York. Where do you sit when we talk?"

"I usually stand." Amanda pointed to the black rotary phone on a corner table.

"Ah, it works?"

"Yes. I also have a cordless in my room."

"That rotary is very quaint. You have a taste of French Classic here, one of my favorites."

"I've never been able to settle on any particular style—I just go for the eclectic things I like. Do you have a place of your own now?" The teapot began a low winding sound that rose to a whistle.

"I stay with a friend in New York." Patricia walked to the kitchen bar and pulled up a stool. "What are you making for dinner?"

"A spinach salad with balsamic vinegar, and fettuccini with grilled chicken and shrimp."

"I never knew my daughter was such a cook." She smiled and rested her chin on folded hands. Amanda had only glanced at her mother as she hurried in. She now noticed her slacks outfit and the light makeup on her face. Her mother had dressed up for this evening.

"I'm really not much of a cook. I have about four favorite recipes that are rotated through the weeks. Otherwise I eat out."

"The things I'm discovering about you," her mother mused.

"Well, we don't know a lot about each other."

"You speak the truth, and as the mother, I accept all the blame for that." Her mother watched as Amanda pulled apart the spinach and washed it inside a strainer.

Patricia had spoken such words before, but they seemed intended to make Amanda feel guilty and say things like, "It's all right, Mom. We're together now." It might work on someone else, but it didn't work on her.

"I'm hoping we can get to know each other better. There are some opportunities here in San Francisco for me."

Amanda paused only slightly as she reached for the kettle and filled a cup with water.

"This is why I wanted to talk to you about your father." Patricia hesitated. "I'm going to ask if he'll rent me one of his rooms."

Amanda looked at her mother sharply. "Why would you consider such a thing?"

"I expected some hostility," her mother stated calmly. "But if you look at it logically, it makes sense. He has that extra room and he doesn't pay rent. The money I pay him can be his play money. I'd be around in case he needs something—as you've known and not told me, his health is certainly in question."

"You have it all figured out. Think about this—you left him and me many years ago and now because it's convenient for you, you'd like to pop back into our lives? It doesn't work that way."

"I appreciate your honesty. Please, Amanda, I don't want to ruin our evening. Just give it some thought. I know it sounds presumptuous of me after all these years, but I also think that if we can let go of the past, we'll see this could be an opportunity for all of us to draw close."

Amanda was silent. She wanted to go through her list of accusations from childhood until the present: the many times her mother promised to visit and didn't; the poetry reading Amanda attended at age seven where she'd fallen asleep and been left in the care of the bookstore owner while Patricia went out to dinner with a group of friends; the missed birthdays and graduations; and the embarrassment when her mother flirted with a guy Amanda liked in college. Once the memories started to surface, more and more came jumbling out.

Her mother was watching her as if attempting to read the thoughts of a daughter she didn't know. "When will you forgive me?"

Amanda stared at her mother in amazement. "Dad says to forgive even when not asked. I've found that difficult to do."

"The bitterness will destroy you."

Their eyes held until Patricia looked away. Amanda suddenly realized that this was the opportunity she'd always wanted—a chance to tell her mother what she felt. How many times had she thought of confronting her mother, but her mother wasn't around to confront? She took a breath and plunged in.

"I'm not bitter, not really. Not any longer. Perhaps the hurt returns when I see you. But honestly, and I truly don't say this to hurt you . . . I just don't need a mother anymore. When I did, you weren't there. As the years passed and I grew older, I realized that most people don't have the ideal family. Probably no one does. My years of needing a role model, a mom to tell me about my adolescent changes and to teach me to bake cookies, are over."

Amanda leaned against the fridge with her arms crossed at her chest. Her thoughts bounced to her father and his words about respecting her mother no matter what. This was the first time she'd ever spoken these truths to her mother, but her father's old warning kept her from going too far.

"Now you arrive, ready to get to know me and come into Dad's life. How do I take that? How long will it last? Next week or next year, you may decide once again that we aren't for you. Or if someday I have a child, maybe grandmothering will scare you away. It's hard to invest yourself in someone like that."

"I did ask you to forgive me. Perhaps I took the pathetic way out by doing it through writing instead of saying it aloud. But it still hurt that you didn't respond."

"I don't know what you're talking about."

"Several Christmases ago I sent that framed poem I wrote. The poem was about forgiveness."

"Yes, I remember. But giving me a poem and asking me yourself are two very different things."

"On the back of the frame, I wrote something about the poem being my question to you."

Amanda tried to recall, then remembered quickly reading the poem and putting it away. She never read the back of the frame.

"It's all right. I come across like I don't know the hurt I cause in people. But I know. I don't want to do it, and I hope to never hurt you or your dad again. I felt like the best way to keep from hurting you was to stay far away. And in that, perhaps greater damage was caused. But could we try, very slowly, to find some middle?"

These were words she'd never expected to hear from her mother. Old grudges rose to remind her of what this woman had done. And yet, this was her mother—the only mother she'd ever have.

"I can try," Amanda said, fearful that her mother would rush over and hug her or do something that would take this intensity over the edge.

"Thank you. Now I wish I could help you cook, but . . ."

"Why don't you put some music on? This won't take long."

Amanda prepared dinner quickly. Her mother went to the CD player. Amanda was surprised when she chose her favorite Benny Goodman CD. Watching her mother's graceful movements, Amanda realized she'd just made a kind of truce with her mother.

"How is your job at the History Show?"

"History Network. It's good, very good."

"What are you currently working on? I saw your papers on your desk."

Amanda suddenly remembered the desk full of papers and the note on her computer that read *Kurt and Hilde Heinrich.* She was sure her mother had seen the note stuck to the top of her computer. But the reference wouldn't mean anything to her. "Just researching a possible new project," she said.

"Wasn't someone in your father's family named Heinrich? His grandparents, correct?"

She stared at her mother's profile, stunned that Patricia would recall such a detail. The woman who couldn't keep track of half of Amanda's birthdays now remembered this. "Yes, his parents."

"Interesting. Are you searching for them?"

"How did you remember their names?"

Patricia turned to face her. "My dear Amanda, it may come as a surprise, but at one time, your father was the greatest fascination to me. You only see the years since our divorce. But before that, I can still picture him at the university. He'd come as a visiting speaker. Handsome, several years older, passionate about changing the world—the way he stared so deeply into me. I was completely enamored with him. I drank in everything about him. Certainly that changed, but I haven't forgotten."

Amanda watched her mother actually flush at the memory. She couldn't imagine, much less believe it. Her father was steady, never passionate.

"If it's a secret, I won't tell."

"What won't you tell?"

"That you are searching for his father."

The chicken sizzled loudly on the stove. Amanda turned the long strips and tried to think what to say. Perhaps she and her mother were attempting a relationship, but Amanda wasn't ready to let her mother know about this part of her life.

"I've pretty much decided not to pursue it, but I'd appreciate you not mentioning it to Dad. Some things are better left alone."

As she said the words, Amanda recalled Uncle Martin saying something similar when she'd talked of searching for their family past during a Thanksgiving meal. The subject arose that Amanda's work at History Network West Coast could offer the opportunity to search for their family background. Her father was intrigued and contributed his own thoughts on such a search, but her uncle was silent until she asked his opinion. His reply simply was "Some places in our lives are better left alone."

"What do you mean?" she'd asked. This was their heritage.

"Sometimes what we believe we know is better than the truth."

"Do you know something?" her father had asked. "Something about our family, our parents?"

"I was told the same stories as you. But isn't that enough? Do you really want to look at photographs of our dead parents or see the mass grave their bodies rest in? Do you want to discover things like that? I think it will only lead to more sorrow."

Her father had defended Amanda's desire to know about her family. When an argument rose between them, Amanda decided to back away from the subject. It wasn't until the Empress Brooch came into the news on its own that she finally began to seek again without telling either brother. Her goal was to find something other than mass graves and stories of sorrow. Possibly a distant family link to the Lange family—the heirs to the Empress Brooch.

But as the conversation returned to her now, Amanda pondered more deeply on her uncle's reluctance to her search. Uncle Martin could already know the truth about their family.

After her mother left, she called and confirmed over Uncle Martin's voice mail that she wanted to meet at their old bench by the museum. She wondered what would keep her uncle from sharing the truth.

CHAPTER THIRTEEN

Duruing Sunday morning church service, Stefan felt his grandmother's hand reach for his. She squeezed it and shared a radiant smile. After enduring many sorrows over the years, today his grandmother had her entire family of four worshiping God together.

It touched him deeply. He'd not considered his jaunts in and out of his grandmother's life. She was always happy to see him and encouraged him toward great horizons as he left. His grandmother was proud of him for all the places he'd gone and the people he'd helped. Yet the joy on her face and her murmured prayers during the minister's prayer would not leave him as they walked slowly home.

Stefan wanted to call Amanda when they returned to the apartment. It would be Saturday night in San Francisco. He found his calling card and began to punch in the long series of numbers, when he realized it was time for Klara to pick him up downstairs.

"I was just about to go up," Klara said when he reached the downstairs doorway.

She had transformed completely since he'd seen her the day before. Her dress was simple yet stylish, her hair in a ponytail, and she wore little, if any, makeup. She looked years younger.

"So you know about my career by now," she said as soon as they got in her car. It was an old Mercedes with leopard-print seat covers, a clean interior, and a cassette player.

"Yes," he said, surprised at her direct statement.

"I am sure you disapprove." She started the car and headed out into traffic.

He considered how to respond. Certainly he didn't agree with prostitution and especially Viktor's sister doing it. Yet it wasn't his place to judge her.

"Stefan, I want to say this now. I am not ashamed of what I do, and I make enough money to take good care of my children." Klara drove through traffic quickly.

"You know about my work?" Stefan said.

"You are some kind of minister, which is as stunning to me as I am sure my job is for you."

"I am sure it is," he said with a smile. "I work for a Christian group who helps people around the world. I have talked with women who give themselves for money. They are abused and desperate women."

"You are talking to the wrong women," she said dryly as she turned the car into a parking lot. "I should not have brought up the subject. I knew you would have a problem with it."

Klara carried a bouquet of flowers into the hospital, and Stefan wished he'd brought some himself. The nurse at the front desk said Klara's mother was too ill for visitors. Klara pleaded, asking that they be allowed for just a few moments.

"He is a minister," Klara said, pointing to Stefan. The nurse gave a tired look of disbelief.

"Five minutes is all," Stefan said.

The nurse relented. They walked down the hallway, the scent of ammonia strong and overpowering, to the curtained-off bed where Ivana was resting with an IV running from her arm. She was three beds down from a window. Klara replaced the wilted flowers in a jar by the bed with the new ones she'd brought.

"Mother, you have a special guest today."

"Stefan," Ivana whispered when she saw him, her hand covering her mouth. Stefan would have never recognized the thin, shriveled woman who had once been like a second mother to him. Tears rolled down her cheeks as she struggled to sit up in the bed. "Stefan, Stefan. You have come to see Viktor. He is not here. Did you know he died? He jumped from the bridge."

"Yes, I know. Tell me how you are doing."

"Of course you know," she said, wiping tears from her eyes. "You were there when it happened. You saw Viktor. You tried to save him."

"I met one of your beautiful granddaughters."

Her eyebrows dropped. "Yes. Beautiful grandchildren, but my daughter, such a disgrace to us. How do I show my face? What do people say? I hear the rumors and see with my own eyes."

"Klara is here with me. She comes to visit you often, she said."

"Yes, I see her. She comes, but if her father knew. Or Viktor. Perhaps my son had a vision of the future, and this caused him to jump from the bridge in disgust."

"No, that is not why."

"Then tell me. No one will tell me why." Ivana choked out a sob and held tightly to his shirt. "I do not understand why my Viktor do such a thing."

Stefan did not want to think of that night. But on her death-bed, a mother wanted the answers to the questions that had plagued her for over a decade.

"I will tell you, but please calm down." Stefan pulled a chair to her bedside. He closed his eyes for a moment, seeing the memory clearly in his mind. "Viktor was being foolish and daring as always. We were all drinking and he wanted to walk the railing of the bridge. He shouted that he could jump into the river and swim across. I could not stop him in time."

Ivana's tears were a steady stream as she nodded in understanding. Stefan heard Klara's soft sniffles behind him. "There was nothing else? He was not angry and wanting to die? He still loved us?"

"He always loved you. But he was being Viktor, brave and unafraid."

"Daring and foolish as he had been since a child. Oh, that boy always made his mother nervous. No fears that child."

"Yes," Stefan said with a slight smile. He noticed a nurse had come around the curtain. She motioned toward the clock that their time was over.

"I must leave now."

"You will come back again?" Ivana asked.

"I will come and read to you my favorite Scriptures—some are ones you would recite to Viktor and me," he said, kissing her on the cheek. "I will come back."

Klara and Stefan walked in silence through the long hall and into the afternoon. "I need a cigarette and a drink," Klara said.

They found an outdoor café and sat down. Klara immediately pulled out a gold cigarette box. With delicate fingers, she opened it and withdrew a cigarette. Stefan watched her snap the lighter to flame. She took a long drag with her eyes closed.

Watching her, he recalled the girl he'd once known. She'd been full of hope and the future—he seemed to remember that she wanted to be a dress-shop owner. They gathered at demonstrations to fight for democracy, sleeping for short breaks on the cobblestone squares as the country's future was being made somewhere in the government buildings. Klara was Viktor's little sister, the tagalong they often tried to rid themselves of. Now she exhibited self-assurance and a hard exterior, though he'd caught glimpses of her vulnerability at the hospital.

Amanda came to mind. The two women were close to the same age and yet so different. Amanda had traveled the world and could pursue any career or dream she wanted. He tried not to envision the men Klara met in her work. He'd heard stories about and seen abused women—both those forced into prostitution and those who chose it.

Stefan ordered a coffee. Klara requested a beer. He thought of Viktor. What would his best friend think—not of Klara but of Stefan, for deserting Viktor's family and their friends when they needed him most? Yet Viktor in his foolishness had deserted them also.

"Why, Klara?" He surprised himself by asking.

She responded as if she'd expected the question. "Do not judge me, Stefan, not you. You had help getting out. Everything fell apart when you left. You may not agree with who I am today, but I am proud that I can raise my children."

"Would you want your girls to do the same?"

"Because I do this, they will not have to."

"There must be some other way."

"Do you hear yourself? This is what I have done for years, since I was still half a child. Where were you to object then? Where were your high morals and great need to protect me? You left us, and we have done what we had to do. Viktor's death destroyed my mother. She did not leave the house for a month, which cost her job. We did not have Viktor's income, and the new democracy brought entrepreneurs who offered me more money than I could make doing anything else."

Stefan felt a sickening knot in his stomach. If only he had known.

"I do not need a big brother, Stefan. Not now. I never wanted you to be my brother. Viktor was enough." A light breeze blew a tendril of hair across her cheek. But her expression remained cynical. "You never figured it out, did you?"

He nodded and noticed a softening in her look. "I knew," he said, "but you were like a sister."

"You would have contacted a sister. Why did we not hear from you again?"

Stefan's guilt ran high. "I don't know. I wanted to get as far away as possible. I should have stopped him that night, but I was just inches away when—"

Tears pooled in her eyes as she puffed on the cigarette. "It is over now. It is many years gone. It does not even matter."

They drove back to the Old Town in relative silence. Before Stefan got out, Klara said, "A bunch of us are getting together tonight. You would recognize a few people. I know it is not the usual minister atmosphere, but you can handle it."

"I will think about it and call you."

She shrugged as if it didn't matter. Stefan watched her drive away. He hiked the five flights of stairs that turned in an ascending square to the highest tower apartment. His grandmother was napping when he entered; he could hear her snoring from the other room.

The fluorescent glow of the computer shone from behind the bookcase divider.

"You are back from the Bible study, Petrov?" Stefan asked as he slid his feet into his old slippers. Seeing the basket, it reminded him again that Amanda was not there.

"There is much to learn on this machine." Petrov peered from behind the bookcase. "There is much to be uncovered with it too."

"Like what?"

"I have spent part of the afternoon trying to get some information for your friend."

Stefan joined Petrov by the computer, dragging a chair up beside him. "For Amanda? What have you found?"

"I have many friends in this city, you know. They owe me some old favors."

"You mean Vlademar."

"Okay, so it sounds good to say I have high connections when I only have one who has his high connections. Yes, Vlademar has been helpful today." Petrov seemed pleased with himself. "You do not think Amanda will find it intrusive that I wanted to help?"

"Not at all. It would be great if we could help her." Stefan pictured her last glance back at the airport and longed to see her, to bring her good news and to somehow move past their many obstacles.

"I wait for the download right now. It has taken twenty minutes so far. Next time, would you give me a faster modem when you give me your old computer?" Petrov winked. "How was Ivana?"

"I would have never thought that Klara . . . I would have never thought . . ."

"That world draws many in, and it is very hard to escape. The money creates the enterprise, and the money often comes from businessmen and travelers from the West." Petrov was thoughtful for a time. Stefan didn't want to discuss it. He couldn't shake the thought that he'd abandoned his best friend's family and the results were far- and deep-reaching.

"And Amanda is safely home?"

"She should be. It's too late in the night for me to call her now. I haven't heard from her yet, but we are in different zones of the earth."

"Yes. A wide space apart."

"In many ways."

Petrov understood the reference. "Let me guess. You were out there, walking and thinking late last night and this morning about that wide space."

"There were a few other thoughts in my head also."

"You care a lot for her, I understand."

"It happened before I knew it. We met and started writing one another. It began like other correspondences, other friendships I've had. But now . . ."

"You are concerned."

"Yes. She doesn't understand what my faith means to me. We don't share that. I should not get this close to that kind of relationship."

"I must confess something to you, Stefan." Petrov leaned forward in the chair with his hands folded between his knees. His eyes closed briefly before he spoke. "You have been raised with the story of your parents. You know much of what pulled them apart was their differing beliefs. Your father believed in the purity of the Communist Party. And yet the corruption and truth of what it became destroyed him. Your father was a good man. Your parents shared a strong love that could have been stronger if they had believed in the same things. This story has kept fear in you about meeting a woman who did not share your faith. And also the Word of God warns of the difficulties such bonds create. But I never told . . ."

He stared at his hands for a moment, then into Stefan's eyes. "There was a girl I once loved. I believed we were all wrong for each other, and I prayed and prayed that God would help me stop loving her. She did not share my faith, and so I told her I could not be with her anymore. Later, she did become a Christian. She married someone else because her father insisted she marry. Her husband abused her for years, and she died because of one of his drunken brawls. I was wrong in my stubbornness to be right, to make her see God by bargaining with my love, and that pushed her away. Our parting was not pleasant, and so she did not come to me once she did find God for herself. Perhaps God had planned for us to be together, but my impatience destroyed that."

Stefan was stunned to hear this revelation. He had wondered why Petrov never married and assumed he'd given his life to ministry and God like the apostle Paul.

"I tell you this story because I want you to proceed with great caution. Many loves have been destroyed because of differing faiths. If Amanda ever finds God, it must be for herself and not because of you. Yet I want you married to a woman who can be passionate about discovering God just as I have seen this passion in you. Be patient. Listen for God. If he seems silent, listen and pursue him even more. He will not let you down or steer you wrong."

Stefan nodded and smiled. "And often God speaks through people—thank you, Petrov."

Petrov nodded and turned back to the computer. "Ah, the file is complete. Let us see if we can help our American friend." He clicked on the new file.

Moments later a photograph appeared. They stared closely, stunned by the image displayed on the screen.

"What is this?" Petrov asked.

Stefan pointed to the name beneath the image. "We are looking at Kurt Heinrich. This is Amanda's grandfather."

CHAPTER FOURTEEN

Ms. Delsig's walker creaked as she leaned against it and pushed down the tile hallway. Mr. Bartlett would be gone on Sunday, but she'd decided to make an appointment for first thing Monday morning. Ms. Delsig must have her own room immediately. If he refused, as she knew he would, she would seek a different care facility and request strong sleeping pills until a move was possible.

The thought of moving to another home scared her—this was one of the nicest, and she'd spent the last few years believing this would be her final home. She'd be leaving her garden, Alfred, her room, and the other familiar faces she suddenly realized she'd miss. Yet a new facility would be a shelter—no rumors would circle around her, no Dr. Matthews seeking her "feelings."

Pros and cons passed quickly through her mind. She shuffled past the hunched figure of Kisser Bob, who was already at his post. Only Candy Banks got in Bob's way and would be heard cackling uncontrollably through the hallways after receiving a kiss or two. Candy Banks really needed help.

Music came to her as she moved down the hall—a sound so
lonely and intriguing that she couldn't stop herself from seeking it. She stood in the doorway of the room designed like a
large, cozy living room. The music came from a television.
Images of the arid and beautiful lands of Israel flashed over the
screen as rich Jewish tones were played.

The music reached inside Ms. Delsig, bringing back her
childhood and the life that had been stolen from her. She
recalled her father dreaming of their escape to Israel. They had
applied for visas, but the British government's strong grip over
the country allowed few refuge in the land of Jewish dreams.
The music played on. She remembered holding her mother's
hand and dancing, her skirt whirling around her knees. Her
hair was long and free. She saw her brother in the circle beside
theirs. He was dancing with overstated movements, bringing
laughter to the crowd.

"Are you going in or out?" The annoyed, blaring voice
brought her back, back to the confines of a metal walker and
a body that groaned with every step.

Candy Banks waited behind her with hands on her lumpy
hips. Couldn't she hear the music? Ms. Delsig felt strangely
confused, unable to answer or move, desiring the music that
was fading. She glanced across the room and saw Alfred on the
couch. She had not seen him there.

"I-I was going somewhere," she sputtered.

"In or out, please. Today would be nice."

She knew Alfred was watching as she turned from the room.
There was no smile on his face, only a terrible sadness. She
believed that if she had a mirror, her look would match his
sorrow. Ms. Delsig pushed the walker. Candy moved behind
her, and the sound of the music clicked off altogether.

As she walked away, Ms. Delsig noticed the tears falling
down her face. It was all coming back in staggered memories
she couldn't keep away. She must leave Oakdale and hope that

somewhere else she could hide from the anguish that sought to consume her.

Since Lilly Parkens had been picked up for church and an after-service lunch, Ms. Delsig had the room to herself. She gazed at the framed print advertising a small Jewish museum in Prague, the cards she'd saved from friends, and the knitted wall hanging Janice had made for her. Twisting the gold locket she always wore around her neck, Ms. Delsig found no sense of peace or comfort. The sun shone too brightly through the curtains. After closing the drapes, she sat on the edge of her bed.

Someone tapped lightly on the door. It was Alfred. "Tonight's the old folks dance. You know what that means." He walked inside and opened the curtains.

"What does that mean?"

"Well, we're a little overcrowded around here, so I can just hear management plotting a way to make some space available."

"What are you talking about?" she said, irritation sharp in her tone.

"A dance. You get a bunch of lonely old folks together in their best duds, turn on sentimental music so they recall the days gone by, memories of youth returning, old feelings rekindled, dancing close—it's a master plot. The old guys especially will be dropping like flies. They'll have plenty of empty rooms by morning."

"Then you better stay locked in your room," Ms. Delsig said.

"I planned to do just that. Unless . . . unless I can get one dear friend to protect me from the wiles of scheming, hormonally unbalanced senior citizens."

"Oh no. You are not getting me to that dance."

"Come on. I already ordered you a corsage and everything."

"I am taking a nap, eating dinner, requesting a bedtime pill, and that is the excitement of my life."

"Be wearing your prettiest dress."

"I am not going."

He just chuckled and shuffled away.

She called after him, "I go shopping so often, how will I ever choose my prettiest dress? I am not going!"

⟶◦◉◦⟵

Lilly's family left after dinner. Ms. Delsig was in the bathroom when she heard her roommate return. Ten minutes later there was a sharp rap on the door.

"How are you doing in there?" Lilly called.

"Fine," Ms. Delsig answered.

"I was ready to call for help."

"Can't a woman use the bathroom in peace?" Ms. Delsig said as she opened the door.

"Well, well, well." Lilly whistled while looking her up and down. "I didn't expect you to be going to the ball tonight, Cinderella."

"The old folks dance is all," Ms. Delsig replied in annoyance. She hadn't made that big of a transformation for this attention. She'd ironed her favorite nice dress that she wore on religious holidays every year. Her hair had taken a lot of time to cooperate, but she'd succeeded in smoothing her curls so they were straight with the ends curled under.

A knock on their open door brought their gaze to Alfred in his baby blue suit with a pressed shirt and navy-and-baby-blue tie. He was smiling and proudly holding a box that must contain her corsage. His bushy white eyebrows had been combed into submission along the top rim of his glasses.

An astonishing flutter began in Ms. Delsig's stomach at the sight of him there.

"You look beautiful, ma'am," Alfred said, bowing slightly.

"Enjoy your evening and stay out as long as you like," Lilly said with a wink.

"Shall we?" Alfred offered his arm.

"After I get my corsage."

"This woman doth protest too much."

In the recreation room the lights were low and a band played an old swing tune. But no one was dancing. Ms. Delsig felt a little foolish pushing her walker with Alfred at her side. Several friendly faces waved at them. Candy Banks swayed at the edge of the dance floor, trying to entice someone to join her.

"Let's be the first to kick up our heels," Alfred said.

"Remember I have something between us." She pointed to the walker.

Alfred took it from her hands and pushed it aside. "We can go slow and I can help you." He took her arm and walked her forward.

"Alfred, people are watching."

"Who cares?" Alfred motioned for the band to slow the song. They ended their number and began a Louis Armstrong song, "What a Wonderful World." Alfred took one of Ms. Delsig's hands in his and placed his other hand on her hip. They turned slowly in a waltz and soon were joined by other couples.

"I was thinking, Ms. Delsig," Alfred whispered in her ear. She noticed he'd put on cologne and smelled quite nice. "Why don't we get married?"

She stopped in the middle of the dance floor. "That is a funny joke," she said, trying to find a glint of humor in his expression. For a moment, she thought the old coot might even kiss her.

"No joke. We're great together. We would laugh until the

grave takes us both." He drew her close to him again and they moved together.

"I suppose you have planned our honeymoon in Mexico, and then we will kick Fred Astaire out of your room so we can live together?"

Alfred chuckled. Charles, his roommate for the past six months, was bedridden and practiced dance moves from his bed during the day. Alfred liked the guy and called him Fred Astaire, a name Charles took pride in.

"We'll keep Fred. He won't bother us."

"Lovely."

"Actually, I thought we'd leave this joint. I've got some money—it was all willed to the children so they'll make a fuss, but it doesn't matter. We'll hire ourselves a full-time nurse, a twenty-year-old babe."

"Named Antonio?"

"How about Antonia?"

"I have a little money too," Ms. Delsig said, thinking that the plan sounded pleasant as a fun fantasy.

The song changed but the slow pace continued.

"Then we're set. It's crazy to pack old people away like this. We need to make our mark on those young ones. That's what's wrong with our world today. Young people discard the old folks like yesterday's news."

"We *are* yesterday's news."

"And the world could learn a lot from old news."

"Anyway, I walked in here on my own. No one forced me here."

"Me too." He chuckled in her ear. "Don't you love my hypocritical soapbox messages? Yep, came in willingly. I didn't want to burden the kids, and someone told me I'd find cute chicks."

"You were tricked."

"What are two people like us doing in a place like this?"

She was thoughtful for a minute as she began to feel herself get tired. "We're escaping our biggest fear."

Perhaps sensing her weariness, Alfred led her off the dance floor to a back table where the music wasn't as loud. Ms. Delsig watched him talk to several people as he poured two cups of punch. He was a cute old guy, and she wished she'd known him years earlier.

He returned to their table and sat beside her, taking her hand in his. "So what's yours?" he asked. "What is your biggest fear?"

"It is the same for most of us who volunteer to enter a place like this." Ms. Delsig returned to thoughts of long ago. She remembered crying and calling for help. And the pain— unbearable and yet inescapable. Even worse than the searing pain was the fear of isolation and the greatest fear she would always remember.

"Tell me," he said.

"I thought it had happened once. I thought I would die out there all alone. That is my great fear. To die alone."

CHAPTER FIFTEEN

Sunday morning, Amanda packed a thermos of coffee, cups, and two bottled waters in her backpack, then went searching the garage for her bike. She found her red street bike, covered in winter's dust and in need of a tune-up, and squeezed the tires to see if they had enough air.

On the seventh day, San Francisco rested. There were few cars on the backstreets as she pedaled toward the upward crest of the park. Her legs felt the burn of the past months' decline from her usual exercise routine, but she pushed on.

A secret garden in the midst of the city, Lincoln Park perched on the sheer cliffs above the waters under the Golden Gate Bridge. The noise of the city and freeways, even the crash of the waves, was blocked outside the quieting trees and wandering pathways. For many years before her father had begun attending Sunday services, they would often meet Uncle Martin at a bench within view of the California Palace of the Legion of Honor. The white, grand arch and ribbed columns drew them inside so often that she felt it belonged to her in some small way—childhood memories bore such possession. Her father would give a history lesson on the construction of the legion or other sites and buildings in the city while her uncle would know the artists and works within the Legion's European galleries. Outside the entrance, Amanda would lean forward with her hand beneath her chin, imitating the massive black sculpture made from the original cast of Auguste Rodin's *The Thinker* in Paris.

"I want to be the thinker too," she had said at age four as she took on the meditating pose—or so her father and uncle had retold again and again.

Riding up the path now, Amanda spotted Uncle Martin waiting at their bench. She watched him remove his blue golf hat, rub the bald area on the crown of his head, and then return the hat. He had been her second parent when she was a child, and yet they hadn't seen each other since Christmas Eve. He'd said he had plans for Christmas Day, though Amanda knew it was his way of seeing her on the holiday without seeing his brother. So the two had met for Chinese food without her father.

"There she is," he said with a large smile as she came to a stop and put down the kickstand on her bike. Her first thought was how unchanging Uncle Martin seemed over the years, even with the slight signs of age lines on his face and the sag of his jowls. He was rounder than her father, something Uncle Martin blamed on his affinity for saltwater taffy and the discovery of gummy worms. As he hugged her with a robust squeeze, again she wondered what she'd wondered half the night: how well did she really know him?

"I'm sure you have new adventures to share with me," he said.

Amanda smiled at the exchange of positions. She'd grown up asking Uncle Martin about the places he'd visited around the United States and his year living on the Hawaiian Islands.

Now they spent much of their time sharing her newest journey.

"Ready to eat?" he asked.

She hesitated, wondering when to ask the pressing questions. "Did you bring sandwiches from Angelina's?"

"Would I disappoint you?"

"Pastrami on rye?"

"Your wish is my command—extra mustard as I recall." He
opened a small ice chest and handed her a sandwich wrapped
in wax paper. She noticed it was indeed from the deli near her
uncle's house.

Amanda poured steaming coffee from her thermos into
small Styrofoam cups. As they ate, they chatted about the
weather and Uncle Martin's remodeling project at his house
across the Golden Gate Bridge in Marin County. The park was
beginning to draw Sunday visitors. An Asian family strolled
by, and a line of runners with numbers on their backs jogged
along the road.

"I hear there are some new art acquisitions inside," he said,
nodding toward the legion.

"Another time, okay?"

"As long as you promise," he said, and suddenly she caught
a loneliness about him that she'd never considered.

"I promise, Uncle Martin. But I wanted to talk to you about
something."

"It was obvious from your messages that something was
up," he said, again removing his hat. He extracted a handkerchief from his slacks pocket and dabbed his bald spot. "I think
I can guess."

"I don't think you can."

"Your dad and I?" He picked up his cup of black coffee and
stared down into the dark brew. "Since your call, I've been
thinking about it and wondering what to tell you. You think it
was the sale of the business, don't you?"

"Dad won't tell, but yes, I assumed that because of the timing. I knew you were having trouble settling a split of everything, and neither of you has talked much since."

"Well, I want you to know that it is more my fault than your father's. You deserve to know that. Your dad and I have always been very different. He's stable, hardworking, content with the simple things in life. I've always been the type to feel like there was something more just over the horizon—another place, another person. It's been evident since we were kids."

"Dad said Aunt Helga didn't treat you very well."

"Interesting that he told you that—he never told me that he noticed. It wasn't like I was abused or neglected. But Aunt Helga was the only mother I ever knew. I don't want to speak badly of her, but Henry was her little boy and I . . . wasn't. I'm not a believer in dissecting that childhood stuff, but there are some small truths to it. Aunt Helga's preference for your dad did cause problems for us as kids, but I got over it as an adult."

"You always seemed close when I was growing up."

"We were. I love your father very much. But sometimes between families or brothers, there are just too many differences. And now I'm not sure how to fix our relationship."

Amanda wanted to reach out and take his hand or wrap her arms around him. Uncle Martin seemed at a loss as to what could help them become close again, and she considered the deeper areas of their family that Uncle Martin knew about.

She tried to think how to phrase it best but finally just spoke. "Uncle Martin, I went to Prague and started searching for your and Dad's parents."

He set down his coffee hard. "You were in Prague?"

"It was a very short trip, but what I found were some inconsistencies in our family story. Dad said you have a steamer trunk that belonged to Aunt Helga. Do you know anything about your parents?"

She'd never seen such inner conflict on his face. He shook his head, resting his face in his palms. "Amanda, please. For me, don't do this. You are opening up a Pandora's box that will only cause more pain."

"I can't stop this now. It would be easier hearing it from you."

He didn't respond.

"What are you so afraid of telling me?"

He looked at her with stubbornness and then resignation, as if he were battling whether to speak the words. "If I tell you about this, you must promise never to tell your father."

"How can I promise such a thing?"

"Amanda, the past is much more connected to the present than you realize. I have carried these things with me for some time now. It has not been an easy burden. I don't want you to carry such things, and yet, I think once you know, you'll understand why I don't want your father to know."

"You must tell me," she said, annoyed at the delay. What could be so damaging for this much wariness?

"I warned you in advance," he said with a sigh. He paused, then finally spoke. "Remember when you and I were tested to be bone-marrow donors for your dad?"

She nodded.

"I wasn't a match; of course, you know that. But I found something out then too." He stared across the sloping lawns toward the trees that lined the cliffs.

Amanda perceived the answer he seemed unable to speak. There was only one thing she thought the test would reveal. "You and Dad are not biological brothers?"

"I couldn't tell him, not then. He was possibly dying. How could I tell him something like that?"

She reached for his hand and felt the shaking fingers of an older man. They stared at one another, her uncle passing to her the knowledge he had held within for the past few years.

She shook her head with the impact of it, the questions arising with the realization that he wasn't her biological uncle then either. That every reference to the brothers' differences in appearance and personality and their similarities in humor and interest were all based upon the projection of their being siblings.

"I didn't expect this," she whispered.

"What did you expect?"

"I searched for Kurt and Hilde Heinrich on the list of victims who died from the Lidice pogrom. They weren't on the list. I thought you knew that story but never did I think . . . never this. Why didn't you tell Dad after he got better? You've known this for years."

"I've tried. I've planned to. But it has never seemed right. Then the problems with the selling of the building arose—his special conditions so we could keep the Levs' apartment. In some ways, those problems made it possible for me to pull away—I felt like I was lying to him."

"This doesn't make sense. You were both sent to Aunt Helga from Czechoslovakia, right?"

"Yes. But our gene code proves that we didn't have even one parent in common. One or both of us are not the child or children of Aunt Helga's sister."

"And you haven't found out?"

He shook his head. "I wanted to know the truth at first, so I went to Aunt Helga. Of course, she wasn't herself any longer with Alzheimer's and such. Yet we would spend time together, and sometimes she would tell me things that conflicted with the stories she'd told us all those years. Like she said that her sister, Hilde, died in 1945—a month after the war. She also would refer to her nephew—not nephews, but singular. I found out that wasn't me.

"So finally I stopped searching. There is only so much a man wants to know about his past. We all want to do our genealogy and find that George Washington was in our lineage. I'm too old to seek birth relatives—they'd be dead or too old for us to try and form a relationship."

"But I'd want to know who my parents were. I want to find out about my grandparents. There are so many questions— why the Lidice story? Did the Heinrichs adopt you before sending you to the U.S. with Dad? Is Heinrich really the family name?"

"You are young, so it is different. It's painful enough to realize my brother isn't my brother. I think about it every time I see him. I've almost told him a hundred times. Then my thoughts began to take over everything. So I pulled away. Your father didn't understand—it ended in an argument about nothing, really. Yet our stubborn pride and my fear that I would tell him has kept us apart. It happens easily enough. And as the years pass, it becomes harder to get back what we had and easier to drift apart. With all that, what more do I need to deal with? What other skeletons do I want to seek? Most skeletons are best left buried. I think it takes age to realize that curiosity can be deadly."

"I have to know," Amanda said.

"Your father must not know. It would destroy him. Think of how we both made all that money selling the apartment and grocery, and yet he lives in his old best friend's tenement. Your father is a man of simplicity who has built his life around the past. It's an honor for him to help others and an honor that he lives in America and can help. There are few people in the world who think like that. I just don't think he would handle the lies of the past. Aunt Helga told us a story to protect us— from what, I don't know, and I don't want to know."

"And he may be sick again." Amanda explained her father's making an appointment with the doctor and his desire to study their heritage. "No, he shouldn't know. . . . We must be sure to not allow that. But I do want to look through Aunt Helga's belongings."

"You have more right to them than I do," he said sorrowfully.

She sighed and noticed what a beautiful day it was becoming as the final bits of fog in the sky burned away. How amazing that one sunny morning could change her life so drastically.

When Amanda left her uncle, his final warning ran in her thoughts: *"I must prepare you, Amanda. You are peering into something dangerous. Once you open it, you can't take it back."*

CHAPTER SIXTEEN

Ms. Delsig awoke with tears on her face. Had she cried out or spoken something from the past?

The room was silent; no groans or snores came from the other side of the room. Lilly Parkens must be awake.

"What did I say?" Ms. Delsig said, her voice shaking and too loud.

"You only cried." Lilly opened the curtain slightly.

"It will not happen again," Ms. Delsig said hoarsely, angry that she hadn't taken a sleeping pill. After the dance, Alfred had escorted her to her room and actually kissed her lightly on the lips. Her thoughts had been of him as she'd prepared for bed, considering whether he truly meant that they should marry and run away together. Of course, it was a fantasy. And now this.

Lilly flipped on a small lamp on the bedside table. "I had nightmares for years. My late husband called them my 'memorymares'—instead of nightmares."

"Memorymares?" Ms. Delsig stared at the ceiling. The word

fit the description—she wished the nightmares were only figments of her imagination and not things from the past.

"You know, Ms. Delsig, we don't have to be enemies. I won't try to replace your old roommate."

"You could not."

"I wouldn't attempt such a feat."

"I appreciate that," Ms. Delsig said, turning to see Lilly's petite face staring at her.

"We have some things in common."

"Such as?"

"We both can be a little too spunky for our own good. Our ages appear to be about the same, and then we've got these memorymares. If we're not careful, someone might mistake us for twins."

Ms. Delsig couldn't help but smile, then chuckle. Lilly's smooth, bronze skin and tiny body compared to her own pale, wrinkled skin and rounder frame—twins? Lilly was chuckling too, their laughter bringing relief between them. The curtain swayed in the air.

"Tell me about yourself," Ms. Delsig ventured.

"Sure. What would you like to know?"

"How does an African-American woman serve during a war back when this was still a segregated nation?" It amazed her to imagine a young Lilly, unable to vote or eat at a Whites Only restaurant, going off to fight for her nation. "What was Europe like for a girl from the South?"

"Pretty boring."

"Boring?" Ms. Delsig pushed a button on the side railing and the bed rose. "How could that be?"

"We arrived in France a few months before the end of the war; then Victory Europe came and the cleanup began. We encountered not even half the racism and prejudice—much less excitement than we'd had in the South. I had spent a lot of time in New Orleans and those people know how to have fun.

Being in the military in Europe was no fun." Lilly's chuckle made Ms. Delsig smile. "Our battle really began after the war."

"I bet it did," she said, recalling the turmoil of the fifties and sixties. When Ms. Delsig had immigrated to the United States, she'd been stunned by life in the South.

"And I want to know about you too. Have you ever spoken of it?"

She knew Lilly referred to the war. And for once, she was tired of keeping it all inside. "I think some things should not be spoken of."

"I found it freeing to speak and to write. It no longer held me captive."

Ms. Delsig nodded. She believed that was true. "But, you see, I do not want it gone. It will not release me, and I would not want to be released."

"What is this 'it' you're talking about? The terrible memories I released have allowed me a free life."

"My life should never be free."

Lilly was silent for a while, watching Ms. Delsig with piercing black eyes. "You lost someone special."

Ms. Delsig couldn't speak. The names were always on her heart but never on her lips. Yet she suddenly knew that they wanted to be spoken of. And then her mouth was speaking the words she'd kept buried within for decades.

"Edgar Kirke. He was my brother. And my father, mother, grandmother, and little sister, Hani. My name was Brigit Kirke then. Their names are always with me."

⊷▭◐▭⊷

Uncle Martin's words stayed with Amanda the entire day: *"You are peering into something dangerous. Once you open it, you can't take it back."*

He had spoken a sobering truth. Innocence lost could not be

found. Though some people, her father included, believed that sins could be forgiven, Amanda wasn't so sure. Even if it were possible, the fact that those sins had been committed would always remain.

From the park, Amanda went to her father's and watched a special program on the San Francisco Giants' spring training. Her father was feeling better, though a box of tissues stayed by his recliner. They ordered take-out Thai and discussed the season ahead. Yet through it all, Amanda felt she was deceiving him. She smiled and acted as if it were any other day together. But her smile was forced, and her laughter sounded false and irritating to her ears. Amanda had lied to her father once as a teenager, going to a party at Half Moon Bay instead of to a friend's house. After two days of guilt, she had finally confessed. Now she didn't mention meeting his brother at the museum bench. And she certainly didn't tell him that the life he believed in was ultimately a lie.

Truth held great consequences.

Amanda returned to her house, took Hemingway for a walk, and watered some plants Mr. Winifred had given her for her front porch. Evening came and she avoided the computer and stacks of books that were tiny doors ready to be opened. The truth about her family could be there. But the fact of Aunt Helga's many lies brought fear of what she would find. Once those doors were opened, she could never close them again.

She ironed her clothes for work and made a salad to take for lunch. Later, beneath the warmth of her covers, Amanda wondered if Stefan had e-mailed, though she didn't have the energy to check. He'd said he'd call, but there was no message on her machine.

Certainly sleep would never come, she thought. There were too many thoughts to consider, memories to return to with this new knowledge: Her uncle and father were not brothers.

Her eyes were blind, but she could hear clearly. First

screaming, then gunshots. Then sudden silence. It would happen again—screaming, gunshots, silence. And then she could see.

She was in the woods, thick and deep. Her feet told her to run, but she felt the gun pressed against her back. The soldier pushed her to the edge of a deep ravine. She was crying. He told her to kneel at the ledge. Amanda crawled on her knees to the very rim, and there she saw them. They were all ages. Men, women, children, the elderly. Some were thin, their bones protruding, others obese with stark white skin. Hundreds of lives were dumped in a gaping hole, arms and legs twisted together. The sun rose with her there. It was bright sunlight shining upon naked bodies. Red blood was splattered and soaking into the hungry earth. A few were still alive. They groaned and clawed at the air and at one another. She realized she was naked too. She knew the gun would blast into her neck and her body would fall upon their bodies.

The gun cocked. A scream. It was her own.

Amanda bolted up in the darkness of the room, sweat running down her back and fear gripping her stomach. The red numbers glowed from her alarm clock, reminding her where she was.

"It was only the dream," she whispered, her voice trying to ward it away.

She had first met the nightmare as a child. It had come in glimpses at first—a gun at her head, ditches filled with bodies, babies crying. Because of her dreams, her father stopped letting her hear the stories of the survivors who frequently came to their apartment or the Levs'. But the nightmare didn't leave her. It understood her weakness in such a way that sometimes Amanda thought her subconscious was a spirit all its own, seeking her vulnerabilities and attacking her lowered resistance.

It was so vivid and lasting; it seemed more real than the

room around her. Even as she turned on the light, Amanda's shaking hands would not calm. Her mind registered that the clock read 4:08 A.M. She should try to sleep. Her alarm would ring in a few hours, and work would be busy after her time in Europe. But she didn't dare. She feared few things but now feared sleep.

Her desk seemed to beckon. Amanda suddenly knew she couldn't avoid what she must know. The nightmare signaled that fact. The truth might await in a book in this very room or only a keystroke away on the computer.

She rose slowly, feeling the lasting remnant of the nightmare as if it were a drug she couldn't rid herself of. The computer hummed awake as she slid a UCSF sweatshirt over her head and slippers over her cold toes.

A therapist once told Amanda that perhaps her dream was really a memory. That she'd died this way in a past life. He thought she should seek hypnosis. Her father was adamantly against the idea, saying to beware of the spirit world, that opening her mind without God's protection could allow spirits or suggestions that were not her own. Amanda had been surprised at his response, and though she thought he was being overly religious minded and fearful of modern therapy, in the end she didn't pursue it. She could live with a recurring nightmare, but she didn't want to live with her father's additional concerns about the welfare of her soul.

While clicking on the icon of her Internet provider, Amanda decided to first search some of the reference books she'd recently picked up at the university library. She'd never thought to search such books—why would she, when her grandparents had supposedly died among the millions of other anonymous war victims? Now she sought her family among the types of books she'd used for countless other research projects. In the fourth book, *Holocaust History*, she found her grandfather's name: *Heinrich, Kurt. pp. 76, 501.*

Slowly she turned to page 76. It listed the SS officers who had attended a secret conference in Germany. She scanned the list and found his name: *SS Haupsturmführer Kurt Heinrich*.

Haupsturmführer meant he was a captain. She rubbed her eyes, then had a thought. With such a common German name, perhaps this wasn't her grandfather. Maybe her grandfather had a different name.

On page 501, she found the answer:

> *Justice did not find many of the men in this group. Among these was Kurt Heinrich, who began his career in the Nazi Party at the encouragement of his mother. He married a young secretary he met at Nazi headquarters in Prague. They would give their lives to the cause—Kurt as a top aide to SS Reinhard Heydrich.*
>
> *After the war, his wife, Hilde Heinrich, killed herself when Allied officials came to the door to seek Kurt's whereabouts. Kurt Heinrich was finally captured, but before his indictment he joined the ranks of other Nazi suicides. A neighbor of the Heinrichs reported that their two young sons had been sent to the United States during the war.*

The story continued but Amanda needed nothing more. She had found her grandparents. They weren't victims. They were among the men and women her father had spent his life refuting and whom she'd always viewed as the most evil of humans. These were the family she'd sought. And Amanda knew that Pandora's box could never be closed again.

What she feared most was that this was just the beginning.

part *two*

Truth Prevails

—INSCRIPTION ON MONUMENT TO JAN HUS
PRAGUE, CZECH REPUBLIC

CHAPTER SEVENTEEN

In one morning, a life could change forever. Amanda knew such moments occurred every day and every hour. Her work of news reports, Internet information, and seeking stories brought her in constant contact with tragic stories. People spoke into the camera the words that stunned their lives:

> *They are still missing.*
> *He was killed right off the train.*
> *I had just left the restaurant when the bomb detonated.*
> *I never saw my wife again.*
> *There was nothing anyone could do.*

Amanda had encountered them in others' lives as she sought newsworthy comments. For the speaker, such moments changed the way of the world and froze a heart with life-changing tragedy as the rest of the world carried on.

The truth of her grandfather's past was minor in comparison. Did it change so much? It could be much worse when she thought of what others had endured. Yet for Amanda and her father, few things could scar their lives more than this. They could face cancer by fighting together, by believing, hoping, and enjoying each minute in case it was the final one. But there was no fighting your own past.

She sat before the computer screen, typing in her grand-father's name. It took time going through various searches. Her mind focused, seeking the information as it always did when she researched, while closing out the repercussions of what this would mean long term. Amanda skimmed through the search results for additional information.

Within twenty minutes she clicked on a site, and an image opened on the screen. The caption read *Kurt Heinrich. June 1942, Lidice.*

Leaning in, she stared at a black-and-white photograph of an SS officer walking among the bodies of the townsmen and boys. The officer was looking at something off camera and seemed unaffected by the carnage at his feet.

Amanda was seeing her grandfather for the first time. He had been at the massacre, but he wasn't one of the dead on the ground. Kurt Heinrich had been one of the killers.

She drew her legs up onto the chair, wrapped her arms around her knees, then stared at the picture for a long time. Her dog slept a few feet away. Sticky notes lined the ridge of her desk with all she needed to do or remember. Outside, an early morning garbage truck moved up the street. Everything appeared the same.

The truth took time to settle in. First the knowledge attached itself to the past . . . to her memories of childhood and the Lev family. What if the Levs had known they had invited the son and granddaughter of SS Haupsturmführer Kurt Heinrich to their Shabbat table? Amanda perceived herself differently. This information reinvented who she was in the worst possible light. How did that change who she was to her employers, coworkers, old friends—some of whom were Holocaust survivors?

In college, Amanda and a girlfriend had traveled Europe for three weeks. They had taken trains from London to Paris to Berlin and Rome. While in Germany, they had stopped at Dachau.

"And your family died in a place like this?" Megan had asked.

"Yes," Amanda whispered. "My grandfather was killed at the village. My grandmother died at Ravensbrück Concentration Camp."

They had walked the wide, dirt walkways, passing the foundations of old barracks. Silence had fallen between them as they mourned the lives of those who seemed to walk there still. Amanda had felt a kinship with the dead, for she'd lost something too.

After gaining the position at the History Network West Coast, she'd taken several trips to camps, including Auschwitz-Birkenau, Treblinka, Belzec, and finally Ravensbrück again. Always the silence of lost lives hung in those places, and she felt an awkward comfort in their presence. In Ravensbrück especially. Somewhere in the earth of that ground was her own flesh and blood.

But it was all a lie now.

In the cold of early morning, Amanda suddenly needed her father. She wanted his wisdom and the comfort of his presence. She didn't want her life to be a lie. Or his. She wanted the story she'd always known—that her family perished at the hands of evil Nazi villains, not that her family members were such villains. She couldn't tell him; Amanda knew this. And if she couldn't tell her father, she lived a deeper lie.

Lies and truths—they weren't so different. Now she had the truth and it shed itself over her past and into her future. The hateful, dreaded truth. What made truth beautiful or right?

In that moment, Amanda found that sometimes truth was much worse than any lie.

⋄═◯═⋄

Ms. Delsig felt as if one domino had fallen as she spoke her family's name for the first time since that dark night with Edgar long ago. She was resting on her side facing Lilly, who listened with the blanket twisted in her tiny, dark hands.

As she began, the stories spilled out, falling one upon another. The images of the past returned with clarity, as if waiting impatiently for her to speak them free. "I should have died. The cliff was incredibly high and I expected death. I did not jump far enough out, so I hit something and tumbled to the bottom. For two days I was alone in agony . . . unable to move, certain that man or some animal would find me."

"You were conscious at the bottom of that cliff? All alone?" Lilly's voice was breathless.

"I was terrified of dying alone or falling asleep. What if I awakened to an animal that had smelled my blood? I could feel the blood everywhere. They should have been the worst days of my life, yet they were not. I had already seen so much, so I waited for death to come. At least I would not die some of the deaths I had seen—the gassings, the electric fences, the beatings. I would die with the wind blowing through the pines. At the bottom of that cliff I found my old belief in God—amazingly enough. I had great anger toward God, even as I waited for death. I told him so and asked to die—why had I not died yet? I yelled and fussed until I had no more left within me."

Lilly nodded as if she understood exactly.

"Maybe I finally admitted that it was not God who had done so many things to me, but man, though I still struggle with that."

"And how did you get out of there?" Lilly asked.

"American soldiers were coming into the area, and one found me there. He just happened to glance over and see a piece of my handkerchief on the rocks. I had over twenty fractured bones in my arms, legs, and ribs, plus a chipped pelvic bone."

"It must have taken months to heal."

"Yes. The war ended within days of my rescue, and I was on a gurney for the celebration."

"I want to hear everything," Lilly said.

Ms. Delsig shivered at the woman's interest; it was as if they'd known one another for years. "I want to hear your story too." She glanced at the clock on the opposite wall. It was well after midnight. "The night nurse will be in soon. She will want us to go to sleep."

"Are you ready to sleep?"

"No."

"Then we'll go to sleep when we want," Lilly said with a firm nod. "We pay their salaries."

"That is what I always say."

They both chuckled.

Then Lilly began her own story. She told of the Ku Klux Klan banging on the door of her childhood home and burning crosses on their lawn. A bomb exploded next door to her father's barbershop, and on her own dark night, Lilly had found her older brother dangling from a tree, his feet still twitching. Both women understood the loss of the brothers they admired.

"My father tried to teach us not to hate. But my other older brother was unable to escape hatred's snare. He killed a white man and was executed at age twenty-four," Lilly said sadly. "I fought back in a different way. I learned to read and write, and write I did. My books are in classrooms and universities now. The men who burned crosses on my lawn are dead and unre-membered."

Lilly told of speaking around the world and of her attempts to influence poets and writers of every race. "At first, this was my revenge," she said. "Then it became my freedom. What was your revenge? Your freedom? Your faith in God?"

Ms. Delsig didn't have an immediate answer. "I suppose it was my survival. The fact that I lived was my revenge. Yet, I must admit, I do not feel completely free."

"Ah yes, but that's not what this world is for," Lilly said. "We can find measures of freedom—freedom of country and civil rights, and freedom from hatred through forgiveness, and for our souls there is freedom in Christ. Yet those memories always are pulling me back down to my flesh and blood with its anger and hate. I fight it, but it always returns to be fought again. That next world will be the place of true freedom."

"I believe you are onto something there."

They continued talking, unable to share enough. Later Ms. Delsig turned on her back and noticed the dim glow of the coming dawn along the edges of the drapes. "We have talked nearly through the night, at least since that nightmare, or memorymare, woke me. I do not think I have done that since—well, since ever."

"Me neither. And I'm still not very tired, but mercy will I be tired tomorrow." Lilly adjusted her blankets around her tiny frame.

"We will have to put a Do Not Disturb sign over our door or something."

They both laughed.

"I feel a weight has lifted that I never knew I was carrying," Ms. Delsig said.

"It's telling about your past. I'm sure there will be more stories that will return now that you've begun talking. How long have you kept it all inside?"

Ms. Delsig knew the date exactly. In one decisive moment

she had sworn herself to silence. And here she'd spilled it all so easily after years of being locked and sealed away.

"Don't you close up on me now." Lilly's voice was firm with authority. "The silence will shut you inside of yourself again."

Ms. Delsig's heart fluttered nervously. She'd already told more than she ever considered telling before. And there was that great final secret she'd thought to carry safely into the grave. The barrier between the two women had opened. Lilly Parkens had in one night broken through walls Ms. Delsig had mortared and maintained for decades. Ms. Delsig didn't make instant friendships. She didn't trust them. And yet, for the first time in her life, she'd found one. It stunned her to realize that she believed Lilly could be trusted with her life. This friendship would be different. Her golfing friends had been mostly surface friendships. Janice was like the daughter she never had, someone to love and protect. Alfred made her laugh and dream. But she suddenly knew that this was the friendship she'd always avoided and always desired.

Petite and full of spirit, Lilly Parkens would not be a friend content to allow Ms. Delsig to yawn her way through her final years. Lilly wouldn't permit her to sketch flowers and birds but would want to see the darkness that wouldn't be still until it was released upon a canvas or sketchpad. Her brother, Edgar, had been the only other person with such dissecting powers.

The prospect frightened her, yet Ms. Delsig felt a thrill at the unexpected. "Do you know what? You are the answer to my prayer," Ms. Delsig whispered as the knowledge made itself known. "When I knew Janice was leaving, I told God I was afraid to be alone. And he sent you. I did not know I was praying for you."

"And I prayed that God would bring me someone to share my final days. You are the one."

Ms. Delsig's eyes filled, and she turned away from the

tenderness in Lilly's expression. "I do not believe I have ever been an answer to prayer."

"I surely don't believe that. God had you live for a purpose."

"Please do not say that. I see the faces of hundreds who did not live, and I know God had a purpose for them also."

Lilly nodded. "This is true. And yet, your work on earth continues."

"I have known something for a long time," Ms. Delsig said, not really meaning to say it aloud.

"What is it?" Lilly asked, sitting up in her bed. She swung her legs over and leaned forward. "Are you all right? I should not have asked that. Tell me only when you are ready. We've had a very long night and could use some sleep."

"No, I need to do this." Ms. Delsig stared at the ceiling for a long while. "It was a brooch. A brooch that once belonged to the empress of Austria. Its value is inestimable, but not worth the blood it cost. There is a line of deaths associated with the brooch that began with the empress herself. People have called it accursed. Every person who has possessed it is now dead—except for me."

"Who else knows about this brooch?"

"I do not know if anyone does. But I know there is only one person who knows where it is."

"And that person is you."

Ms. Delsig nodded. A bright shot of light streamed through the crack in the drapes as the sun rose from the sea and awakened the earth. The night seemed to make it right to speak of such things, but daylight brought the fear of what she had done.

"It must never be spoken of again," Ms. Delsig said anxiously. "So many died for the Empress Brooch—my brother was one of them."

"And I will die with that secret."

CHAPTER EIGHTEEN

The cold stung Stefan's face as he flipped his collar up and leaned into the light wind. Soon he might leave chilly Prague for humid Guatemala. When Stefan called the mission headquarters that morning, the director, Paul Dutton, had told him about a small missionary group in Central America in need of temporary support. Paul had explained how three missionary families, including the district leader, were suffering from a tropical illness. If Stefan agreed, he would help them through the sickness, making sure medical and physical needs were met, and continue the work with the locals.

Stefan asked for a few hours before deciding, which he knew surprised Paul. Stefan never hesitated but he hadn't felt ready to explain. He still hadn't reached Amanda. Now he walked toward the documentation center to get the file he'd volunteered to pick up. Not only did he feel both urgency and reluctance in reaching Amanda, Stefan wasn't mentally—or spiritually—prepared for Guatemala. "I'm sure they could also use some encouraging in the Lord," Paul had stated as they discussed what preparations would be in order.

Stefan recalled those words as he walked toward the river along streets he'd walked with Amanda only days earlier. He had allowed Paul to speak without saying what he was thinking. Who was Stefan to be encouraging someone else? For the first time in years, Stefan felt that God was far from him. There seemed to be a huge void between him and heaven, a lasting silence and slices of doubt. It was as if he'd worked his way up Mount Sinai to find what God had to say to the world, but God had disappeared. Stefan had somehow climbed the wrong mountain, or he'd tumbled down to the bottom without the energy to try again.

Perhaps that was why he should go to Guatemala. Often when he journeyed on a commercial jet to a small plane that landed on a dirt runway and then by boat up a river to a crude village, he would find that the people he'd come to help—the villagers living the simplest of lives and the missionaries who'd given up everything to join them—were the ones who encouraged his life.

But this ran deeper than a need to cheer up. Stefan was wrestling within himself. He needed to reach Amanda and tell her what Petrov had found. Yet he dreaded revealing what had shocked even him. Stefan had thought he couldn't do it, couldn't be with someone whose heritage held ideals and bloodlines that had caused his own grandfather's death. He saw his grandmother's continued sorrow whenever anniversaries and holidays came and went. But Petrov had read his thoughts: *Amanda is her own individual. And she'll need you now.* Greater than Stefan's own pain would be Amanda's devastation—and he must deliver the news. How would she react? What would happen when she knew? Now there were two things tearing them apart—their beliefs and their pasts.

But first the documentation center. It took much longer

than expected. Stefan had to fill out papers for the request, talk to one secretary and then another. They finally called Amanda's office and received authorization for the information to be given to him. Stefan entered a small room where an archivist discussed the two files that were presented to him.

Hours later he carried the papers Amanda had requested, believing he'd asked the right questions he thought she'd ask. He wondered what she was doing now—probably sleeping safely in her bed far across the ocean. In one evening and morning, he had obtained two pieces of information that Amanda would want. But he wished he didn't have to tell her.

Stefan left the documentation center and walked toward the river. He passed street musicians, artists with their sketches and paintings, and tourists as they captured a sunny Prague with their cameras. He paused at a small square and looked toward the blue ripples of the Vltava River. How easy it would be to drop the papers into the deep, flowing waters. Yet these were mere copies. Amanda would know soon enough; she might already know some of what he held. And he must take it to her, the information she sought and would wish she'd never known.

⊶⟹◑⟸⊷

Amanda squeezed into the elevator full of businesspeople and went to the fourth floor where the History Network West Coast buzzed in full operation. Usually one of the first to arrive, today she was late. She waved at the front-desk secretary and hurried down the line of cubicles to her office. It felt strange to walk in as if everything was normal and unchanged.

Tiffany, her assistant, wasn't at her desk, but Amanda picked up a stack of messages before opening her door. Her office smelled stuffy after being closed off for a week and a half. She adjusted the vertical blinds and walked around her desk to the wood-and-leather office chair she'd found at an antique store. Sitting down, she gazed around the room as if something should be out of place or different since she'd left for the Budapest convention. One side of the room was lined with bookcases full of historical books and reference video-tapes; the other side had files and a long shelf with framed photos of her family and some of her favorite travels. Nothing had changed. She sifted through her messages, including one from Stefan. They were playing phone tag. Another message was from the Prague Documentation Center. She noticed the name *Heinrich* in the message just as Sylvia Pride tapped on the door and sauntered in.

"We need to talk," Sylvia said, closing the door behind her.

"Okay." Amanda moved the Prague message to the bottom of the stack and set the stack in her in-box.

"Welcome home, but will you please call me back when I leave two messages on your machine?" Sylvia Pride, self-proclaimed, quintessential professional woman, had risen up the career ladder and anticipated Amanda doing the same. Somehow Amanda had become Sylvia's pet project of bringing another successful woman to the upper levels of the corporate offices.

"Did something happen? You said we'd talk today."

"I know what I said, but yes, something did happen, and I'd hoped to catch you over the weekend so you could prepare. We have a production meeting Wednesday morning at eight."

"In two days? I thought we had another week and a half."

"Wallace is going to the Caribbean for three weeks so he wants to see what stories are progressing. When he gets back they'll take the projects to the executives. Did you get any-thing in Prague?"

"Well, a little," Amanda said, hoping that the message from the documentation center was something other than informa-tion on her family.

Sylvia was silent as she picked up one of Amanda's framed photos—the profile of the city of Florence at sunset. With long fingernails she tapped the glass.

Amanda watched as the woman, with her styled, short hair and tailored shirt and jacket, narrowed her small eyes and turned to face her.

"You didn't find anything then."

"I have several leads, but nothing definite."

"We must have a strong lead, something that can carry at least a thirty-minute broadcast about this Empress Brooch. You have until tomorrow night."

"That shouldn't be a problem," Amanda said with confidence, but she knew it was riding on hope alone.

"You have a lot going for you, Amanda." Sylvia's tone was serious. "There have been a lot of meetings with the executives in New York. They're making some changes in the programs that will be announced soon. We need to keep our professional quality, and especially as women, work twice as hard if we want to advance."

"What kind of changes?"

"It's all rumors right now. I've heard it all—everything from a more cutting-edge image of the History Network to a few programs with women and family appeal. I've even heard talk of budget cuts and layoffs. But who knows? The rumors get wild. How about reality TV hits History Net?"

"Something like who can survive the history lesson without getting voted off?"

"You never can tell anymore. But what keeps us through the changes is when we become valuable to the company—when no one else can do what we do."

Amanda had heard similar talks from Sylvia before, but the news that changes were happening in New York pushed her to consider how valuable she'd made herself.

"Your work reflects on me and on all of us," Sylvia continued. "You must have something concrete on Wednesday morning. I've enlisted a few assistant researchers already on this project and then there are your expenses in Europe."

"I tacked that on to the Budapest convention—it cost very little. I even stayed with a friend."

"Good, that is good. Our budget is being looked over and books audited. This is a precarious time. Wallace liked the original proposal. Wednesday he's expecting the presentation. Be ready."

"I'll do what I can."

"Do a little more." Sylvia turned and walked out.

Amanda waited for Sylvia to be fully down the hallway before she went to find Tiffany.

Her assistant was making coffee in the small kitchen. "There you are!" Tiffany said with a perky smile that vanished when she saw Amanda's face.

"We have work to do."

⤙⟹◉⟸⤚

The hours of the morning hurried by. Amanda's work at the History Network was an exercise in historical fact mixed with the stories—some truth, some legend. It was her job to research and cross-reference and sometimes improvise when minor details were lacking. The stories would be brought from the page into visual form to be broadcast into the world as history.

First came the preliminary production meeting, where she would present a computerized display of her idea—a miniature version of what would be produced into a full program. Amanda would scan photographs and do the voice-overs. The still photographs she used for the presentation would be replaced by interviews, and the historical dates would be enhanced by film footage, if available. All of that would come later, if she got the green light for the idea.

Before launching into the work, Amanda took a moment to focus. She picked up the two faded and scratched photographs of the Empress Brooch—one showed the Austrian empress wearing the brooch and the other was of the brooch itself.

The sounds of a typical office day drifted through her open door—fingers tapping on keyboards, distant chatter and laughter, chairs shuffling, and phone conversations. Within her comfortable office, Amanda was about to dive deeply into the story and discover all the links with her own now-tainted history. How many people had sought, touched, or hidden the Empress Sissi Brooch? Lives had been taken, blood shed. *Where are you?* she wondered. It was a story similar to ones she'd read and researched again and again. She must keep that usual detachment to do the story and not be overwhelmed by the sorrow such digging had uncovered. She would fight to keep that detachment, or else this assignment would surely sink her.

Clearing her desk, she went to the large corkboard above her framed portraits. She turned her family photos facedown, not wanting the smiles of her father and uncle in view as she worked. After removing notes and articles, she set the corkboard on her desk.

Time to storyboard. She took three-by-five-inch index cards and pulled up a chair, then began writing every idea she'd developed for the program "In Search of the Empress Brooch." She wrote what information was missing and any contacts they already had or needed to find.

Tiffany returned with a carafe of fresh coffee and began organizing files of information about the Empress Brooch, from Empress Elizabeth herself to the Lange family possessing the piece of jewelry. Amanda had to be careful to keep all information about Kurt Heinrich away from everyone working on the story. She'd already contacted the assistant researchers who had been put on the story while she was gone, and they had e-mailed their information to her. The story was unfolding.

The information written on the index cards was organized in a timeline across the corkboard, beginning with Empress Sissi in the 1800s.

"We need to reach Darby Evans Collins to find out how her family got the brooch from the empress—when did it become their heirloom?" asked Amanda.

"I have that in a file already. It was in the story about the Lange family." Tiffany went to a cardboard box and pulled out copies of a newspaper story. "Hey, can we order in some lunch? I'm starving." Tiffany looked up from the newspaper and awaited Amanda's response.

"Sure, order me anything." Amanda continued to stare at the newspaper story. The many pieces of what she'd been told as a child were falling together into a picture she didn't want to see. Lidice, the Empress Brooch—they were truly parts of her family's past, but not in the way they'd been told to her. Amanda wanted to talk to her uncle and go through her great-aunt Helga's belongings to see if what she suspected was true—that even before Kurt Heinrich, her family had hated a Jewish family and wanted the Empress Brooch.

An ambulance siren sounded from the street below. Amanda stood and looked out the window as the red-and-white vehicle sped around cars and drove past.

I must focus on the presentation and put everything else aside, she told herself. Sylvia's warning had been clearly understood. If the presentation failed, her job could be in jeopardy.

A far-off ding of the elevator brought Amanda away from the window. The time on the clock reminded her that Troy Donley would be by anytime. The assistant editor for *History Network on the Net* stopped by almost daily when she wasn't traveling to quiz her on his next "question of the day" for the Web site. If she easily answered his trivia question, he would work on a harder one. If she didn't know the answer, Troy would do a crazy victory dance. Every month they tallied up the points, and the loser bought lunch for their group of office friends.

Amanda had prepared for today's question before going to Europe. She expected Troy to walk in and say, "Tell me. How quickly do things fall?"

Amanda hadn't cracked his computer password, but she had discovered the book he used for the question. Months of side research had uncovered *The How and Why Around Us*, an out-of-print book from 1950. Troy was going right down the line of subjects.

She knew he'd be stunned today when she knew the answer. But somehow the thrill of her victory had worn off. She no longer had the humor or desire to play their game.

Suddenly she remembered the pile of messages she'd put in her in-box when Sylvia had come in this morning. She found the one from Prague: *Prague Documentation Center confirm records for Heinrich and Kirke.*

"Tiffany," Amanda called to her assistant, who had just ordered a vegetarian pizza, "what does this message mean?"

"Oh, I forgot—I have a million things to go over with you since you've been gone and then with—"

"Tiffany, first this note."

"Oh yeah. The Prague place confirmed that Stefan Keller was there to retrieve records for the names *Heinrich* and *Kirke*. That's your boyfriend, right?"

"And what did you say?"

"I told them that yes, they should give the files to him—you faxed me that I was supposed to if they called."

"Yes, yes, of course."

"Is everything okay?"

"Yes, fine," Amanda said.

Tiffany stared at her strangely but began labeling file folders.

Amanda moved boxes and papers around on the floor to her desk chair. She closed her eyes and turned toward the window. A wall of fog was rising to block out the blue sky. It was late night in Prague. But the documentation center had information on Kurt Heinrich. So Stefan now knew the truth about her grandfather.

"Hey, Amanda." She could see Troy Donley's reflection in the window. "Got a question for you. How quickly do things fall?"

He was leaning against the doorjamb with his usual smile. It took a second to gather her thoughts. "It depends upon the height. The higher you go, the faster and harder you fall."

"Hmmm. Too easy, then." Troy turned with furrowed brows and walked away.

Not easy at all, she thought. Days earlier she had been riding high on what the future held. Now she had plummeted. What worried her most was that this wasn't over. She must face Stefan. She must face her father. And Amanda knew she must face her grandfather.

Would she be able to rise from such a fall?

CHAPTER NINETEEN

Ms. Delsig rolled over to see Lilly already in her wheelchair with a determined expression in her jaw and eyes. Ms. Delsig blinked at the effects of their two nights of late talks and only short afternoon naps. She believed she could sleep through the evening and into the next dawn.

"I have an idea," Lilly said.

"Can I wake up first?" Ms. Delsig yawned and stretched, struggling to escape the snare of sleepiness.

"Wake up fast."

"You are a tyrant," Ms. Delsig said, slowly rising to a sitting position. "What is it?"

"Not if you're in a grouchy mood. I'll just tell you later."

Ms. Delsig pursed her lips and focused on the petite woman in her slacks, white blouse, and furry pink slippers. She tried to keep the stern look on her face but found herself losing the battle to a smile. "Okay, okay, what is it?"

"Well," Lilly said, eyes sparkling like a teenager's about to reveal her crush on a boy, "Alfred and I discussed some things about your past and he looked up some—"

"Alfred and you discussed my past!"

"Don't get your muumuu in a bunch—I didn't tell him anything you wouldn't want me to tell. That man is in love with you. If you had any sense, you'd snatch him up before someone else does, like that Candy Banks."

"Quit lecturing me and just tell me why I am wakening from my afternoon nap with you staring at me and babbling away about something."

"I'm trying, for goodness sakes." Lilly sighed and crossed her arms firmly. "Now if I can speak without interruption . . ."

"Fine," Ms. Delsig said, crossing her arms too.

"Fine." The two women stared each other down until tiny grins rose from the edges of their lips. Lilly's teeth shone bright against her dark face as they began to laugh together.

"Well, this is what we think," Lilly began, then paused.

"I am waiting . . ."

"I don't want you to take this the wrong way."

"Lilly."

"I think, and Alfred agrees, that you need to get your story on one of those Holocaust video testimony things. Thousands and thousands of Holocaust survivors have done it already, and several groups are doing it to preserve the truth of what happened. Alfred and I found one foundation through a university and another started by a Hollywood filmmaker. But I think you should really consider this. It could take time, but your story should be kept as a record for what has been done. There, I said it."

It was as if a door had suddenly opened. A door Ms. Delsig had known was there yet not been able to really see. "I cannot. I could not."

"Alfred thought it might be too soon."

"What did you tell him?" She was terrified that all of Oakdale knew her story.

"Calm down. You can trust me. But yesterday he asked me what happened to you. He said there was something different about you. I just said that we'd confessed all to one another. He seemed very pleased by that."

"He did?" Ms. Delsig smiled and slid her feet into her slippers.

"Yes, he said that he'd hoped you'd find your way, and then we started talking about these Holocaust programs."

"You two sure became friends quickly."

"It doesn't happen often, but sometimes those kindred spirits are easily identified. Oh, and Alfred is still waiting for an answer to his marriage proposal."

"What?" Ms. Delsig's hand covered her mouth. "I thought he was joking."

"Oh no, he was quite serious. Except I'm not sure if he really wants to move to Mexico—wouldn't put it past that old fella though."

"You really know how to wake someone up from a nap."

Lilly wheeled toward her and reached for her hands. "Listen to me. I want you to think about this Holocaust taping thing. It's important. And think about Alfred. Take your time. But remember, we're old. We don't have forever."

⊷⊶⊷

Ms. Delsig worked on the computer, checking the Web sites Lilly had told her about. Survivors were dying every day and their stories were being lost. She was shocked when she began to find articles about the Empress Brooch and the Lange family—a family she remembered from childhood who were the true heirs to the brooch. Ms. Delsig had always believed the family had perished during the war. Now she discovered differently.

"Ms. D," Lilly said, interrupting her.

Startled by the fear in Lilly's voice, Ms. Delsig turned toward her.

"Something happened to Alfred," Lilly said softly.

"What happened?"

"I don't know, but the paramedics are here and taking him to the hospital."

Ms. Delsig hurried out of the resource room and down the hall as quickly as she could push the walker. She reached the main lobby in time to see the top of Alfred's balding head as the paramedics hurried him out to a waiting ambulance.

Standing in the hallway, Ms. Delsig knew she didn't have as much time as she'd hoped.

⊷≡◒⊏≡⊷

Amanda's office was a disaster after two days of working, with a quick trip home to sleep a few hours and shower. It was night again. Amanda flipped on her desk lamp and leaned back in the chair. The building was silent except for the night janitor vacuuming somewhere down a hallway or in an office. Tiffany had volunteered to stay longer, but Amanda had finally sent her home. After a second day working late into the night, Tiffany deserved to go.

The meeting was in the morning. Amanda wasn't ready.

Her computer presentation would run the story idea, but she knew Wallace would see the holes in it. She had a brooch that disappeared during WWII—what was so compelling about that? The files from Prague might have given some information, but Amanda hadn't heard from Stefan and no one answered her call to his family's apartment. For the sake of her meeting, Amanda had needed to reach him, but her fear of facing him had grown. Their relationship had begun with the shared history of family persecution. Everything else about their lives was different. Now what did he think of her, and what would keep them together? Amanda hoped Stefan would simply send the files FedEx with a letter telling her why their relationship wouldn't work.

Amanda decided to just go home. She'd do the presentation in the morning, tell Wallace that more information was coming in, and hope for the best. There was one detail that would sell the idea. It was intriguing and hit their demographics. A Nazi officer obsessed with an empress brooch that belonged to a Jewish family—Wallace would love it. But Amanda could never reveal it.

Stepping over boxes and files to get around her desk, Amanda realized she'd have to get back early to straighten up. But tonight she was too tired to do anything more than check her voice mail before leaving.

Her father's voice came over the line. "It's Dad. Wanted to talk to you about something, so give me a call. I've missed you the last few days. Love you."

His voice brought it all back. Amanda sat on the edge of her desk, feeling the weight of what she knew. She'd tried not to focus on the information during the past two days. But through it she had found bits and pieces related to her grandfather. What she'd thought was stunning news a few days ago was now shockingly beyond belief and getting worse. When Amanda came to the transcript of the interview she'd done with Darby Evans Collins, the heiress to the Empress Brooch, she'd found another piece of the puzzle. Darby had been raised by her mother and grandmother, who escaped Austria during WWII. And the transcript had stated clearly what Amanda had originally missed in her first interview with Darby over the phone.

> *My grandmother said there was a Nazi officer who was seeking the brooch, though I don't know why. My grandmother's best friend, Tatianna Hoffman, was taken to Mauthausen Concentration Camp because the Nazis*

believed she was my grandmother. Tatianna purposefully
traded places with my grandmother, sacrificing her life so
that my grandmother might live. As a result, she was held
and tortured in the camp prison by the orders of this Nazi
officer in an attempt to gain the location of the Empress
Brooch.

The transcript described the girl in Mauthausen Concentration
Camp, but it was the mention of the Nazi officer that stopped
Amanda. She needed to confirm her suspicion but feared this
Nazi was her grandfather Kurt Heinrich. The link was too close.

It was too much. Amanda couldn't call her father back
tonight. She didn't have the energy to pretend everything was all
right. Her thoughts moved from her father to Stefan to the meeting in the morning to a man who long ago had held his own
child and believed it was right to murder another man's child.

Amanda carried her satchel into the elevator and leaned
against the wall, her blonde hair falling over her eyes as the
elevator dropped to ground level. Her footsteps echoed across
the marble lobby as she passed security cameras and exited
through the glass front doors. Cars and taxis zipped by and
groups of people moved down the sidewalk.

Amanda began to walk. She passed a homeless man, then
turned back and dumped all the change from her coat pockets
into his empty tin cup. Around a corner, she sifted her way
through crowds just released from a concert or play. This late
at night Amanda usually took a taxi, but she wasn't ready to go
home. She kept walking up the staggered streets of San Francisco, then turned down the steps toward the bay. She felt
people surrounding her, heard the laughter and jokes among
teenagers, sensed a child beside her legs. She stopped at lights
and crossed with the crowds, moving in an apparent destination. The lights of the city shown from headlights and
streetlamps and buildings.

Amanda saw faces—her father, Stefan, Benny, Stefan's mother, Sylvia Pride, her mother—but she always returned to her father.

Much later she found herself between Pier 39 and Fisherman's Wharf. The walkways were busy with tourists and locals out enjoying the clear, cool night. Amanda sat on a bench beside a street performer, who stood straight and erect like a robot, and she pulled off one shoe, revealing a bright blister on her heel. The black dress shoes weren't made for hiking the streets of San Francisco.

She'd been to the Wharf a hundred times—with her father as a child, with a visiting friend or a boyfriend. Amanda would complain about the tourists though she acted like one herself, peering into shopwindows with their seashells, cable car souvenirs, and saltwater taffy. It all felt different now.

Naïveté was a gift, she decided. She'd always scorned people who hid their heads in the sand, who ignored the news because it was too depressing, who read only romance novels and not literary works. The loss of intellectual innocence was a curse. It created a fork in the road. Amanda must make a choice; there was no going back to who she had been. Such knowledge changed the way a person saw herself and the world. It caused either courage to go ahead or defeat that might never be overcome again.

The sound of boats rocking on their mooring lines was like a lullaby in the night. The salty bay breeze and scents of batter-fried fish, sourdough bread, and clam chowder whirled around her as she resumed walking. Amanda wanted to listen and feel the security of life again. She wished for rain to fall from the clear, dark night. Rain that would drench her clothes and hair and wash away all that she felt.

Amanda wanted joy again. But she did not believe she'd ever have it.

◆≡◎≡◆

It felt like hours had passed. Amanda walked and walked until her feet ached and the streets were too silent. Settling against a run-down building, Amanda realized she'd gone too far. She was unsure where she was. Pushing her hair back from her face, she sought a street sign. Fear crept in. She dug her cell phone from her satchel, but the battery had gone dead—she'd forgotten to recharge it. She hadn't been thinking at all. Amanda knew the rules of living a single life in the city. You never took safety for granted or believed yourself beyond harm. This city was home, and yet it held its own evils.

She saw a phone booth up the street and hurried toward it. Passing an alley, she noticed a group of people warming themselves over a small fire in a barrel. She reached the booth and shut herself inside, searching her pockets for coins. Then she remembered the change she'd given to the homeless man and instead fumbled in her bag for some money.

The line rang and rang. Amanda glanced at her watch. It was almost midnight. She almost hung up when she heard him.

"I have new work hours," Benny mumbled in a groggy voice.

"Benny, could you please come pick me up?"

"Amanda? What's wrong?"

"Can you just come get me?"

"Where are you?"

She leaned her head against the booth and started to cry. A few tears hit the glass and made their pursuit downward. "I'm not sure. I found the sign for Broadway but the cross sign is missing."

"I'm putting my shoes on as we speak. You can give the directions while I drive."

"Hurry, Benny. Please hurry."

They didn't speak when she first got in his car. Benny stared at Amanda with an expression of amazement and great worry, but she turned her face from him. Amanda closed her eyes against the comfort of the bumpy leather seats and Benny's aftershave that permeated the worn and faded Porsche.

"How did you get down here?" he asked with a thread of anger.

"I don't know. I was walking . . ."

He put the car in gear and started to drive. "Do you want to stay with me tonight or go home?"

"I don't care," she whispered. Her feet and legs pulsed with dull, deep aches, and her shoulder felt like a knot had formed from the strap of her satchel.

"I can probably get a substitute and you can call in sick tomorrow," he was saying.

"No." She opened her eyes. "I have to be at work tomorrow. I need to go home."

"Whatever you say." Benny drove faster on the empty backstreets. He seemed upset with her, something that rarely happened. Amanda might get irritated at him, but Benny didn't get angry often. He didn't speak again until he stopped suddenly at Mr. Winifred's tiny driveway.

"Okay, let me guess; you want to be Jewish again?" he asked, turning off the engine. "Huh, my little Gentile?"

Amanda was so surprised that she smiled. "I forgot that you knew about that."

"Grandfather took it seriously."

"I just wanted to belong with all of you," Amanda said, recalling what a child she had been—so innocent and blinded by what the world would hold.

"That was why Grandfather wouldn't let you pursue it. He wanted you to want God, not our family."

"God—Stefan's grandmother mentioned God to me before I left Prague. She told me to seek him with all of my heart."

Benny turned, pulling a knee onto the seat. "We don't spend enough time seeking him, I'm sure. I don't quite know how to change that or if I should change it."

"I don't know much of anything anymore."

"So it's about your family, is it?"

She nodded and stared out the window. A streetlight down the road flicked off.

"It's bad, I know. I can tell—it's not every day that Miss Professional, Have-It-All-Together Amanda Rivans is found hiding in a phone booth in the bad part of town. You can't keep it from me. You can try to hide from Daddy, from your coworkers, girlfriends, and Boy Wonder, but I'll sit here until I starve unless you tell me what is happening to you."

Amanda smiled wearily at his dramatic display, but her smile quickly vanished. She turned to face him.

"Your family didn't die at Lidice. You found out what happened. Are they still alive?" Benny asked.

"No, I'm almost sure of that, if I can be sure of anything now."

"They weren't victims and this is bad. So what—your grandparents were Adolf Hitler and Eva Braun? Come on, Amanda, tell me."

"You aren't that far off."

He furrowed his eyebrows. "Nazis?"

"Yes." Her voice was monotone as she spoke what she still didn't quite believe. "Kurt Heinrich was a captain in the Nazi Party who took part in the Lidice massacre. The reason I've heard stories about the Empress Brooch since childhood is probably because Grandpa Heinrich tortured and killed at least four people, maybe more, in his search to obtain it—one of whom was a nineteen-year-old girl named Tatianna. I don't know much about my grandmother yet except that she was married to a Nazi officer. My presentation for the Empress Brooch is tomorrow morning, and I have no leads except my own family connection which, of course, I'm trying to keep buried. And now I'm hoping that the story will fail when I present it to Wallace. The worst that will happen is that I'll be demoted or lose my job. If Kurt Heinrich is revealed as the officer after the brooch, my father will certainly know all about the parents he has tried to make proud all these years by helping Holocaust survivors."

"Unbelievable," Benny whispered. "Beyond my worst imaginings."

They sat in silence as a car passed by. Time seemed to march around them.

"I don't know how to be this person, Benny," Amanda stated.

"You are still the same person." He took her hand and she looked at their fingers intertwined. His flesh with its Jewish heritage and hers with Nazi.

"No, I'm not the same. I'm not. I never realized how much easier it is to be the child of a victim than the child of a murderer."

He squeezed her fingers hard, too hard. Benny wouldn't tell her lies; he understood. "Amanda, I want you to hear something. Remember after the gallery turned down my paintings and I was dropped from that band—all in the same night?"

"I remember."

"Well, I had already been kind of depressed and directionless. Those two things were the final straw. I was going to kill myself that night."

"Benny, you never told me this."

"I know. I couldn't. I got really drunk and I had it all planned. But I called you to hear your voice one more time. You said something that changed my mind."

"What did I say?"

"You told me that in the morning the dawn would come, just like every other morning of my life. You said that soon enough a morning would come and everything would be all right again. Then you told me to go to bed and get some sleep."

A tear fell down Amanda's cheek.

"Well, now I'm saying it to you."

Amanda wanted to believe it and felt a glimmer of hope.

"But, Amanda, you will have to tell your father."

"You were the one who said I shouldn't tell my father."

"I was wrong. You can't carry something like this alone. It doesn't have to be today or even soon. But eventually, you must tell him."

She knew he was right, but she couldn't fathom actually doing it.

"Now to bed with you for some sleep."

As she got out of the car, he took her hand and carried her satchel on his shoulder. Benny opened the gate and closed it behind them, putting his arm around her as they walked toward her cottage house.

"Amanda, there's someone on your porch," Benny said abruptly, holding her back.

The light from Mr. Winifred's porch shone into the tiny yard and was the only light to see the man by. He was rising from a chair on the porch, a long duffel bag beside him. Amanda knew who it was in a strange otherworldly sense, like the time she'd found a penny in the waves of the sea—he didn't fit with the location.

"Stefan?"

He gazed at them awkwardly. "Your landlord said I could wait for you. I guess I fell asleep."

"What are you doing here?"

"I had to come. There's something I need to tell you and so I got on a plane—it was too important for a phone call or e-mail."

"I better get going," Benny said, turning away.

"No," Amanda said, staring at Benny, "wait."

"Then I'll make some coffee. I'm Benny, by the way."

"Good to meet you," Stefan said as Benny found the secret key in the porch eaves and disappeared into the cottage. There was an awkwardness between them.

"You came because you know about my family," she said, unable to meet his eyes—those clear, blue eyes that looked deep inside her.

"Yes, I didn't know if you knew. I brought that other information."

"The Kirke file."

"Yes, and a file on your grand—I mean, a file on Kurt Heinrich."

"My grandfather." Amanda stared at the white flowers in the flowerpot beside her door.

"Yes."

"And you've read through it."

"I read enough—there was a lot of information." He was staring at her.

"I can't talk about this right now, Stefan." She wanted to run away from him, tell him to go home. But his presence—the fact that he was here, that he had flown around the world as soon as he knew—said more than words could express.

Benny peered back out the door. "What kind of information? Because, Amanda, you have a very important meeting in the morning."

"It doesn't matter anymore," she said.

"She says this now," Benny stated to Stefan, "but down the road when she's making laxative commercials, she'll wish she'd given this her best shot."

"He sounds right to me," Stefan said, taking her hand.

Amanda walked into her cottage with Stefan leading the way and Benny flipping on the living-room lamps. Coffee was soon brewing, and Amanda knew they wouldn't let her lie down yet.

CHAPTER TWENTY

I am not leaving this spot until I hear something," Ms. Delsig stated firmly to Mr. Bartlett. Lilly sat beside her on the long reception couch by the front door. Mr. Bartlett seemed more nervous about their presence so close to the door than about Alfred's condition—as if the two would make a prison break.

"Mr. Bartlett, is there a reason why we can't wait right here until you get the call?" Lilly asked in her sugar-sweet voice.

He glanced at her, as if suddenly remembering his awe of the local celebrity. "No, no reason at all. I'll have someone bring down some food and drink for you ladies. And I'll call the hospital to see if there is any word on Alfred's condition."

"Thank you," Lilly said with a polite smile.

Mr. Bartlett adjusted his glasses, then went back to his office across the lobby, closing the door behind him.

"That man is quite a character," Lilly said, patting Ms. Delsig's hand.

"Why haven't we heard anything?"

"We will. Surgery takes a long time. And no news is good news sometimes," Lilly assured her.

"I should have told him yes. What keeps me so afraid of doing things out of the ordinary?"

"Don't start with the 'should have's.' Just look at the 'can do's.' You can do a lot of things. You can marry that man when he gets better. You can do some praying to God Almighty. You can take care of yourself so that you can do many more things in this life."

"I think you could take over the world, Lilly Parkens."

"And I've considered it," Lilly said with a firm nod that made them both chuckle.

"I think that you and Alfred may be right about this Holocaust thing," Ms. Delsig said softly.

Lilly's eyes widened. "Well, Ms. D, I'm so glad to hear you say that—that's a 'can do' in action. Alfred will be proud of you."

"He will, yes?" She felt her skin flush a little. "I do not know what has been stopping me all these years. Pride? Stubbornness? No, it has been my fear of facing the past. And yet it has never left me anyway."

Ms. Delsig tried to imagine actually sitting with a camera pointed her way and speaking of what she'd only recently revealed. It frightened her. And there were some parts of her story she would never reveal. Yet, in the setting of her days on earth, this seemed right. It would be the children she never had, her legacy to the world.

"Alfred and I found one group in Florida who does the taping."

"Actually, I already know who must do this. Perhaps you and Alfred can help me locate them. If Alfred is all right."

"We'll do whatever we can."

Richter carried his new life in his wallet. He would soon have even more money and would find a place in one of the great cities of America—he'd decide which city when he got there. He drove the dark, narrow road in his new, forest green SUV, like those so many Americans drove, and headed straight for the Canadian–U.S. border. Within days he had received a perfect-looking U.S. passport, driver's license, and social security card.

All he had to offer them was information. They already knew about the Empress Sissi Brooch, or at least they'd found out about it after his initial contact with them. Richter perceived that they already had a grudge against some recent failures to locate old Nazi loot. This was important to them. They wanted everything he knew.

Richter's contact, his grandmother who had known the Lange family, had told him that there was one last possibility for the location of the Empress Brooch. The Langes had had best friends—the Kirke family. If the other leads proved wrong, she always believed the Empress Brooch might be found with one of the Kirke family members.

The border station came into view. Richter slowed the car and stopped for the border patrolman, who walked toward him. This would be easy; in a minute he'd be on U.S. soil. Perhaps Richter would settle down somewhere, or perhaps, just perhaps, he'd go after the Empress Brooch himself. Sure, it had cost him dearly once before, but it always irked him that it was out there and that someone else might find it first.

"How long are you staying in the States?" The dark-haired man looked stiff in his uniform.

"I'm an American. Just went into Canada for a few days of skiing," he said with a smile.

"Then why the Canadian plates?"

"I just bought it. Got a good deal."

Richter wondered why the guard looked him over so closely. "Any fruits or plants that you purchased and have with you?"

"No, none."

"May I see your driver's license or passport?" The patrolman glanced over the car and through the back window.

"No problem. You can have both if you like." Richter opened the glove box and handed the passport to him.

"Rich Doe, huh? Any relation to John Doe?" The patrolman snickered to himself, but Richter didn't get the joke.

"No, not at all. And it is Doe with an *e*," Richter pronounced.

"And you are an American citizen?"

"Yes. For two years now. Proud to be an American," he said.

"Originally you are from . . . ?"

"Germany."

"Doe or Do-ee doesn't sound German."

"Well, that's a long story. But I was born in Germany."

"I need you to turn off your engine and step out of the car."

"Is there a problem?"

"Someone called and said to watch out for a German-accented American who might be carrying illegal contraband into the U.S. and who was a fugitive in Austria for a kidnapping. Would you know anything about that, Rich Do-ee?"

Richter's hands went cold on the wheel. He considered accelerating right through, when another border patrolman walked from the small building.

"No, I do not know what you are talking about."

"Turn off your engine and step out of the car." The border patrolman's voice was firm and threatening this time. His hand rested over the gun on his belt.

"I'm sure this is all a mistake," Richter said, shutting the engine off.

But he knew it wasn't a mistake. He'd been set up.

⭠⮕⚬⮕⭠

Amanda watched Stefan from across the room. In the commotion of the last few days, she'd forgotten how much she was drawn to him. The way he flipped through papers and leaned back to look them over, the hair that fell across his forehead, how his long fingers wrapped around the coffee cup as they discussed the files—he had a way about him that she couldn't pull her eyes from, except when he glanced her way.

Stefan and Benny were trying to help her—these two important men in her life. She'd explained to them about the missing holes in her morning presentation. Now they were forcing her to go through the Kirke file to close up some of them.

Neither mentioned Kurt or Hilde Heinrich.

Studying the paper that Amanda had found with Jirik in Prague, Stefan explained the meaning of the dates and numbers.

> CZ45000K5
> Kirke, Jan (Linz, Osterreich 30/11/98 Praha, CZ. 21/06/42)
> Kirke, Ilsa (Linz, Osterreich 07/02/05 Praha, CZ. 21/06/42)
> Kirke, Edgar (Praha, CZ. 10/10/23)
> Kirke, Brigit (Praha, CZ. 27/07/26 Auschwitz)
> Kirke, Hani (Praha, CZ. 14/01/39 Auschwitz. 14/12/43)

"We know the CZ stands for Czechoslovakia, and the rest of those numbers are just the file's serial code. Now after each name in parentheses, we have the birthplace and the birthday. In Europe they do the day of the month first. So for Jan Kirke, he was born November 30, 1898, in Linz, Austria, or Osterreich, and he died June 21, 1942, in Prague, Czechoslovakia," Stefan explained.

Benny was sitting on the floor beside the coffee table. "So you have the birth and death records of the parents—Jan and Ilsa—and of one of the children."

"Yes. The child was gassed at Auschwitz on December 14, 1943."

Amanda calculated the dates of Hani Kirke. "She would have turned five years old a month later."

They were quiet for a moment.

Stefan continued, pointing at the names. "There is no record of Edgar Kirke other than his birthday, not even in the rest of the file. However, here are papers showing that Brigit Kirke was deported to Auschwitz-Birkenau with her little sister and grandmother. Hani and the grandmother perished there upon arrival. The file does not list a death date for Brigit."

"I can get some information by contacting the archive center at Auschwitz-Birkenau. They might have her death record, but a lot of people were killed without it ever being recorded. There is nothing else in the file about Brigit Kirke?"

Stefan shuffled through the pages. Benny tried to help, but he made little progress because the words were in German and Czech. Amanda knew she should be going through the file herself, but she couldn't bring herself to touch the copies of original Nazi records. The ones with handwritten notes churned her stomach as she imagined the writer as someone on her grandfather's staff.

"There is nothing more on her," Stefan said.

"Then Edgar Kirke is the best hope for the next lead. Did you go through all these papers?" Amanda asked.

"No, just a few," Stefan said. "They do have some of the information obtained through the interrogation of the parents—Jan and Ilsa. But, Amanda, we need to talk about this."

"Talk about what?" She was tired, more tired than she'd ever been before. Benny's and Stefan's prodding and sensitivity were starting to annoy her. She didn't need protecting; it was too late for that.

"You want to talk about my grandfather being a Nazi, a

murderer? How will talking change anything? Let me just see the interrogation sheets."

She grabbed them from Stefan's hand and flipped through the pages quickly, perusing what she'd need to study later.

"I only read the beginning . . ."

Amanda saw the name on the page. She had avoided the file on Kurt Heinrich and did not expect to find his name here.

"No," she whispered. "He was their interrogator. Of course, I should have known that." She leaned against her folded hands. "Don't you see? It doesn't matter now."

"It does," Benny stated. "Your job is important to you."

"But what if the story is taken to production? If I don't reveal all of this about Kurt Heinrich, I become a greater liar. And what if someone finds out—we had to really search for these, but there will be researchers assigned who might find the exact information. How will I explain if the connection is made? I've had enough. I'm going to bed."

She had to get away from their concern and the tumultuous feelings that moved through her with Stefan in her cottage, becoming fast friends with Benny, and her grandfather's files sitting on her coffee table. Her room would be a refuge from them, even for a few minutes. Hemingway scratched on the door and she let him inside, then went straight to bed without taking off her makeup or even brushing her teeth.

⋯⊶◉⊷⋯

"Wake up." Benny was shaking Amanda against her pillow. "Come on. You look terrible and need a shower. You don't want to be late."

"Benny, leave me alone."

"Up you go." He tugged her to a sitting position. Amanda realized she was still in the clothes she'd worn the day before. The clock read 6:45 A.M.

"I've hardly slept in the last—I don't know how many days."

"You can't just ignore this. You'll go in to work and tell them that the story isn't worth pursuing or that for personal reasons, you need to can it. Then come home and sleep. But I won't let you pull a Benny. You *will* be there and face this—and someday you will thank me."

Amanda grumbled and tried to lie back down, but Benny started jumping on her bed. Stefan chuckled from the doorway.

"Come on, Stefan; let's get her awake."

Stefan ran and jumped on the bed beside Benny, both men bouncing around her.

"The two of you are in cahoots!" She leaped up and hurried to the bathroom, hoping Stefan didn't get a good look at her in such an awful morning condition.

Within an hour, Benny had called a cab, Stefan was handing her a cup of coffee at the door, and she was leaving her house.

"Will you be here when I get back?" she asked Stefan.

"Unless you want me to leave."

She shook her head and he smiled. "I'll see you later then."

⋯⇒◉⇐⋯

Tiffany was waiting by the elevator. "I'm so glad you're here."

Amanda glanced at her watch. "I'm not late."

"I know, but Sylvia came in early and was in your office when I got here. She said she'd take the presentation disk to the conference room."

"Why?" Amanda stood in the middle of the hallway, stunned.

"She's all nervous about the changes they're making in New York. Wallace is stopping there before his trip to the Caribbean. I thought you'd be here earlier to get things ready."

"I've been up late for days."

"I know and I told that to Sylvia. But she said to meet them in the conference room when you got here. Wallace is in a big hurry to get out of here today."

Amanda hurried down the hallway, stopping only to take a breath. She straightened her black suit jacket and smoothed the white shirt beneath. The clasp on her silver necklace chain had flipped around and she quickly adjusted it.

She walked in with attempted confidence. "Good morning, Wallace. Sylvia."

They were sitting around the table, facing a lowered video screen. One of Wallace's assistants sat beside him, with Sylvia on the other side of the table. Michelle from marketing and Bryan from advertising were waiting there also.

"Glad you could make it," Sylvia said with a cool smile. The clock on the wall said two minutes to eight. Amanda rarely felt intimidated by the long table or the faces that watched her presentations. Unless she came in unprepared. These were no fools. They knew their show, and they were there to rip holes in ideas to see if the structure would hold. Amanda had to pull off her own confidence first—creativity, poise, and a touch of humor. Then she needed the unbreakable story. This time she had the story—a great story—but one she couldn't reveal. She had come to apologize and tell five people that she hadn't done her job, that she was wasting their time. It wouldn't be pretty.

"Good morning," Wallace said, glancing at his watch. "I apologize but I have ten minutes tops before I head to the airport."

"We already watched your presentation," Sylvia said from her seat, setting the remote control on the table. The presentation had been arranged to show photographs with her voice-overs, but the element needed for an actual program was missing.

"You already watched it?" Amanda paused as she walked to the end of the table, setting her satchel on the chair. She told herself to remain calm. "I was hoping to—"

"I think you have an interesting story," Wallace said, "but I have some concerns. It's just not there for History. You can take it to Fine Arts or Women Today channels. We don't compete with affiliated channels, and I think they'll be interested."

"I wanted to keep it here," Sylvia said. "Amanda and I will lose all creative influence. They'll take it and run."

"Your names, both of yours, will be in the credits."

"Not enough. Amanda has been working under me on this project from its conception."

Wallace pushed back in his chair. "This isn't debatable. You haven't hit our demographics. Sylvia, you've been here too long not to know that."

Sitting down, Amanda felt relief. The story wouldn't go. The History Network's demographics were males ages thirty and up. Advertising targeted these viewers with sports car, SUV, and men's clothing commercials. Most of the shows were war related, which had saved the History Network by playing into their viewers' interests—facts, blood, battle. In fact, Amanda had gone into this story of the Empress Brooch concerned as to whether it would be compelling for the demographics.

"And that is why we kept the best angle for last." Sylvia rose from her chair, dropping a manila file on the table. It was like any other file that could be found in every office on the fourth floor that comprised the History Network West Coast. But Amanda suddenly knew it hadn't come from just any office. It had come from hers.

Amanda stared at Sylvia, unable to sit or move, too stunned to speak.

"She's too humble. Amanda uncovered the link in the entire story that will make it perhaps an award winner—if only we could find that brooch it would be guaranteed. But this is almost as great."

"What is it?" Wallace pulled his chair back up to the table. "Amanda?"

"I'll let Sylvia explain," Amanda said warily.

Sylvia opened the file, withdrawing a photograph. "I printed out a great photo from our own archives. His name is Kurt Heinrich—an officer in the Nazi regime."

Amanda stared at the head shot of Kurt Heinrich in full SS uniform. She felt her stomach knot and her face flush. What should she do? She wanted to grab the photo and run or confess everything.

Sylvia explained the life of Amanda's grandfather. "Kurt Heinrich became obsessed with finding the brooch, and that obsession led to the deaths of many Lange family members. He never found it and committed suicide to avoid arrest in 1945, soon after the war."

"Good. Very good," Wallace said, picking up the photograph of Amanda's uniformed grandfather. "This changes things."

Someone knocked on the door. Tiffany peered inside and motioned for Amanda.

"Can it wait just a minute?" Amanda asked, glancing at the others watching them.

"I think you'll want to hear this," she said with a smile.

"Then tell all of us, Tiffany." Sylvia gestured her inside. "You are part of this team and you should also be in here."

"I just had a phone call from one of our current-affairs researchers. He discovered a link in our story. It could be like the modern-day man obsessed by the brooch."

"What modern-day man?"

"Richter Hauer—remember he was trying to get the Empress Brooch from that Darby Collins lady, though I think her name was Darby Evans then 'cause she wasn't married yet. He threatened and kidnapped her, then escaped. He was just arrested at the U.S.–Canadian border in Idaho."

"Great, this guy can parallel our Nazi from WWII. Maybe something along the lines of two men obsessed . . . I don't know. You all work this out." Wallace rose from his chair.

"I apologize for the deadline I gave you. Michelle, Bryan, any objections or concerns?"

"Some things to work out, but I think it'll go," Bryan said.

Michelle added her input, but Wallace was already bidding good-bye.

"I'm leaving for vacation. I'll check my e-mail only twice daily and I'd like to be kept in this, along with the other three programs we're working on. And . . . no, I'm just leaving. You are all competent, and I'm going to think white sand and my wife in a bikini, who is threatening to toss all electronic devices once we arrive. Ciao."

Amanda watched Wallace leave and the others follow. They congratulated her on a nice video presentation but especially for uncovering the Nazi. Amanda tried to smile and act natural.

Sylvia spoke as she passed. "That was too close, Amanda."

Amanda's hands shook. The photo of her grandfather remained on the table, his eyes staring at the ceiling.

"Sylvia, you went into my office and went through my files—"

"Wait a moment. I just saved you. I told you to be ready and you weren't. I couldn't believe you didn't have that information about the Nazi in with the presentation. That's what sold it to Wallace, and you almost lost that chance for us. You know what it takes around here to sell a story. It wasn't that you didn't have the key element; you had it right on your desk."

Sylvia would have launched into a tirade, but Amanda stood suddenly, the chair falling with a crash to the floor. "I don't need this right now, okay?" she said.

Tiffany stared, obviously surprised.

"Okay." Sylvia tried to pacify her. "Just next time have all the information together so I don't have to pick up your slack. But it was a good discovery."

Sylvia headed for the door and motioned for Tiffany to

follow. She began discussing a woman's role in the corporate world, telling her to spit out her gum as they exited the conference room.

The door closed, and Amanda stayed behind in the windowed conference room. The sun was rising over the city on a clear, blue morning. Anger pulsed through her as she leaned on the table—frustrating anger that had no place to go. And fear came with it. Fear of what lay ahead. She had no choice now. It had been decided for her. Amanda must tell her father. He had a doctor's appointment at the end of the week, so she'd wait until those results came in. And somehow she wouldn't let this destroy them. She'd find some way to fight it, work through it, move on. Somehow.

For now, Amanda knew what she had to do—get some answers. Why did Aunt Helga lie to the family? That was easy—she wanted to protect them from a truth that was hiding in wait until the perfect time to attack.

Who were Uncle Martin's parents, and what had happened to them?

What was the deeper story behind Kurt and Hilde Heinrich?

She'd begin with her research files and Aunt Helga's steamer trunk. If she had to, she'd return to Europe to find the answers. It wasn't enough for her to know her grandfather's crimes. She needed to know him. Then Amanda would tell her father.

CHAPTER TWENTY-ONE

Sender: JaniceT@albanycitinet.com
Recipient: MsD@oakdalenet.com
Subject: I did it!

My dear Ms. Delsig,
Guess what? I went to the mall! Can you believe it? It was even my idea! I did let out one scream when a cashier forgot to remove the alarm tag on this lady's purchase, but the rest of it went great. It was really fun, like watching TV but being there. I can't thank you enough for believing in me all of these years. I really look up to you and miss you a lot.

Love and hugs and new adventures,
Janice

Ms. Delsig printed out the e-mail and held it against her chest. Janice had done it—she'd really faced her greatest fear and conquered it. It was late evening and Ms. Delsig was alone in the resource room. Alone and full of peace.

Alfred was still in ICU after heart surgery. They had great hope for a full recovery—he might be back at Oakdale within a month. Soon she hoped to see him and perhaps even tell him that she wanted to marry him. God had heard her many prayers for Alfred, and even if she lost him, she felt a closeness with God that she hadn't felt in a long, long time.

And now she was going to face her own greatest fear. *If Janice can go to the mall . . . I can do this too.*

Later Lilly came in and helped her with the computer to find the phone number in Salzburg. Ms. Delsig went to bed with two printouts in her hand—Janice's and the number in Austria. She waited the hours until late that night, then shuffled past Lilly's snoring form and down to the lobby telephone.

It took a while to go through the series of numbers and begin to hear the dialing. She imagined her voice zipping through the line to the city of Salzburg, a city where she once spent her childhood summers. Not far from the city was a village she had loved. Ms. Delsig remembered those times with her parents and brother and later with baby Hani. Much of the summer was spent with her parents' closest friends—the Lange family. Ms. Delsig's family had split their time between the city and the village where the Langes lived. She had been Brigit Kirke then, a girl full of dreams, a girl untouched by the coming war that would destroy her peaceful life.

A woman answered the phone in German.

It stunned Ms. Delsig to hear the language. "Uh, uh, English please."

"Certainly. This is the Austrian Holocaust Survivors' Organization."

"Thank you. I live in Florida, USA, and would like to speak with Darby Evans Collins about getting my survivor testimony on tape—they do that service now, I read."

"Yes, they do. But I am sorry, she is unavailable at this time. I take a message, *bitte?*"

"No, I must speak with her right away."

"Herr and Frau Collins will leave for America in few days,"

the woman said. "But they are going to West Coast. We do have contact with great interviewer in Florida."

"No. It has to be Frau Darby Collins. Please, it also involves some information about her family."

The woman paused. "One moment, *bitte*."

Ms. Delsig waited a short time before someone picked up the line.

"Hello, this is Darby Collins. Can I help you?"

"My name is Ms. Brigit Delsig, but before the war, my last name was Kirke. I want to have my story taped for the Holocaust archive. But I also would like to meet you. I read about what happened to you. And I knew your grandmother in Austria many years ago. I knew your grandmother Celia Lange and her best friend, Tatianna Hoffman. My family was the Kirke family—we were very close with the Langes."

The woman hesitated. "I think I remember my grandmother speaking of your family. Please, Ms. Brigit Delsig, tell me about yourself. I did not know any of the Kirke family survived the war."

"Only one did," she said softly. "I am the only one."

⋰⟴⟵⋱

Amanda left work early, citing a headache—much to Tiffany's amazement.

"Are you going to be okay? You didn't even clean your office—I'll do it for you."

"No. Leave it. I'll get an early start tomorrow."

Later Amanda entered the back courtyard to find Stefan talking with Mr. Winifred in the garden. Stefan was leaning over a large, flowering plant, the sun bright upon his ash-blond hair, as Mr. Winifred explained something in the root system. Brushing off dirt from his hands, he turned his head toward Amanda, apparently trying to gauge how the meeting went.

"We're doing the program." Amanda felt as if her face were frozen in a blank expression. "Good morning, Mr. Winifred."

"Morning, Amanda."

"Why don't you get some sleep," Stefan said, taking her bag from her arm. He had a smudge of dirt on his cheek that she felt compelled to wipe off and then touch along his jaw and rest her head against his chest. And yet another part of her felt strange in his presence, with his knowing her family's past. She blinked away her tired stare.

"Come on," he said, taking her hand.

"Stay here with Mr. Winifred. Finish your tour," she said. "Will you be here when I wake up?"

"Do you want me to be?" he asked with a smile.

She nodded, went inside, and made a straight path to her bed. There was no way she'd actually sleep—not with the million thoughts buzzing in her head. Stefan was outside her cottage—Stefan. He knew everything and they hadn't talked about it at all. Everything was up in the air; her life had never been in such unresolved shambles. It would take too many sticky notes to make some semblance of her thoughts.

⋯⫷◉⫸⋯

Hours later, Amanda awoke to evening. She smelled something good in the kitchen and stumbled out in her wrinkled white blouse and black pants. "What smells wonderful?" she asked.

"Grilled cheese, fried eggplant from Mr. Winifred's garden, and tomato soup," Stefan said with a smile. "Nothing spectacular."

"Thanks, Stefan."

"I didn't answer your phone—but you had some messages."

"Let me guess. My father, my mother, and Benny?"

"Exactly."

"I need to go see my uncle tonight. You could help me translate if anything is in Czech. Would you come with me?"

"Sure."

"I still can't believe you are here," Amanda said in a bit of wonder. He looked up and turned off the stove. "How long are you staying?"

"I was supposed to go to Guatemala tomorrow, but I'm changing those plans."

"Why?"

"Well, it depends on how long you want me in San Francisco."

"It depends on how long you want to stay. I have an empty couch."

"Actually, I was going to a friend's house tonight."

"You have a friend here?"

"Benny."

Amanda blinked. "Benny. You're staying with Benny tonight? What—you don't trust yourself here with me alone?"

He looked at her steadily. "No, I don't."

Amanda didn't quite know how to respond. She knew Stefan had strong beliefs, values, morals—she understood that. But he was struggling with those, is that what he meant? He had hardly even kissed her and yet there was this powerful connection between them—it was stronger than anything she'd felt before.

"Amanda." He said her name softly and with the slightest accent. He walked toward her and took her hands in his own. "Amanda, we need to talk."

"I can't right now. Please. Let me find out what is at my uncle's house. Then . . . then we'll talk."

Later they stood in front of the black steamer trunk. Amanda had seen it many times in the corner of Uncle Martin's living room over the last few years. He'd put books and a CD player on top of it; it had been just another piece of furniture. Yet all along it held their family secrets inside.

Uncle Martin didn't want to open it, but it had stayed closed long enough. Stefan helped remove the CD player and the books.

Uncle Martin took a deep breath. "Amanda, I want you to understand. It was hard for me growing up with the story of parents killed in Lidice. Your father seemed to accept it, and he used it for good—listening to Mr. Lev's stories and helping people. I just wanted to be a normal child. I wanted a mother and father, not an aunt and uncle, and I wanted to live in a little house with a yard and my own dog in the back. Your father loved to talk to the old people who would come by. Those people scared me with the things they'd seen and gone through. In the summer I'd get on my bike in the morning and often stay away until dark. I hope you understand why I don't want to be here for this great unveiling. I will have to know, but I just can't stay for this."

"That's all right, Uncle Martin. Come back when you're ready."

"Thank you." He bent down and kissed her cheek. "Nice to meet you, Stefan. Would either of you like me to pick up a sandwich at Angelina's? Best grub on the North Bay."

"Stefan cooked for us already," she said.

Uncle Martin nodded as if impressed. "Sounds like a keeper," he said with a wink as he put on his golf hat and grabbed a jacket.

"Great meeting you, Martin," Stefan said.

Amanda was already trying to pull the large steamer trunk away from the wall before Uncle Martin closed the door. Dust had accumulated between the wall and along the top where the books and stereo had sat. Stefan took the other side. Together they stood it up on end and unclasped the locks.

"This belonged to your great-aunt?"

"Yes."

The trunk opened in half. One side had an area for hanging clothing and storing shoes with a single drawer beneath; the other side had three drawers of faded green fabric over thick cardboard. It smelled like mothballs and old papers.

"They had to make it as light as possible for the journey overseas," Amanda said, poking the inner dividers. "Let's see what she has in here."

The top drawers were filled with old cards, loose photographs, theater ticket stubs, children's drawings, and school papers from her father and uncle. She found one picture of a little girl jumping rope beneath a smiling sun that read in a child's handwriting: *To Aunt Helga, Love Amanda.*

At the bottom of the lowest drawer and beneath crocheted doilies and embroidered dish towels, Amanda found a stack of letters wrapped in two large rubber bands.

Neither of them spoke as she pulled the rubber bands away from the worn edges and yellowed areas. The envelopes had been stuck together so long they snapped apart when separated. Amanda lined up five letters in a row on the coffee table.

Four of the letters were dated 1937, 1940, 1943, 1945; the fifth was undated. All were addressed to Mrs. Helga Rivans in San Francisco, California, USA. The first return address read *Hilde Schmitz.* The rest were from Frau Hilde Heinrich.

Amanda leaned forward, pinching her temples. This was real. Amanda stared at the letters again, as if they might disappear without warning.

Opening the first letter, Amanda found it written in Czech. "So at least it is true that we are German Czechs, I suppose. Will you read it to me?"

Stefan took the letter and pointed to the line he was translating. "She writes to her dear sister Helga. She has a new job as a government secretary—a very good job, she says. She misses

Helga and wishes she had not left with her husband to go to America. But she understands. If she found love, she too would go across the world for him. This part here is talking about a new dress she bought with matching hat and shoes. Money from her first paycheck. And then she closes with much love and says that someday they will go shopping together, perhaps in Paris or Rome or New York."

"A sweet letter from one sister to the other." Amanda opened the next one dated three years later. She could tell that Hilde was married now by the return address, and this letter was written in German. Amanda laid it out so they both could read it and translate it into English.

> *Greetings Helga,*
>
> *How are you? I am as good as can be expected. It is diffi-cult bringing a child into the world at such a time as war. But I hold my little Henri in my arms and sing him songs of happier times. We are not suffering at all, of course. Prague is hardly changed. Yet I do allow my worries at times. I apologize if my last letter sounded as such. Winter always gets me down, but now spring has come and I will begin to grow my flowers once again.*
>
> *Your last letter showed your concern for us—I am sure my complaints did not help. But I could not have found a better man than Kurt. He is so passionate about his beliefs and his love for me. You should see what a wonderful father he is. I know you and Hans do not agree with our politics. I would not have agreed if not for finding the truth. Someday we will discuss it, but we will never let it divide us as sisters.*
>
> *How I wish you could see my sweet Henri. He is walking now, though a little wobbly. What a wonderful smile—much like his father's, though his eyes are certainly my own dark hazel color.*
>
> *Kurt and I wish to have more children immediately. We*

believe it our duty to bring more beautiful children into the world. But the doctor has given us tragic news after losing the baby. I am not able to have another child. Kurt tells me not to worry. We have one son to carry on our name. But it does hurt. I should not say such things to you as I know you and Hans have also wanted a child of your own. Please forgive my foolish ways.

Someday we will shop in Paris.

Always,

Hilde

Amanda immediately opened the next letter. It was dated 2 January 1943.

My sister,

I hope this letter reaches you.

It has been terrible times since the awful death of Reich Protectorate Reinhard Heydrich. I could not write; Kurt forbade it. We have censors, of course, and it does not look good for an officer of his position to have his wife writing letters to our enemy nation. Please forgive me that I cannot write often now. This letter will reach you only if my closest friend, the kind wife of a Prague businessman, is able to mail it from their trip to Switzerland. I would not dare trust the wives of the other officers. Trust is difficult to find in these precarious days.

I want you to know that you are an aunt again. We have adopted a handsome young boy. His parents were enemies of the state, living in a village outside of Prague. I am so thankful the Reich sees fit to put children of Aryan appearance into the care of a good German family such as ours. He looks like a pure German, not any Slovak markings that I can tell. Henri is already fascinated by him. He soon will become happy in our home, I am certain.

This must be short. We are all well and safe and much

> *calmer now that those assassins have been caught and*
> *executed. The citizens here are afraid to look us in the eyes*
> *now—I think nothing like this will happen again. I hope you*
> *can be happy for us as now we are a family of four. Kurt*
> *seems very pleased and his position has advanced remark-*
> *ably in such a short time.*
>
> *Someday, my sister. Someday.*
> *Hilde*

"What is this?" Stefan said as a folded-up newspaper clipping fell to the floor.

"It's an article from the *San Francisco Chronicle* about the Lidice massacre. I imagine this means Uncle Martin's family was from there. Perhaps Aunt Helga told part of a truth when she mentioned the village of Lidice."

"I think that is a good assumption."

Amanda wondered how this would affect her uncle. The brother unable to process his family being murdered in Lidice was the brother whose family was killed there. Then he was taken to a strange home where the woman looked at him for any "Slovak markings."

The letter without a date or postmark on the envelope had been stuck to the back of the next letter. It simply read *Helga Rivans*.

> *Sister,*
> *I can never thank you enough for agreeing to take the*
> *children. I would not want anyone but you to have them at*
> *this time. Some believe the war will end soon, those shame-*
> *ful ones who have lost faith. It is strange to write such things*
> *when you are most likely hoping for the loss of our side. But*
> *I believe the war will continue and the tide will turn back in*
> *our favor once again. You do not understand, I know. You*
> *left before this began and only heard, and still hear, of the*
> *evil of our cause. I will not deny that horrible things have*

occurred, but it is the terrible loss for a fine and wonderful future. There is nobility and honor and this is a righteous cause—I believe that with all of my heart. I want you to understand me just a little.

My boys will need you for just a little while. Kurt does not yet know that the boys are with you. He is gone again to Austria and Germany for months at a time now, instead of the shorter trips he made before. He will be angry, but I believe he will soon understand. I beg of you, my sister, to care for my boys as I would care for them. Speak German to them and only a little English. I believe within the year we will be ready for them to return home to us. Once Kurt recovers that old brooch, everything will be good again, he will want to be home, and the war will be in a better place. I believe these things, and I know I will hold my boys again.

Someday,

Hilde

Amanda read the line about the old brooch several times to herself, then went immediately to the final letter without speaking.

9 May 1945

My sister,

This may never reach you. The war is over and everyone is fearful. Many have been executed, others have killed themselves, and I await that fateful knock on my own door. Kurt has been gone for months now, and I do not believe he will be back. He was so angry that I had sent the boys to you. I thought he might kill me. I have hardly seen him in the year since. His obsession with finding that Austrian brooch puzzles and frightens me. He says it is the only redemption he can find. It is all he would talk about except that I had sent our children to the den of the enemy. Well, now I see that I was right. Conditions are very difficult and I

*would not want my boys here. They are safe—that is all that
matters. I hope they will always know that I loved them. I
hope to be with them again, but it just does not seem possible
anymore. Please love them as I have loved them. Tell them
whatever you believe is best for them to have a good life in
America. Teach them English and take away the past that
will only tarnish their lives.*

*My arms ache to hold them again. Please forgive me for
everything. I have loved you, my dear older sister, and
admired you all my life.*

Always,

Hilde

"And she died that same month," Amanda said.

"What's amazing is that she sounds like a wonderful
person." Stefan settled back against the couch.

"Frightening, isn't it? She was married to a top Nazi, and I
actually kind of feel for her." Amanda folded the letters carefully.

"It shows the real people who were blinded by visions of
grandeur and allowed themselves to destroy others for their
own advancement."

"Well, it's a lot more than I had before. I'll have to ask Uncle
Martin if there are other things he found belonging to Aunt
Helga."

Through a further search inside the steamer trunk, they
found her father's and uncle's immigration papers that stated
they were brothers, photographs of them as young boys, two
worn baby blankets, and dried, pressed flowers in a book of
German prayers. Amanda soon felt a return of her headache,
and a thick wave of fatigue washed over her. She watched
Stefan carefully turn through the prayer book. Again, the
conflict surfaced within her—she wanted him here, yet she felt
a sudden fear—or was it knowledge—that there was no way

their pathways could stay together. Now, even more than ever, they had nothing but a mixed-up mess of feelings to keep them together.

"I'm ready to go. Are you?" she said, rubbing her head and looking away when he met her eyes.

"I'm with you. Your wish is my command."

Her eyes filled with tears. "My father says that."

"I'd like to meet your father." Stefan closed the steamer trunk.

She rose slowly and gathered her grandmother's letters. "Yes, perhaps," she said, but now she didn't believe it would ever happen.

⊷⊛⊷

They parked outside Benny's apartment complex on the summit of a San Francisco street. The lights of the city glowed and twinkled down the hill and around them. Stefan's duffel bag was in the backseat. They didn't speak as she turned off the engine.

"Did Benny actually make it to class this morning?" she asked. It was strange to ask Stefan about Benny's day.

"Yes, but when he called at lunch, he said he'd fallen asleep during a test and awoken to about ten spitballs in his hair."

Amanda smiled at the thought of teenagers doing exactly what Benny undoubtedly had done in high school.

"Tell me what you are supposed to do in Guatemala."

"Some missionaries are sick and they need someone to take over. But I'm calling my director in Amsterdam tonight to tell him I'm not going."

"You have a bigger mess here. Is that it?" Her voice was tired.

"No. I want to be here, and you still owe me a night to get some crème brûlée."

"It must bother you. We came together because of our similar backgrounds—my family from Prague and the Nazi atrocities against them, just like your family."

"We came together because I couldn't stop myself from getting in line behind you at that vendor in Paris."

"And I dropped my purse." A tear fell down her cheek.

"And you dropped your purse." He reached for her hands. "I haven't been completely honest with you. I want you to understand me. You need to know that my beliefs are not separate from who I am—I am what I believe. God isn't a religion to me. I don't want shared religions or for you to feel like you must convert so we can raise our children the same. I want us to share faith in Christ and discover the amazing things he can do in our lives."

He was trying to make her understand, but it was too much, too great and lofty for her to make sense of. There was fire in his eyes as he spoke, and all she wanted was to run from it, to get away and hide from what he might perceive in her. What past was living inside her, ready to crawl out?

"I can't even comprehend this right now. Please. I have so many decisions to make and it's only complicated by your presence. I have this mess now, and I just need to get through it. I've spent my adult life pursuing histories and pasts. Now I discover this about mine. And I have to find the strength to tell my father."

"The past doesn't matter. You don't have to do this alone."

"It matters to me. And sometimes I do have to do things alone—this is one of them. I think you should go to Guatemala and do what you're called to do. It will give me time to sort this out."

"Are you serious, Amanda? You want me to leave?"

"Stefan, this is something I must face alone. I know you pray for me, so don't stop. If I ever needed it, I need it now."

She saw the pain in his eyes. It went deeper than she'd expected, and Amanda believed he hurt as much as she did.

Perhaps she should take it all back. But he'd become so important to her, too important. She didn't want life without him, yet she feared if she didn't get out now, she'd never survive. She felt tainted somehow, as if every area of her life from childhood to the present was a lie, and she needed to sift through and see if there were any truths to be recovered.

"Stefan, this is the hardest—"

"Don't say it. Don't say, 'This is the hardest thing I've ever done. Let's be friends and stay in touch. You'll always mean a lot to me.' Don't say those words, Amanda. I'm leaving. I have a flight in the morning that I was going to change, so if you change your mind . . . otherwise, just say good-bye."

He opened the car door and grabbed his bag from the backseat. One last look, then he was gone.

"Good-bye," she whispered.

CHAPTER TWENTY-TWO

H

er cottage was cold, but Amanda didn't put a blanket over herself as she sat on her couch in the darkness. She could call Stefan. It wasn't too late. But in a way it was.

She finally listened to her messages and heard her father say, "I need to talk to you about something." A terrible thought popped into her mind as she grabbed the phone in panic: Had he gone to the doctor early and gotten the results?

"I thought you'd gone off on some trip you forgot to tell me about." Her father's voice was calm and cheerful as usual. The last of his cold had left.

"Dad, I'm really sorry. It's been so busy—" She stopped. One of her promises during his illness was that she'd never be too busy to call him. She was using the old line, but it wasn't exactly the truth. Avoidance—she was afraid to face him with all she knew and couldn't tell. "Sorry, Dad."

"It's all right, honey."

"Are you okay? Did something happen?"

"It isn't health related. It's your mother."

"Oh. Her."

"She'd like us to attend her reading in a few weeks. And she's decided to move back."

"Wonderful," she said sarcastically.

"Amanda." The father tone again.

"Sorry."

"But this is what I wanted to discuss with you because I don't want you to flip out or anything. Maybe we should have dinner."

"I can't. I have to get to the office. You can't just tell me? Me, flip out?"

"Well, it's just that your mom is spending all her money moving out here and—"

"You aren't loaning her money, are you?"

"No. She's going to stay with me for a month or so until she gets on her feet."

"Dad, you can't let her—no way!"

"I knew you'd flip out."

"I'm not. I'm not flipping out. Well, maybe a little. But, Dad—"

"Listen to me. I didn't want to say it this way but, Amanda, I am making this decision and you don't need to protect me from your mother. I'm well aware of our past, and I don't want to be used again. But I also don't mind helping her for a while. I've helped a lot of strangers in my life, so I should help my ex-wife and the mother of my child."

"So this isn't a discussion?"

"Sorry, honey. Dad can handle it."

Amanda stared at the phone for a long time after hanging up. He didn't know just how much he needed her protection right now. But Amanda couldn't do it all. Her mother had won this round while Amanda was preoccupied. Once she finished her work, she'd make sure to talk to the woman.

For the next few days, Amanda poured herself into her job. She worked with Tiffany and two researchers on the production of "In Search of the Empress Brooch," while also digging up more information on her grandfather. She tried to keep all thoughts of Stefan and her parents behind her, but she'd find herself staring off and remembering or wondering if she'd made a huge mistake. Stefan would be gone by now. Benny had dropped him off at the airport. Suddenly she noticed Central American things all around her—from magazine advertisements to a new intern who'd come from Nicaragua. On a large framed map of the world in the History Network foyer, she found the small country of Guatemala and wondered where Stefan was located and for how long. At every pause, she ached with missing him. But then she forced herself back to work.

Which archival films and photographs should be inserted and at which precise moment? What music would fit the era, culture, and class of each segment just right? Much like poetry or music, Amanda's work was the perfect combination of a story told to the beat and rhythm of sound bites, commercial interruption, and spoken testimonies.

Late hours—when the offices had closed down and the comforting sounds of vacuums and cleaning were the only noises around her—were Amanda's favorite times to work. Research was more than her job; it was her love. She searched for clues in testimonies from the Nuremberg trials and from recently opened files of the CIA, German government, and other countries around the world. On-line auctions and advertisements offered German uniforms, SS handbooks, photographs, written journals. A search engine could provide thousands of sites to visit. Anything might uncover a piece of the puzzle. Amanda knew many tricks, but the amount of information was huge and one person could easily be lost in it.

For most of the week she shut herself inside her office and her house, taking trips to the library and antique bookstores. She called her father every night, and much to her chagrin, her mother was already staying in his extra room. Sometimes Patricia answered the phone and Amanda spoke with her for a few minutes. Amanda buried everything beneath the discipline of reaching her goal. But research always left its mark. The testimonies and photographs were more scars added to her memory. And now she carried the additional guilt that her grandfather was one of the men who had inflicted such pain.

A week later, she thought she'd feel better about Stefan. She didn't. But she'd compiled a rough journey of her grandfather's life. After decades of silence, Amanda was about to meet Kurt Heinrich for the first time.

⊶═◉═⊷

Why do I do what I don't want to do? Stefan remembered the apostle Paul saying the words that he found himself praying again and again. He'd told himself he'd never, ever fall in love with someone who didn't share his faith. And yet, over the years of dating and even a few times considering if he'd met the "one," he'd never felt the way he did for Amanda.

He expected his work at the Guatemalan village would keep his thoughts away from her. Several family members were already recovering, but there was a lot of work still to be done. A major spring in the area, the main source of water into the village, was drying up, so Stefan and some villagers had hiked through the dense, tropical growth to find the problem. It had taken two days in the jungle to find the spring and remove the rocks that had fallen over the mouth, diverting the water. Back at the missionary huts, he worked long days and then would lie awake at night beneath the mosquito netting, unable to find peace. He thought of Prague and wondered again if he should return home.

Amanda was foremost in his thoughts. He should have called one last time before leaving the States. She was struggling and he should not have let his bruised pride stop him. The thoughts kept him tossing and turning until dawn.

A young man who had recently returned to his native village from seminary sat beside Stefan at breakfast one morning. Emilio was known as Smiley because of the joy that characterized his life.

"You pray when you not sleep," Emilio said.

"Am I keeping you awake at night?" Stefan asked Emilio. He hadn't noticed anyone else awake in the bunkhouse.

"No, but I notice you no sleep. You pray."

Stefan nodded, and they began discussing the plans for the day. But he knew Emilio had touched on his problem. He wasn't praying. He hadn't been praying much in the last many weeks. Instead, he'd been trying to sort out his life and the lives of those around him all on his own. It wasn't working very well. Stefan felt sick to his stomach when he looked at his breakfast, so he quickly got up from the table and started working.

Why do I forget to do what I know to do?

That night when he couldn't sleep, Stefan got out of his bunk and went outside. Beneath the clear, brilliant sky, he tried to pray. He knew why he'd avoided God. It meant surrender. And Stefan feared surrendering Amanda to God—he didn't want to let her go, not even to the Lord Almighty whom he'd served for so many years. He went back to bed.

Stefan still couldn't sleep. It felt like a million pebbles were stuck in the back of his throat. The world moved around him in a great swirl that wouldn't stop. Feeling sick, he jumped from the bed. Barely outside the door he began retching, but his stomach was empty. Later he heard shouting and lights. Someone was shaking him, and he couldn't wake up.

"Get him to the hospital. He has it. Stefan! Stefan, can you hear me?"

"Stefan!" someone else called into his face.

Stefan tried to respond, but his mouth wouldn't open. And though he moved his arm, he didn't see it reach for Emilio as it should have. Then he drifted to places he'd gone before . . . to an African mountain and the familiar streets of Prague. He saw Amanda sleeping in her bed and called to her, but she didn't move. He opened his eyes and saw a bright glow at the end of his bed. It was a man in white, a man who looked like the sketches of Jan Hus he'd seen. Stefan's mind recited the facts of Jan Hus' life as if a liturgy. A hundred years before Martin Luther led the Reformation, Jan Hus had been a reformer in the Czech lands. He was one of Prague's great historical figures. And yet he had once been only a man, someone like himself.

"Jan, what are you doing here?" Stefan asked wearily.

"Remember, Stefan, what you are to do," the figure said.

Then the image was gone, and Stefan was reaching for the space where the white glow faded away. Time was passing, he knew. He realized it by the glimpses of people who came and went, the injections he felt, the darkness and light of the room.

It was at first light on a day he didn't know that Stefan, exhausted and aching, woke up with his head beginning to clear. The roof of the outdoor hospital came into focus and Stefan knew what had happened. He had been sick, but also he'd finished his wrestling with God. In a way he'd spent the last few years running from his calling. He'd been doing good things, great works in the eyes of men. He could fill his life with them.

Through his foggy thoughts, Stefan recalled a missionary couple who were returning to the United States to take over a coffeehouse in their hometown. And he'd never forget what they told him: *"We fill our lives with good works. But God calls us to be close to him—that comes before everything else."*

He tried to sit up but the room began to swim. With his head against the pillow, Stefan prayed: "My life will be in you . . . not in my work or my desires. I'm letting her go, Father. I pray that you would bless her and guide her. Hold her close to you and let her see who you are. With everything in me, every-thing I have left, I pray for Amanda. I let her go into your care. She is yours and not mine. If you want us together, bring her back."

CHAPTER TWENTY-THREE

Darby Collins and her husband, Brant, arrived at Oakdale within a week of Ms. Delsig's phone call.

In preparation Lilly had ordered a white-carnation corsage for Ms. Delsig's nicest dress. They had done her hair in hot rollers and taken her pearls from the Oakdale safe. All was ready when the couple arrived late morning with their camera equipment.

The man entered first, a handsome young man, and held the door for his wife. Darby had a new shorter haircut than what Ms. Delsig had seen on the Internet—she also had a warm smile that had been missing from the screen images. Darby wore a pretty dress that flowed softly at her knees. She hesitated shyly, then walked quickly toward Ms. Delsig, enveloping her in her arms.

"This is a great gift to meet you," Darby Collins whispered.

Ms. Delsig felt as if she were greeting a long-lost friend. There were tears in Darby's eyes, and Ms. Delsig found there were tears in her own. She couldn't understand the emotion; it was unexpected. And yet as she held the young woman tightly, she realized that Darby was the first living link to her family and childhood that she'd met since the war. Her lip quivered and her body began to shake. Not since that night so long ago, that dark night when Edgar had told her to go and she saw the outline of him in the darkness . . . not since that moment decades ago had she touched someone connected to that person she had been.

Ms. Delsig was unsure how long Darby held her, for she had begun to cry. She was overwhelmed with the grief of lives long lost, lives she'd buried within herself and who now rose to be loved once again.

"Why? Why am I doing this?" she muttered, wiping away tears that overflowed her hands. The powder she'd applied so carefully was washed away.

"It's okay. I understand," Darby said. "I found my grandfather and I didn't even know I had a grandfather. I was a mess."

"Thank you so much for coming."

Mr. Barlett appeared and softly cleared his throat to get their attention. "Please, we've prepared the entertainment room for your use today." His voice actually portrayed concern. He led the way a little too quickly, making Ms. Delsig feel like her walker was even slower than usual. Darby walked with her hand beneath Ms. Delsig's arm. Her touch felt good and comforting in the strangest way. She wondered if it was what a grandmother felt when touched by one of her own.

They entered the empty room that was usually filled with the TV watchers who enjoyed *Good Morning America* over coffee. Ms. Delsig realized that Mr. Bartlett had gone to a lot of effort once she'd announced that the taping people would be arriving. Dr. Matthews was in the room also. Introductions were made all around. Lilly stayed close by, acting as a miniature bodyguard.

Ms. Delsig stared at the young woman, examining her for

Lange family features. The shape of her chin and fine lips reminded her of the Langes. "I remember your grandmother playing with me—she was older than I was and very nice, though I believe I bugged her after a while. I broke a bottle of her perfume after she told me not to touch it."

"I wish she were alive to meet you," Darby said, "and to know that one of the Kirkes survived. She told me about many of her childhood days in Austria—hiking the Alps, swimming in Lake Hallstatt or Hallstattersee. She said that the Kirkes would come every summer with their younger children."

"Our mothers were neighbors as children. The men met after they were all married and became very good friends. I always looked up to your grandmother and her friend Tatianna. They were both very pretty and I wanted a girlfriend like that. It has taken many years to have a girlfriend." Ms. Delsig smiled, glancing toward Lilly, who was talking with Brant and Dr. Matthews.

"Did you ever meet my grandfather?" Darby queried. "He is alive still, you know. We found each other only recently."

"I did read that in the newspaper on the Internet. But I never met him. My family could not leave Prague to attend their wedding—there were difficulties before the war. We lived in Austria for a time, though we mainly went there for summer visits. My father went to see the Lange family once after the war had begun. That was the last time any of us saw them. I remember my parents were very worried about the family, but then the worries were just beginning." Ms. Delsig studied Darby with great thought. "I also read that you searched for the Lange inheritance—you found some coins but not the Empress Brooch. Do you search any longer?"

Darby folded her hands and rested her chin upon them. "No, we've decided to leave that one alone." Her eyes drifted to the window, then back to Ms. Delsig.

"It is said that a curse surrounds the brooch," Ms. Delsig said softly.

"Do you believe in such things?" Darby asked.

"No, I believe human greed surrounds the brooch. Human greed is more powerful and consuming than a curse. I know that firsthand, and you know it even more fully."

The women stared into each other's eyes. They understood one another in the silent connection of two people crossing generations. Ms. Delsig knew of Darby's search for her grandmother's story and the great danger it had brought her. And she knew Darby had heard enough survivor stories to perceive some of Ms. Delsig's losses.

"I suppose something within me wants to know. I tell myself it is with pure motives. I'd put the brooch in an art museum or the Holocaust Memorial Museum in D.C."

"Interesting," Ms. Delsig commented.

"But then I wonder why I want to find it," Darby continued. "Is it to have what belongs to my family as retribution? But an object can never repay lives. I may want it for some inner greed I don't quite perceive at this point. Perhaps some things are better left undisturbed."

Ms. Delsig smiled softly and nodded.

"Do you feel prepared to start the taping today?" Darby asked.

"Yes, I have my best outfit on," Ms. Delsig replied, primping her collar dramatically.

"Wonderful. I am due in Northern California for an interview of my own and to see my mother—she left Austria a few months ago. All of us have been dividing our time between countries with my grandfather living in Salzburg. He has trouble traveling often, and my mother has her house in California."

"I would like to meet your mother someday—the child of dear Celia." Ms. Delsig sighed as she realized many things. "If

I had not been afraid all these years, I might have met Celia again. There have been so few people from my childhood who survived the war. It would have been good, very good, to see her."

Ms. Delsig watched Brant and Darby, studying how the couple worked together—setting up the equipment, talking quietly, and understanding some things without words. They reminded her of another couple, but who was it? And then she knew. Of course, they recalled memories of her and Josef as they'd been in the beginning.

It was the one time she'd fallen madly in love. It was as if the world could barely be seen beyond one another. She was consumed by the sight of him and he of her. The demons of the past had fled to the background for a short time beneath their intensity. She hadn't thought she could love again after Edgar had died, and this was such a love. After Edgar's death and the discovery that her parents and other family and friends were all dead, gone forever, Brigit's emotions had numbed and died. Until she met Josef. Josef Delsig had lost as she had, yet his father had invested in foreign markets and created safeguards. The family had lost a fortune, but it had been worth many fortunes. Josef said he loved her the instant he saw her. That was at the refugee center where she worked, taking down names of survivors searching for someone, anyone still alive whom they might know. She and Josef had married within a month, and Brigit had believed for the first time that she might be happy forever.

But it couldn't last for them. The demons waited for their time and began coming through the cracks. Human love didn't remain. She wondered if this couple knew that. Did they know that only a divine bond could keep them beyond life and death? Only as her Josef was dying years later—years after they'd shared a bed with nothing between them, years after they'd settled into a comfortable existence—did they remember how they'd once loved and how they'd lost what brought them together. Mere hours before he left her forever, a pastor had sat with them and prayed. And they had both found what could have saved them all those years—the bond that would have kept them as one, the balm that could have soothed the wounds. But it was too late for their life together.

Somehow Ms. Delsig trusted Darby Collins. She so often wanted to believe there was good in man. Yet Darby herself had admitted her hesitance about the brooch. Ms. Delsig knew that if she told such a secret, it would unlock a door without her knowing if good or evil waited behind it. Wasn't it better to simply hide such a key?

❖═◯═❖

The camera had been set up, the lighting in the room adjusted, and photography lights added. Darby and Brant did several tests and then led Ms. Delsig to the couch. For a second she considered attempting an escape. The eye of the camera appeared ominous; her heart and stomach fluttered nervously.

"We will start with just talking," Darby said soothingly. "Brant and I find it's better to just get comfortable in front of the camera as you talk. At some point we'll turn it on and just keep the same pace of you sharing your story. There is no hurry. We can take several days if needed or even come back if you don't feel good about the results."

"All right," Ms. Delsig said, adjusting her cream jacket and the corsage.

"Please start at the beginning."

Ms. Delsig paused, journeying back in time to the girl she had once been. She realized as the testimony taping progressed that it was even more difficult than she had expected. Her partial desire for the taping, other than to tell her story in a lasting way, was to meet Darby Evans Collins and decide what to tell her about the Empress Sissi Brooch. This was much different. Sunlight shone outside. A camera faced her. People heard her story and gazed at her face. They asked questions that she didn't want asked. It was all flooding over her, coming fast in remembered images. She could smell the disease, death, and ashes. Hunger and thirst weighed upon her tongue. Ms. Delsig tried to stay composed, but it was growing inside of her, pressing to get out. The old knot of tension she felt at remembrance had formed as soon as Darby and Brant had arrived. Now she only wanted to make it through to gather her composure once again.

"In July 1942 my parents were arrested. After the death of SS Reich Protectorate Reinhard Heydrich in Prague, every last Jew was terrified. One night it was our door that was pounded upon with orders for my parents to come immediately with the soldiers. My brother had been told to go into hiding if this happened, but he would not leave my grandmother, little sister, or me, except to search for extra food or try to gain information. Then our summons came. Already many Jews had been taken away—that had begun in the fall of 1941. Now it was our turn. Edgar had gone to the forest, where his friends were hiding, to try to find a way to escape out of German-occupied lands. He was gone when we were sent to the cattle cars. There was nothing he could do. I was sixteen years old. I could not believe that I was leaving Prague—for a work camp in Germany, we were told. My parents had been gone for weeks, and my brother would not know what happened. Our summer would not include our usual trip to Salzburg and the Alps."

The camera continued to focus on her, but Ms. Delsig barely noticed it. As the story unfolded, each detail became a domino that knocked down the next one in a wall of secrecy. And she began to recall what had long been covered up.

"People wonder why more people in the camps did not

revolt. The number of camp inmates was vastly greater than the number of guards. Yet after days in a hot cattle car, pressed together with the dying and the dead, with human feces and urine at your feet—oh, if you could see what I see. . . . Then we arrived at the camp to guns, beatings, fear you cannot imagine. Fear is a mighty force, much greater than weapons. And we still had hope then, that it would get better. Who would guess that it could get worse?"

"Please explain your rescue at the end of the war."

"Okay. Well, let me see."

"An American soldier found you, correct?"

"Yes. It was a miracle, he said."

"What did you do after you healed?"

"The war had been over for months. I worked at a refugee camp, helping survivors and refugees locate family members. During that time, I was trying to find out about my parents. I knew my brother was dead. I had even told some soldiers and they recovered his body.

"While working at the camp, I listened to story after story. I heard about mothers who had seen their children taken to be gassed, young people who survived by hiding in the woods eating potatoes, roots, bark—anything to survive. I heard of entire families wiped out, husbands searching for wives. Every story imaginable and beyond belief was told to me as I helped compile names and origins for circulation throughout Europe. Oh, the stories. It became too much for me."

"Because you'd been there yourself," Darby interjected.

"Yes, I had been at the camps."

Ms. Delsig realized her hand had involuntarily moved to cover the tattoo on her arm. "I was on a death march. Miles and miles in the snow with rags for clothing. Only a few of us had shoes. The Russians had come too close to Auschwitz, and there were still too many of us to murder before their arrival.

And so the death marches began. Every woman who fell behind was shot right there in the snow."

Ms. Delsig continued through her thoughts and memories with only an occasional pause. Darby asked a question from time to time to open a new memory, then allowed Ms. Delsig to tell what she found inside.

"And the officer who killed your brother. What happened to him?" Darby asked.

"I had information that helped the Allies track him down after the war. He was captured and awaiting trial. I gathered my courage to face him and to be a witness against him. I believed that, at last, justice would be served. But he killed himself before justice found him. It troubled me deeply for many years, and I did not know how to overcome that. Yet I know the nature of God now. I know that you may escape human judgment, but no one escapes God's—for both the evil and the good things man does."

"Why was the officer after you and your brother?" Darby asked.

"You don't know?" Ms. Delsig responded, surprised.

"Should I?"

"Yes. He was the same officer who almost captured your grandmother. The man who ordered Tatianna Hoffman's execution, along with having your great-grandfather and great-uncle killed."

"He was the one after the Empress Brooch?"

"Yes. An evil man, a very evil man. He killed my parents and my brother. His name was Kurt Heinrich."

CHAPTER TWENTY-FOUR

Amanda had stepped into the mind of evil before. She'd studied the paintings of a mediocre artist named Adolf Hitler and wondered how a painter became the greatest mass murderer of all time. Her work brought her in touch with serial killers from history, the ritualistic human sacrifices of various tribal peoples, and the pious murders of the Salem witch-hunts. Focusing on the WWII era dropped her into Nazi official orders and the biographies and thoughts of camp kommandants, camp doctors, and SS officers. Though troubling, this was different. It broke beyond curiosity and fascination.

Amanda was about to resurrect a man who had committed atrocities against other humans. She'd never hesitated at that door before. Yet this was a resurrection of one of her own family members. Her father's father. She'd see what he saw and feel what he felt. This was her own flesh and blood. From the grave, he would rise and she'd learn all about him. He would be speaking to her, his own descendant. But was Amanda ready to hear what he would tell her?

In addition to Kurt Heinrich's service records that Stefan had brought from Prague, Amanda had retrieved several testimonies from war-crime proceedings and made the greatest find of all in a small museum in Austria. The museum Express-Mailed copies of a stack of journal-style letters that SS Officer Kurt Heinrich had written to his mother. When Kurt's mother died in 1958, the letters had been kept by an archivist at the museum.

Amanda tried to prepare herself to face all the papers at once. She'd skimmed the records and then put everything in a file box. Taking everything home, she set the box on her coffee table and lifted the lid. Hemingway had moved from his usual spot in her bedroom to the floor beside her feet, as if sensing her need for another presence nearby.

With the box opened, Amanda saw the neat words written in her grandfather's own hand and in those words she heard his voice. For the first time she wished she didn't know German, couldn't translate it into English, and could close her ears to the words he'd written:

> *8 October 1929*
>
> *I am a man today—eighteen years old—and I have come to my woods, the woods of my childhood wanderings. It is strange to be considered a man when inside I am not far from the boy who loved to explore these old pathways. The yearning to be a man has left me today, and I long for boyhood adventures. Yet I will enter the world soon and seek adventures on a larger scale.*
>
> *I see people everywhere I travel. My eyes follow them as they walk their paths and follow to destinations I will never know. I want to know them, to hear about their families and what joys and sorrows are folded inside their lives. There are so many people, each with a life unique unto themselves. If I could know them, know what they carry, know the loves*

*and heartbreaks—it would be too great a burden. Only God,
yes, I believe that God alone can carry such a thing as
knowing each individual. It makes me return to my disbelief
in God, which should please you, of course. And yet I see
your point. How can God be so great? Yet if I do believe in
him and recognize his enormity beyond my comprehension,
should that not make my wonder of him that much greater?
I am awed.*

Amanda read about a young man who wanted to be a writer.
He secretly read and wrote in the woods when his mother
believed he was getting fresh air and exercise. His writing of
poetry frustrated him; finally he gave it up when his mother
found the writings she called "primitive and useless." University and military service were better pursuits and then the
place that held the key to the future—the Nazi Party. Kurt was
welcomed, despite his inner hesitance, and there he found his
place within a uniform that made him something.

> *31 July 1933*
>
> *Mother, you were right. You said this was the place for
> me and though I listened and followed your advice, it was
> not until today that I fully understood. The winds have
> shifted, and I find myself believing in something for the first
> time. Not just believing but embodying, consuming those
> beliefs.*
>
> *Just two months ago I doubted the party. I watched the
> burning of books, great works that were deemed un-German.
> The flames from pages of words flew high into the air of
> Unter den Linden. It seemed madness to me. Yet now my
> doubt is relieved. The German spirit had been raised and
> some difficult choices must be made at that cost. I saw that
> after I attended the SA rally in Dortmund. If only you could
> have seen it. The red flags waved in the light wind, and we*

stood in our perfect formations. Power and greatness were felt within each man, such as Germany has never seen before. Then Hitler himself appeared before us, standing as if a god upon that platform, watching us, studying us—and we understood before he spoke a word. We are the New Germany, the future of all mankind.

Mother, you could see the opportunity and direction I did not want to see. I beg your apology for my reluctance and my anger. Our world will never be the same. We have a glorious and righteous future. I will be part of that future.

Amanda read of his views of the Jews. His family had bred in him the worldview that Jews were greedy and malicious behind their masked smiles. Just look at what had happened to his mother's family—prominent within the emperor of Austria's personal service, promised the brooch, and then it was stolen by the conniving Jew—Herbert Lange. It was clear the Heinrichs believed that Jews were to be watched and kept at a safe distance. Their odd secret practices were feared by the young man raised by a dominant mother and father who had died for the Fatherland in the Great War.

There were many pages of writings. Some Amanda skimmed as her grandfather wrote about a new posting, rallies, his first friendships. Other pages she read more carefully, discovering his slow but steady descent into evil.

2 November 1935

These pages must never be seen and yet I risk the writing of them. It seems I cannot stop myself.

My training has taken me to Esterwege KZ—a concentration camp for political enemies. We were trained by Papa Eike on how to deal with enemies of the people. I believed I would fail every moment. My mind must not think or hear the cries. If we even flinch or show a pause of compassion as

*the prisoners are beaten and executed before our eyes, then
we fail. Just as I believe I must go to Papa Eike and admit
my failure, that my sympathy for the prisoners is too great,
that I am not strong enough for this, then my memory
returns to Father and his loyalty to the Fatherland, even
unto death. I will not fail him or you this time, Mother.
Later, as the blood of the criminal flowed at my feet, I
pictured Father's approval and stood strong. I have passed
the training and I am an SS officer.*

*It is strange to say, but now I cannot give up this uniform.
I see people everywhere I travel. I am seen when I walk the
street. They glance at me with their deep eyes and quickly
look away. Eyes of fear, hatred, and curiosity. They see me.
I come to them in their dreams and cause them to walk
faster as night falls. Even if I am already in another city or
country, I remain with them. This uniform, my endurance to
be strong through all training, has earned the hatred and
respect I see in their eyes.*

*And how do I see them? Their faces run together like so
many grasses along the road. They live for a time, then die
beneath the searing sun. I wonder about it. What makes
some men born to be seen and others born only to be grass
beneath the feet?*

9 March 1938

*I have discovered a most amazing development. During
some work in Austria, of which I cannot yet reveal, I found
the Lange family in Salzburg. Mother, they still have the
Empress Brooch that was rightfully to be given to your
father. It is well known that the Lange family have the heirloom. Simon Lange was working in Salzburg. He, like his
deceiving father, believes that the brooch belongs to their
family.*

We will march into Austria within days. Austria must

*belong to the Third Reich. And such Jewish crimes will not
be tolerated when Hitler walks Austrian soil.*

⤞══◅═⤝

Ms. Delsig could see again the gray world as the doors of the
cattle cars opened. They could breathe for a brief second and
then the sound of shouting and dogs barking erupted like
gunfire blasting in their ears.

"Hani, my little sister, was with me. She was holding my
hand. Her hand still soft, yet clinging so strongly. I was crying;
she was not. An almost-four-year-old child, the little sister I
wanted so badly. I would carry her around and pretend she
was my baby doll. And . . . I failed her."

The knot in Ms. Delsig's stomach grew and expanded in
sharp pains. She gasped, suddenly dizzy. In an instant, Lilly's
arms held her. Someone said they'd take a break. Voices murmured as tears exploded out of her eyes and ran down her face.

"I betrayed her," she sobbed.

"No, no, honey," Lilly said softly. "You didn't do anything
wrong."

"I did. I sent her with my grandmother. She did not want to
go. She begged and started to cry when I made her go."

"It's okay. It's okay," Lilly soothed.

"No! It is not. I killed her. I sent her to the gas. My little
Hani."

"You didn't know."

"What if I did? What if somehow deep inside, I did know? I
thought they would be kinder to the old, the sick, the babies. I
told myself this. But how could I not know by the way they had
already treated us? The old, sick, and babies were already dying
in the cattle cars. They were being shot by the tracks if they did
not line up. How could I think it would be better for her?"

Lilly held her, rocking back and forth with her gently.

"Perhaps we should not do this," Lilly said. "Perhaps it's too much for you."

"Just give me . . . ," Ms. Delsig said in a cracking voice, "a few minutes."

Finally Ms. Delsig took a breath to calm herself and tried to focus her mind away from what she spoke, keeping her voice sounding matter-of-fact. "My sister, Hani, was with me at Auschwitz. I sent her to be with my grandmother. My grandmother said, 'Remember, Brigit, remember who you are. Remember.' The last time I saw them, my sister was calling for me. My grandmother gave a brave wave good-bye. They went one way; I went the other. By the time my hair was shaved and the delousing complete, my baby sister and grandmother were both dead."

⊷═◦═⊷

Amanda could barely bring herself to read more, but she plunged on. . . .

> *13 June 1941*
>
> *I am at Mauthausen KZ, this dreadful place. I watch her, this Celia Lange who believes herself brave. I have seen others with the same spirit. It does not take much to change them. To have their tears and blood and to gain their begging pleas. I wonder at this power I have and consider the man I once was, blind to these things. Sometimes I envy that man, myself, then filled with hope and innocence. What the world is, is not what I wanted it to be. Ideals, hopes, loves are but childish follies of Old Saint Nicholas, the Magic Flute, and the wolf in the closet.*
>
> *I watched the girl today. She is still innocent of what is. I felt a sadness, strange that it was. A deep sadness of what I have lost and that it cannot be. We have only the quest of*

ourselves. The animalistic drives to survive, destroy, and mate to produce ourselves again. What is, feels futile. But it is what I am. She will learn soon enough.

2 July 1941

My frustration cannot be denied. While the war is going well, my position advancing, I am troubled throughout my assignments by this girl. I have insisted that she be left alone in the jail unless I am there, especially after the deaths of the Lange father during a torture I was not present for. Ziereis is now camp kommandant of Mauthausen and owes me a few favors from before his assignment. Yet my work in Czechoslovakia keeps me away. Reich Protectorate Reinhard Heydrich has more work than I can do, so it is difficult for me to get back to Austria and this girl who will not surrender.

However, I must get the answers soon. I will not continue to go to this camp of walking skeletons where the worst brutalities are congratulated. I understand the beast who thirsts for blood has risen within me as well. What is the human condition? I do not quite understand it. I try to place us in the category of mammal, but we are different. There is this love of poetry and music and of good food, and the desire to be admired and feared. And there is something in me that is never satisfied for long, yet I seek to find it. I do not see that in other creatures. I see it only in man.

9 August 1941

I am finished with her. This Celia Lange. Today I set her execution date. She has two more days of life. Two days to change her mind if she does know the location of the brooch. I must have that brooch. I feel the obsession burn within me. Mother, I am not blind to it. But you would want me to not give it up. And I cannot. It is for you, myself, our family, and

the German people. It symbolizes the greater cause of
Germany to not be overcome by the connivings of a Jew. It is
insane in some ways. I know that. And yet it will not leave
me. I believe somehow I will find it.

10 August 1941

She will die tomorrow.

Outside the door to her cell, I waited, thinking, seeking a
way to make her speak. I heard her praying. The words
would not come to me, for she spoke too softly. I wanted to
hear them. Did she ask forgiveness for her lies? Did she
speak of the truth I have been unable to gain from her? Or
did she beseech a God to save her from me?

I went into her cell and stood with my back against the
stone wall. She seemed small, sitting there with her legs
drawn against her chest and her head bent low. I told her
that when I die, I will not beg God for help or forgiveness.

She glanced up at me quickly. I believe it was the first
time she really looked at me. There was something akin to
pity in her eyes. It made me laugh.

I told her she could save herself. It was in her power. If
she would speak the truth I know she keeps from me, she
could live. And suddenly I promised her and meant it. If she
would speak, I would release her.

But instead she stared at her hands.

I stayed there for a long while, feeling the mystery of it
all. There have been moments like this before. A face of
peace in the midst of pain that I always took for resignation,
acceptance of defeat. A human mechanism that prepared for
death.

Yet for this girl, it is different. Perhaps I am too close and
something inside me wants her to live. I tell this to myself,
but it does not quite fit. It is not desire for her. I know those
feelings well enough. For a minute I believed I envied her. It

angered me and I hit her. She fell upon the mattress and covered her head, curled in a tight ball. I hit her several times, but it brought me nothing. I stopped abruptly.

She does not fit with my attempts at philosophy. I am certain she knows where the Empress Sissi Brooch is located or at least knows something. She is half Jew—half deceit and lie.

Tomorrow she will die. There is nothing more to be done. Once she is gone, I have lost the brooch, perhaps forever.

11 August 1941

The girl is dead.

I watched from the tower. She walked in silence and did not close her eyes.

There was no reason for me to watch. Yet it seemed beyond my control. I had to see it. I could not sleep all the night before until it was decided.

And now she is dead.

12 August 1941

Mother, I am stunned at the newest event.

I returned to the girl's cell. Anger seized me. I grabbed the mattress and threw it on the floor, kicking the frame again and again. Then I saw something that caused me to stop. Beneath the bed, cut into the wall by some object.

A name. Scratched into the cement. It was not her name. Not the name of Celia Lange. Why would she write the name of Tatianna Hoffman? I knew she had scratched it into the wall. I knelt close and saw the dust on the floor.

A thought came to me. What if it was her name? I went over it all again and again. I went to my office and found all my notes about her, her family, friends. And that is where I found the name. Tatianna Hoffman. Celia Lange's friend from Hallstatt. She had confessed that Tatianna had been in the car with her at the border.

At last I knew. The girl who had died was Tatianna. I had somehow lost the Lange girl at the border, and all this time I had had the friend. Tatianna was not a Jew, and she had not lied. She did not know where the brooch was located.

But why? What brainwashing had the Jewess Lange performed upon this one who would die such a death? Why would she die for her friend?

CHAPTER TWENTY-FIVE

M y brother, Edgar, and I made a promise."
Ms. Delsig was again in front of the camera, seeing the past in
her eyes. "If we ever separated, no matter what, we would live
and get back to Prague. There was no way to know how long
it would take, how long the war would last, or what would
happen within our city during that time. My parents' apartment had been a gathering place. My brother and I would
listen to their late-night talk. They discussed the fate of our
city beneath Nazi control. We had heard rumors about Jews
being transported somewhere to the West or being confined
to walled areas of other cities.

"On one of those nights, Edgar and I made plans, feeling a
bit excited about it all. If ever separated, we would meet in the
woods above Prague. We knew the people who could be
trusted. My father made us memorize their addresses, and we
discussed routes of escape through the city, to their houses,
and out to the countryside. Among the most trusted was my

father's old friend Kozel. They had been in the Czech Army together years earlier and were both at the university.

"I have heard people tell their stories and show their tattoos. It seemed wrong to me. Why answer the questions and probe back to those places? How would I explain it? What is it like to survive a concentration camp? What things will a person do to survive in such conditions? You pray that the person beside you will die instead of you. Then the prayer comes true and you take the shoes from your bunk mate before saying the prayer of the dead.

"At night I would dream of home. My promise to Edgar kept me alive when I was ready to lie down and close my eyes—for good. I discovered that it is harder to die than I thought. In the years that followed, I found that suicide can happen on a whim. But torturous death clings to life. We did not know anything else to do. We knew our enemies, for the most part. The SS guards, both men and women, were enemies, and some of the ones we knew in our barrack. You trusted no one, though you called a few 'friends,' with loose attachment— anyone could be dead by next roll call. Prague was my goal. I would dream of standing on a bridge over the Vltava and watching the slow waters for hours and hours. No one would disturb me or make me stand in line or work without food and water.

"And I did escape, right from a death march. A woman from the front tried to escape. While the guards went after her, I took that split second and slipped into the bushes. I heard gunfire as they shot the woman and then the quick footfalls as they moved away. A sign on the road pointed to Praha going the opposite direction. It took me a week to get home. Only by the help of a Czech farmer and his wife did I make it. I found my father's friend Kozel first. He opened the door and did not recognize me. Then shock covered his face. 'What are you doing here?' he asked. There was no shred of happiness at seeing me, though I did not realize it immediately.

"'I came home,' I said.

"He yanked me into the house. I felt like a dirty animal entering his clean parlor. There were beautiful rugs and I remember noticing the paintings . . . of course I would notice the paintings. They were the first art I had seen in so long.

"'My father's,' I said, staring at a particularly favorite oil painting that hung in his study. 'I never would have thought to see it again.'

"'You cannot stay here,' he said quickly, almost fiercely. 'If I see you again, I will turn you in.'

"'Why? You were on the list. You were first. Most trusted. My father—'

"'Your father is dead. So many are dead. Do you understand? You have been gone and do not realize what has happened.'

"'Where do I go?'

"'Just go away from me. Go as far as you can.'

"So I did. But I kept searching and finally found Edgar. He had been fighting with the Resistance. Night after night, I went to our hiding place, and one night he was there. He'd believed every one of us had died, and there I stood like a ghost, he said. We thought we'd made it then and would hide in the woods until the war ended, even fight when necessary.

"Then we heard that an officer named Kurt Heinrich was looking for us because of some valuable brooch. We knew what that was about. Our father had told us that if he was taken, we were to hide it and use the information of its location only to save each other's lives—not his or my mother's, for he said they would be beyond help of a simple brooch. But it might be helpful someday. We had forgotten about it—there was so much more to be concerned about. I had met this officer before my deportation, though he would not remember me. He was a handsome man, proud and fearful. He would walk the streets and people moved aside. I followed him once to hear his voice. Because of this man, Edgar and I fled Prague. We went to a cabin across the border in Austria, believing it would be safe. But Kurt Heinrich found us there."

✦⟹◎⟸✦

By now, tears were streaming down Amanda's face. But she couldn't stop herself from reading more. . . .

4 June 1942

They have killed Reinhard Heydrich. I saw his body and still find myself unable to believe that the man I knew is that one. He was ambushed on a street and wounded severely. It took several days, but now he is dead.

I had attended a concert in Prague and saw Reinhard and his wife, Lina, there the night before he was ambushed. We spoke briefly afterward and that was the last time I saw him alive. You do not realize attachments until they are gone. Everyone is fearful now. Hilde wants to take Henri away from Prague, but I will not hear of it unless she comes to stay with you, Mother. But she will not. It is all so shocking, and the Führer is mad with rage and anger. They will wish they never did this.

9 June 1942

The orders have been given, and I will be one of the commanding officers. I find it ridiculous but, of course, would not say that. We must destroy the village of Lidice. It is a show of Nazi might and ruthlessness. The terror will do its work upon the Czech people, though we have yet to capture the ones who murdered Heydrich.

11 June 1942

I am weary through my entire being. The killings are maddening and affect my men. It did not sit well with me either. I can understand the Jews, though it rarely brings me any pleasure even to see a Jew die. But these men were Czech villagers of all ages . . .

And then there is the matter of the young boy whom we have named Martin. Hilde was thrilled to be a mother again, though of course, she knows nothing of the truth. She is too sensitive for such things. The boy's parents are dead now, though I could have adopted him with them still alive—the power of the Nazi fist on occupied lands. He is surely an Aryan by his appearance and will never have to face the degrading facts of his life before us. Yet I wonder which corpse on the ground was the father of this child we have brought into our home. I have thought too often in this life, and it only brings more anxiety.

1 July 1942

I have a lead. And in Prague!

Jan Kirke, another Jew, helped the Lange father before his capture. And I discovered Jan lived right beneath my nose in Prague. He was an artist and only his connections helped him through the first deportations. His wife, Ilse Kirke, died too quickly. Jan was not allowed death. When he thought death would come, we pulled back until he finally gave the information. He was a stubborn one indeed. And then he sobbed and sobbed, for he had betrayed his own son and daughter into my hands. He told me they were the last to have the brooch. Now I know the brooch was in Prague and who can give it to me. I gave him the gun to finish his life, but in the end I had to do it for him. Jews—cowards and betrayers to the end.

The boy, Edgar, has disappeared. The girl, Brigit, is at Auschwitz. I will find the girl and make her tell me the location of the Empress Brooch.

Something to live for again.

⋆══◉═⋆

Ms. Delsig looked into Darby's face, wanting someone to understand, if only in a small way. "The cries of children come to me most often. Sometimes in the screech of tires or the way the wind moves through certain trees I hear them. Do you know what it is like to hear a child cry in terror? to watch a mother's anguish when her baby is murdered before her eyes? Can you even comprehend how the emotions fight one another when you see bodies of old women, children, and infants pulled out? The sight . . . it is in my eyes so often."

⋆══◉═⋆

Amanda's hands shook as she picked up the last letter. . . .

30 November 1946

This will be my final letter, Mother. I send this journal of works, and you can do as you will with them. Only you understand. Only you know why I have done what I have done, and what I have sought so hard for.

I recall the night before Tatianna Hoffman's death. The look in her expression after I told her I would not beseech God on the day of my death. I have thought of that look often and I remember how it angered me. A half Jew to see me in such a way. But then she was not Jewish. What was that in her eyes? What made her look at me like that?

Even at my end, I seek the answers I will never find.

It is strange to be in a cell. This time I am the one imprisoned. It is not fitting to my sense of who I am.

I read something in the Bible . . . but do not fear, Mother; I am not falling into religion. Yet it is amazing what you turn to when death comes knocking. The writer spoke of how everything is meaningless and like searching after the wind. I wondered at that and recalled my life. There were so many things important to me. I was so determined to fight for beliefs and ideals that now, alone and facing the end— the end of the only life a man gets to live—it seems meaningless.

If I had given up the search for the brooch, I would be free now. But what is worth anything in life? I am but an organism that now meets the end of his days. This is truth, yet I am uncomfortable with it. I want to be more, to believe that human life has value. Yet if I do, then I condemn myself. I want to at least believe that some lives have value—I want that to be for myself.

I read further in this Bible . . . the concluding thoughts of the writer of this strange and pondering book. This writer is one I identify with. He says that he collected proverbs, classified them, and sought the sayings of the wise. Yet he writes that there is no end to the opinions of man. Is not that the truth? All mankind has opinions and the thought of the day is only that—a momentary thought that will change beneath the words modernism *or* neomodernism.

His final conclusion about life is to fear God and obey his commands, for this is what every person should do. God judges everyone for the good and the bad.

Then I find that this writer I understand was King Solomon. King of the Jewish people. A Jew himself. The ironies never end.

Mother, all I can say in conclusion is that I know nothing for certain. Through a life of searching and delving into good and evil, I have found nothing.

My life has been. That is all. My life has been.

Ms. Delsig closed her eyes as she sang.

> *Our strength cannot carry another step.*
>   *And so we die tonight.*
> *In the darkness, forgotten from the world.*
> *We die tonight.*
> *We wanted to walk the fields of spring. We dreamed*
>   *and hoped in vain.*
> *We die tonight.*
> *Who will remember if we all die tonight?*
> *We die for nothing.*
>   *And yet, we die tonight.*
>   *Tonight we die.*
>   *We die.*

The others clapped in solemn memory to the ones who had sung such a song. Ms. Delsig sighed and even smiled. The weight of memories had lessened—because, for a time, the weight was shared.

"But you didn't die—you lived, Ms. D," Lilly said with a sparkle in her eyes. "You lived."

Amanda was not one to cry easily, but she'd cried until there were no tears left.

This man had become real. A murderer, her grandfather. In his words, she found pieces of herself, of the questions she had asked and continued to ask herself. A man who had begun somewhere and ended with her own life. Through his journey, he'd destroyed himself and everyone in his path while believing it was the way of life.

Amanda had seen into the mind of Kurt Heinrich. Going through his files and research on the Internet, she found information on his fate. Kurt had been captured a year after the war. His trial was set and witnesses called.

The charges were long and extensive, with many witnesses on the docket. Amanda found the testimony she was looking for. Soldiers in her grandfather's unit told of the cold-blooded murder of a young man in the woods within days of the war's end. This was not an order; it was a personal mission that Kurt's men did not understand. They knew of a sister hiding in the woods also. When Kurt returned without her, he told another soldier, "She is dead."

Amanda found U.S. Army reports of those who had investigated. They did find the body of a young man in the woods. But the woman had survived and was there to testify against Kurt Heinrich. But Kurt killed himself before the trial could proceed further.

The woman who had come to testify was the sister of Edgar Kirke. Brigit Kirke had not only survived the war; she had survived Kurt Heinrich.

∗══◎═══∗

"I'm worried about you," Benny said when he stopped by Amanda's after work a week later.

"Just tell me about your students."

"You've lost weight. Have you talked to Stefan?"

She shook her head.

"You can't let this stupid thing destroy you. It doesn't matter what a grandfather you never knew did decades ago. It doesn't matter."

"That's not what you said before."

"I was wrong. Look at you. You have talked to your dad for only a few short conversations; you haven't talked to me or Stefan. You can't pull away from everyone."

Amanda closed her eyes. She was tired lately, always it

seemed. And yet she could hardly sleep at night. She was afraid of the nightmares and the many thoughts wrestling within her mind. At work she continued the program development, but she stayed away from the office gossip and didn't go to lunch with her friends. When Troy Donley came in with his trivia questions, Amanda wouldn't have an answer—she hadn't dug out *The How and Why Around Us*. She just didn't care.

Her nights were spent on the computer, searching and seeking links to Kurt Heinrich and the Empress Brooch. And yet she'd find herself staring for long periods of time at nothing, wondering where her thoughts had gone.

"I'm fine, Benny. It's a lot of things at once."

"Just call him."

"I can't."

"Tell me why. You love him, don't you?"

She glanced at Benny and noticed his worry, something she'd never seen in his eyes.

"I know you love him."

"It's not enough," she whispered. And yet how she longed for Stefan Keller.

"You sound like me."

"I can't be his next charity case. I don't understand his faith in a God I don't know if I even believe exists. And Stefan hasn't called, so he knows it too."

"Amanda, you've always believed in God, so don't tell me that. And remember that he was in Guatemala or could still be there."

"With everything else, the last thing I need is to be grappling with theological issues."

Benny stared at her intently. "Perhaps that's exactly where you should start . . . and let go of everything else."

"You are sounding quite spiritual. What—did Stefan convert you on his night over there?"

"We had some good discussions. But I've been grappling for quite some time."

"Benny, please." She stood up slowly. "I'm going to bed now. I made it through today; now I need to make it through tomorrow."

"You can't stay like this. Something has to happen."

Those were the words that kept her up into the night. Something must happen because she couldn't continue on her current path.

Suddenly Amanda knew. She had fully seen her grandfather's journey into evil. That would destroy her father once he learned the truth about his family. Yet with the History Network production in full swing, Amanda must tell him soon. But within her grandfather's writings she had found the answer for redeeming her family. She must find the Empress Brooch. She must somehow uncover the place where it lay, waiting. And with that token—which Kurt Heinrich had become obsessed with gaining and caused so many deaths— returned to the Lange family, Amanda would find a semblance of redemption.

Amanda knew she must first find Brigit Kirke. Then she would find the Empress Brooch.

part *three*

There was no one to be seen for miles around; there was
nothing but the wide earth and sky and the larks' jubilation
and the freedom of space. I stopped, looked around,
and up to the sky—and then I went to my knees. At that
moment there was very little I knew of myself
or of the world—I had one sentence in my mind—
always the same: I called upon the Lord from my narrow
prison and He answered me in the freedom of space.

—VIKTOR E. FRANKL, Holocaust survivor, *Man's Search for Meaning*

CHAPTER TWENTY-SIX

Ms. Delsig's careful world had come undone.

She had spent a steady succession of years where she knew what to expect out of life. When Ms. Delsig had entered Oakdale, she knew she entered until death. Her garden and art were outlets, her friendships were a source of comfort and laughter, and her last days were relatively secure, containing moments of happiness. She had never expected to revisit the past or journey to places long tucked away.

The video testimony taping was to conclude on the second day. Brant and Darby's plans to stay and then go to California were interrupted when her grandfather in Salzburg had a medical emergency. Darby apologized again and again but said she had to leave for Austria immediately. She would call and reschedule as soon as possible.

Ms. Delsig felt the unrest of an unfinished project. She was still unable to see Alfred, though he was improving and had taken a short phone call from her.

"Break me out of this place, will you?" were his groggy words.

For days she seemed to wander without direction. What should she do now?

Finally Lilly was the one who produced the answer. "What is that print on your wall?" she asked.

Ms. Delsig didn't need to look up. The print was a mosaic artwork that she knew well. "It's advertising my favorite museum in Prague."

"How long have you had that print?"

"My husband bought it in the seventies."

"When was the last time you were at your favorite museum in Prague?"

Ms. Delsig looked at her strangely. "It must have been October 1946, before I left the country."

"That's a very long time."

"Yes, it is." Ms. Delsig let her mind drift back to the small museum of Jewish art.

Lilly interrupted her thoughts. "You need to go back. I'll go with you."

"What? You cannot be serious."

"I'm more than serious. It's decided."

"Wait a minute. What makes you think I want to go back to Prague?"

"You've had the same print since the seventies."

"Do you know how hard it would be for us to travel? Impossible! Me with my walker and you with your chair?"

"I'll bring my daughter, or we'll hire a handsome helper."

"Lilly, this is insane."

"No, I think it just might work. After we visit your birthplace, we'll go to Salzburg and finish that interview of yours. I've always wanted to see where *The Sound of Music* was filmed. Such a magnificent place it seems from the movie."

Ms. Delsig walked to the window and stared outside over the

fence to the thread of silver sea. What would it be like to leave Oakdale, even for a little while? What would it be like to drive along the beach roads and perhaps stop and get out? to walk across the soft sand and put her toes in the salty sea? What would Prague look like after so many years? And would the old places remain—the home of her childhood, the streets she once played in, and the museum that had been her favorite?

"What are you doing to me, Lilly Parkens?"

"What I would hope someone would do for me, but I have seen the places of my youth and made my peace with them. Now it is your turn."

Tears sprung from Ms. Delsig's eyes. "I was quite content with my life before you came along. I have cried more in the last month than in the past twenty years."

"And you've never been happier."

⋆═◉═⋆

Within a week the plans were set. They had contacted Darby Evans Collins, who said she would stay in Austria for some time, even though her grandfather had improved. She also told Ms. Delsig that she looked forward to welcoming her back to the place of her childhood summer journeys.

The day before leaving, Ms. Delsig was finally able to visit Alfred in the hospital. She had expected frightening tubes and machines, but instead she noticed only the clear tubing of one IV stuck in his left hand. He looked thin but healthy. Ms. Delsig had paid for fresh flowers to be delivered every few days, so a bouquet of white lilies filled the room with a sweet aroma.

He smiled as she entered. "Mexico might be too far. How about two decrepit old people running away to the Bahamas?"

"Who is old and decrepit?"

"Not you, of course." Alfred reached slowly for the button

on the bed and raised up slightly. White bandages covered his chest, peeking out the top of his shirt.

She wrapped her fingers around his.

"Ms. D, you are such a wonderful sight, let me tell you. Somehow I've been assigned only male nurses or grouchy female ones."

"So they added insult to injury."

"You got it."

"How long until we have you back?" she asked. "You have your own room, I see."

"Yes, for today. But I'm not sure when I'll be back. Everything moves on hospital time, which means one day they might boot me out, or I could be in for weeks more."

"Alfred, I came to tell you that I'm leaving Oakdale for a short time."

"The escape plan is in order?"

"I'm going to Europe for two weeks with Lilly."

"Actually, a little bird already told me," he said with a smile.

"A little bird?"

"A very small dark-colored bird."

"Hmmm, I wonder who that could be. And what do you think about it?"

"I think it's a great idea. Just don't stay gone forever."

"I can't. I have a marriage proposal to contemplate."

"It shouldn't be so hard to consider." One bushy eyebrow raised in wonder. "Go to Europe, come back, and say yes."

Ms. Delsig smiled. "Yes. I will."

⊹⇒◉⇐⊹

Amanda enlisted the help of her favorite researcher in her search for Brigit Kirke. Sam Wallingham had been her boss when she worked in research. He had no desire to move up and leave the world of "PI of the past," as he called himself.

Sam had eagerly taken on the project, drumming his fingers on the pages as he quickly perused them.

"So you know this woman was alive after the war and appeared to testify against this Nazi officer." Sam thumbed through the report Amanda had put together. "Kurt Heinrich. This is a good lead."

For the next few days, Amanda conducted her own searches between working on the program. She e-mailed Sam back and forth as they found a trail. Soon they knew that Brigit Kirke had married Josef Delsig in 1946 and the couple immigrated to the United States. Records were found of the Delsig ownership of several businesses and of Josef's death.

Sam called Amanda's office with the real news. "I found her," he said excitedly.

"She's still alive then?" Amanda felt a rush of excitement— the first in a long time.

"Our dear Brigit Delsig is alive and well in Florida."

"Florida? Guess it's time for me to get some sunshine."

⋅—⟹◯⟸—⋅

The breeze came from over the waters of the sea. It touched her face as Ms. Delsig paused at the double wood doors of Oakdale, looking down the uneven brick walkway to the awaiting luxury car. She gazed around at the great big world, a world that suddenly felt much larger than she remembered.

Lilly's daughter, Lorraine, held the car door open. She would be their escort across the sea. After their first unfortunate meeting, Ms. Delsig had spent time with the woman, finding her to be a determined lady with a tender heart. Lorraine was excited about seeing Europe for the first time and had packed more than they'd ever need.

As they drove onto the coastal highway, Ms. Delsig spotted

the long line where blue sky met blue ocean. "Could you please pull over for just a minute?"

Lorraine glanced in the rearview mirror. "At a rest room?"

"No, no, just for a moment, right in that parking lot." She pointed to the sign that said Beach Access.

They found a place beside an old VW bus with a surfboard attached to its top. Ms. Delsig opened the door and stared down the concrete path to the white sandy beach. She was there, at that place between the sky and the Oakdale fence. The breeze picked up, as if welcoming her.

"Let's put our feet in the water," Lilly said, popping her head up on the other side of the car.

"We can't," Ms. Delsig said, thinking of her walker and Lilly's wheelchair. But *can't* was Lilly's action word. Lorraine helped greatly after their metal aids were left on the side of the concrete trail. They leaned heavily on her stocky arms the last fifty feet to the water's edge. It took half an hour, but soon they were standing in wet sand with their knee-high stockings peeled off and stuck in their shoes. Lilly rolled up her slacks and Ms. Delsig lifted the hem of her dress and frilly white slip as the cool waves rolled in. The water touched their feet and ankles, wrapping gently around them, pulling the sand from around their feet.

Ms. Delsig began to giggle and then laugh as the waves came in. She wished she could run again. The light wind in her face and the water pushing around her ankles took away the years. For a brief time she was young, and the world was a beautiful place. All on a sunny afternoon.

⋯⟾⊙⟾⋯

Richter Hauer entered the room separated from Amanda by a glass wall. Orange jail garb, hair unbrushed and hanging to his shoulders, weeks' worth of growth on his face, and a deep blue bruise on his cheekbone—Richter appeared the quintessential criminal with a cocky attiude displayed in his easy walk and casual way with the guard.

In the cubicle beside Amanda, a woman spoke Spanish in an agitated voice to "Miguel" on the other side of the glass. The sounds of a prison surrounded them—the hard clang of metal doors and the occasional high buzz before doors opened on automatic locks. Amanda, wearing a visitor badge on her shirt, waited with notebook and pen in hand.

When Richter approached, Amanda could tell he was looking her over. She caught a twitch of a smile as he sat down and leaned close to the window, picking up the telephone on his side of the glass as she did on hers.

"You are doing a television program about the brooch?" he asked, smoothing his hair with one hand. "What is your name?"

"Amanda Rivans."

"Amanda," he said, drawing out the name as if enjoying the sound of it, "nice to meet you."

"I appreciate your agreeing to speak to me," she said, noticing the features of a handsome man beneath the beard and scraggly hair.

"So what do you want with me?" he asked.

"We'd like an on-camera interview with you. Would you be willing to discuss how your search for the Empress Brooch led you from a normal life into this place?"

"Tell me about yourself first."

"Okay," Amanda said hesitantly. She told him the basics of her work and then again asked him about the brooch.

He leaned back, as if contemplating. "It was obsession. I have always become easily addicted to alluring things—and people." When his eyebrows raised slightly, Amanda realized he was flirting with her.

"At first I wanted it because I was in serious debt to a man who does not like you to owe him, if you understand my meaning. Then, amazingly, the debt was forgiven. It was my chance to escape, but my suspicion of why my debt was forgiven made me think I was close to finding the brooch. It brought me to do what I never thought possible."

"Kidnapping?"

"I did not really consider it being that, but yes, it was. Then I got another chance. I was supposed to be caught in Austria. Did you know that? I was taken to the police station, but I got away. I was able to get out of Europe and all the way to Canada."

"But now you are caught once again."

"I get a new chance and tend to make a new set of mistakes. Is this what you want for your interview?"

"Yes, and some other questions."

"I am being sent back to Austria."

"We'll do the interview before that. Extradition may take some time." Amanda jotted down a few notes as he watched her. "How did you get caught at the border?"

"I am very unlucky."

"From my information, you were given identification papers that would be immediately suspicious at the border. Sounds like this was planned."

"It is possible." His expression told her that he knew it was exactly that.

"Who gave you the papers?"

"These questions do not sound like matters for a history program."

Amanda smiled slightly. This guy was in prison, but he was no fool. She wondered if he had his next escape plan all figured out. "Where do you think it is?"

"Ah, this is what I thought. I see it in your eyes," he said, then paused. "Be careful."

"It is a question for the program."

"And so much more. The brooch is said to have a curse—and since I am in here, I tend to agree. It gets a hold on you. Obsession begins with the denial of obsession—this I know. Do you deny obsession?"

"I would like to know your opinion."

"My opinion, huh? Well, I have often wondered if Darby Evans—or Collins, I believe it is now—actually found the brooch when she recovered the other items of her family heirlooms, even though she denies it."

"Why would Darby do that?"

"To keep people from trying to steal it—I do not know."

"You don't really believe she has it, do you?"

"Who knows?" He shrugged.

"Who gave you the identification papers?"

"I think you asked that question."

"My thought is this: If you paid someone to make fake papers, then they would not have been intended for you to get caught. So, I wonder, who would you trust who would betray you? Of course, my thoughts return to the Empress Brooch—it's the only illegal activity I've found connected with you."

"A woman who does her homework. Did you receive good marks in school?"

"As a matter of fact, I did." Amanda set her paper aside and moved closer to the window, her voice quiet. "Richter, why are you protecting these people?"

At these words, he stopped smiling. He stopped trying to flirt. She could see him carefully considering his answer.

"This is off the record, yes? I will deny it if you write or tell any of what I am about to say. This is for your search only."

"Okay," Amanda said as calmly as possible.

"This brooch thing is not a buried subject, and I am not just talking about myself or Darby and Brant. There are groups in Europe and in your country who are taking an interest in it."

"Why?"

"From what I can tell, these groups see it as an undeclared war between the Jewish people and themselves. They feel that the Jews have regained power since the war, taking control of Hollywood and many of the governments in various nations."

"You're talking about neo-Nazi groups."

"Yes, but I will not speak of specific groups. These people are angry at the reparations being made to families of Holocaust survivors and to survivors themselves. The group I spoke with feels it personally whenever another survivor is returned artwork, money, land—anything. They feel the Nazi Party gained these things through their righteous fight, and they are now being taken away. The Empress Brooch is one in a list of previously Jewish-owned items that this group wants to gain for themselves . . . or at least keep any Jew from reclaiming."

"We've done a few programs on neo-Nazi groups before," Amanda said cautiously, "but this is interesting information. So you are saying that there is at least one group who is searching for the Empress Brooch at this current time?"

Richter hesitated. "Yes, that is what I am saying. Perhaps it will be information for your program, but I will not be put on camera stating any of it. I will need as few enemies as possible."

"You should consider telling this story to the FBI. You might get some leniency on your charges."

"I have no evidence that this group committed any crime except giving me papers that would get me caught at the border. Believe me, I have thought of any way to help myself." He looked up at the clock on the wall. "You did not give me an answer to my question."

"What question?"

"Are you obsessed with finding the Empress Brooch?"

"No."

"That's what I thought you would say." Richter smiled and said farewell. He hung up the phone and then picked it up again while moving close to the window. "Be careful, Amanda Rivans. This is bigger than you realize. You don't mess with this group—even in here, I'm not safe."

Richter turned to show the bruise on his face. "That was my warning. And this is my warning to you." One last long look and Richter returned the phone and left the room.

Amanda watched the door close behind him, then jotted down the notes that filled her head from their discussion. At the end of the second page she wrote his final words of warning.

After collecting her purse and notepad, Amanda rose from the chair and passed the woman now crying in the booth beside her. Amanda had a long journey ahead of her. Next stop was Florida, to see the woman she believed was Brigit Kirke.

CHAPTER TWENTY-SEVEN

At the airport Stefan was greeted by his family, who appeared concerned. His mother held him tightly for a long time—just as she had when Stefan was little and had followed a puppy down the street and gotten lost for several hours. Petrov watched him and carried his travel bag, seeming to note the slowness in Stefan's steps. The journey to Prague had taken any strength he'd gained in Central America. His grandmother sat him in a hard chair for several minutes as she fussed over him, touching his forehead and staring into his eyes.

"I'm all right," he said, trying not to sound annoyed. A wave of nausea swept over him as he stood up and pushed himself toward the doors to the parking lot.

They talked little on the ride home. It was late afternoon and traffic clogged the roads. Stefan leaned his head against the window of the old, faded Fiat. He closed his eyes from time to time and would open them to a feeling of great relief. Yes, this was home for him.

At last, Petrov let them off in front of the tower apartment before going to find a parking place. Five flights of stairs awaited them. Petrov caught up with them on the third-floor landing and took his grandmother's hand for the last flight. Stefan was the last to reach their door.

His mother had food in the refrigerator, but Stefan couldn't eat. Instead he went to the loft stairs and said good night. Half-way up, he paused. "Have I had any phone calls?" He'd been afraid to ask, afraid to find out that Amanda hadn't called.

"Only Klara," his mother said, wiping her hands on a towel. "Her mother died and she wanted you to attend the funeral. It was yesterday."

Stefan went upstairs and fell into his bed. It was the place Amanda had been not long ago, and the place she would most likely never be again. He closed his eyes, first wondering where she was and then replaying the image of Klara's mother when he'd told her that her son had not committed suicide so many years ago. Sleep mixed with memory wrapped around Stefan and took him away.

⊷⟹◐⟸⊷

Two days passed before Stefan called Klara.

During much of that time he had remained in his loft bedroom, reading, sleeping, and praying into the silence he'd begun to seek. He stood at the windows and opened them wide, feeling the crisp morning air flow against his face and bare chest. He left bits of bread on the windowsill and watched the pigeons come, cooing and prancing as they pecked at the crumbs. The loft was safe from the jungle delirium and a cottage in San Francisco that he wanted to quit thinking of. Stefan wanted to find his strength, but he remembered that in his weakness, God could be strong in him. It was something his nature fought against; he'd been strong for so long. And yet he knew the mysteries of God's ways included this—that less of himself meant more of God in him.

Stefan met Klara at a park a few blocks from the tower apartment. He recognized her daughter Viktorie as she stood beside the swings watching the other children. Klara waited on a bench. There was a deep sadness about her that dissolved the hardness he'd seen in her face before his trip to Central America. Today she wore little makeup and was dressed casually, looking even more like the Klara he remembered.

"Thank you for meeting me," she said. "Your mother sounded very worried about you when I called. Are you better now?"

"Getting there." He watched little Viktorie, who stared at the children, laughing and playing, with those large, dark eyes. She smiled at something they said but remained on the sidelines with her hand on a metal pole. "I am sorry about your mother. I wish I could have been here."

"Of course. You just seem to miss being here when I need you most." There was no bitterness in her tone, though Stefan felt the pang of guilt. "I wished so many times that you would have stayed. If you only knew what I have gone through, what I have done. It would all be different, everything."

"You think *I* am responsible for your choices, Klara?"

"I was so hurt after Viktor's death. And I was in love with you."

Stefan felt her eyes upon him. He'd known it, he admitted to himself, but she was just a child. What did she know then of love? What had she ever known of love? Reaching for her hand, he saw the tears in her eyes. She was a child like her daughter, watching and yearning to be seen. He took her hand and felt the small, soft fingers.

"You could never love me now," she whispered, laying her head against his shoulder. He didn't know what to do or say— didn't know quite how he felt. Her tears soaked his shirt as they watched Viktorie shuffle her feet in the gravel while glancing at the other children.

"Don't think that I could never love you because of what you've done—what you do. It's not like that. Klara—" He dropped her hand, pulled away from her, and lifted her chin. She tried to look away, but he turned her face toward him again. "I can't say what will happen. Everything I planned has been falling apart. I've learned that people will always let you down at some level."

"The religion talk," she said dryly. She opened her purse and took out a compact with a mirror. With a few touches of makeup she put on her hard independence again. "If I needed that, I would talk to a priest."

"Right now it's all I can give. And, Klara, it's the best of me that I can give you."

She stared at him for a long time. "Perhaps I will take whatever you give me. It is more than I have now."

And so he talked. He told her about his own journey of finding God while in the States, of his ministry work, and then of his recent descent into doubt and the silence. All he could do was tell what he knew to be true and why—the moments of God's great movement in his life and why sometimes the silence was a blessing, because it brought him searching all the more. It would be for her to find her own path to God if she chose to seek him. Klara was silent as he spoke. But he saw in her times of tears and times of hardness.

Later, as Stefan pushed Viktorie on the swing, he was happy when she began to giggle and laugh. Soon afterward a few other children took tentative steps toward them as he began a game of tag. Then Viktorie found herself in the midst of boys and girls who called to her like an old friend.

Seeing Viktorie was a bridge, Stefan suddenly realized. A bridge that filled the gap between his guilt and sorrow over Viktor's death—the death he'd run from for so long. Now, at long last, he could feel the sorrow he had buried and find laughter with the niece his best friend had never known.

⊶≡◉≡⊷

Ms. Delsig had gone to Europe, the secretary informed Amanda when she arrived at Oakdale. Amanda chastised herself for not calling and making an appointment before flying all the way to Florida, but she'd feared the woman would refuse to see her. And how could she have guessed that Ms. Delsig, a woman confined to a nursing hime, would be gone from the facility?

Amanda almost turned away in disappointment but then asked to see the woman's room. She just had to know if Ms. Delsig was indeed Brigit Kirke. At first, Amanda didn't think they would let her; after all, it was someone's private quarters. But then Amanda flashed her History Network credentials and said she was interested in doing a story on her if Ms. Delsig was the woman she sought. Finally the secretary relented, asking a young woman in the office to take her there.

The smells of age and illness were barely present in the hallways and rooms of Oakdale Home of Senior Living, yet Amanda still recognized them.

The office assistant didn't speak until they reached a closed door. "This is it," she said, opening it. "Both women who live in this room went to Europe for two weeks."

"Do you know where in Europe?"

"No idea."

"Which side is Ms. Delsig's?"

The woman glanced at the names on a chart hanging on the wall. "Window side."

The bed was made with a cream eyelet bedspread. There were paintings on the walls and some figurines on the windowsill. But it was the print in a gold frame that caught

Amanda's attention. She examined it closely. The background displayed a mosaic picture of a woman from a museum in Prague—it could not be a coincidence. This had to be Brigit Kirke's room. Somehow Amanda was sure of it.

As they left, Amanda noticed a woman watching them from the hallway. She smiled at Amanda. "I believe Ms. Delsig has had more visitors in the last few weeks than during her entire stay here."

"Really?"

"My name is Candy Banks, and I never get visitors. Ms. Delsig never did either."

"Nice to meet you," Amanda said.

"Her new roommate's daughter has come a lot as they planned their trip to Europe, so that's understandable. And then we had those camerapeople and the couple who came— more new people to visit Ms. Delsig. Perhaps there is someone who wants to video my story."

"Camerapeople?"

"Yes, they were taping her story, or started to, for some Holocaust thing."

"Do you know the name of their organization?"

"No, no, I don't pay that much mind—though they were from some place in Europe—Australia or something."

"Darby and Brant Collins from Austria?"

"That was probably their names. . . . Yes, I do believe so."

"Thank you, Ms. Banks; I appreciate that," Amanda said.

On her cab ride back to the hotel, Amanda began to make plans. She wished she'd asked Candy Banks more about the couple who had visited Oakdale. However, her next step was clear. She was already packed, but Sylvia Pride was the one to speak with first.

"I need to go to Europe." Sylvia was still at the office when Amanda called from her hotel room. Amanda's date book, along with a map of Austria and the Czech Republic, was open beside her on the bed.

"When?" Sylvia asked quickly.

"Tomorrow."

"Should I send a cameraman?"

"Not yet. I'll call when I'm ready. But can Dirk be prepared? I'd like it to be him shooting this project."

"I'll let him know. But, Amanda, the budget is being watched right now. If you don't find anything, then this trip is out of your pocket."

"Fine," Amanda said, thinking of her dwindling savings. "I'll get the locations figured out, interviews lined up, and everything ready for Dirk in a week max."

"Let's make this good, all right? It's important, essential really."

After making plane reservations for the next morning, Amanda made a note to call Darby Evans Collins in Austria at dawn—they'd be sleeping now. There were many details to plan out with Darby before leaving. Amanda wanted the locations of Darby's search for the Empress Brooch, and she needed to set up a face-to-face interview with her in Salzburg.

Amanda's next call went to her father.

Her mother answered. "He's napping right now. Would you like me to wake him?" Patricia's voice was cool and distant.

"No, just have him call me on my cell phone later tonight." Amanda almost said good-bye during the awkward pause on the line, then asked, "How are you?"

"I am fine, actually, doing pretty well. My new job starts next Monday."

Amanda couldn't remember what day it was, then recalled it was Tuesday. "I didn't know you got a job."

"It's in a bookstore—perfect, is it not?"

"You can read all the poetry you want on your breaks."

"That was my thought exactly."

"I'm happy for you—Mom. Very happy for you," Amanda said, realizing she truly was. She didn't like her mother in her father's home, and she prepared herself to one day call and find her mother gone again. Yet a small hope fought within her—a hope to believe in her mother.

"Your dad got the results of his tests."

Amanda's heart tightened. Why hadn't her mother told her immediately? "I thought that was tomorrow," she said.

"It's okay, Amanda. He is all right. He might have arthritis, but it's not cancer."

"Are you sure?"

"That is what the doctor says."

"Oh, thank God," she whispered. And yet with her relief came the reminder of what she needed to tell him. "Mom, take care of him. I'll be gone for a short time." She briefly explained that her work was taking her to Europe again.

Her mother asked a few questions, then tried to reassure her. "Amanda, you don't need to worry about your father so much. You'll be happy to hear that he's asked me to find my own place to live as soon as I can. See, he certainly can take care of himself."

Amanda smiled, feeling both pride for her father and surprise at his show of resolve. "I've thought it was my job to take care of him."

"It's never been yours, Amanda dear. He's a lot stronger than you think." There was an air of annoyance in Patricia's tone, which calmed as she spoke. "But I will take care of him for you."

"All right, thanks."

"No, you don't understand. I will because I want to, not only because you asked."

Taken aback by the steady tone in her mother's voice, Amanda hit the End button and rested the phone against her chest. She lay down, gently pushing the map to the other side of the bed. Her stomach growled and she hoped they had something decent at the hotel restaurant. She checked her voice mail at work, at home, and on her cell phone. Benny had left his usual frantic messages, but Stefan's voice wasn't there. Though she didn't expect him to call—he was most likely still in some jungle village without a phone—she felt sad that he hadn't. She had told him to go and that it wouldn't work between them. She had hurt him—it was the only way he would leave her. But she missed him. The map on the bed contained one sliver of the world where he could be. His family would be sleeping right now on that dot on the map that said "Praha." What was Stefan thinking? Was he thinking of her?

Amanda shook herself mentally. She had to stop thinking of him. Someday she would realize that an entire day had passed without a thought of him—hopefully soon, though it hadn't happened yet.

CHAPTER TWENTY-EIGHT

Stefan was surprised to see Klara leaving the small blue building. He was waiting as Petrov finished a food delivery to an elderly couple who were fearful of new people—the man was sure Stefan was a Communist spy.

At first he was unsure if it really was Klara. He noticed she was wearing her "professional" clothing—short skirt, tight blouse, and tall boots—clothing she didn't wear for their meetings at the park. She walked the kind of walk that said the whole world should bow before her. She didn't act like the woman he'd met for the third time in the park. But it was Klara. He started to call out to her but stopped himself. She paused to light a cigarette without looking around and continued down the street. He almost followed her to see if she went home to her daughters or to some other location he could only imagine. The anger surprised him. But after her tears and seeming eagerness to talk to him, he felt like a fool. And he was angry at himself for agreeing to meet her and a group of their old friends tonight.

✦═◉═✦

The evening came too fast. Stefan met Klara and their friends at a café across town. Petr came without Leona as Stefan had expected. They had married soon after Stefan left for the States and had divorced several years later. Zigmund brought his girlfriend, and Kubas came alone. They greeted Stefan with hearty hugs and pounds on the back without asking much about his life or his time away. Zigmund ordered beer after beer, and the group got louder with ever-exaggerating stories of their youth. Stefan listened and watched them, feeling an even greater loss of Viktor. Viktor would have been the story-teller of the group, then would have led them on some outra-geous adventure—something similar to what caused his death.

Stefan caught Klara watching him throughout the night. She asked him to drive her home afterward. He hesitated but agreed when Petr, with a drunken, hungry smile on his face, looked Klara up and down without discretion and offered to take her home.

"Did you enjoy tonight?" she asked as Stefan drove Petrov's car along the narrow streets into the Old Town.

"It brought back a lot of memories."

"And you are glad you are not like them, correct?" Her voice had a raw edge. "You are glad you are not like us anymore."

"I never thought that, Klara," he said. "But no, I don't want to be there. I don't want to go back to that."

"That is why you cannot get close to me. It is not this woman in America as you say. Have you even spoken to her since your return?"

He drove the car into a parking place in front of Klara's apartment. "No, I have not spoken with her."

"I will leave you alone, Stefan. You can follow that God of yours and be by yourself for the rest of your life." Klara opened the car door and slammed it shut.

He quickly turned off the engine and got out of the car. "Klara, stop."

She waited by the steps to her apartment. The sidewalk and street were empty. Once he was there in front of her, he didn't know what to say. He looked at the ground, to his shoes on the cobblestone sidewalk.

Her feet, long boots beneath another miniskirt, moved close to him. She reached to adjust the collar on his shirt, then kept her hands there. "Stefan, will you ever see me as anything other than Viktor's little sister?"

Feeling her body moving closer, he held her away from him. "What do you want from me, Klara?" he demanded. "One minute you act like my lost sister, then this. I don't like games."

"I just want to be with you," she whispered. Her dark eyes were a mixture of need and want. "I have always only wanted you."

He pushed her away. "Is that what you said to the client you were visiting this afternoon?" he asked.

"What are you talking about?" She reached for a cigarette case in her purse and snapped it open.

"Today I was near Karlovo namesti. I saw you."

Klara held the cigarette in her fingers but didn't light it.

"What do you want from me?" he asked again. "You try to deceive me."

"He was not a client."

"Okay, Klara. I'm leaving now."

"Stefan, it was not a client. It was a doctor." She dropped the cigarette into her purse. She looked up at him and spoke cynically. "I was not careful too many times, and every gambler eventually loses. I will lose in the biggest way of all. The doctor told me today that I have six months to a year until I join Mama in the grave."

He stepped back. Was she telling the truth? She didn't appear ill that he could tell.

"I watched Mama die in that hospital. The same thing will happen to me. Except no one will be with me as I die."

"How long have you known?"

"Several years."

"Do you tell the men you sleep with? You just tried to seduce me. Would you have told me?"

"I insist that they use protection—I would have told you the same."

Stefan shook his head. She didn't even perceive the wrongness of her words. It was all laid out—what was best for Klara was justified as right. He wondered what had made her this person who changed her color to fit her surroundings like a chameleon. His anger mixed with horrible sympathy.

"And so you want me to be by your bedside. Is that what this act has been about?"

"It is not an act. I can be myself with you. No one else has ever let me be myself. Please, Stefan, you are the only one who knows me even a little. But I do not know how to make you love me."

He turned away from her and walked toward the car.

"My daughter will be an orphan," Klara stated flatly. "The other girls have fathers, but not Viktorie. She will be sent to an orphanage or worse when I am gone."

He walked faster.

"Who will take Viktorie?" she called as he slammed the car door, turning the engine over.

He sped down the narrow street, trying to escape her. And yet he already knew the answer to her question in a strange sense, as if he knew this was meant to happen. *I will take Viktorie.*

⊷══◐══⊶

"I need some time in Prague. I'm not sure how long." Stefan held the phone, imagining the reaction on Paul Dutton's face.

He could picture his friend and boss in his cramped office in Amsterdam, propping his feet on his desk or picking up the photograph of the two of them in Africa together. It was a snapshot Stefan had given Paul for Christmas several years earlier.

"All right, I understand."

"But I am leaving you with problems—the trip to Tanzania in a few weeks, and then did you want me back in Guatemala?"

"We'll get someone for both places. This might be just what you need."

"What do you mean?"

Paul paused and Stefan thought he heard a chair creak. "Stefan, Kathy and I have prayed for some time now that you would find direction. You are such a valuable part of International Missions, and you know what we think of you on a personal level. It's impossible to replace you. You've been perfect—going anywhere, willing to do anything. But it was Kathy who first noticed it and so we've been praying for you even more. You seem to be wandering. It's time to find home."

"If you knew what a mess I am in, this doesn't feel like an answer to prayer." Stefan wondered what Paul and Kathy would think if they knew he'd fallen in love with a woman who didn't share his faith—or any faith at all—and that he now spent more time with a prostitute than in his ministry.

"Tell me about it."

Stefan held back—what would Paul think? Then suddenly he explained everything. He told about wanting to call Amanda every day, how it wasn't getting better, and about the night he wrestled with God during his illness in the jungle. He'd promised God that he would care for little Viktorie but he didn't know when or how, though he was meeting her and Klara at the park and taking the child for ice cream, just the two of them. Though he could see God opening the path before him, Stefan still felt like he was making his way in the dark. Paul listened. It was exactly what Stefan needed. And yet he awaited a lecture or chastisement from Paul. After all, shouldn't Stefan know better by now?

"My brother, I will pray with you. And I want you to remember that though Christ didn't spend his time in the synagogues but among the people, remember who he was. You must be careful. You are only a man. Listen carefully for the still voice that speaks to your heart. Listen and hear and follow. Let's pray together."

After they prayed together, Stefan set the phone down, feeling renewed throughout his being. His future was unclear, but it looked as if he would be staying in Prague for now, perhaps for good. That was all he could see, and at last, he felt at peace that this was all he needed to see.

⁖═◉═⁖

Ms. Delsig had returned to her homeland. They arrived at night, exhausted and ready for their hotel beds. Air travel had been just as difficult as she imagined, if not worse. Hours in a tiny seat that made the bones ache, lines for the many bathroom trips she had to make, food that just didn't sit well with her stomach, and turbulence—something she'd never experienced and thought she wouldn't survive. Everything they did was slow in the airport world of superspeed. People raced by them or waited impatiently behind them. Even Lilly was at the end of her goodwill by the time they descended into Prague Ruzyně.

As they deplaned, Ms. Delsig was hit by the realization of where she was. The signs were in several languages including Czech—her first language. She heard Czech spoken over the speakers before the other translations. Though she'd heard German occasionally, it had been many years since she'd heard the first language she'd learned before taking German lessons at age four.

Ms. Delsig moved as if unaffected as they found a taxi to take them into the city, but as they entered Prague and she returned to the city of her youth, the tears came in long streams and her hands covered her mouth. There was Hradcany Castle, shining and brilliant along the northern hills. They entered the Old Town, busy and pulsing with traffic that hadn't been on these streets when she left. But it seemed unchanged in the important ways. Prague had endured the centuries . . . and life away from it. She thought she'd feel a stranger to the streets, but instead Ms. Delsig experienced the pleasure of returning to childhood memories. No one spoke as the taxi sped through the streets. Lilly stared out her window and Lorraine held on to the dashboard in the front seat.

Ms. Delsig had come back. And she knew that both pain and joy remained in the memories of this city where the world she'd known first had lived and died.

CHAPTER TWENTY-NINE

Vienna—Hallstatt—Salzburg.

It was the pathway of cities Amanda mapped out and scheduled for the first few days of her journey in Austria before going to Prague.

Amanda was familiar with the cities of Europe. She'd long ago lost count of the times she'd had her passport stamped. London, Berlin, Zurich, Paris, Dublin, Rome, Copenhagen, Moscow—the list went on and on. Benny had asked if the cities all ran together into one. "After all," he said, "they all look the same. Each has Gothic, Baroque, perhaps some remnant of Rome. A few cathedrals for certain, perhaps a synagogue if it hadn't been burned, a river through the middle, and some cobblestone streets. Most now flying the European Union flag beside their own."

But Amanda knew the differences of each one. Each city had such unique characteristics that it was hard to describe.

Stefan had mentioned it on that first weekend in Paris. "Can you feel it?" he had said as they walked a busy street at midnight. "I love that about Paris. The quickened pulse that keeps her ever young."

Stefan understood. Each place had its own pace and pulse. The people, the history, the scents, and the food. She'd walk the streets and feel the personality of each city wrap around her as if she became a small part of it for a little while.

Vienna was no exception. The monarch jewel of the old Austro-Hungarian Empire, Vienna had lost its power as the throne capital, but the remnants of its beauty remained. Amanda enjoyed hearing the highbrow name-dropping of the Viennese musical giants who had once roamed and played in the streets—Strauss, Mozart, among a few. Culture and sophistication had survived beneath the crush of two wars and the long struggle to rebuild. And yet there was a youthful strand beneath the architectural wonders of palaces, cathedrals, and fountains; it was found in clubs, galleries of art nouveau, and trendy coffeehouses.

Amanda rented a car at the Flughafen Wien Schwechat when her flight arrived to a breezy Austrian morning. She followed the Zentrum signs toward the center of the Ringstrasse, passing the Rathauspark in front of the city hall and then the universitat on the Dr.-Karl-Lueger-Ring Street. She took the first parking space she found, knowing from experience that she could drive for hours without finding a place. She needed only a short stop in Vienna before leaving the city for country roads into Upper Austria.

The narrow Viennese streets were already teeming with delivery trucks bringing their shipments of wines, crystal, vegetables, and meats for the restaurants and shops in the center of Vienna. Amanda walked through squares and streets quickly to avoid the morning commuters. She found Altes Rathaus, the Old Town Hall, along busy Wipplingerstrasse. Amanda gazed over the Baroque palace and found the entrance. It took a while to find the Austrian

Resistance Museum upstairs. She was greeted by two young men who looked like college students. Amanda was specific, and within twenty minutes, she had information on her grandfather's birthplace and his influence in Vienna before he went to Prague. His initial entrance into the Nazi Party was while he still lived in Austria. Kurt Heinrich's service records were printed, including another head shot of him in his uniform. Now Amanda had documented information on Kurt's rise in rank, training, and assignments in the Nazi Party.

On the walk back to her car, Amanda paused when she entered a simple square that had cars parked along the rim. Tall buildings surrounded the square; several streets were veins of escape. She recognized the statue of writer Gotthold Ephraim Lessing frozen in his trench coat, feet striding forward as if to cross the generations. Amanda knew the history of this place. The Judenplatz had been the site of the 1421 pogrom when Viennese citizens drove fearful Jews from Vienna and burned at the stake the two hundred who remained. Amanda recalled that the first pogrom was under the accusations that the Jewish community supported the young Hussite movement that Stefan had mentioned to her— the movement that had begun with Jan Hus and his martyrdom by fire.

It wouldn't be the last pogrom against the Jews of Vienna. The next one had come with the Nazis. They had knocked down the original Lessing statue and forced the Jews to scrub the streets—and that had been only the beginning. Amanda had been here before. Yet she hadn't known then what she knew now—that her grandfather most likely had stood here at one time. The record from the archive told of his presence here.

It was strange to walk on stones her grandfather had walked on. What would he think of a granddaughter who had wanted to be a Jew as a child? She wished he could know. Amanda would have gladly told him.

⋯⇒◎⇐⋯

Amanda left the city and drove several hours past farmland and rolling hills into the winding alpine roads of Upper Austria. The road would take her to the village of Hallstatt and then to Salzburg, where she would meet Darby Evans Collins. Amanda had spent less time in the villages of the countries she visited, venturing out only for an interview or a camera shot, then getting straight back to the cities that represented the culture of a region or country.

Now as she drove the ribboning highways of Austria, Amanda was surprised by the vibrancy of colors in the sharp, deep blues of sky and lakes, the greens of new leaves, and hillsides dotted with wildflowers. Amanda could envision a young Maria from *The Sound of Music,* twirling with arms out wide on the crown of a grass-covered slope. Jutting from the slopes were the towering ridges of range after range of Alps, already ablaze with early spring colors.

Amanda's family on her father's side had supposedly come from the lands of Bohemia. It was what she had always believed. Now she knew her grandfather had come from this nation—a place that birthed great writers, artists, musicians . . . and also men like Adolph Hitler. Kurt Heinrich had been born a few hundred kilometers away and yet had traveled among these imposing peaks and deep-cut valleys in his quest for the people he sought. Amanda wondered what these roads had looked like with German military vehicles rumbling through the narrow mountains that later became the hiding places for many runaway Nazis, their treasures, and their secrets, many yet to be discovered.

How could people not feel their own insignificance in such

a place? Had Kurt wondered at his? Or had his own greed and tainted beliefs kept him blinded? His journal indicated his constant thoughts and grappling with it all, and yet, he had still become an instrument of mass murder.

Amanda realized that she was taking a journey not unlike the one Darby had taken to find the story of her grandmother's life. Their stories entwined—Kurt had sought Darby's grandmother, causing her to flee Austria. And he'd killed the woman's best friend by mistake. It was a journey Amanda had read in another story—and one that was her own.

⋯≡◉⟨⋯

Amanda entered Hallstatt by early evening. She recognized the village—one she'd seen in many photographs. Hallstatt was the perfect photo opportunity for Austrian brochures. Such photos were often cropped for optimum advantage as Amanda had experienced in a brochure for a South American beach resort that had cut out a line of makeshift shacks on the outskirts. Yet in Hallstatt the real image was even more breathtaking than a photo. The village rested along the narrow shore of Hallstattersee, Lake Hallstatt, and its gingerbread houses grew up the sharp slope of the mountain in staggered steps. Amanda drove the one street that ran through the village along the lakeside. She left the car in a small parking lot beside a dock where two ferryboats regularly delivered passengers to and from the train that rumbled along the mountain edge several times a day.

Everything was there, just as Darby had told her when they'd spoken the day before. The gasthaus on one corner of the main square was a perfect place to stay. "Be sure to request a room overlooking the lake," Darby had said. But instead of going inside, Amanda took her notebook and camera straight toward the cemetery before the sun fell too far over the mountains.

The climb was steep, and the walkways and stairs wound back and forth between cottages and miniature gardens. A gate separated the cemetery from the Catholic church. Small red candles glowed on the concrete edgings of the graves as she walked through the cemetery. The small roofs over the wood-and-iron grave markers pointed heavenward, and each grave had well-tended flowers inside the cement border.

Amanda stopped at the Bein Haus, the white cylindrical building that housed the bones of Hallstatt residents who'd been recycled out of their graves as new arrivals took over their spaces. It was a tradition started hundreds of years ago that Amanda wanted to research further when she returned home. Inside, the skulls stared at her with their hollow eyes, as if wondering about another visitor who paid two schillings to see her own future state.

Leaving Bein Haus, Amanda remembered what Darby had told her about where the grave would be—past the Bein Haus, then around another building to another row of graves near the foot of a steep stairway. Amanda moved along the trail that went straight up the mountain and saw a bench that must allow an incredible view of the mountains, lake, and village below. The bench would have to wait for another day. For now she approached the grave, opening the wrought-iron door.

Inside it read *Tatianna Hoffman,* and there was a Scripture reference. Amanda jotted down John 15:13 to look up later. Then she took several photographs from different angles. This grave was an important marker in the search for the Empress Brooch. Within it, Darby had recovered a portion of her family inheritance buried here by her grandfather after the war. Darby's grandfather said he'd hidden nothing else there. But Amanda wondered about that. He had made the iron head-stone. She looked at the depth and width—there was just enough space to hide something inside. And it made sense to keep the brooch at the grave where no one could find it. Tatianna Hoffman had been one victim of the search for the treasure; perhaps the site that marked her life and death was the perfect place to hide it.

Amanda heard a noise behind her. An old man glanced her way as he watered flowers behind a tiny fenced yard.

"*Entschuldigung*," Amanda said, walking toward him.

He quickly turned away and moved up the short walkway toward the house.

"Please, *bitte*." When Amanda spoke in German, the man slowly turned back toward her. "Have you lived here for a long time?"

"My entire life," the man said gruffly, looking at her suspiciously. He'd certainly know by her accent that she was an American. The sympathies of a man his age could go several ways—he could be an old Resistance fighter, an avid Nazi believer, or somewhere in between. Amanda could choose from several approaches to gain this man's confidence. If she suspected his beliefs aligned with a more tolerant view of the world, she could use her work at the History Network to draw him out. If he longed for the days of the German reign, she could speak of her grandfather's life. Yet caution rang within her. She was afraid of stepping into lines of deceit, especially with the continued reminder of Richter Hauer's words in her ears: "*Obsession begins with denial.*"

"Do you know about that grave?" she asked, pointing toward Tatianna's headstone.

"I know some things," he said. He shuffled along the stone walkway to the fence. "What old men know matters little now. We have seen too much in our lives. Much more than can be told."

"It matters to me."

"Many wanted her and yet she did not belong to them. May she rest in peace forever. May she ever rest in peace."

He turned toward his small doorway again, walking hunched and with careful steps. Amanda wanted to stop him but thanked him instead. He only waved his arm behind, as if shooing her away. She had wanted to ask what he meant—whom did he want to rest in peace? Was it Tatianna Hoffman, who had lived her short life in this very village, running and playing along these mountain stairs and pathways and who, as a young woman, had given her life to save her best friend? This man had surely known Tatianna. Or did his words imply not only the girl but the item so many of them sought—the Empress Brooch?

◆═◆

That night Amanda slept in a drafty room overlooking the dark waters of Hallstattersee. The down comforter warmed her chilled feet as she melted against the mattress. She wished to sleep for endless hours. But each time she closed her eyes, her thoughts would not find rest. She kept hearing words from her grandfather's letters.

My mind must not think or hear the cries. . . . She walked in silence and did not close her eyes. . . . I must have that brooch.

Fitful dreams and wide-awake silence were her night curse. And then the nightmare came again. The darkness, the cries. Then the images of white bodies, twisted and bloody. Her knees were trembling as she knelt at the edge of the mass grave. The gun was cocked. She turned to see who held the gun. But it wasn't a man or a soldier; it was her own face she looked into above the black SS uniform. Her own cold stare.

The gunshot woke her.

Amanda got out of bed in the dark coldness of early morning. She didn't want to sleep; once again her determination prodded her onward. She must find the brooch. It was her only means of escaping the nightmare. It was her only means of redemption.

CHAPTER THIRTY

The city of Salzburg was awake when Amanda
arrived. She drove toward the medieval, white fortress that
overlooked the city and through the tunnel beneath the mountain Monchberg to find a hotel. Old Town was cushioned
between the towering Monchberg cliffs and the river Salzach.
A tunnel ran through the mountain connecting old and new
Salzburg and providing parking for visitors and tourists. In a
few hours Amanda was scheduled to attend the dedication of
a new memorial. She was already tired, and it was only ten
o'clock.

In her cozy hotel room, Amanda reviewed profiles containing Internet articles of the people she would interview today
and those she needed to set up appointments with before Dirk,
her History Network cameraman, arrived to start taping.

Darby and Brant Collins were first on the list. They worked
with a Holocaust group, taping and reviewing videos for a
Shoah testimony archive. Both were involved in several muse-
ums and in the construction of the new memorial. And Darby

herself was working on a book of photographs about survivors and their families.

Next was former Austrian minister Lukas Johansen. Herr Johansen had spent the past year dealing with the scandalous revelation that he had been an SS guard at Mauthausen before becoming a spy for the Austrian Resistance. He also had spent the past year donating money, first to a small museum near the village of Hallstatt and now to the memorial in Salzburg that commemorated the Austrian Jews who died during the Nazi regime.

Marta Olsen would also be there. Her deceased husband had been in the Resistance with Lukas Johansen, and now she worked with him on the current projects.

Darby had mentioned a few others who would be in attendance, including Kate and Jack Porter, a married couple and their daughter, Abbie, from Oregon. They had their own recent tales of old war Nazis.

The memorial opening and banquet following would have been a perfect opportunity for Dirk to be filming, but Amanda wasn't ready for him. Darby said that their organization would be covering the event and that the History Network could obtain the film from them. Usually Amanda had Dirk with her during the fieldwork of program development. Dirk had been a cameraman for thirty years and his instincts often added a new twist to an interview or a shot that she wouldn't have considered. She tried keeping an even focus on her reading but found herself more consumed with her grandfather and the search for the brooch. If she found the priceless heirloom, it would be a landmark ending for "In Search of the Empress Brooch." Amanda knew she was justifying everything now— but it seemed the path she must take. Find the brooch for her father . . . and for herself.

Amanda dressed in a black knit shirt and comfortable gray suit. She wore her favorite vintage black jewelry. Before leaving Hallstatt this morning, she had curled her blonde hair but once more touched up her hair and makeup. Her profiles of the people she'd soon interview were in a portfolio in her satchel along with a handheld tape recorder, business cards, and notepad.

⋯⟾◉⟾⋯

"It's great to finally meet you in person," Darby Collins said as Amanda entered their second-story office. As they shook hands, Brant Collins stepped in from the hallway and welcomed her.

"Another Californian, I hear," he said, sitting on the edge of a desk. Darby and Brant Collins were one of those couples you could mistake for brother and sister, with their brown hair and fair complexions, but especially their welcoming expressions as both smiled. Both talked warmly as they got past introductions. Brant invited her inside a wide conference room that Amanda suspected also doubled as a taping room, judging by the equipment in one corner.

"We have coffee and some sandwiches. Let's spend some time getting to know each other."

"Sounds perfect," Amanda said. She'd done this time and time again—the casual lunch that was really pure business. But she appreciated the couple's genuine interest in her work. They talked about favorite restaurants in San Francisco, since Darby had grown up an hour north of the city and had gone there often over the years. Amanda explained the History Network program and some of the information she was seeking.

"Would you mind if I asked a few questions right now?" Amanda ventured.

"Certainly not," Darby answered, glancing at Brant with a smile. "I'm not used to being the one interviewed, but I'll try my best."

Amanda took her mini tape recorder from her satchel and set it on the table between them. "I'll be easy on you. Everything we use for the program will be done with your approval. The tape will be used for my own notes, and then we'll get our cameraman here to do the actual interview used on the air. Would you like to be referred to as Mrs. Collins, Frau Collins, or Darby?"

"Let's stick with Darby."

Brant pulled up a chair at the table after refilling both their coffees.

"Interview Darby Collins at office in Salzburg. Okay. Darby, I've read about your search for your grandmother's friend, Tatianna Hoffman, and for your lost family heirlooms. Before we get into that, why are you now working solely within Holocaust organizations? Why devote yourself to this era?"

Darby folded her hands and rested her chin above them. Her eyes drifted outside as she considered the question. "Recently, I was told that this is all history, that it's over and I should devote my life to stopping the inhumane acts of today. I struggled with that . . . actually Brant and I both did. But we believe that much of what is happening today is because of what has happened before—old hatreds that haven't been destroyed, ignorance and fear and a loss of compassion toward other peoples. Perhaps a look at the past—and getting people to really see other people—will help some of these present situations. What do you think, Brant?"

Brant turned from watching Darby and spoke to Amanda in an even, determined voice that held her attention. "The stories are not buried. They are living, breathing stories that must still be heard. There are hundreds of thousands of individuals whose names will never be recognized on this earth. Their ashes will never be distinguished from the soil of a million places throughout Europe. They will not be remembered. So we do what we can and record those who can speak. We do our small bit in a vast world of need. But we must. It won't leave us alone. Surely you understand."

Amanda stopped, startled. Somewhere along her journey she'd lost what Darby and Brant had—the driving passion for her work to be more than just airing a compelling program that would be played for an hour, maybe go to video, and help promote her team. It was futile to believe that her work was the voice of those who could not speak. Yet Brant and Darby didn't seem to see this futility.

"Doesn't it overwhelm you—the weight of it? Being the voice of those who can't speak?"

"It does," Darby said. "We both go through stages of wanting to give up. Especially when we see how the past has devastated so many people. Last week, an elderly man wept in this office, telling us that he's never gotten over what happened to his family sixty years ago. That's not something you leave at the office. But the weight isn't for me to carry. I have to give it up to God because he's the only one who can take it. I know, because I've seen God moving in my life beyond what I could do or imagine. But that's another subject all its own."

Darby glanced at her watch. "We'll have to resume a little later. Right now it's time for the dedication."

⋖═◉═⋗

During the memorial ceremony Amanda especially watched former minister Lukas Johansen. She expected him to give a speech and unveil the huge sculpture of twisted bones with the names of Austrian camps and subcamps. He was the main financier of the project, yet he stayed on the sidelines, even though cameras often turned his way.

After the dedication Amanda went to the elegant banquet room across the Salzach River near the sweeping gardens of Mirabelle Palace for her meeting with Herr Johansen. The sun

hung in a bright blue sky, warming the chill from the day.
Amanda waited outside, near the garden of stone dwarfs, and
admired the ornately patterned flower garden. Its wide aisle
framed the cathedral domes and Hohensalzburg fortress on the
mountain at the south.

An imposing figure, former minister Lukas Johansen did not
simply occupy an area; his presence filled the space. His age
revealed itself in the age spots on his hands and forehead, yet
his eyes showed the strength of his character and intelligence.
He'd once been Bruno Weiler, Nazi, who chose to serve time
in prison for his crimes as a camp guard. A person of infinite
intrigue—a Nazi who turned against the party he'd pledged his
life to in order to spy against the Third Reich and fight with
the Resistance—Lukas Johansen was worthy of his own two-
hour special at least, and Amanda wanted to hear all about this
fascinating figure.

"You are interested in an interview for American history
television?" Herr Johansen said after they greeted one another.

"Yes," Amanda said. She'd planned to use her tape recorder
but now kept it tucked away.

"This story is about the Empress Brooch."

"Yes, it is."

His gaze and abrupt manner intimidated her. Would this
have been her reaction if she had faced Kurt Heinrich, her own
grandfather?

"I assume then you already know my past."

"I do."

"And do you have any questions, or do you just have one-
and two-word comments?" As Lukas smiled slightly, Amanda's
nerves calmed.

"How does someone like you become a camp guard?" she
asked suddenly, a little embarrassed after she'd asked it, yet
knowing it was directed not at Herr Johansen but at Kurt
Heinrich. *Grandfather, how did you become a mass murderer?*

Lukas Johansen crossed his arms and nodded as if satisfied she'd asked something of value. "It is becoming easier to speak about this. Now that I can speak it, I search for what makes a young man turn to evil. If a man could see himself at the end of it, that would make all the difference in the world. Yet it is not the place of man to know the destination—only to choose the right paths at the crossroads.

"Evil is beguiling. Sometimes you walk in voluntarily. The hatred was already there, or the determined lust for power and success. Man believes he controls the evil. He will decide upon, choose for himself, and leave behind evil at will. The truth is, evil takes control of a man and does not easily let go. It owns you."

He gazed at a bird that hopped along a branch, then flew away. "The other way a young man turns to evil is by compromise; it is like quicksand. You know it is something controversial, dangerous, exciting, but you stick your foot in, thinking you will draw it out if or when the danger becomes real. Before you know it, you are stuck and there is no way out except deeper in—unless someone throws you a rope."

"Who threw you a rope?"

"Tatianna Hoffman."

Amanda was surprised to hear that name again. So often it came back to Tatianna.

"You know I was in the firing squad at Tatianna's execution," Lukas said somewhat sadly.

Amanda tried to recall if she had known such news. "You were at Mauthausen when Kurt Heinrich came to interrogate her about the location of the Empress Sissi Brooch?"

"Yes. You know of Kurt Heinrich then?"

Amanda nodded. "Did you know him personally?"

"Not personally, though I saw him arrive and leave, and I heard stories about him while there." Lukas churned his hands.

"What do you know about him?"

"I know he was obsessed with getting the Empress Brooch. He was obsessed to such an extent that he did not know he had the wrong girl in prison."

"Yes," she said, trying to imagine the memories inside Lukas' mind. She wondered what he'd think of her next question, then spoke it. "Are we all capable of evil, Herr Johansen?"

"Yes."

"Why do you believe this?"

"Because I know it to be true. We all have the propensity to do wrong. With every wrong, it becomes easier. Without a moral standard, what keeps anything from being wrong? Without a higher force or God, what reason is there for a moral standard? Animal instinct and survival of the fittest destroy morality, making the Holocaust acceptable. For a time I lived in a world where God was not welcome, where the strong survived in the rawest, most instinctual world that has ever existed. There was allegiance to a power of evil only. All good was sought to be destroyed."

Amanda studied the man's face, the deep lines around his eyes that deepened as he spoke. She found it strange that the people who dug closest to the horrors of man were grappling the most with issues of theology.

"Is evil found more strongly in some than others?" she queried. "Perhaps it is something passed through DNA codes. They say mental illness is hereditary."

"Every man is born with his own choices. Despite what is pressed upon his life, there comes a time when every human chooses his or her own path. I would not think my daughters are more prone to evil because of my past. Perhaps they will see it more closely because of what I have done, yet they make those crossroad decisions for themselves."

"How do we get free from evil?"

Lukas' eyes strayed to the glass windows of the foyer into the banquet room. An older woman in a pretty violet dress waved from behind the glass, then turned back to a group she was speaking with. Lukas smiled slightly, a smile that warmed his face. "A friend of mine would say that only God coming in can get the evil out."

Amanda wondered about that. Lately she had felt as if she could step into her soul and see the blackness, the beating evil growing inside, the love that fought against it but seemed to be losing, always losing. "I think those are wise words."

"I do agree."

"Do you believe in the curse of the Empress Brooch?"

"I believe in the curse of man's greed. That is all." Herr Johansen sighed. "You do know that this is very much Tatianna's story?"

"What do you mean?"

"The story of the Empress Brooch is really about Tatianna. It may seem to be about a lost heirloom or human greed or another story from the war. Yet it is about a girl who gave her life to protect her friend. Kurt Heinrich believed that he murdered her, but her spirit lives on. I would say that Tatianna overcame Kurt Heinrich, though I also know the spirit of Nazism is found in many forms today. We all know in our spirit what is good and beautiful and pure. The story of Tatianna. Perhaps the strongest do survive, yet it is the word *strong* that is up for discussion."

Amanda could only nod. She told herself to remain professional and composed. "I would say that the good and beautiful and pure are the strong that survive."

When Lukas looked at her oddly, Amanda realized a tear had burst down her cheek. In that instant she didn't care. She paused with the sudden desire to run—and run quickly. Yet a longing to be understood filled her as she gazed into the eyes of a man who had met her grandfather, who had been at

Tatianna's execution, and who was loved by Darby. He was a link from yesterday and also understood the consequences yesterday had on the present and the future—the scandal surrounding his life was proof of that. Perhaps he was the one person who could understand.

"Herr Johansen, I must tell you that I always believed my grandfather died at the hands of the Nazis. I found out last month that he was actually a Nazi. My grandfather was Kurt Heinrich."

Visibly surprised, Lukas Johansen opened his mouth to respond, then stopped.

"There you are," someone said behind them. It was Darby. "I meant to tell you. We began interviewing a woman for the Shoah Library. As a child, she knew my family before the war. She played with my grandmother. It has been quite extraordinary finding her."

"I know who this woman is," Amanda admitted.

Lukas watched them without comment.

"You know her?" Darby asked.

"I know of her. My research tracked her down from the account of a soldier who found her at the bottom of a cliff."

"She believed no one has known her identity all these years."

"Perhaps she knows about the brooch."

"She was just a young teenager when she went to the camps. I doubt she would recall much . . . except she did know that her family was targeted because of their friendship with my family. That's bothered me since meeting her. They were Jews so they would have been sent to the camps anyway, but her brother and parents were specifically killed in the Nazis' quest for the brooch."

"I would like to speak with her," Amanda said. "But first I must tell you what I just told Lukas. The time has come for me to speak the truth before I return to Prague."

CHAPTER THIRTY-ONE

The tiny hotel was charming, tucked into a corner in Malá Strana—the "Little City" that connected itself to Old Town by the famous Charles Bridge. Ms. Delsig stood on a balcony outside her hotel room. Lilly and her daughter, Lorraine, were still sleeping after struggling with jet lag. From her hidden view above the street, Ms. Delsig watched a woman and child walk hand in hand down the sidewalk.

She remembered walking that same street with her mother and crossing the Charles Bridge, its railing lined with stone Catholic saints. Some of the towering figures awed her and others frightened her as she had stared into their frozen faces. They had come this route every Friday to the market in Malá Strana and her mother's favorite vendor of fresh vegetables. Her mother said the quality she found there was worth the long walk.

Where did this child and mother walk this morning in Praha? Ms. Delsig wondered. What was their conversation? Did they cherish the precious feel of hands held together—

hands of mother and daughter? Ms. Delsig knew she had not treasured it enough until she longed for her mother's hands again.

The sights of Prague were altogether different from those in Florida. She'd forgotten, or perhaps she could not have known until she left and returned. Prague exuded a feeling of the ancient, as if the whispers of priests, courtesans, and peasants could be heard in shadowed corners and beneath wide stone archways. Rock squares had been hand cut and hauled to where castles, bridges, towers, and churches had been built along the wide, deep Vltava River. As a child born in such a place, she had seen the beauty of morning light reflecting over the water, upon dark stone structures, and over the green tree-tops along the hillsides above the city. Ms. Delsig wondered who lived in the apartment of her childhood memories. For years, she hadn't allowed herself to remember. She didn't want to recall the creaky gate or the green vines that grew up the sides of the courtyard. The burgundy door had surely been repainted during Communist decolorization. Yet someone had gone in and out all those years, talking to neighbors who were not the ones she'd known, going to shops and to market.

Ms. Delsig left her balcony perch and went downstairs. As she sat at a table in the hotel breakfast room, she continued to ponder the places of her youth that waited just across the river. Through a part in the curtain she could see the wet stones outside and the sprinkled dots on the glass from an early morning rain. She took a bite of the warm bread, the taste itself bringing her a great sense of home. America some-how failed to imitate the flavor that filled her nose and melted on her tongue.

The door to the breakfast room opened, but it wasn't Lilly or Lorraine, though she hoped they were finally awake. Instead a handsome couple entered and nodded at her. The man was tall with light hair, and the woman's long hair was pulled back, displaying her sharp features. Ms. Delsig noticed that they spoke English as they went through the line of yogurts, granolas, cheeses, and rolls, selecting only juice or milk. Ms. Delsig continued to take slow bites, gazing out the window.

"Did you ask him how to get there?" the woman asked as they sat down.

"He gave me a map. We'll find it."

Ms. Delsig wondered which tourist site the couple was going to visit for the day.

"I hope I can do this," the woman said. "What will it be like to see where my father lived?"

"It will be like finally finding him," came the response. From the corner of Ms. Delsig's view she saw the guy take the woman's hand. "Like coming home in a sense."

"Yes, I think you are right," she whispered. The man opened the map, and they discussed the best route to Bilkova. It was the same street Ms. Delsig had lived on as a child.

"You are looking for Bilkova?" Ms. Delsig asked suddenly.

They looked at her, obviously surprised.

"Yes, yes, do you know the street?" the young woman asked.

"I once lived on that street and today will return there."

"When did you live there—perhaps you knew my father?"

"I left in the late forties."

"Oh," she said with disappointment in her voice. "He settled there after the war and was killed during the Communist era. My mother escaped, and I was born in America."

"So you never met him?"

"No, I only heard the stories of his life. What about you? Why are you here?"

"I have come to see my childhood home on Bilkova. I have not been back in over fifty years."

"Perhaps we could go together?" the man suggested. "Such

an amazing coincidence to meet you, so there must be a reason for it."

Ms. Delsig hesitated. "If you do not mind some old ladies slowing you down."

"Not at all," the woman said kindly. "I fear this day will be difficult, and it would be wonderful to have someone share it with me. My name is Ilona, and this is my husband, Kane."

"This is a true pleasure meeting you both," Ms. Delsig said, taking the hand the woman extended. "Let me get some more tea. Then please tell me about yourselves."

"Let me get your tea, and we'd like to hear all about you too," Ilona said, rising quickly and taking Ms. Delsig's cup.

Ms. Delsig moved to their table as Ilona returned with the tea and began to tell about her life in America and the longing to see where her father had died. Ms. Delsig also shared about her recent reconciliation with the past that led her back to Prague. Lilly and Lorraine later joined them in the breakfast room and became acquainted, discussing the best time to cross the bridge or to take a cab into the Jewish Quarter and Bilkova Street.

As they set up the day ahead, Ms. Delsig smiled. Yes, there was strength in numbers, and she was happy to share this visit with the young couple. As Ilona had said, "This day will be difficult."

-+≈◎⊂=+-

Richter Hauer read the letter for the third time. He sat on the bed in his cell, then stood by the barred window and went over it again. It was postmarked from Florida, and though unsigned, he knew exactly who had written it.

> *Hope your trip to the U.S. is going well. We appreciate all you did for us and wish you would have joined us. Prague won't be the same without you.*

They were mocking him. He was being punished for his unwillingness to join their insanity—he'd suspected that, but they wanted him to know for certain. And they were going to Prague. That didn't mean anything to him. If they'd named an Austrian city, he would have known they'd found the brooch. But they were on the trail and might even know where it was.

Richter crumpled the letter and threw it against the opposite wall. They were laughing at him, believing him incapable of anything now. The letter was intended to be the twist of the knife they'd already plunged into him. Yet they didn't know he had more in him than that. He wouldn't give up. Instead he would pull out the knife and strike them back. Perhaps he couldn't get out of here, but he must make sure they didn't win.

Richter pounded the metal door of his cell. "I need to make a phone call!"

⊷⊜⊶

Amanda crossed the border from Austria into the Czech Republic after showing her passport to the border patrol. Not many years earlier, there had been lines of cars waiting to go through the long approval process to gain access across the invisible line that separated the Communist East from a "Western" nation.

Wispy gray clouds hung in the sky. The Czech country roads were bumpy asphalt lanes in the midst of green fields over rolling hills, and bundles of budding trees along the edges of crystal streams. She followed the Praha signs through quaint villages and wide rolling spaces.

Lukas Johansen and Darby had spoken to her long into the night. Amanda told of her own journey that reminded her of Darby's search for her family's history but had ended with devastating results. Lukas shared telling his daughters about his past and their continued work in finding a new closeness together. Darby said she would speak to Brigit Kirke; perhaps they could meet soon.

But it was Lukas' parting words that stayed with Amanda as she left Austria behind: *"It is better to face it than to run."*

Amanda had explained that she had little choice with the History program getting the green light.

"But you must face it for yourself also," Lukas had added.

As she drove, Amanda began to feel the pressure of the deadline pushing her along. Sylvia would be expecting her to report in—usually Amanda would have called or e-mailed by now. Sylvia would want something new and great for the program—something to impress Wallace, especially during "these precarious times." Amanda thought Sylvia needed to get away from the office to become fully aware of what a precarious time really was.

Even more important, Amanda kept thinking of her father. She needed to get back to him. The days since she had discovered their true heritage had pulled her away from him. She knew he thought it was her mother's appearance in San Francisco. He wouldn't understand the real reason. Yet she must have something, some token that would calm the storm she'd soon release upon his life. Amanda stopped at a drab gas station for coffee, since her need for rest must be conquered. After all, "that's what coffee's for." Amanda smiled at Benny's line that made her miss him and home even more.

As she continued down the road, Amanda noticed two women beside a parking turnout. They stood beside a van. Hair and clothing were immediate indications of their profession. But what were they doing out here? Amanda drove on, and within a few miles she again saw women on the roadside. One diesel truck had pulled over and the driver was leaning out, talking to one of the women. She was pretty, with thick, dark hair tumbling down her back. She turned to glance at

Amanda as she drove by—their eyes meeting for the briefest second. Amanda wished she could stop and tell the woman she didn't have to sell herself to any man who stopped along the country road. There was a world of opportunity beyond her barred life. Amanda passed a few more groups of women. She wondered about them—what had brought them to such a place and what would happen once their beauty faded?

The road sometimes narrowed into two-lane streets through towns; then she'd catch a wide freeway, newly constructed. She saw a road crew using hand tools and Skil Saws at one site over a bridge—a symbol of the fact the new republic was still attempting to catch up with the modern age.

With every mile closer to Praha, Amanda thought more about Stefan and his family. She remembered his mother, grandmother, and cousin in their tower apartment with the broken elevator. What Bohemian dance or song had Pavla taught her students? What gentle Czech words of advice and guidance would Ruza have for Amanda now? What ministry work did Petrov pursue for his struggling countrymen?

And, most of all, she found herself thinking, *What is Stefan doing? And where in the world could he be tonight?*

⊷⊶◉⊷⊶

Tiffany nearly dropped the phone. She looked around the offices, wondering whom to tell, who could do something. After a minute, she called Benny Dunn's work number and told the school secretary that it was urgent.

"Benny, this is Amanda's assistant, Tiffany. Remember we met at the concert . . . ?"

"Tiffany, I was in the middle of a music lesson."

"Sorry, but I just had a very strange and scary message, and I didn't know who else to call."

"What is it?"

Tiffany's hands fluttered in the air as she spoke. "It was a man in prison. Amanda met with him before she went to Europe. He just contacted me and said he must speak with Amanda as soon as possible. When I told him she was somewhere in Europe, he got upset and said she could be in terrible danger. I didn't want to worry Amanda's father, and I didn't want to tell my boss yet. What should I do? Should I call the police or FBI?"

Benny's voice was calm and assuring. "I'll think of something. But tell me all the details first."

◦═◉═◦

Their voices and the sounds of the city bounced off the stone courtyards and walkways as they walked the narrow sidewalk from Staroměstské namesti, the Old Town Square, and through the maze of streets toward Bilkova. Ms. Delsig kept reminding the others to look up at the many surprises found in the architecture and sculptures above eye level. Kane and Ilona walked ahead, reading their map and travel book at street corners as they waited for the women.

It amazed Ms. Delsig how little she could do. Her feet had once skipped happily over these very cobblestone streets that now she slowly trod, pushing the rattling metal walker as she went. Thus far, the city had warmed her with longing and reminiscence as they had eaten lunch at the Old Town Square, watching the Astronomical Clock on the tower as it turned the hour and displayed the season, moon phases, zodiac, and time of day. As a child, she had always stopped to watch the clock, in awe of the hourly entrance of the figure Death. He would ring a bell and turn over his hourglass before the parade of apostles passed two windows. And yet now, Ms. Delsig's stomach churned sickeningly as the memories of this place returned with vivid clarity.

Then she found it. The doorway along the sidewalk was decorated with vines and flowers around the arched opening. Beside the entrance was a small courtyard where she and Edgar had played as children, and where later she had watched Hani explore. Flowers were tended in neat containers, and children's toys were scattered inside the fenced area. Through the doorway would be stairs leading to their three-room apartment on the second floor. Ms. Delsig could see white lace curtains in the windows—her mother had bought thick drapes a few years before the war and closed them tightly every night. Ms. Delsig shuddered.

With the many happy memories of celebrations, Shabbats, and friends who had lived on this street came the other memories. The sound of boots on the stairs, the dreaded midnight knock on their door, the promise from her mother that she would be back as she hastily packed a few items in a bag, her father being hit and falling to the living-room floor. Her father, a man of great kindness and a lover of art and beauty who had never known violence, was hit in the face by one of the Nazi soldiers. Later she'd found drops of blood on the rug where his nose had been bleeding. It had been her last glimpse of her parents.

Ms. Delsig looked for a place to rest. There were blisters on her hands from pushing the walker, and her feet ached.

"Is this it?" Kane asked from beside her. "This is where you lived?"

She nodded. His voice sounded too loud. Her thoughts went to the great leaving of people. They had all carried suitcases of various sizes down the street but all with their names clearly marked on the sides. She'd been frantic to get word to Edgar. Her grandmother was like the prophet of doom, stating that this was the end as they'd been told it would come. Hani was irritable, wanting to play in the garden. They had carried their luggage and enough food for several days toward the exposition hall. It would take two days before they boarded the trains that would take them away from Prague—most of them forever.

Just then Kane sneezed.

When Ms. Delsig put her hand on his shoulder, he jumped back as if burned. "I was going to offer you my handkerchief," she said kindly. "Or I think I have a tissue in my purse."

"No," he said quickly. "Thank you, but no."

An instant later she saw him wipe his hands off on his pants. It sent a sickening wave through her, and she wondered why. Somehow it reminded her of another time but the same place. Ms. Delsig tried to brush the uneasy feeling aside. Surely she was wrong; surely she was misreading Kane.

Ilona stepped up beside them, linking an arm through Kane's. "How long did you live here?" she asked. That's when Ms. Delsig realized they had not seen Ilona's father's house.

"From birth until I was almost thirteen years old. Your father's home should be down the street a few houses. Perhaps the people who live there will remember him. Would you like us to go with you?"

Ilona smiled. "No, but thank you. Do you think the people who live here will remember you?"

"I will not ask," Ms. Delsig said. She'd hoped that the occupants would not see them. "I do not want to know them."

There was a restlessness about Kane, she noticed, as Lilly tried to talk to him. He kept glancing around and pulling away from the others. He whispered something to Ilona. Perhaps he had tired of being with old women, Ms. Delsig thought. She couldn't blame him. And yet the young couple stayed with them. Kane seemed bored with the casual chitchat and only became interested again when Ilona asked about the city during the war and about Ms. Delsig's own history.

"Did you lose many friends?" he asked.

"Almost every one," she replied sadly.

"What happened to your family's belongings?" he fired back.

"I never knew." His questions felt like an inquisition.

Finally Kane and Ilona walked down the street to the number Ilona claimed was her father's home. But they didn't stay long, and Ms. Delsig noticed they didn't even try to speak with neighbors. Soon they were back, and this time Ilona was the one asking Ms. Delsig questions.

Then in the middle of Ilona's questioning, Kane spoke abruptly. "They say a lot of Jewish art and things are still missing. Do you have anything from your family like that?"

A great weariness fell over Ms. Delsig as she looked at Lilly, asleep in her wheelchair. Lorraine, herself tired, leaned against the handlebars. "I did have some things not returned, many things. But, Kane, would you mind walking to the corner down there and hailing us a cab? I think it is time for a late-afternoon siesta."

Kane didn't seem especially happy about his errand, but he did it.

Back at the hotel, just before her nap, Ms. Delsig realized that she had faced her greatest fear—seeing her home again. And yet, amazingly, she had found she could leave it without bitterness. Although the past would never leave her, she knew she could go on and be just fine.

CHAPTER THIRTY-TWO

Stefan had taken to walking the dark streets of Prague again. The evening brought clouds and a cold breeze. He walked with his head lowered and his coat buttoned tight.

He had decided to talk to Amanda. They couldn't leave things with that good-bye in San Francisco. Though it would probably never work between them, Stefan had to tell her the truth of what he felt, of who he was, of the child he would someday care for, and then they could go their separate ways. She'd be at work right now. It was afternoon in San Francisco; the fog had probably burned away and the sun would be shining in the vibrant blue sky. He had wanted to see her office, to picture her there. Instead of calling at work, he decided to wait until he hoped to find her at home. Maybe she'd be sitting with her legs pulled up on the couch, her slippers covering painted toes, her dog curled on the floor beside her.

A car zipped by, splashing water on the sidewalk at his feet. Stefan paused. He was at the river again, as he often found himself. The Charles Bridge was quiet, with few wanderers. Beneath the Staré Město Bridge Tower, he walked to the first stone saints along the bridge railing. He counted the statues on the left until he could barely see the stone profile of St. Christopher against the low lights along the bridge. A part of him wanted to go there and stare into the dark waters below. It was at Saint Christopher that Viktor had jumped. The image was carved forever into Stefan's memory. Viktor had stood on the stone railing with arms held high, as if he too were a statue.

"Watch this!" he had shouted before leaping over the edge.

The Saint Christopher statue—the patron saint of travelers—was where Stefan had last seen his best friend alive.

But for the first time, Stefan was no longer overpowered by the guilt and sorrow that had always accompanied this trek to the bridge. Instead there was peace. His return to Prague was like coming around to a new beginning. The past was gone, brushed away. The years of his journeying were over, and now he knew his place was here in Prague. The only area still unfinished was his relationship with Amanda. He must talk to her and know where she fit into his tomorrows.

With this thought Stefan turned away and began his walk toward home.

◦━◉◉━◦

After returning from a small restaurant, where their total extravagant dinner cost less than a trip to Denny's in the States, Ms. Delsig was surprised to receive a message from Darby Evans Collins at the hotel desk. She expected it to be about the Holocaust taping, but the note said to call her at home. Ms. Delsig found phone calls in Prague a great challenge. The line was fuzzy when she had called Alfred in Florida, and there had been a pause between their voices. Phoning Darby was another difficulty involving her calling

card and using the correct country code. Ms. Delsig sighed, sat
at the antique desk in their two-bedroom suite, and pushed a
long series of numbers. At last she heard the call go through
and Darby speaking a German greeting over the phone.

"Your German sounds very good," Ms. Delsig told Darby.

"I'm getting a lot of practice."

"How is your grandfather?" Ms. Delsig asked, afraid of bad
news for the young woman she'd grown fond of in just a short
time. She knew the loss of the grandfather Darby had recently
found would surely devastate her.

"He is much improved. He's given us several scares, but he
continues to amaze us. He says he has too much to live for
now, so he's fighting off the grim reaper. And how is Prague?"

"It brings back memories, as I am sure you understand. Is
everything all right?" Ms. Delsig doodled tiny images on a
piece of scratch paper. She'd noticed her hands wanting to
sketch and create since they'd arrived.

"There is someone I must tell you about. A woman
contacted me about the Empress Brooch. Her name is Amanda
Rivans. She works at the History Network—are you familiar
with that cable channel?"

"Yes, it is a favorite for many at Oakdale."

"This woman began working on a program about the
brooch for two reasons. One was after the recent information
about my search. The other was because as a child she'd been
told about an Austrian Empress Brooch. This began both her
personal search to find some answers about her past and also
her professional search to develop a program about the
Empress Brooch."

"Interesting."

"Yes. However, she discovered some startling details as she
researched her heritage."

"Go on."

"I'm struggling with the best way to tell you this. But

Amanda discovered that her grandfather was not who she'd been told. Instead of being a victim of Nazi atrocities, he was a Nazi himself."

Ms. Delsig nodded, wondering what this had to do with her and why Darby seemed so concerned.

"Ms. Delsig, Amanda Rivans found out that her grandfather was Kurt Heinrich."

Ms. Delsig blinked. And blinked again. "This woman who works at the History Network and is doing a story on the brooch . . . Kurt Heinrich has a granddaughter?"

"Yes."

Ms. Delsig thought of her brother, sister, parents, and grandmother. When her death came, her family bloodline would end. And yet Kurt Heinrich's had continued. She remembered his voice, so calm as they stood on the cliff ledge in the deep night. Now it returned to her over the years, much louder than the voices of her own loved ones. His tone seemed to say, *"Yes, you will die tonight. But it will be fine."* Yet she had survived. If only she'd had the chance to tell him that.

"Ms. Delsig, are you all right?"

"Yes." She nodded again and again. "Have you told her about me?"

"I told her a little, but she already knew about you." The phone line was quiet for a long moment; then Darby said, "And she is in Prague."

Ms. Delsig turned toward the window. "Of course she would come here."

"Ms. Delsig, she seems like a very good person. She is searching, and it isn't for the brooch, though this is what she believes will make things right."

"No. He said that he would get us if we did not give it to him. We never did."

"He's dead, Ms. Delsig."

"He has a child or maybe more?"

"A son."

"He has a son and a granddaughter? One of them will take over his work now that they know I am alive."

⋅⇒⊜⇐⋅

Amanda had returned to Prague. She reserved a hotel with a locked garage—a requirement for bringing her rental car to the Czech Republic—and mapped out her location in relation to the tower apartment where Stefan's family lived. The pricey hotel was near Wenceslas Square, the long rectangular center of politics for the city of Prague, and a long walk away from Stefan's house. Finding Petrov's name in the phone book, Amanda almost called him. Even without Stefan, Amanda would love to see them. There was a warmth and feeling of safety within their walls. She wished to stay in Stefan's loft bedroom and to awaken to church bells and the scent of Pavla's cooking.

Amanda left her luggage at the hotel and ventured out into the night. It was chilly and rainy, though not the snowstorm as on her earlier visit to Prague. She yearned for time to just explore and wander in the city on a warm summer evening. Her first stop was on the list of five sites she'd chosen for Stefan to show her—if the storm had not kept them away. Amanda read the history of this area in her guidebook as she walked.

Wenceslas Square had begun as a horse market in medieval times and was later the place of celebrations and riots, death and triumph. In 1918, the new Czechoslovak Republic was announced to citizens here. The new nation was taken over by the Nazis in 1939, finding brief independence in 1945 before becoming a Communist country a year later. In 1968, there was a surge of hope as citizens sought the end of Communism. Jan Palach, a student at the university, lit himself on fire at the square to protest the Russian invasion. Over two hundred thousand people honored him the next day, though Palach would die before the week's end and the hope for freedom crushed beneath Russian tanks.

Amanda stood before the small wooden crosses of the memorial to victims of Communism—the exact location where Jan Palach had burned himself. It was something she could not understand—giving her life for something she believed in. She recalled the verse she'd looked up in Austria from the reference on Tatianna Hoffman's grave in Hallstatt.

> *Greater love hath no man than this, that a man lay down his life for his friends.*
>
> —John 15:13

Amanda wandered from Wenceslas Square toward the river. She stopped at a familiar square and realized it was Betlemska namesti. Bethlehem Chapel stood just across the street. She stared at the Gothic windows of the church Stefan loved. The doors would be locked, but how Amanda suddenly wished for the comfort of the church.

A light drizzle was falling as she continued down narrow Lilova Street and then Karlova. The cobblestones of the bridge were wet with rain, and her hair was damp. Darkened stone saints stood as sentries along both sides of the bridge, each with a unique inscription and image in their design. Hradcany Castle stretched along the hillside above her. The towers of Malá Strana rose on the opposite end of the bridge. The rain brought a soft haze to the world around her, giving the castles, cathedral domes, and church towers a dreamlike quality. Lights on the castle and stone monuments reflected an orange glow into the blanketed sky, covering the world. The bridge was like every magical place she'd ever read about—the wood between worlds, the yellow brick road, Alice's wonderland.

She wanted to stay here forever. It didn't feel new to her. It seemed she'd always known it. She certainly didn't want to claim to be a visitor, a tourist of all things. Prague. This bridge was the center of a city that brought them all together. Her grandfather and grandmother had certainly stood on this very bridge, as had Brigit Kirke and Stefan. Perhaps that was how something inside her recognized it as if it were a part of her. Amanda stood at the crest and thought about raising her hands to heaven. She wanted to cry out, *Do you see me here? Do you know how to help me? What can I do? What can be done?*

But Amanda didn't raise her hands upward; they were pressed into her coat pockets as she turned and walked away.

She determined to stay alert on the way back to the hotel. After her night walk in San Francisco she tried to remain on populated roads and keep her travel smarts. A great compulsion pulled at her feet as she stayed on the busy streets, making a wide arch that brought her to Stefan's tower apartment. Several floors had lights in the windows, and she tried to figure out which window belonged to Petrov, Ruza, and Pavla. She remembered gazing from the loft as the snow fell on the street. Following the sidewalk to the streetlamp, she looked up. There was a soft glow of light from the window that would be Stefan's. What if it was him? What if he was really there, reading by the lamplight or sleeping on the box spring and mattress? Amanda stood there for a long time as a chill ran through her.

She turned away for the long walk back to her hotel.

Finally I discover the magic of Prague, Stefan. But you are not with me.

⋆≡◯≡⋆

Amanda awoke, sitting straight up, wondering if she'd really slept. What had caused her sudden alertness? It wasn't the nightmare. There had been no knock on her hotel door. She heard a few cars outside but nothing else.

And then Amanda knew. Somehow it was clear. She knew exactly where the Empress Brooch was located. She had seen it before. It was right where anyone could see it.

Kicking the comforter from her legs, Amanda flipped on the lamp above the wooden headboard. She grabbed her satchel and went through her files until she found the packet of photographs. She flipped through them until she held the pictures of Brigit Delsig's room.

At last the pieces of the mystery were fitting together. Amanda read the inscription at the bottom of the mosaic print; it was barely visible beneath the large letters advertising the museum. The inscription was like a mockery to all who passed by it.

Amanda felt sure she knew now. But tomorrow she would know for certain.

CHAPTER THIRTY-THREE

What would you die for?

The question was whispered in her ears though no one was there to speak it.

Amanda had hardly slept the rest of the night. She wrapped her coat around her nightgown and stood beneath the eaves of her balcony in chilled, bare feet, watching the rain falling upon the city. The brush of low clouds that had swept in the day before was the prelude to thick, rolling clouds that brought fingers of cold stalking the new green meadows and budding leaves. Bell towers began their morning ringing, heralding another day. They chimed and boomed as morning travelers walked the sidewalks and drove the wet streets.

What would you die for?

The question hung in the air.

Amanda huddled inside the wool coat, her back to the balcony door. She sought an answer to that question. She knew the people she believed she'd die for—her father, Benny, even her mother. And Stefan. But *what* would she die for?

Stefan's cousin, Petrov, had nearly been imprisoned and had risked his life to bring Bibles into his country during the Communist era. Jan Hus had been burned at the stake for his beliefs in God, and Amanda believed Stefan might go to such a death for his faith also. Tatianna Hoffman died that her best friend might live. It was said that Jesus died for all of humankind, repaying the debt of sins that man could not pay himself. Even Kurt Heinrich had died for the pursuit of the one thing he couldn't have.

What if this day Amanda found that thing her grandfather sought and had given his life for? It would mean peace for her, she hoped. It would be the crucible overcome. The horror of their story, the truth she would tell her father, would be righted and restored.

Yet, even as Amanda left the covering at the corner of the wet balcony, she knew restoration was only a hope. Once found, the brooch would prove its value in her life and the life of her father. It might not restore enough. But she could hope.

As the warmth of her room welcomed her, Amanda thought she heard the question again.

What would you die for?

<hr />

The museum was closed. Of course she should have known a Jewish museum would be closed on the Sabbath. Amanda peered inside the darkened windows but could see nothing. Settling against the glass with a sigh, she glanced out onto the wet street. There was one place she'd wanted to see on her last trip that she now dreaded seeing. Yet Uncle Martin deserved to know who his parents were, especially once her father knew the truth about his past. And Amanda knew it was part of the journey she must take.

Before leaving the city for the day, Amanda went to an

CINDY McCORMICK MARTINUSEN

Internet café. She made a few Web searches and found further evidence of what she suspected. Then she sent notes to Sylvia Pride's and Tiffany's home e-mail addresses.

> I will know for certain tomorrow, but be ready for confirmation—I found the brooch. I'll call Sunday.

Amanda didn't include the details as to how she knew the location. She'd tell that story once she saw the brooch and touched it with her own hands.

It was afternoon by the time she drove her car from the locked garage. Amanda had hoped for Stefan's presence when she took the country roads to the remains of the village of Lidice. That had been the hope before—before the world had turned upside down.

✦═◉═✦

When Amanda stepped from the car at Lidice, she vowed to keep this place distant from her—to put it under the face of research and of finding some information about her uncle's family. Yet her heart made odd leaps that took her breath away, and a knot formed in her stomach as she walked toward the row of buildings.

The Communist government had built a long, curved wall and walkway toward the museum. The granite portraits in the wall depicted Communist comrade helping comrade in a show of how the great Fatherland would keep such evils as the Nazi Party away. She followed the stone walkway to the small museum, pausing before she stepped inside. There was a driving force that wouldn't let her run away. Amanda needed to know this.

She paid the admission fee to a bored, older woman so she could view the work of her grandfather's hands. Something within her wanted to scream to the woman, *Do you know who I am?*

One room told the story and showed the pictures she'd already scrutinized. This time Amanda's compulsion was to study not only the dead but also the soldiers who walked among them. One of those men was probably her grandfather. The other men followed his orders or met him for Czech beer after the killings.

Personal items from the victims were within the glass display cases. Amanda stared at the wire-rimmed glasses, a silver spoon, a comb, shoes, a doll, and photographs— remnants of people's lives.

She was the only one in the tiny cinema downstairs, where she watched a movie of the village's destruction—taped by Nazi cameras. Buildings were demolished one by one into huge heaps of rubble, and fires burned what could be consumed, until a world of people's lives was nothing but charred remains.

An SS officer turned and for a moment his eyes met Amanda's. Across time and space and generations, she recognized her grandfather's face. And then he was gone.

The movie ended but Amanda couldn't leave. She waited for the next showing, hoping to see something in the officer's eyes. It was impossible, she knew. But if she could see something, a glint of evil, a menacing smile, a look of recognition— something, anything. He came into view again, the camera panning over the destruction and then came to SS Officer Kurt Heinrich, who stood as if overseeing it all, his back to the camera, then turning, looking into her eyes. Then he was gone again.

Amanda had never known she'd had a veiled pride in the fact that her family had died at the hands of the Nazis until it was taken and replaced by shame. She'd felt owed something because her grandparents were victims. Now she owed the world. The debt was too much for her to pay—ever. That truth was confirmed at Lidice.

…

"Amanda is here? In Prague?" Stefan asked, stopping halfway down the loft stairs. He'd heard the worry in Benny's voice when he picked up the phone, but the idea that she was here, so close, stunned him.

"She's been withdrawn since you left. I was worried about her; she's never been like this. Her dad is worried too. I finally reached her right before she went to bed last night. Today she was going to a museum and some village where she was told her grandparents died or something."

"She was going to Lidice?"

"Yes, that was the place. She'd been wandering the city in the rain. I would have called you sooner, but I didn't know you were in Prague—she doesn't think you are." Benny talked quickly. "Then just a while ago, I got this frantic call from Amanda's assistant. I guess this guy from jail is trying to reach Amanda—says it's urgent. He seems to believe that Amanda or some other woman in Prague could be in danger. He received a letter from a fanatic white supremacist who is in Prague right now. I'm trying not to get panicked over this, but I was about to catch the next flight over."

"I'll find her," Stefan said. His grandmother had set her knitting on her lap and was watching him with concern.

"I tried the hotel, but she's not there."

"She's probably at Lidice then. And she shouldn't be there alone—not after everything," Stefan said, looking outside at the rain splashing against the window. "I'm leaving right now."

…

Ms. Delsig had sat beneath the tower of Saint Nicholas, watching the people of Prague, the tourists from around the world, the children holding the hands of parents and looking at her and her walker with curious eyes. Lilly and Lorraine had found a shop of hand-knitted, wool clothing. The prices were incredibly low for the beautiful-quality sweaters, shawls, and scarves. Lorraine dug through boxes and racks, picking out Christmas and birthday presents for the next year. Ms. Delsig smiled at their excitement as did the older woman who owned the shop. Yet the square was where she found her place, among the pigeons and travelers she watched.

She needed the space to think and try to process the idea that Kurt Heinrich had a son, and that son had a daughter, and that daughter would someday have children. One part of her wanted to cry for the injustice of it. Yet another part fought to reason with herself, to remind herself that these were lives that could be reached with truth even when Kurt Heinrich couldn't. What better justice was there than for Kurt Heinrich's children to hate all that he believed in? These were her thoughts as the morning passed and her friends explored the shops of the Malá Strana, the "Little City."

Ilona found her there and sat in silence beside her as if to comfort her. She bought them each a cup of coffee, and they discussed the various people around them.

"What do you think of when you watch these people? Is it strange being back in the city of your birth?"

"I was thinking of a song. It was one I believed would be my song of death a long time ago. My brother died that night, but I would survive."

"What is the song?"

Ms. Delsig spoke the words in English as best as she could translate, finishing the last line, "'Tonight we die. We die.'"

She could see the images of death around her. Slowly she became aware of Ilona beside her, cars driving around the square, and people moving toward their own destinations. Weariness tugged at her. Through the crowd, she spotted

Lorraine pushing Lilly's wheelchair, though Lilly could barely be seen above the pile of purchases. They looked as tired as she was.

They were napping, each on their own bed, but Ms. Delsig found only short breaks of sleep. Finally she rose. Ilona had invited her to dinner and said she wanted to discuss something with her. Ms. Delsig decided it would be nice to get away from the city center and see some of the metropolitan side of Prague—a side she'd never known.

"Do you mind if I go to dinner with Kane and Ilona?" Ms. Delsig whispered to a half-awake Lilly. "They found a little place on the outskirts of town, but they do not have room for all of us in their car."

Lilly mumbled something in response before falling back into the grunting sleep Ms. Delsig was rapidly getting used to.

She decided to leave a note. And in the corner she scribbled a note to herself. She wanted to find the song she'd heard long ago at the camp. She wrote the words: *We die tonight.*

CHAPTER THIRTY-FOUR

A map directed Amanda's path toward the mass grave. Down the stairs, across the meadow, there would be a tall wooden cross. Beneath the earth would be the bones of men and boys her grandfather had ordered murdered—five at a time as the others awaited their fate, watching neighbors and brothers and friends die before them, standing above their corpses before a bullet brought them to the ground. Her uncle's father most likely could be found beneath that earth, his bones mixed with those of his countrymen, not knowing that his murderer would take his child to be his own.

Amanda walked to the ledge where the village had once rested at the cradle of the meadow below. The light of late afternoon was too bright, even beneath thick clouds. A stairway led down to the meadow where she saw the wooden cross. There was the mass grave.

Pausing, she glanced back at her car and the road behind it. The rain was light upon her head and she was cold, so cold already. She could leave without going down there. But instead, she turned toward the stairway.

The meadow was beautiful with wet green grass. It sloped down, then back up to a tree-lined vista where she could see monuments similar to those she'd seen at the concentration camps. In the bow of the slope was the cross, but suddenly her eyes caught something else in the meadow.

Children.

There was a large group of them—unmoving, silent, and still. She made her journey toward them.

Her steps slowed as she approached. She felt as if she'd come to holy ground, that her shoes should be removed and her head covered. There were dozens of them. Life-size and caught in a moment of time, each statue child was individual and unique in his or her expression of grief and silent plea for help.

The rain gave the appearance of tears running down the statues' faces. Amanda walked close to the young boy in front, who was grasping the hand of a young girl. The tears ran down the little boy's face in long, wet streaks. Some dripped from his chin; others trailed from his head to his feet. He was covered with tears, this little boy of stone. They were all covered, the boys and girls, the children.

Amanda felt the tears or the rain, she wasn't sure, falling down her own face. She wished to cry it all away. The rain came down harder. Her clothes stuck to her skin, and strands of wet hair fell in front of her eyes. Her knees weakened as she carefully examined each child. She wanted to reach out and touch their smooth baby skin, to touch their hair and feel the sunlight warm each strand, and to dry the tears and keep them from ever falling from their eyes again. But they were stone, not real. The once-living children were gone now, flesh fallen from bone, tears dried into the dust of the earth.

Nothing on this earth could compensate for these tears. Finding the brooch would not do it. Nothing could redeem.

Amanda felt the futility of everything, the hopelessness of living. She cried in a wide green meadow at the feet of the little statue boy. She cried until there was nothing left inside her. But the rain continued to fall, now in a slow, soft drizzle. It touched her hair and forehead, washing over her face and skin.

Then Amanda realized that the rain was not the tears of stone children or the many children who had cried a thousand tears—these raindrops were the tears of God. They poured from the sky and upon the earth, a river of tears that brought hope to the ground. She recalled Stefan's words: *"I am what I believe."* Amanda had been what she had believed also—family stories and the past. But they couldn't sustain her. "I want us to share faith in Christ," he'd said when it was beyond her sight or comprehension. Yet before these children of stone, Amanda could see.

The world could not redeem, but she could find redemption in the rain from God's own eyes.

⊷≡◉≡⊷

The usual traffic blocked the roads out of the city. Stefan drove around cars on the shoulder and honked until others moved over. He finally left the city behind and sped down the lonely country road. A million thoughts and worries spun through his mind. He spoke prayers aloud and feared what he didn't know. Had this group found Amanda? Why did they want her? What would the reality of Lidice do to her, knowing that her grandfather had been one of the executioners? Would she want him to come?

Stefan found her there. She appeared small and alone, kneeling in the field of green in front of the gray stone children. He ran down the steps quickly and followed the long pathway across the meadow. He slowed only a few yards behind her.

He spoke her name in quiet reverence. She was soaked through, and for a split second he wasn't sure it was actually Amanda. The shivering of her body was her only movement.

"Amanda," he said again. She didn't turn to him.

Stefan took quick steps toward her, taking off his jacket. He covered her shoulders and knelt beside her.

"We need to get you warmed up," he said, suddenly fearful. Her skin was pale and her hands ice-cold. He wondered how long she'd been here. It appeared quite a while.

"Amanda," he said gently.

She looked at him, her green eyes widening with recognition and surprise. "Stefan?"

"Yes. I'm here." He felt a wave of wonder as he helped her stand and cradled her in his arms. He held her tightly, not wanting to let go. She was here, and she would be all right.

"Did you see them?" she asked, pulling back to look at the statues.

"Yes," he whispered, pressing his mouth against her wet hair. He looked over the top of her head to the monument of children. "Let me take you home now."

He kept her wrapped tightly as they made the long, slow walk up the hill to the parking lot. After setting her in the passenger's seat, he turned on the engine and the heater.

"I'll bring Petrov out later, and we'll get your car. First we need to get you dry and feed you something hot—some tea, perhaps? My mother has the best tea, or would you rather I took you to your hotel?" He was babbling and she was silent. "Amanda, I was so worried when Benny called."

"Benny called?" she asked, her throat cracking.

"Yes, your assistant called him." He relayed the message as best he could from Benny's telling.

"Richter Hauer called from jail?" Amanda sat up straight. "They aren't after me. But I know who they want."

⋆═◎═⋆

After changing into a nice dress, Ms. Delsig took her long wool coat and umbrella and waited in the hotel lobby. Just as she believed they had already left for an early dinner, they entered the lobby. It appeared they'd been arguing by Kane's forced niceties and Ilona's red-rimmed eyes. Ilona kept looking away, hiding slightly behind the long curls she'd let down from the severe ponytail she'd worn earlier.

"Are you okay?" Ms. Delsig asked Ilona while Kane went up to their room to get their jackets.

"Yes," Ilona said quickly.

Ms. Delsig put her arm across Ilona's shoulders and at first felt her flinch, as if unused to such a touch. "You have beautiful hair, Ilona. Do you have a grandmother?"

"No, my grandparents were dead by the time I was born."

"And I do not have a granddaughter. We should adopt one another."

Ilona stared at her with a wide, amused expression. "Well, wouldn't that be something," she said, her amusement fading as she studied Ms. Delsig's face. Ilona was about to speak again when the elevator dinged and the door opened to Kane.

Outside in the parking lot, cameras kept a close eye on the cars through the night. Ms. Delsig pushed her walker behind Kane and Ilona and noticed again the stiffness between them.

"Oh, I wanted to write down the name of the restaurant," Ms. Delsig said, stopping. "Can we wait a moment? Lilly and Lorraine might want to meet us later."

"I don't remember," Kane said, opening the passenger-side front door for Ms. Delsig.

⋯═◯═⋯

Amanda used Stefan's cell phone to call Austria. She tried Darby Evans Collins' office, then her home, then back to the office, where she insisted on getting Darby's cellular number.

"I need you to tell me where Brigit Kirke is staying in Prague." After Amanda told Darby the story, Darby promised to call back with the number in ten minutes.

"What do you think they'd do to her?" Darby asked, worry in her voice.

"I don't know," Amanda said, but she remembered Richter sitting in jail because he didn't agree with their teachings—and Ms. Delsig was of Jewish descent.

⋯═◯═⋯

"You seem very close to your two black friends," Kane said almost as soon as her walker was in the trunk and the car doors closed.

"What do you mean?" Ms. Delsig asked.

There was an edge to Kane's words that hadn't been there previously. Somehow they caused a nervous flutter in her.

"Kane, let's go eat and then talk to Ms. Delsig." Ilona's voice sounded small coming from the backseat.

There was an expression, a slight smirk, Ms. Delsig caught as Kane glanced her way. She felt that sickening feeling she'd experienced so many times over the years—first as a young girl when forced to wear a yellow star and later when she watched reports of racism in America. Trying to brush away the tension as imaginary, Ms. Delsig thought about specific instances since Kane and Ilona had been with them—Kane jerking away when touched, some of their strange remarks. She'd trusted them because they had seemed like friendly Americans. But how well did she know these people? She thought about her walker locked in the trunk.

"I forgot something," she said suddenly as Kane started the car.

"What?" Kane asked, turning to stare at her.

"My . . . my camera." She tried to smile sweetly. "I would not want to miss photographs of this restaurant."

Kane put the car in gear. "We'll be late for our reservation, and Ilona has a camera. She'll send you doubles."

"But—" Ms. Delsig couldn't think of anything else to say as Kane backed out of the parking space.

Evening was falling fast over the city. A car came around the corner and stopped suddenly in front of them. The doors flew open.

"Idiot drivers!" Kane laid on the horn as the passenger and driver hopped from the car and hurried toward the hotel entrance, their car still blocking the narrow street.

"Ilona, get out and tell those people to move their car."

Ilona didn't say anything but opened her door and got out. Ms. Delsig put her hand on the door handle.

"You just stay in here with me." Kane put a firm hand on Ms. Delsig's arm.

Ms. Delsig hit the button to roll down the window. She saw the couple coming out of the hotel. The young woman spoke to Ilona in German. "Have you seen an elderly woman with a couple leaving this hotel?"

Ilona put up her hands. "I don't understand—no comprends."

Kane turned to peer through the window.

Ms. Delsig pushed down the latch and her door opened. "I am an elderly woman with an American couple," she said, putting one foot, then the other, out the door. Kane seemed too surprised to speak.

"Is everything okay? Is it Alfred?" Ms. Delsig stepped slowly forward.

"You are Brigit Kirke?"

Ms. Delsig's hand rose to cover her lips. She had not been called that name in decades. The woman stood in the rain, her blonde hair straight and damp against a petite, pretty face, her green eyes staring at her. "It is you. You are the granddaughter."

"Yes, my name is Amanda Rivans. And I am the granddaughter."

Ms. Delsig glanced around, wishing for someone familiar other than Kane and Ilona. She felt off balance and reached for the side of Kane's car for support. The woman, Amanda, took a few tentative steps closer. There was a mixture of emotions in Amanda's expression. Ms. Delsig searched for something, some glimmer of Kurt Heinrich in her face, in her eyes, or in her features. Ms. Delsig remembered the cliff, his voice, the darkness. The granddaughter of Kurt Heinrich reached her hand toward her. Hadn't he done the same?

"You are scaring her, and her name isn't Brigit Kirke," Ilona said, coming up beside her. "Ms. Delsig, are you ready to go?"

Amanda Rivans' eyes had not wavered but stared directly into Ms. Delsig's.

Kane, who had still been looking through the window, now got out of the car. His quick steps on the pavement approached from behind. "Let's get out of here," he stated, taking Ms. Delsig's arm at the elbow.

The young man slightly behind Amanda stepped forward. "She won't be going with you," he said firmly.

Ms. Delsig felt sudden fear, but Amanda continued to hold her stare. "These people know who you are. They came here to find you. Please. Trust me."

"What are you talking about?" Ilona asked in a strained voice.

Ms. Delsig's feet were frozen in place. Amanda's hand reached for her again.

"This woman is crazy. Let's go," Kane said, again trying to turn Ms. Delsig away.

Ms. Delsig looked at Ilona, who glanced from her to Amanda. Suddenly Ms. Delsig realized that Ilona knew exactly what Amanda was saying. Amanda's outstretched hand waited. She thought of Edgar, dead in the darkness, and how she had thought it would be her last night. Ms. Delsig wavered, her thoughts in turmoil, but decided she had to trust her gut. Reaching out across what felt like an eternity, she took Amanda's hand.

"I know who you are, and why you're here," Amanda said with a steely stare at Kane. She drew Ms. Delsig closer to her side. "My grandfather was Kurt Heinrich—a captain in the Nazi Party. He spent his whole life looking for that brooch and died in his pursuit of it. It was never found."

Kane stepped back quickly, looking around them. "I don't know what you're talking about, but we're getting out of here. Get in the car, Ilona."

Ilona hesitated. She couldn't meet Ms. Delsig's eyes. Then she turned, hurried to the car, and got inside. The engine roared to life.

In a second, Ms. Delsig quickly moved away from the car with the help of the young man's arm around her.

"Are you all right?" he asked in a strained voice as the car sped down the narrow street.

"Fine. I am fine."

"Amanda, help Ms. Delsig. I'll call the police."

There was a quick switch of arms around her, and then the young man ran to his car and grabbed his cell phone. He jogged down the street in the direction of Kane's car as he shouted an explanation in Czech into the phone.

"Who were they?" Ms. Delsig asked, wondering what had been planned for her if she'd gone with them.

The young man returned and spoke. "We believe they are members of a neo-Nazi group in the United States."

"They went to all this trouble for the brooch? Just like—" Ms. Delsig shivered.

"Just like my grandfather, yes." Amanda Rivans was trembling, and the young man put his arm around her protectively.

"Let us get you inside," Ms. Delsig said without moving, suddenly noticing Amanda's soaked clothing. The rain was light, as if to send wet kisses upon their cheeks.

"I am so glad we found you. But I hope you can—" Amanda seemed unable to find the words, but Ms. Delsig understood. This was the granddaughter of Kurt Heinrich, but she didn't follow his ways. And it was clear that she felt the weight of the Nazi's sins on her shoulders.

"His sins are not yours," Ms. Delsig said softly.

"I am alive when so many that he murdered have no grandchild. Doesn't that somehow make me guilty?" Amanda asked, her eyes bright with agony and tears.

"I can understand how it is put upon your head and conscience. What we do will affect others, and it will affect the children of other generations."

"Is it possible for one person to take the sins of another and bring healing?" Amanda pleaded.

"That is what my faith is based upon." Somehow, at that moment, Ms. Delsig felt as if there were no one in the world but this young woman and herself. Like the night on the cliff when the world fell away and it was only the two of them there. "You have been searching, yes. And I have been too, though I did not know how much until now. I want to know you, the granddaughter of Kurt Heinrich. I want to see an end to this. The brooch is not important, Amanda. It is you and your life—what you will live for." She took Amanda's hand, feeling the coldness in her fingers. For a moment, her heart skipped at the contact with Kurt's grandchild—and yet, in so many ways she was not of his blood.

"What I will live for?" Amanda asked as if it answered a question.

"It is raining again," the young man said.

Amanda looked up and the rain hit her face.

They were women who spanned two generations of lives and deaths. They stood together with their faces toward the sky. Ms. Delsig smiled. "The rain comes and makes everything new and clean."

One Month Later

"*The story of the Empress Sissi Brooch involves not only a missing piece of jewelry that disappeared during the Nazi Occupation of Austria and Czechoslovakia. This is also the story of innocent lives lost for the pursuit of the brooch, and the story of one man who murdered because of his desire to obtain it. This historical journey began in the 1800s with a beautiful empress of Austria and continues through the last century until present day. A man currently awaits extradition in a U.S. prison for his recent crimes involving the brooch. Many have said that the Empress Brooch is cursed and that no one should find it. If the quest has cost so many lives, what would the discovery bring? And yet, will it ever end? Man searches for what he cannot have while missing what is right before his eyes. . . .*"

Amanda sat at her desk with the San Francisco day shining brightly through the window. She continued working on the opening and closing for the program. "In Search of the

Empress Brooch" would be a two-day series. People would watch from around the world. Then they'd go on with their lives, turning the channel or watching the next program. Amanda didn't really mind; the story would be there. Perhaps it would change a life or two or many. Perhaps some class-rooms would play the video version.

Brigit Kirke Delsig would speak toward the end of the program. "I saw the brooch in the early 1940s, and I hope it is never recovered." Her statement would provide Ms. Delsig the safety to live her days in Florida, to travel or do whatever she wished without looking over her shoulder or fearing a new friendship.

"It's going to be a great program," Sylvia Pride said, leaning against Amanda's office door. "The only thing better would have been the discovery of the brooch itself."

Amanda simply nodded. After receiving Amanda's e-mail stating that she had found the brooch and then a phone call the next day explaining that she'd been mistaken, Sylvia had seemed somewhat intrigued by Amanda ever since. "You wouldn't have e-mailed us if you weren't almost positive you'd found it," Sylvia had said when they met in the office. Amanda kept with the story.

"I'm glad you approve of the program," Amanda said, turn-ing back to her computer screen.

"You may find it interesting that the History Network East-ern Europe is moving forward. They've chosen the city. It's Prague."

Amanda looked up. "Technically, Prague isn't Eastern Europe," she said with a smile, recalling how Stefan always corrected her about it.

"I'm aware of that. But should I be prepared—are you going to put in for a position?"

Amanda paused at the keyboard. Stefan would be at her office soon. They were going together to listen to her father give his first living-history speech to a classroom of college students. Her father was telling his story—their story. She'd been so afraid of the moment when she told him the truth, but now the worst was over. Her father had been devastated, and they'd forever struggle with the aftershocks of such knowledge, but Amanda was witnessing the remarkable strength in her father's spirit. Uncle Martin was now seeking his biological parents, and the two men who were brothers in life but not by blood were finding a new path together. The next evening they were all attending her mother's second poetry reading at the bookstore where she worked. Stefan would finally meet Amanda's father, and they would go out for a "family" dinner afterward. Her patchwork family was finding its way after all.

"Guess I have some thinking to do about that, even some praying," Amanda said.

Sylvia raised her eyebrows. "Whatever it takes, but I'd like to know ahead of time."

After Sylvia left, Amanda exited the program and shut her computer down. She did a quick brushup on her makeup and hair and straightened her desk.

"What am I going to do with you?" Stefan was standing at the door. He'd come straight from the airport. They hadn't seen one another in weeks and it had felt like years. As he walked toward her, he dropped his duffel bag to the floor and tossed his coat on a chair.

"I keep wondering the same thing." She came around her desk, and he drew her into his arms. "Nothing really works in our lives."

"It makes no sense at all." His words were whispered into her hair. "We live on opposite sides of the world."

"And our pasts have nothing in common." She pulled away and gazed into his clear eyes. "A therapist would say we're doomed."

"Really?"

"Probably."

He touched her hair and cupped his hands around her neck. "Long distance relationships can't last for long. And I'll be a single father someday—baggage, you know."

"I want to meet her. Viktorie," she whispered.

He kissed her and held her as if they would never part again.

"Amanda, I'm not sure how to make this work. But since I've met you, my entire life has fallen out of my own hands. When I'd get lost in the woods as a kid, I'd search for the North Star. It always brought me home. So I'm trusting that God has some plan for me—and for us."

"I'm trusting in the same thing."

"Then tomorrow and all the rest after that will work out just fine."

⋯═◯═⋯

Brigit Kirke Delsig knew she would never come here to Prague again. She had spent over a month now in the city of her birth, and much of that time had been spent alone. It had been a time to remember the old and to discover the city anew. But she would not be back. There were too many years upon her for such a delusion. This was the place of her birth, but Prague was no longer home. Ms. Delsig had wanted to remember it and see all the old places before she returned to Florida.

She would return to Oakdale Home of Second Chances, as she'd decided to call it. If Alfred would still have her, she'd be planning a small wedding soon. She would splurge on a laptop so they could play solitaire together from his bed if they needed to. Lilly was already back home, working on Mr. Bartlett to give them neighboring rooms. Ms. Delsig wondered how her garden was surviving under the touch of Agnes the librarian, and she looked forward to e-mailing Janice about her own adventure into the world. But it was time to go home.

This was her final day among the ancient streets and ringing bells. Prague would continue on without her, and yet the city would forever be engrained within her. Somehow she believed it would remember her too.

A taxi took her to the Jewish museum. It would be her last time here, though she'd come several times in the previous weeks. She paid her money and entered the small museum, winding through the exhibit until she reached the place she knew so well.

"And there you are," she whispered to herself. Brigit settled on a wood bench against the opposite wall, where she could watch the people in groups or singles as they worked their way through and perused the artwork.

It was a mosaic of objects—broken glass, stones, and jewelry—all shaped and placed to form the face of a woman. The piece was signed simply *J. K.* The museum had little information on Jan Kirke, the unknown artist, except for the fact that he'd been a local Prague artist who was killed during the war. Since there were works in the room by more famous artists, many eyes passed the mosaic merely en route to the Marc Chagall painting in the next room. Some paused and gave it a momentary look.

"You must seek to find," Ms. Delsig said softly. It had never been lost or buried or stolen. The mosaic had hung in one of Reinhard Heydrich's residences during the war—he hadn't known it was the work of a Jew. After the war ended Brigit had recovered the papers to reclaim her father's works. She had then donated the piece, along with Jan's other works, to this Jewish museum. Not even the museum knew what they had— the Empress Sissi Brooch hanging right on their wall.

Brigit could see it. The largest emerald was in her right pupil with two lesser gems on each side. The emeralds could only be identified by a knowing eye, since they blended with the other green gems that hid the gold brackets of the brooch and perfectly matched the gem cuts within the other eye of the woman's face.

Ms. Delsig had been shocked in the seventies when her husband had given her a print advertising the museum. They'd used this mosaic as the backdrop. Her husband had not known what he'd given her. And yet there was a remarkable irony that the object sought for so long was copied on prints and placed all over the city.

Ms. Delsig stood to leave, taking one final look at the mosaic. It had been in full view, hanging here for decades. People thought they looked every day, yet few could see, and even fewer would understand.

She read the inscription so many passed by:

Those with Eyes Will See

I'm here at my laptop, staring out my window at the tops of black oaks and evening sky. And beyond those trees, my thoughts journey across two continents and an ocean to a gathering of stone children who stand in a lonely Czech meadow. These statues remain through the seasons, through wind, rain, and snow. I recall their features, the sorrow in their expressions, the unspoken questions of *why?* I attempt perspective—they are only works of sculpture made of stone and only symbols of the long-lost children of the village of Lidice. Yet their faces remain with me.

Recently I attended the 59th Reunion of the U.S. Army's 11th Armored Division to interview war veterans with a friend. We heard stories of the 11th's landing in France, combat in the Battle of the Bulge, and then as they reached the war's end, these battle-worn men discovered the walking dead within Mauthausen Concentration Camp. The night before the 41st Cavalry arrived in May 1945, camp prisoners of many nationalities learned "The Star-Spangled Banner" in hopes of liberation by the U.S. Army. As we talked, each veteran looked across the table and right through me, where he saw once again thousands of starved and dying men singing and cheering them on, bringing the knowledge of what our boys were truly fighting for. Those hollow faces remain with them.

I wonder about this world, about yesterday, today, and tomorrow. The loss of children continues. Memorials will rise from the dust of tears and ash. People will make their descents into evil, and others will rise to be heroes. The turbulent times are far from being pages in the past. And that brings up the words a man long ago once spoke: "How frail is humanity! How short is life, and how full of trouble! Like a flower, we blossom for a moment and then wither" (Job 14:1-2a). In the midst of futile moments we proclaim words like these: "God, why? Life is all for nothing. We don't learn. We aren't getting better."

The evening turns to dusk outside my window as my thoughts return home. My eyes catch the photographs on my desk of stone children and my WWII vets. Their stories and questions and tears are with me always now.

I once thought I understood this world. Then I prayed for wisdom. Now I seem to have less figured out and more questions I'm seeking answers for. But some truths rise above the questions; some things I know for sure. Thankfulness is a child's soft hand within your own after standing with stone children in an autumn rain. Respect is sharing tears and stories with men who gave up their youth to fight for humanity. And I know about a love, peace, and joy that only God can give. Love is greater than hatred, and truth prevails.

In your quest through life, I hope you look toward the North for guidance. I wish you moments of tears and moments of joy that change your life forever. I pray the vision given through Christ will be fulfilled. God is God—sovereign and just. And we have great need of him. The Lord's blessings upon your journey—both today and tomorrow. And may the vision remain in you always.

In my two previous novels, my acknowledgments have been quite long, to say the least. It's necessary due to the debt of gratitude I feel to many people in my writing endeavors and in my personal life. I hope my appreciation to those I've listed before and those I've told in person will be fully understood because I truly mean it when I say, "Thank you."

But particularly during the writing of *North of Tomorrow* there are some people I must give an extra amount of gratitude.

My husband, David, you provide daily love and faithfulness (and many dinners during the completion of *North*), and without you I would still be wondering if someday I could be a writer. My children, Cody, Madelyn, and Weston, who were understanding when I couldn't do some end-of-the-year field trips. You've been excited over these publications and the letters received by readers. But most of all, you fill each day with joy.

Janet Kobobel Grant—my super agent who is a friend first and foremost. Ramona Cramer Tucker and Lorie Popp—excellent editors who added much more than just your expertise to *North of Tomorrow*. Tricia Goyer—you have my unending gratitude for your manuscript advice and your friendship. We've been on some amazing adventures over the last few years.

Some special people who helped with research, prayer, support, my children, and travel: Dad and Mom, Eleanor

Martinusen, Tony and Katie Martinusen, Shawn and Jennifer Harman, Anne de Graaf, Kim Burns, Kimberly Shaw, Serina Martinusen, Shelley Chittim, Jenna Benton, Amanda Darrah and the Kincaid family, Cathy Elliott, Maxine Cambra, Laurie Williams, and Mt. Shasta House owners (Mike Chittim and Joe Gazzigli) along with Shawn Chittim. Also *Quills of Faith*, my writer's group, and my Cottonwood church family, including the great pastoral team of John Roland, Terry Johnson, and David Martin. I hope each of you knows how valuable you've been.

Men of the 11th Armored Division, you welcomed Tricia Goyer and me into your reunion with open arms and you shared your stories—something I will never forget and deeply appreciate. Each of you became a part of our lives. Thomas Nicolla, Tony Petrelli, Charlie Torluccio, Arthur Jacobson, LeRoy Woychik, Ross Snowdon, David Wofsey, Joseph Lawolki, Al Dunn, Tarmo Holma, LeRoy Petersohn, Bert Heinold, David Pike, Ray Stordahl, Alfred Ferrari, Bill Mann, Lester Freeman, Charles White, Roy Ferlazzo, Darrell E. Romjue, Margaret Gerace, and all the others.

In Austria, this novel found guidance through Professor Reinhold and Elisabeth Wagnleitner (of Salzburg), Martha Gammer (St. Georgian/Gusen), and the Ebensee Museum (Dr. Wolfgang Quatember, Gabriela Eidinger, and Andreas Schmoller).

I'd like to thank Tyndale House Publishers for their commitment and belief in these stories: Ron Beers, Anne Goldsmith, Rebecca Nesbitt, Ken Petersen, Curtis Lundgren, Danielle Crilly, Mavis Sanders, Dan Balow, Travis Thrasher, Jan Pigott, Julie Huber, Sue Lerdal, and many others.

Most of this manuscript was written while listening to Third Day's Offerings. It helped through those long nights to remember what this was all about and to Whom it was for. Because, above all, I am most grateful for the Lord God Almighty, who was, and is, and is to come (my true North of Tomorrow).

For more information or for survivors to connect with these camps, please contact:

Concentration Camp Memorial Ebensee
Museum of Contemporary History
Kirchengasse 5
A-4802 Ebensee
Austria

Mauthausen Concentration Camp—
http://www.mauthausen-memorial.gv.at/engl/index.html

Mauthausen/Gusen Information Pages—
http://linz.orf.at/orf/gusen

Under a Cruel Star: A Life in Prague 1941–1968 by Hega Margolius Kovaly

Licensed Mass Murder: A Socio-Psychological Study of Some SS Killers by Henry V. Dicks

War Letters: Extraordinary Correspondence from American Wars edited by Andrew Carroll

A Surgeon in Combat by William V. McDermott

From World War to Waldheim: Culture and Politics in Austria and the United States (Austrian History, Culture, & Society, Vol. 2) edited by David F. Good and Ruth Wodak

Here, There, and Everywhere: The Foreign Politics of American Popular Culture by Reinhold Wagnleitner

Coca-Colonization and the Cold War: The Cultural Mission of the United States in Austria After the Second World War by Reinhold Wagnleitner

The Camp Men: The SS Officers Who Ran the Nazi Concentration Camp System by French L. MacLean

Concentration Camp Ebensee, Subcamp of Mauthausen by Florian Freund

An Illustrated History of the Gestapo by Rupert Butler

Hitler's Silent Partners by Isabel Vincent

Piercing the Reich: The Penetration of Nazi Germany by American Secret Agents During World War II by Joseph E. Persico

Yes, We Sang!: Songs of the Ghettos and Concentration Camps by Shoshana Kalisch with Barbara Meister

The Holocaust Chronicle: A History in Words and Pictures— Publications International, Ltd.

Cindy McCormick Martinusen lives in Northern California with her husband, David, and their three children. Cindy and her husband were both raised in the small town of Cottonwood and continue to live there near their extended family and longtime friends.

Over the past few years, Cindy has traveled several times to Europe to research her novels, particularly focusing on Austria and the Czech Republic. She also includes many of the settings in California that are not only close at heart, but close to home.

In addition to fiction, Cindy enjoys coleading a writer's group, studying history, and hearing the stories of others.

North of Tomorrow is the sequel to *Winter Passing* and *Blue Night*.

Cindy appreciates letters written to her in care of Tyndale House Author Relations, P.O. Box 80, Wheaton, IL 60189-0080.